Freedom Fo

A curious teenager's experience with designer drugs.

Bryson P. Connolly

By three methods we may learn wisdom:
First, by reflection, which is the noblest;
Second, by imitation, which is the easiest;
And third by experience, which is the bitterest.
-Confucius

Copyright

ISBN:
978-0-692-85086-2:

Dedication

Something strange happened to the world between 2008 and 2011. It tormented me that this chapter of history could be forgotten, so I decided that a book needed to be written about it. If one thing was to come of my life, it was that this story be told. That was my original intent in 2011.

Had I not come to prison, I would never have been able to gather the organization to write this novel. This book is dedicated to everyone who experienced MDPV. As a witness to their experience, I have assumed the duty of recording this side of reality and expressing it through fiction.

I give thanks to my parents. They have gone through an incredible amount of emotional distress through my visit to prison and the creation of this book. Their unconditional love and support has been a blessing I will never take for granted.

I also thank my Aunty Deb for the recommended readings. Sylvia Brown's books have had a huge impact on my life and the outcome of this novel.

I would also like to thank all my friends who unknowingly contributed to this book. I thank them for all the adventures of my high school years. Those experiences had the greatest impact on the shaping of my reality and the inspiration for the scenes in these pages.

Preface

"They've finally come to capture their lab monkeys. This is real. This is life or death. The Monkey Police are out to get me." -p.272

Some drugs cause spiritual revelations while others become the object of psychotic obsession. This story is about both; the slippery slope from spiritual seeking to mental slavery. Luke Baker is a high-school student with a passion for exploring the mind. For the past several years he had been able to balance school, work, family and friends along with psychedelic adventure. His life is soon changed upon discovering a whole realm of newly invented and not yet illegal drugs.

"Research chemicals' (sometimes sold as 'bath salts') come in many varieties and can be purchased through the internet. Luke is blindsided by a highly addictive psychosis inducing drug called MDPV (methylenedioxypyrovalerone). The peace-and-love is replaced by fear. Hippy-friends are turned into treacherous speed freaks. Luke, seeing this evil, struggles with himself searching high and low for a way to undo the damage he's done.

My intentions are not to glorify drug use. They did not work for me. But to avoid misleading, I had to include the bliss along with the horror. I chose to write without prejudice in order to give the reader an authentic experience.

~~~

The drugs in this story are real; The characters are not. This story depicts a hideous descent into addiction and an unexpected but feasible method to recovery. My intention is to expose, not to bring comfort or reinforce common belief. This story is narrated with sympathy to the characters perspective, where the line between good and evil is not always clear.

Once I began this book it seemed to take off and write itself with no effort. It felt as if an external force was aiding its creation. Now that it is complete. I question the nature of that force. Even as I write this preface I worry that
~~~

humanity may be better off without it. I am strongly considering sealing and hiding the entire novel in fear that it may be harmful.

My greatest hope has always been that this story would benefit all beings who encounter it. My greatest fear is that it will do the complete opposite. In saying this, I caution readers to proceed with a guarded heart.

It is a strange desire, to seek power, lose liberty; or to seek power over others, and to lose power over a man's self.
-Francis Bacon

Chapter 1: The Experiment Is Over. Dirty Underwear.

"They're out there!" Jared whispered, "A whole fucking squad of them got out of an SUV that's parked down the street. They're wearing all that gear and everything! They mean business, Luke. What are we going to do?"

He grabbed the clip from Jared. "Get under the stairs and keep an eye out that window." Luke found a different spot to keep a lookout.

This is it. The experiment is over, Luke thought. We've taken it too far; pushed it to the breaking point. Now it's decided, they're finally going to put an end to this. "Jared, what's happening out there?" Luke said from the far corner of the basement.

"The SUV is still parked down the street and another one just drove by real slow." Jared was terrified. They were in complete darkness except for the streetlight coming through the dirty windows.

Luke shivered, mostly from fear, but partly because he was only wearing the dirty underwear. *Fuck this shit. I shouldn't have to go through this. I'm not ready to die. I'm just a kid. Should we surrender? Can we surrender?*

"What do we do, Luke? I think they're at the front door. I can hear them."

"If they come in without announcing we have to kill em." There was no other option for Luke. *Where's Zuri? I should have listened to her. She tried so hard to convince me that this would end horribly.*

Luke had a friend who's grow operation was raided and robbed by fake FBI agents. This would be Luke's defense in court. He didn't trust sneaky black clad militia looking groups. He would kill them all, legitimate law enforcement or not, and get away with it.

Luke noticed one of his spare gas masks on a table. He strapped it on and hid under the table, keeping the sights of his AK-47 pointed at the top of the stairs. Fat Jared adjusted his position under the stairs. He looked ready to start shooting through the steps at the potential invaders.

"They're outside the back door!" said Jared. "I can hear them talking, they're coming in."

"Are the doors locked?"

"All of em, I even locked the bathroom doors on the way down."

Good, thought Luke. There was only one way they could come in, unless they came through the windows, and Luke hoped they would. It would make them easy targets. Luke was ready for anything, even tear gas, but he would have to be careful of flash bangs. He would probably lose Jared, and that was acceptable. Jared would make a good decoy.

Tension rose as things got quiet. Minutes went by as condensation built up in Luke's mask. *Any second now, they can't wait all night.* Thirty minutes went by. Neither Jared nor Luke moved a muscle. They both had the same mind set. They would not be caught off guard.

Maybe they think we'll forget about the situation. Maybe they think we'll attribute it to the drugs. If they've been studying us properly they would use these tactics. They should know how our brains operate by now. If it's a waiting game they want. They've met their match.

Jared's breathing changed. It was labored. Luke suspected he was trying to inject himself, but didn't risk asking. *Go ahead you fat retard, make a distraction of yourself.* There was rustling under the stairs. Luke expected this to prompt the invasion. He tightened the grip on his rifle.

There was a flash of light at Jared's end. Jared looked out the window. "Hey, that SUV is leaving. We're safe now, right? Luke? Does that mean its over? Luke? Luke, where are-"

Glass broke upstairs. It was all coming together. Jared had given up his position. Luke was still under the radar; still under the table, right where he wanted to be. There were footsteps upstairs; three people, maybe five. They checked the living room, then the bedroom; back to the kitchen. Luke could visualize them trying to open the bathroom door. They couldn't get to the basement without going through the bathroom. Not unless they came from outside through the back door. The front door opened. They went outside.

Jared looked at Luke waiting for instructions. Luke gave him none. Jared had served his purpose as a diversion. Luke's face was sweating terribly, but the mask refused to fog. They would be coming through the back door and straight down the staircase. *Here it comes the moment we've been waiting for.* There was a tap on the back door as they tried the handle. SMASH! The door flew open followed by gunfire.

Everybody's youth is a dream, a form of chemical madness.
-F. Scott Fitzgerald

Chapter 2: School Problems and Normal People

Monday 5-6-2010

"Luke?" a girl whispered, "Hey Luke."
"Huh?" he looked up from his abstract painting.
"What did you do this weekend?"
"Well..." Luke thought as the rave music echoed in his mind. *How can I begin to explain what happened this weekend? This freshman girl has probably never even smoked pot, let alone dropped acid or X.* "I partied in Missoula a bit. Also did some camping I guess."
"That sounds like fun. What kind of parties? My friend Jaime just got a car and we want to do something crazy next weekend."
"Umm... I think you gotta be eighteen to get in to most of these ones." *Crap. Math class is next. Did we have homework? Of course we did. I guess I can add another to the list of missing assignments.*

~~~

Math class was horrible. Mondays like these make numbers look Japanese. On the way out of class Luke was pulled aside by his teacher. "Luke, I need to speak with you for a moment."
"Sure," said Luke as the last of the students walked out of class. Mr. S
~~~

grabbed a piece of paper from his desk and showed it to Luke.

"Do you realize that you have twenty-six missing assignments? Fifty percent of your grade in this class is based on homework. You've done well on all of your tests but you have a thirty-seven. You need at least seventy percent in this class to graduate and finals are coming up quick. I can give you half credit for late assignments. You'll need to turn all of them in if you expect to pass this class."

~~~

Glad that's over with, thought Luke as he started his car. *Less than a month till school's out, what a nightmare.* He lit a cigarette as he looked around the parking lot; people laughing and talking with their friends as they walked out of school. *Why can't I have friends here? Why did all my people have to drop out?* He turned up the stereo as he drove away in his old Chrysler.

~~~

Luke pulled up next to his mom's Subaru. His mom and Stacy were on the front porch. "Hi hunny, how was school?" Stacy said as she ran up and gave him a kiss.

"It was great. You should try it sometime," he said.

"Ha-ha, very funny. Alice and I were just talking. She's gonna teach me yoga. Don't need no education to be a yoga teacher," she said with a smile.

"Sweetie I've missed you all weekend," said Alice, "I'm glad you made it to school." She gave Luke a hug and kiss on the cheek.

"I missed you too, mom. Is dad still at the shop?"

"Yeah. He should be home any minute now," she said.

"Well, if he gets here tell him we're in the garage. I'm gonna go heat up the vaporizer. You want to come?" he said.

"No, no, I've got things to do around the house. If I do that I'll be useless."

"If you say so, I've got some new stuff that doesn't make you sleepy," Luke said as he walked around to the side door of the garage.

Luke pulled out a big bag of pot as Stacy came in after him. He plugged the cord into the outlet on the workbench and set the temp. "So, how was school really?" said Stacy.

"Couldn't pay attention to nothin. I feel so burnt out and I'm getting further behind every week. You have no idea how bad I wanted to take one of those Adderall," he said.

"Oh hunny, I'm sorry. Should we go to sleep early tonight?" she said.

"I definitely need to go to sleep early. I should also try and do some homework," he said.

"Well, before you do that can we make a run up to Whitefish? My sister's in town and her friends need some bud," she said.

Dang it. If I do it there's a good chance it will be another day wasted.

Just don't let them talk you into playin any beer pong or nothin stupid. Homework. First priority. No excuses. No distractions. "I suppose we can do that. Just don't expect me to stick around a long time," he said.

A few minutes went by before the garage door opened. Luke's father pulled in with a big smile. "Hello children," Allan said as he stepped out of the car.

"Hey dad you're just in time. It's at 390 right now," said Luke.

"Very nice. Good to see you, son. I see you survived the weekend," he gave Luke a strong hug.

"Well, its time. Shall we partake?" said Luke with the vaporizer mouthpiece in his hand. The smoking went on for a few minutes. Allan noticed Luke's tension. "Is everything okay?" he asked.

"Yeah, I'm good," said Luke.

"You seem down. Have you tried taking any 5-HTP?" said Allan.

"No, I haven't. I should though. My serotonin levels are probably all whacked out."

"You were out molly houndin, weren't you? Bad stuff. You've been doing too much of that. What's up with school? How are you doing?"

"It sucks. I'm doing crappy, just barely scraping by. I think I have ADD. I need a prescription."

"Everyone has ADD and you don't need amphetamines. What you have is brain fry."

~~~

Stacy lit up a cigarette as they pulled out of the driveway and headed towards Whitefish. "You really need to clean this car," said Stacy as she kicked the beer cans on the floor.

"Yeah. That's what happens when everyone treats it like a mosh pit. It was spotless on Friday," he said.

"Well, maybe we can clean it together when we get back?" she said.

"Yeah. I suppose we could do that," he said. Stacy pulled out a Sublime CD and put it in the player. Luke turned up the volume and spaced out the rest of the drive.

~~~

Luke and Stacy pulled up to the mansion in Whitefish. Stacy's sister would be here often when she visited from Spokane. The place was chaotic most all of the time. There were parties every night, and big ones on the weekends. *God I hate this place,* thought Luke, *snobby, rich, drunk people are the worst. Pill fiends at that. Full price for them. No deals. If they can afford to smoke oxycontin all day, they can pay top dollar.*

"Why the weird look?" said Stacy.

"I just get disgusted by some of the people here. Do you know how much they want, or should I just bring it all inside?" said Luke.

"Better bring it all. They don't even know what kind they want," she said.

"Alright then, let's do it." He grabbed his brown paper bag, got out of the car and locked the doors. The street was packed with rich people cars. Luke's faded 91 Chrysler Imperial sat low to the ground on broken suspension; obviously out of place in a yuppie neighborhood like this.

Before they made it to the front door, Cindy came running out and gave Stacy a hug. "Hey sis, I've missed you so much! Hurry up, let's go inside."

Luke and Stacy followed Cindy up the stairs to a giant room. In one corner were a group of guys playing X-Box 360 on two huge television sets. In another corner was an oddly placed kitchen where another group of people were gathered around. There were already bottles of alcohol opened, and even a few lines of white powder (presumably some form of opiates) on the counter.

"Jeff. Lee. Get over here!" said Cindy. Luke set his bags of weed on a ping pong table and pulled out his scale. Stacy was already off in conversation with her sister and the group of people in the kitchen.

"Alright, I got Train Wreck, Afghan Goo, Blueberry, Buddha Cheese and G-13. Take a look, tell me what you want. Same price as last time," said Luke.

They took their time admiring the selection. One guy was drunk and already getting on Luke's nerves. "I want a quarter of that," the drunken guy pointed at the Afghan goo.

The other guy's order was more complicated. He wanted three kinds; an eighth of each. Luke weighed it out and the guys handed over two hundred dollars. Before Luke got his stuff put away there was a circle of people around him. Three fancy glass pipes and a bong already in rotation. Stacy came up behind Luke and gave him a hug and kiss on the neck. Luke smiled as a pipe was handed to him.

After a half hour of good conversation Luke decided it was time to go. The sober guy's name was Justin. He said he wanted to get bud from Luke in the future. Luke gave him his number and went over to Stacy and Cindy who were laughing together. "Stacy, I gotta head out."

"Oh," she hesitated.

"You don't have to come with. I know you probably wanna spend some time with your sister," said Luke.

"Well, I'd feel bad. We had plans together. Are you sure you can't stay a while? I think we're gonna play a game of quarters," said Stacy.

"Definitely can't do that. I gotta go home and get my life together. It's gonna be boring. You're not missing out."

"Alright hunny. I love you." She gave him a hug and kiss.

"I love you too. Call if you need anything." Luke made his way out. The volume was much louder than when he arrived. *Don't get jealous, thought Luke, she's not gonna get wasted.* He received a text message when he got in his car.

(From Fat Jared): Need U at the skate park

(From Luke): no

(From Jared): yes

(From Luke): NO

(From Jared): I have 80 dollars

(From Luke): 20 minutes

Lame. Obstacle after obstacle keeping me from doing what I need to do. Damn it Stacy. It's okay. She's not gonna get wasted, or do pills. Actually, she will probably do both. At least I know she won't cheat on me. Well, I don't really know that either, and neither will she if she gets too effed up.

~~~

The drive to Kalispell was full of bad feelings. When Luke drove to the back of the park he saw Jared sitting on a bench, looking greasy in his dirty clothes.

Luke pulled into a parking spot and Jared squeezed in. Jared could make any vehicle feel crowded, even a luxury size car like Luke's. "I'm out of selection for today, so here's a quarter of G-13," said Luke.

"Can I give you seventy? It's for someone else, so you can take a little out. They don't have a scale and I'm really hungry," said Jared.

"Fine. You didn't get it from me. I don't want people getting ripped off and thinkin I did it," said Luke.

"Thanks man, I fuckin love you. Can I have a cig?"

"Here, take three. I gotta go. Get outta here you bum."

~~~

When Luke got home he grabbed his backpack and went up to his room. The house was old, but Luke's parents kept it clean and well decorated. Luke's room was another story. It was something between an attic and bonus room. There was a narrow wooden staircase leading up to his room. The railing was broken and there were holes in the walls from drunken friends falling down the stairs.

He pulled out his math textbook and sat at his desk. After a few blank moments staring out the window he started thinking about Stacy. *My life would sure be easy if I had no responsibilities. If she would do something with her life I wouldn't feel so miserable. Sure, she has her own hustle and makes her own money, but if she keeps living like this she will turn out just like her mom. God I hate those pills. Her whole family is hooked on opiates and benzos; except maybe her dad, but he's still an alcoholic. It's pretty much inevitable she will end up the same. She's probably already doing that stuff behind my back. Her pupils get pretty tiny sometimes, a sure sign of opiate use. On the other hand, my pupils are abnormally large most of the time. But that's because of all those times I overdosed on cold medicine. Or could it all be genetic? Maybe it's only genetics. I'd sure like to believe that.* Concentrate damnit, Luke said to himself.

He started to read about multiplying fractions and lost it again. The harder he tried, the harder it got. After thirty minutes of wasted effort his mother walked in. "Hi sweetie, your home," she said.

"Yeah. I left Stacy in Whitefish. She's gonna kick it with her sister."

"Well that's nice, I hardly see you anymore. Is everything okay?" she said.

"Mostly good. I'm a little behind on my homework; math especially."

"Well, maybe you're smoking too much pot. Or it might be all those parties."

Luke knew she was right, no denying it. What was he supposed to do? Stop partying? A lot easier said than done. "Yeah. I know your right. It's just hard because all my friends are out of school. I wanna be where the fun's at and it's hard to balance school and work into that."

"Well, there's hardly a month left till school is over. I know you can do it. The harder you work early in life, the less you have to work later."

"Thanks mom. I should really get to work on this stuff."

"Okay my smart boy. I love you."

"I love you too."

Alright, time to get to work. Better get comfortable and take this stuff to the couch. Luke laid back and started working on an old math assignment. Easy stuff. It should have been easy. He got frustrated and fell asleep after a half hour of struggle.

There are only two ways to live your life.
One is as though nothing is a miracle.
The other is as though everything is a miracle.
-Albert Einstein

Chapter 3: 2C-B and Fred the Tree

Friday 5-10-2010

Luke walked into his first period art class five minutes early. He sat in his assigned seat next to the freshman girl. "Good morning, Natalie."

"Aren't you in a good mood," she said.

"Of course I am, it's Friday. I've got wicked awesome plans for tonight." Something was clearly bothering Luke's classmate. Natalie was usually the instigator of conversation while Luke was half asleep. "What seems to be the problem?" he said.

"I got grounded. Last night I snuck out of the house to hang out with my friend Mike. When I got home all my stuff was either broken or missing. Then my dad came in and started yelling at me. He was drunk, as usual. I guess I'm grounded for the summer. The only friends I can see have to come over. He made all these other stupid rules I don't even want to talk about."

"You're kidding. That's effed up! It's unacceptable. I won't have it. You're coming, with me, tonight, Spirit Quest, bring your boyfriend," Luke demanded.

"Are you serious? Then I would get grounded for years."

"You're not gonna let him get away with that cruel punishment. Are you? It's an outrage! These are the best years of your life. He's gonna ruin it all for you if you don't do something about it."

"Well... Alright. Mike is not my boyfriend by the way," she said.

"There was a time when I had to sneak out, too. I know you don't usually go out just to be friends," he said.

"I guess I've had a crush on him for a while. I've known him since junior high, but never got to hang out with him much outside of school. You'll probably get along with him. He smokes pot, too."

"Good, so he won't be a party pooper. Do you smoke?"

"Are you kidding? If my dad ever found out... it wouldn't be pretty. Mike always talks about it. I almost tried it last night but I chickened out. I had a bad feeling my dad knew I left."

Luke's brain started to catch up with the impulse decision he just made. *So innocent*, he thought, *I hope I'm not making a mistake.*

She's curious. She will probably end up doing this stuff anyway. I'm doing her a favor. She needs this.

What if her dad calls the cops? She's only fifteen or something.

That's fine, remember what you used to do when you were her age? It's fine. It's all for the good. We're seeking spiritual enlightenment. Is that a sin? It's not like you're taking her out to the woods to do meth and triple C's. It's fine. This will go great.

"What's a spirit quest anyway?" said Natalie.

"Hmm... I won't lie, it's a magical experience. We cleanse the ego by eating mushrooms and becoming one with the universe."

"Mushrooms?" she whispered, eyes wide.

"Yeah. It's a ritual people have done for thousands of years; nothing to be scared of. To be honest, it will probably be the most profound experience of your life."

"Well... if you put it that way it sounds pretty innocent. I'm gonna text Mike right now," she said.

~~~

Luke sat anxiously in history class, hoping to avoid the inevitable talk with his teacher. He narrowly escaped his Government teacher in his previous class. This teacher is more involved; more likely to give the "you're not going to make it" speech. *I will make it. I just procrastinate. There is still time to make up all the work. Don't need the speech. Spare the awkwardness; I know what I need to do.* With less than a minute left, Mr. Anderson was already eyeing Luke. *If only I sat at the front I could get away faster. Here it goes.*
~~~

The bell rang. Luke followed the crowd, avoiding eye contact. "Luke, may I speak with you?" said Mr. Anderson. Luke stopped and looked up. The rest of the class rushed out and he was left with his teacher. "I'm afraid I need to go over missing assignments with you." Mr. Anderson motioned Luke over to the computer.

"I know about them," said Luke, "I have them all written down and I will finish them before finals."

"This is a big list. You're the furthest behind in the class. The only way you can pass this class is if you get all these in and get at least an eighty percent on your final."

"I got it. I'll get it," said Luke.

"Alright, I'll see you on Monday."

Brutal, Luke thought as he walked to his math class. *That is worse than I thought. I'll have to become some sort of superhuman if I have a fighting chance. Gotta get focused... after tonight.*

~~~

"Thank you, Jesus," Luke said. The final bell rang and he almost ran to the parking lot. He didn't bother to let the engine warm up or even light a cigarette. *It's 3:15. Got to be to work at 4:30. First stop, Dave's.*

Dave's apartment was only five minutes away from the school. This was one of Luke's more common stops. They had been friends for three years, ever since Luke wandered onto Dave's back porch one night. Luke had been blacked out on triple C's and Dramamine. He didn't even know his name, so Dave took him in. When Luke sobered up the next day they became friends; and have been ever since.

Luke pulled into his usual parking space. He grabbed his herb and went inside. Tim and Jack were in the living room playing X-Box. Both were so absorbed into the game they didn't look up to greet Luke. "Hey guys, where's Dave?" said Luke.

"In his room watching TV," said Jack.

Jack and Tim were Luke's friends; about the same age too. Luke introduced them to Dave and they'd taken full advantage of his hospitality. Dave was almost fifty. He had just moved to Montana when he met Luke. Since then, most of his friends had been young people he met though Luke.

Luke knocked on the bedroom door and Dave told him to come in. The air was smokey. The sitcom, Two and a Half Men, was on the television. "Hey Luke, how was school?"

"Not too bad. You wanna smoke?" Luke said as he sat down and loaded the
~~~

pipe. Of course Dave did. It was almost a daily routine for Luke to stop by Dave's after school. Before they could pass it twice, Tim and Jack were knocking on the door.

"Come on in," said Dave. They came in with hungry eyes, never missing an opportunity at a free smoke session.

"Well you guys… I have an announcement to make" said Luke, "Spirit quest tonight. It's mandatory."

"What kind of spirit quest do you propose?" said Jack.

"I'm thinkin Ashley Lake. I'm gettin an ounce of shrooms, so feel free to bring anyone you want," said Luke.

Dave wasn't quite as excited as Tim or Jack. "I don't know about the mushrooms. It tears my gut up so bad," said Dave. "Can you get any of that LSD we did a few weeks ago?"

"No LSD. Tonight is mushrooms. These came from Washington. They're awesome. You'll only need to eat a gram or two," said Luke.

"I'll think about it. No guarantees."

After the smoking was over, Dave gave everyone a Marlboro. They sat anticipating their adventure. "I'll get glow sticks," said Tim. "Do we need alcohol?"

"No alcohol. It's a spirit quest. Plus, we don't need the unnecessary risk. If cops come and we're trippin, we're fine. If we're drunk, the party is over," said Luke.

"Good call," said Jack. "Who's all gonna drive?" asked Tim.

"Don't worry. The universe will conspire to our purposes," Luke explained.

Tim and Jack went back to the video games after a while. Luke looked at the clock. It was almost four. Dave reached under the bed and pulled out a mirror with lines of methadone on it. "You wanna get high? It will make work go by in a flash," said Dave.

"No thanks. I'd better not."

"Suit yourself." Dave snorted one of the small lines. "Where's that girl of yours been anyway?" Dave asked.

"Her sister has been in town for the past week or so. She's been with her a lot lately. I'm pretty sure she's coming with us tonight; might even bring some friends."

"Tonight might be my last fun night for a while. I'm so far behind in school. If I don't pass my classes I won't graduate. Then all this time I've spent in school would be wasted. So I gotta get it done, no matter what. So it would be super cool if you would come on our adventure tonight."

Dave looked at Luke with a smile. "You're a good kid. I really am proud of you. All your friends have no ambition. I still love em and all, but you're different. That's why I like you so much. If it means a lot to you, I'll come on your spirit quest."

"Awesome. Thanks Dave." Luke looked at the clock again. It was four. "I better get going. Gotta meet dude before I go to work. Told him I would be at Super 1 at ten after."

"Alright. we'll see you tonight."

Luke said goodbye to his friends and left in a hurry. It wasn't until he got into his car he realized how stoned he was. *Super stoned on Friday night. Smart thinking. Aren't I working sauté tonight? Better pay attention. Actually you better take an Adderall. That will make you think straight. No. I don't need to wear out my dopamine receptors for work. Better save it for homework.*

~~~

When Luke pulled into Super 1 parking lot, Shawn was already there. He was parked in the far corner in his big Silverado. Luke pulled up next to him and climbed in the passenger side. Shawn has an intimidating appearance. He's huge, muscular, and looks serious most of the time. Also he's rich. He's got nice cars and some good connections. "How did everything go this week," said Shawn?

"It went good. I got rid of it all. Only got personal left," said Luke.

"Good deal. I got another QP for you." Shawn set a paper sack on Luke's lap. "I also got another surprise that came in with the shrooms. You ever done 2C-B?" said Shawn.

"You're kidding! I love 2C-B, that shit's hard to find."

"So you want some?"

"Of course I do. How much you got?"

"Well, it's all in capsules and its ten dollars a dose. There's a limited supply so that's the best I can do this time. The shrooms are $120 an ounce. They're even better than the last ones I got you," said Shawn.

"Hell yeah. I want twenty capsules of the 2C and one and a half ounces of the other," said Luke.

When the exchange was done, Luke hopped out with his merchandise and got into his car. Luke had a lot to lose, so he crammed as much of it as he could into his glove compartment and locked it.

Luke got to Sizzle Steakhouse five minutes late. The parking lot was filling up already. It was going to be a busy night. He ran inside and clocked on, making apologies to his co-workers. After he changed into his work clothes he found his
~~~

place on the line. He was still stoned. The situation was intimidating even though he had done this for years. *First thing: make sure my station is stocked...*

Luke made it through the evening rush. It was 8:15, time for a smoke. He went outside, lit a cigarette, and pulled out his phone. *New message?*

(From Stacy): Subject: What are you doing tonight?

(From Luke): Spirit Quest. Remember?

(From Stacy): You should come to Whitefish

(From Luke): I need spirit quest. Plz come.

(From Stacy): Maybe. idk yet

Luke replied to his other messages then put his phone away. He sat down on a milk crate and looked at his cigarette. *Damn. I really need to spend some time with Stacy. She's been over at that mansion way too much. Before long she'll be shootin heroin. I seen those track marks on her sister; pretty freakin obvious.*

"Hey Luke. You need a truck?" It was Andy, one of Luke's co-workers.

"Umm... maybe. Why?" asked Luke.

"See that brown Suburban in the back of the parking lot?" said Andy, "My grandpa just gave it to me for replacing the head gasket on his Chevy."

Luke looked at the SUV suspiciously, "How much do you want for it?"

"From you? I just wanted to see if you would give me some pot for it. It's in pretty good shape actually, good tires even."

"What year is it?" said Luke.

"85. C'mon, take a look if you're interested." They walked out to the truck. Andy got in and started it up. The engine roared as he revved it up. Luke looked under the truck. The muffler was gone, it was straight piped.

"This belonged to your grandpa?" Luke was skeptical.

"Yeah. I did the exhaust a few years ago. All the dents and scratches are from my brother. He stole it when he was drunk one night," Andy explained, "It's yours for a half ounce."

"Deal! I'll even throw in some mushrooms or 2C-B."

"Too see what?" said Andy.

"You haven't tried 2C-B? You should come with us tonight. Parties on me," said Luke.

"Well, I can't think of anything better to do," said Andy.

~~~

The rest of the night at work dragged on terribly. When he finally got off work at 11:30 his phone was flooded with texts and missed calls. He knew most of his friends would be waiting at Dave's so he called Natalie first.

"Hello?" she answered.
~~~

"Hey, I just got off work."

"I'm at Albertson's with Mike. When are you going to come get us?"

"Pretty soon. I'll text when I'm on my way," he said.

The next call was Stacy... No answer. *Probably drunk already, Luke thought, Fine. This is my night. It might even be healthy for me to be away from her for this.*

Luke went to his car, grabbed his drugs and stashed most of the pot in his secret hiding place under the dash. He would only bring a half ounce with him, any more than that would be a liability. After that, Luke and Andy got in the Suburban. Luke pulled out his Crown Royal bag of goodies. He handed one capsule to Andy and swallowed one himself. "Eat it now and we will be trippin in less than an hour."

Now the clock was ticking. Luke needed to hurry if he planned to make the drive sober. Luke drove out of the parking lot and made another phone call. *Since Stacy won't be coming I guess I can call my cousin she hates so bad.*

"Hello?" he answered.

"Blue! Where are you?" asked Luke.

"I'm at Walmart. What's up with you?" said Blue.

"I got some 2C-B. We're goin' to Ashley Lake."

"2C-B?" said Blue.

"It's like LSD and little like X. Can I pick you up or what?"

"Sure bro, I got a couple friends with me."

"That's fine, I'll be there in twenty," said Luke.

Luke drove and texted frantically on his way to Dave's. When he got there everyone was waiting outside as he instructed. Dave, Tim, Jack, and Fat Jared got in. Andy loaded a pipe and started the circle as Luke headed towards his next stop.

By the time Luke got to Albertson's there was Dubstep blaring in the Suburban. Andy had hooked up Luke's I-pod into the tape deck adapter. His ghetto-rigged sub was performing well considering the sloppy setup. Natalie and Mike were waiting by the entrance. Fat Jared opened the back door and told them to squeeze in behind him. They got in with nervous looks.

A bag of mushrooms was being passed around on the way to Walmart. Luke was the first to take a pinch and munch them down. When the bag got to the back Mike did not hesitate. Natalie ate them more cautiously. There were still pipes going around when they arrived at Walmart. Luke parked next to his cousin who was talking with some people in a Ford Explorer. Fat Jared opened the door again, this time a cloud of smoke poured out. Blue and two girls climbed in, almost piling on Mike and Natalie in the back.

The SUV was full. The quest had begun. There were ten people. They were headed to Ashley Lake. Three capsules were passed back to Blue and his two friends. Natalie was now on Mike's lap as they watched in amazement.

For Natalie, this was sensory overload. She had never even imagined a scene like this. These people were crazy; reckless with their mysterious capsules and loud music. *Is that the pot or the music making me feel so good? Am I high? I only took two hits. Did I just eat mushrooms? What does that even mean? What is that fat guy doing? Is he arguing with that old guy? He looks so stupid.* Natalie started laughing and pointed at Jared. Jared looked at her with a worried look. His concern made her laugh even harder. "I don't even know what you're talking about. I'm sorry," she said.

Jared shrugged it off and continued to talk over the music. The mood was good. The energy was chaotic.

~~~

After twenty minutes on the highway Luke turned onto Ashley Lake Road. He could feel it in his stomach; the chemicals were kicking in. He looked over at Andy. There was a mental exchange. They would not make it, not sober anyway.

The winding gravel road was becoming treacherous. The music was getting fuzzy. The lights on the dash were bright and blurry. Luke could feel his senses expanding, reaching out, and inviting the forest to communicate with him. He was leaning forward in his seat, focused on the trees. Luke was no longer a driver; he was the rumbling machine that propelled itself through the forest.

"Luke," said Tim. He was leaning forward between the two front seats, "You're going really fast and I think you've almost gone around the entire lake. We passed a really good spot a few minutes ago."

"Oh." He slowed down and looked for a place to turn around. The turnaround was much more difficult than it should have been; a six point turn. He approached the campsite with caution and turned down the uneven dirt road toward the lake. The tire tracks were deep, making the vehicle shift violently as it creeped down the trail.

Before long they were parked right next to the lake. Luke shut off the Suburban and got out. Everyone else followed suit, except they were already wearing glow accessories. It was quiet. Luke turned the music back on.

"Come help us get firewood," said Blue from a distance. Glowing people spread in all directions. Tim was throwing glow sticks in the trees. Fat Jared was the first to bring over a big pile of mossy branches. It caught on fire quickly. Soon more branches were being thrown on top.

"That's probably enough, guys," said Luke as he stared at the huge pile. In a couple minutes the fire was high and the music was blaring.
~~~

Dave was next to Luke with a flask of whiskey in his hand. "Hey Luke... that 2C stuff is good."

"I know. We really lucked out this time. I've never found this stuff in Montana. Only done it at big festies outta state," said Luke.

Luke went to check on Natalie. She was sitting on a log by the fire. Luke sat down next to her. "How are you doing?" he asked.

Natalie started laughing, "I can't stop looking at this fire. It's really weird. As long as I look at the fire I won't go crazy. I can't look at anyone. That fat guy had hair growing out of his face," she said.

"Well, that's perfectly normal. Weird things happen."

"Are the trees always... just chillin?" she said, "I can feel them."

"Yeah. They are always just chillin." They both laughed.

~~~

Tim was sitting on the ground in the forest with a pocket knife and a box of glow sticks. From here the music was quiet and the fire barely visible. He tore up the box and cracked all the glow sticks. When they were all glowing he cut off the tops and handed them to Jack, Mike, Jared, and Andy. After that they ran around laughing while splattering glowing juice all over the trees.

Everyone else was by the fire. Blue saw what was happening and pointed, "Hey look." There was the glowing forest and he ran towards it. Tim was still cutting up glow sticks. They all took some and helped splatter the trees. Jack came running through, his clothes and face covered with glowing juice.

"Where did he come from?" one girl asked.

"Where's he going?" said another.

Was that fear on his face, thought Luke, *or was it just glow stick juice? I'd better check it out.*

Luke walked in the direction Jack had run. He could hear branches breaking ahead of him but could see nothing. As he got closer to the lake he could hear splashing. His heart pounded, he panicked.

"Jack!" He saw a splash and jumped in the water after it. It wasn't deep. He walked out neck deep and grabbed Jack. "What are you doing?" said Luke.

Jack stared at the shore from the water, "I can't go back."

"You can't stay out here. What the hell are you thinking?" said Luke.

"There's evil trees out there. They grew teeth and claws. They tried to grab me!" said Jack.

"It's in your head, I promise. We're trippin, remember?" That brought him back a little. He followed Luke and they went to the fire. Luke took off his clothes and laid them on a log next to the fire. Now all he wore was his blue
~~~

Smurf boxers as he stood close to the fire.

Luke saw headlights. *Oh no, this could be weird. Please don't come here.*

They came. Luke stood all alone in the headlights. Jack was on the ground huddled by the fire. The vehicle stopped right in front of Luke. The lights turned off and the doors opened. Four girls got out. Luke recognized one of them but knew none of their names.

"Luke!" one of them squealed as she ran up and gave him a hug. One of the other girls gave him a hug also, "I don't know you but I fuckin love you!" she said. The other girls ran to the glow sticks that were on the ground and started waving them around dancing with each other.

"So, where is everyone? Tim told me you guys were out here," said the girl Luke recognized.

"Umm... Yeah. they're somewhere out there." He waved his arm at the forest.

"Hmm, Tim also said you have some awesome stuff," she said.

"2C-B?"

"We want to try it."

Luke went to the Suburban and grabbed four capsules. He handed them to the girls.

"Can we snort it?" she said.

"It sucks, but you'll be trippin' immediately."

"I'm doin it!" They poured the fluffy powder on the hood of their Subaru and sniffed it up with a twenty. They moaned in pain. One of the girls gave Luke a capsule of MDMA.

By the time they recovered from the pain they were hallucinating. "What happened to your clothes?" said one girl.

"I jumped in the lake." She went to her car and came back with a foil emergency blanket. "Thank you," Luke said as he tied it around his neck as a cape. "Should we go find the tribe?"

~~~

Natalie was following her new friends down the gravel road. They had just been exploring through the trees along the lake. Their musical anthem was playing from Tim's phone and the trees were dancing with the beat. *So much personality,* thought Natalie, *Angry tree, sad tree, happy tree. I love you friendly tree. Mean tree, don't look at me!*

Moments later there were green, blue, and yellow lights bouncing around in the distance. When they got closer Natalie wondered if she was hallucinating. Luke still wore the Smurf boxers and the foil cape. The girls and he began to run. They collided into a group hug. "I freakin love you people!" Luke shouted
~~~

while hugging the group. "This way you guys!" He ran into the woods, away from the lake. Everyone followed.

"The quest goes on," said Dave from the back of the pack. Natalie was walking next to him. They climbed over branches in the un-tracked wilderness. The foliage was lit up by glow stick and cell phone light; everything was growing, twisting, and vibrating with energy.

The hike went on, full of laughter; much more laughter than conversation. The trees changed and Luke came to a stop. "This is where we need to be. These are the wisdom trees. Let us learn from them." The trees gave of an aura of peace and understanding.

"It's true," said Tim, "This is no accident. We were meant to find these trees."

Everyone felt it; they were in the presence of a guru. One tree even started to grow a mossy Fu Manchu. They all found places to sit around the trees. A girl hugged one of the trees and held it for some time. "I love you tree."

They eventually wandered back to the campsite. It was quiet. Jack was standing by the fire. "Your battery died."

"That sucks," said Luke, "sorry we took so long. We got side tracked, literally." Luke's boxers were dirty and his cape was torn. A group of people were down by the lake, laughing carelessly. The sky was showing signs of daylight.

Blue and his two girlfriends hopped out of the Suburban. They looked evil. "I can get us some jumper cables," said Blue. "Ask your friend if I can borrow her car."

"Sure," Luke went to ask the girls. The girl gave him the keys.

"Alright. I'll be back soon." Blue left with the two girls he brought.

Luke went to see what everyone was doing by the lake. He sat down next to Andy who was smoking a cigarette. "Can I please have one of those?" asked Luke.

"Sure, bud." Andy handed him a Marlboro and a lighter.

"How you feelin?" said Luke.

"Trippin'."

"Yeah… me too."

The sky had a pink tint from the sun getting ready to creep over the mountains. "Smoke time," Andy pulled out his pipe, still loaded with a half burnt bowl. He took a hit and passed it to Luke. Natalie joined them with a smile. "I love it here," she said, "It's so beautiful."

"We are a part of a very loving universe," said Luke.

"Thank you for showing me all this. I've learned so much."

"I'm glad I could share it with you" he said.

The smell of weed traveled well. Clusters of people came and gathered around the circle on the beach. Even Jack and the other two girls came from the warmth of the fire to partake. Andy loaded the pipe again and continued the rotation. Before the session was done the sunrise was at peak intensity. There was a vivacious blend of red, orange, and pink that flooded the senses. They all sat in silence hoping it would last forever.

Blue came back at 7am. He jump started the Suburban. Dave was asleep in the passenger seat. Everyone else was huddled around the dying fire. "How'd your trip go, guys?" Blue asked.

"Awesome," said Tim, "How was yours?"

Blue made an impression of an airplane pilot, "We are three thousand feet above sea level; no oxygen is needed."

"I can't believe I let you drive like that," said the owner of the car.

The SUV was beginning to look inviting. People started climbing in. *Well, I guess it might be time to go,* thought Luke. *We need food. Where should I take these people?*

Tim got in a few minutes later. "Carly and them are heading out."

Luke looked back as the Subaru was creeping down the dirt trail. A few minutes later Luke drove back to town as well.

Luke dropped everyone off except Jared, Mike, and Natalie. The drive was treacherous because Luke was still hallucinating. He drove to the restaurant to pick up his Chrysler. Jared followed it to Luke's house.

It was noon when Luke pulled into his driveway with both of his vehicles. He went inside with his friends. His parents were in the kitchen. "Hey mom, hey dad, this is Mike and Natalie."

"Nice to meet you two. Hello, brain fry," Alice greeted Jared.

"Hi, Alice," said Jared. Alice knew him as 'brain fry'. It was a nickname that stuck after the first time she met him when Jared had eaten a bottle of Dramamine before he came over.

"Are you kids' hungry? Help yourselves to whatever you want. Luke, get them some food," said Alice. "Feel free to take showers if you'd like."

"So, how did your night go?" said Allan, " Do anything exciting?"

"We did a spirit quest," said Luke. "Got some people up to Ashley Lake and ate mushrooms. I also got a new truck; it's in the driveway right now. I got it for a couple hundred bucks."

"Oh wow," said Allan, "let's go see!"

Luke set three boxes of cereal down on the kitchen table and went to the fridge. "You guys like cereal? If you want something else just look around."

Jared started digging through the pantry, "Where's all the fruity sweet stuff?"

"We like to eat healthy around here. None of that marshmallow fruity junk. You need to cut down on that stuff anyway," said Luke.

"Hey! This is my survival suit." Jared grabbed his stomach and jiggled it around, "I worked hard for this. It's what keeps me going when I don't have any food."

"Good plan Jared," Luke replied.

They ate in silence while Natalie thought about her situation.

"Mike, what are your plans for the day?" Natalie asked.

"I was thinkin of going home to take a nap. Then maybe goin to the skate park later. You can come with me if you want."

"Sweet." *Problem solved. For now.*

~~~

Luke barely made it to work without falling asleep. He knew that as soon as he walked through those doors he would be on autopilot. At work he didn't have to worry about being tired; making it there was the challenge.

Around 5pm he started getting texts form Stacy. On his eight O'clock smoke break he called her.

"Hello?"

"Hi, Stacy."

"Luke, I miss you. We need to hangout tonight."

"Well, okay. Are you still in Whitefish?"

"Yeah. Will you come get me when you're off work?"

"Sure. I can do that. I'll call when I'm on my way. It will be around midnight."

"Okay. I love you."

"I love you too. I'll see you later." Luke hung up. *Crap. I guess I'd better go take an Adderall unless I want to crash into a tree later.* Luke walked out to the parking lot and got into his truck. He grabbed the pills from under his seat. *Thank god for Jared. He might be a lazy bum, but he's sure good for giving me his script every month.* Luke took one out and swallowed it. *If I took two I'd probably be up all night. Plus, Stacy would probably accuse me of doing meth.*

Luke drove to Whitefish with a fresh supply of energy and a sense of euphoria. Combined with the after-work smoke session and sleep deprivation, Luke enjoyed a comfortable loopiness. He drove down the fancy Whitefish street, this time in an even trashier vehicle.

Stacy walked out into the street looking confused. Luke flashed his lights and waved his arm out the window. She walked over to the Suburban and got in. She scooted next to him on the bench seat and gave him a long hug and kiss. "Whose truck is this?" she asked.
~~~

"Its mine. I got it last night," he said. It roared as he accelerated down the street.

"I like it." She had her head on his shoulder and hand on his thigh. "We should go somewhere," she said.

"Time to take its virginity?"

"Definitely time."

Luke turned up the music and they drove to one of their secret places. They went up a mountain and turned off on an old, almost non-existent, logging road. It came to an opening that overlooked the town of Kalispell.

Luke parked the truck and put his arms around Stacy. They held each other for a few moments. Stacy kissed him, "Mmh, I missed you."

"I missed you too, gorgeous," he kissed her again.

The kissing became passionate. Stacy's hand went for Luke's pants. Luke reached for Stacy's back and began to undue her bra strap. The bra came off. He caressed her breasts. She reached beneath his thin chef pants and felt him as well.

Stacy stopped kissing him and looked him in the eyes, smiling. She pushed him back against the driver's side door and pulled his pants down just enough. She went down, teasing with her tongue at first. Luke gripped her hair with ecstatic anticipation, then she went for it, mercilessly.

In less than a minute Luke was quivering, trying to warn her. She persisted, ignoring his attempts to pull her away. Then he came, tense and helpless. She continued, finishing him off for a few more unbearable moments, then came up kissing him repeatedly on the neck.

"Oh, you're terrible," he said, pulling off her shirt. He pushed her down onto her back, and began kissing her bare, beautiful breasts. His kissing ventured lower. She knew what was happening and guided him in anticipation.

He began to unbutton her pants while kissing her waistline. Finally, he pulled her pants off, leaving her with nothing on. His kisses continued at the waist, making their way to her inner thigh. The teasing was unbearable. She was wet with desire.

Finally his tongue made contact, starting slow and passionate. Then he dug deeper, showing the same determination she had shown him. She moaned with pleasure, digging her nails into his hair.

This went on until she couldn't bear it any longer. She wanted him inside her. Stacy tore off his clothes and pulled him to the back seat. She climbed on top straddling him and initiating the penetration. They bounced off each other with vicious determination until her legs seized up from the climax. She was helpless, that's when Luke took control and flipped her onto her back.

"Oh, you asshole," she said as he put her legs into a criss-cross position. He rested on top of her with her legs crossed against his chest. She guided him in, as it was difficult from this position. He began the motion gaining momentum. She tore at his back as the intensity escalated. Then another orgasm, this time simultaneous, she looked helplessly into his eyes as they shared the peak experience. Luke went a few more moments until his efforts finally failed him. He rolled off next to her. They held each other, naked, in a beautiful silence. Those concluding moments were of supreme peace; total freedom, without a care in the world.

"How was your time with your sister?" he asked.

"Well, we smoked a lot of weed. Also drank a little. I didn't get wasted or anything. We went to a bonfire last night; it was kind of a hick party."

"Right on," said Luke. He didn't want to ask anymore. Most of their fights started with questions. Too many questions meant he was being over possessive. He had been trying hard to give her space, no matter how bad he wanted to interrogate her.

"When was the last time you slept?" she asked?

"Thursday night," he said.

"So you're on Adderall?

"I took one at work after I called you."

"Just one?" she said.

"Yeah, I promise. Do you believe me?" he said.

"I believe you. So are you gonna stay up all night?" she said.

"I wasn't planning on it. Why? Do you want one? I'm not tired at all."

"Yeah, give me two," she said.

"If you take two, I'm gonna take another. And if we take two we might as well take three," he said.

"Okay, gimme three." They put their clothes on and went for a drive.

~~~

"Wow. It's almost two, and we need gas," said Stacy.

"Yeah, we'd better fill up and head home before bar close. Too many cops out here."

When they got to Luke's house his parents were asleep. They snuck up to his room and turned on the lights and locked the door. Stacy went to the bed and jumped in. She pulled the blanket up to her nose; her dilated pupils were peeking at Luke invitingly. He took his clothes off and got in with her. She went down on him. He went down on her. They had some sex.
~~~

Later Luke worked on homework while Stacy played around on the internet. She played music and downloaded new songs on Luke's I-pod. When the sun came up they cleaned both of Luke's vehicles.

Good and evil, we know, in the field of this world grow up together almost inseparably.
-John Milton

Chapter 4: Desperate Measures

Monday 5-13-2010

Luke came into art class feeling well rested. He slept ten hours Sunday night, but that was all the sleep he got over the weekend. For him, it was a typical Monday morning after a typical weekend. When he sat down next to Natalie, she was bursting with excitement. She looked at him, waiting for him to ask. "Good morning, Natalie, how did your weekend go?"

"It was great! I stayed with Mike all weekend after you dropped us off. His mom is super cool. I told her about my situation and she said I could stay as long as I needed. She even let me wear her clothes, see? She's the same size as me, only a little taller."

"That's great. Did you ever talk to your parents?"

"I did call my mom. She said my dad was pretty pissed. Guess he doesn't want me to come home until I've learned my lesson. She thinks he will get over it and lighten up, so I'm just gonna stay with Mike until then."

"That's good, I'm glad it all worked out. So you're glad I invited you on the adventure this weekend?" said Luke.

"Yeah. Friday night was a mind blow. I would never have imagined anything like that could have existed. I wish I could show everyone," she said.

"Well, I don't think everyone is quite that open minded. Also, I don't really like being labeled as a druggy. So I keep it on the down-low at school. I already kinda blew my cover; you've still got your super innocent reputation. Keep it as long as you can."

"That's good thinking Luke. I like that." She paused for a moment and worked on her project. "How did the rest of your weekend go?" she asked?

"It was pretty good. I got a lot done; spent some time with my girl. I gotta call off all the partying until school is over. I've got a stupidly huge amount of homework I need to do. I gotta make up for an entire semester of neglected assignments."

"That's terrible. How are you gonna make it? School is almost over," she said.

"Yeah. It sucks. I'll make it, no matter what it takes."

On the way to history Luke began to panic. *Three weeks? I'm fucked. Finals start on the 29th. That means I need to have all my work in by the 27th. How many Adderall does it take to make this possible? More than I could ever get my hands on, that's for sure. Maybe I should go see Blue. Yeah. That would ruin things with Stacy for sure. She's gonna be on my ass about eating all the Adderall anyway, might as well go all the way. Extreme circumstances call for extreme measures. My future depends on this.*

~~~

On the way out of school Luke called Blue.

"Hello?"

"Blue, where are you?"

"I'm at the tent."

"Can I come by?"

"Yeah bro."

"I'll be there soon." Luke hung up the phone and got in his truck. His phone exploded with text messages. Lots of people needed weed; three messages from Stacy; missed calls from Stacy. *Can't talk now. On a mission to finish school.*

Blue's tent was in West Valley, about thirty minutes out of Kalispell. It wasn't just a tent, it was a circus tent; A tent with carpet, couches, refrigerator, microwave, TV, and a wood stove. Running water was right outside next to his landlord's cabin. It was also hidden; hard to find with no neighbors nearby.

Luke turned off the gravel road up a rugged dirt driveway. He winded through the trees until he saw the tent. The tiny cabin was barely visible behind the tent. Blue was out front working on an old Toyota Camry. Luke pulled up next to him and got out. "Hey Blue, what's up with you?" he said.

"Same shit, dude. Let's go inside."
~~~

The tent was nice as ever besides the clutter of stereo speakers and electronics in one corner. They sat down at the couch, "So, what's goin' on with you?" said Blue.

"Well actually, I was seein if you got any criss."

"Hell yeah buddy, let's get high." Blue grabbed a glass pipe out of the night stand next to the couch. "You gonna get in trouble with that girl of yours?"

"That doesn't matter right now. You see, I've got less than three weeks of school left and I'm way behind. If I plan on graduating I'm gonna have to get really focused and skip sleep altogether."

"You sure picked the right time. I just made a run to Oregon; got back last night. All that bunk crap around here's got me about to start robbin people, so I figured it was time to see a dude back home," said Blue.

Blue took a hit off the glass pipe and handed it to Luke who did the same. "How did you get there?" said Luke.

"I drove. Took that Toyota you saw outside," he said.

"You're freakin nuts! With those crappy tires and temporary paper license plates? You could have taken my Chrysler. How much shit did you pick up?"

"I got a lot, but it's all on front. So I gotta send some cash after I flip some of it."

Luke was high. The one hit got him quick. "Wow. That is some good shit."

"Yeah bro, it's the best. I'm gonna have to cut it just sell it to these stupid junkies around here." Blue took one more hit and handed it back to Luke.

Luke took one more hit and handed it back. "Could I bum a QG? I'm outta cash for the moment."

"Don't even trip. I got you covered bro." He handed Luke a tiny square zip-lock with devils on it.

"Thanks Blue, I appreciate it."

They went outside to smoke a cigarette. Being high made the cigarette more satisfying than usual. Luke examined the rusted out car his cousin had risked his life and freedom in. He pictured him cruising down the interstate with the sun rising, paper license plates flapping in the wind. The rear passenger window was broken and covered with a piece of garbage bag. Blue was the drunk driver who always made it home.

"It's really a miracle you made it," said Luke.

"Sometimes you just gotta take a chance. It felt right, so I did it. You can't run around being paranoid, that's what will get you in trouble."

"Whatever you say, dude. I'd better get going. Lots I need to do, very little time. Need anything? Want a nugget for later?"

"Yeah. Sure bro," said Blue.

Luke gave Blue some weed and drove off. He turned the music up; Rob Zombie this time. *Now we're freakin motivated! No deliveries today, time to kill some homework.* He glanced at his phone on the passenger seat. It was full of missed calls and text messages. *Fuck em.*

~~~

When Luke got home he grabbed his backpack and ran to his room. He pulled out his history textbook and planner where all the missing assignments were listed. First assignment: Read Chapter 3, answer questions 1-6 p.47; 2, 4-7 p.56;1, 3, 5 p.63. *Alright, I guess we will start here.*

He read to page 47 with lightning speed and perfect retention. He answered the questions then glanced at his phone. Lots of people needed weed. He gave them all the same reply: "If you need. Come to my house."

Moments later his phone flooded with either complaints or confirmation. He didn't care about the complaints, the message was clear. What he did care about was the missed calls from Stacy. *I'd better call her.*

"Hello," she answered quietly.

"Stacy, hi," he said.

"Where have you been? I called you ... earlier."

"Homework. I've been frantically doing homework. My phone exploded so I ignored it altogether." There was a long pause. "Stacy, are you there?"

"Yeah, sorry... just tired."

Tired? Yeah right. "Alright, I'll let you go then. I'll just be working on homework all night." *Oops,* "I mean, not all night," *crap* ,"I gotta go. I love you, bye." He hung up the phone. *That was stupid. Eh, who cares? She's so high on pills she probably won't even remember talking to me. I'd better pre-weigh some bags. That way they can get in and get out.*

~~~

People started showing up and he would tell them to go in the garage. The first people were a young couple. They showed up ten minutes after he told them they could come over. The next showed up two minutes later. She was a waitress from Luke's restaurant. They were enticed by the vaporizer and insisted on loading it. *Alright, they can loiter until the last person gets here. Then they gotta go.*

Fat Jared was the last person to show up. By then Luke's pockets were packed full of cash and there were nine people (including Luke's parents) in the garage. Luke's parents were talking with them as if they were their own friends. It was a comfortable setting and people did not want to leave. Luke's anxiety began to build, *Homework*, he thought, *gotta get to that homework. It would be rude to tell all these people to leave. Plus, they loaded that vaporizer; they should be able to finish it. Maybe I could just sneak away.*

"Okay guys," said Luke "I gotta go work on somethin. Go ahead and finish smoking, I'll see you all later."

"Bye Luke," said one person.

"Thank you," said another.

He retreated up the stairs to his room and sat down at his desk. Back to chapter 3, page 48...

~~~

It was ten o'clock when Stacy showed up without warning. Luke was sitting at his desk and looked at her with dilated pupils. "What the fuck, Luke? First you ignored my phone calls, and then you fuckin hang up on me?"

"I'm sorry, I-"

"Are you high? The last time you tried avoiding me it was because you were high." She came closer and looked into his eyes. "You are fucking high!"

"You're fucking high! Look at your pupils, They're fuckin pinpricks," said Luke. "Don't yell at *me*, I'm just trying to do my homework."

"Don't try to turn this around on me. You promised you wouldn't do that shit anymore," she said through tears.

"Oh come on, what even makes you think-"

"Don't even try to lie," she cut him off, "I know when you're lying and I can tell you're about to now."

"Fine. alright, I panicked. I'm sorry. School's almost over and I'm about to fail. I needed some serious stimulation. Is that so bad? Will you forgive me?" he said.

"Are you gonna do it again?" she said.

"Honestly? Can I be honest with you?" She nodded. "If I tell you, will you be honest about your pill problem?" Luke added. She nodded again, "Well, I was only planning on getting high until I graduate; Just a desperate measure for a desperate situation."

"Thats fucking horrible. How can you possibly think doing meth is going to help you graduate?"

"You have no room to judge. All you do is drink, sell your pills, and hang out with heroin addicts. At least I'm trying to do something with my life. You're just gonna turn out an alcoholic pill junkie just like your mom." Luke felt immediate regret. She looked at him for a moment. Her tears turned into sobs and she ran out of the house. By the sound of the car he could tell it was her sister who drove her. Luke didn't dare to look out the window to see.

Great, I really messed that up didn't I? That's probably the meanest thing I could have said
~~~

to her. What a fuckin prick.

Luke loaded a pipe and took it out to the front porch. After one hit his dad came out. "Hey Luke, is everything alright?"

"Yeah. Kinda. I don't know. I said something really mean to Stacy."

"Well, you want to tell me whats going on?"

"Sure." Luke paused, took a hit, and handed the pipe to his dad. "You know how I've been stressin over all my homework? Well, I took some Adderall today so I could get a bunch of work done. She thought I was avoiding her so she came over. When she saw that I was high she accused me of being on meth. I got mad and told her she has her own problems to worry about; except I said it meaner than I meant to."

"Why would she think you're on meth?" said Allan.

"It's because of some of the people I hang around, I guess. Just because she hangs with heroin addicts doesn't mean she does heroin, does it?"

"The bible says something about that. It says to take a close look at your friends, because that is what you will become. Something like that, anyway. You get the message," said Allan.

"Yeah dad, it does make sense." Luke lit a cigarette.

"Are you gonna be alright with all your school work?"

"Yeah, I will. Without a doubt." Luke made his decision. There was no turning back. After the cigarette Luke went back inside. "Good talk, dad. Gotta get back to homework."

~~~

Luke worked on homework until eleven. There were a few text messages and missed calls which he ignored. He was in no mood for people. Just then his mother came upstairs and knocked on the door. "Yeah?" he answered.

She opened the door, "Hey buddy, how are you?"

"I'm good. Really busy. I would rather not be interrupted."

"Okay sweetie. Do you need anything? Are you hungry? I'll get you something."

"I'm fine! Would you please go away?" She paused, the door started to close. Luke got up and walked towards the door, "Hey mom, I'm sorry," he gave her a hug, "I don't wanna be mean. I'm just stressed out. I know you just want to help. I'm sorry."

"That's okay. I know you're having a tough time," she said.

"It's all gonna be fine. I just need to work hard and not worry about Stacy for a while."

"Yeah. Just worry about yourself. You're always doing everything for that girl.
~~~

Plus, time apart can be good."

"I agree. Thanks mom. Now, I've got all my work scheduled out and there's still a lot I need to get done tonight."

"Alright my sweetie, I love you," she said.

"I love you too, goodnight."

~~~

It was Thursday, three days since Luke had talked with Stacy; three days since she left his house crying. Luke had gotten plenty of work done. He was still high and finished the last of his supply early that morning.

Luke was proud of his progress so he decided he could pay a short social visit with Dave. First thing was first; he needed to make an important pot stop. After school, Luke headed to Albertson's to meet Justin. He had never sold to Justin since the time at the mansion. It was an important meeting for Luke because Justin might have known what Stacy was up to.

Luke was driving the Suburban. He had already become attached to the vehicle; they had grown a bond when they shared the psychedelic experience on the spirit quest. He found Justin easily.

Justin got into the Suburban and set three hundred dollars on the seat. Justin wasn't as talkative as he was at the mansion. It made Luke suspicious. Luke grabbed the ounce from under his seat and handed it to Justin. "So what's new with you?" Luke asked.

"Not too much, man. Think I'm gonna do some skatin today."

"You seen Stacy lately? I kinda bitched her out the other day. Is she doing alright?"

"I seen her at the mansion a couple days ago. There was some drama going on so I've been staying away. Are you guys still together?"

"I'm not really sure. We got some issues I'm not sure we can fix. Why do you ask?"

"Well, she's been over at my buddy Logan's place. I guess they're not dating or anything, he just said she could live there if she needed to."

Luke clenched his fists to keep them from shaking. "Alright, thanks man."

"Sure. Thanks for the bud. I'll call you when I need more." Justin got out of the truck and Luke headed for Dave's. *That bitch,* thought Luke, *she's gonna try and get me back by moving in with the biggest heroin junkie in Whitefish. No doubts now, she's on heroin. Now that I'm not around, she has no reason to try to control herself. She's a goner. Best accept it now.*

~~~

Dave was home alone. "Where is everyone?" said Luke.

"Just missed em. Tim and Jared left with some people. What's happening? You want to get high?"

"Yeah, that's exactly what I want to do," said Luke.

"Right on." Dave enjoyed sharing his methadone with Luke. Luke would almost always turn it down. Dave would still ask, and always looked surprised when Luke declined. He pulled out the mirror with lines of crushed up pill on it. The first line was his, and then he handed the mirror and pen tube to Luke. Luke did one of the lines. "Take another," Dave instructed. Luke took another.

Luke pulled a pipe out of his pocket and they smoked. "I need you to do me a favor," said Luke,"Let me take you to the liquor store so you can get me a bottle. I have a craving to drink some Evan Williams."

Dave had no objections. He was a sucker for bourbon. They drove to the liquor store. Luke was already in a better mood. "Luke, are you high?" said Dave.

"Yeah, of course I'm high," said Luke.

"No, that's not what I'm talking about. You been doing speed. I can see that much."

"Why... what makes you think that?"

"Don't worry," Dave said with a smile, "I've been around the block a time or two. I could see it in your face when you showed up. I just hope you don't think you're gonna get away without sharing." They both laughed.

"That's cool, man. I'm actually getting more today. Just don't tell no one about it," said Luke.

"Don't worry. I don't want that kind of reputation any more than you do," said Dave.

They got back to the apartment and had a mixed drink: Squirt, bourbon and ice (Dave insisted on ice). Dave asked about Stacy. Luke explained the whole thing. They made another drink. Luke asked about Dave's history with meth. Dave explained that he had some biker buddies when he was in his thirties. They used to do crank; the 'old school' stuff. Dave had only gotten high a few times since those days. He's tried crystal meth twice, but nothing could beat that old crank.

"What happened to all the crank?" said Luke.

"From my understanding, some of the ingredients became extremely hard to get. I guess you can still get that stuff in Mexico, but you can see why it's become so rare," Dave explained.

The time came for Luke to leave. "I'll come by tomorrow. We'll get high."

"You staying up tonight?" said Dave.

"All night every night until I get done with school."

"Stop by in the morning. I get up around six and go to work at seven," said Dave.

~~~

Luke should have been drunk. Two of Dave's drinks always got him drunk. The alcohol felt good. The opiates felt good. The sleep deprivation made it even better. Thoughts of Stacy had faded away and the bad feelings were gone. Luke loved this feeling.

He arrived at Blue's and went into the tent with the bottle in his hand. Blue wasn't there. A girl was sitting on the couch and looked up from her cellphone, "Hey Luke." It was one of the girls Blue brought on the spirit quest. "My name is Kimmy if you don't remember."

"Right on, nice to see you. Where's Blue?"

"He's inside talking with his landlord. He'll be back soon." Kimmy was the prettier of the two that Blue brought to the spirit quest. She was skinny with pale skin and blond hair. Luke stood there for a moment and looked at his bottle. "You can come sit," she said. He sat on the opposite side of the couch. "I didn't know you did dope."

"Yeah. I don't usually do it very often," he said.

"What do you got there? Can I have a drink?"

"Sure," he handed her the bottle. She took a swig, and then a gulp. She handed it back and Luke took a drink. It was horrible; much better with squirt.

"Have you ever shot up before?" she asked.

"No, don't plan on it either. I hate needles."

"Well, last weekend you showed me something amazing. That 2C-B was the shit, I thank you for that. Now I want to show you something amazing. You only have to try it once and I promise you won't regret it," she said.

"I don't know about all that. For me, that's going way too far to get high."

"I feel like I owe you. You have to try it," she said.

"I appreciate it, but no," he said.

"Don't be a pussy," she said.

"Oh, that's dirty. Fine, I'll try it one time," he said.

She smiled and started digging in her purse. She pulled out a bag of syringes, a spoon, a Q-tip, and a bag of crystal meth. A chunk of crystal went into the spoon; the cap came off a syringe. The syringe was filled up in a glass of water; the water squirted on the crystal; a piece of cotton from the Q tip was rolled up and thrown on the liquid; the liquid was sucked into the syringe through the cotton. It was ready. "Give me your arm," she said. He forced himself to do it.
~~~

She slid a rubber band around his arm. His elbow was straight. His wrist was resting on her leg. When the needle came close he looked away and closed his eyes.

"What the fuck!" said Blue. He took the syringe away from Kimmy. "That's my fuckin cousin; he doesn't want to do that shit."

"Yeah he does," she said.

"Do you?" said Blue.

"I'll try it once," said Luke.

"Are you sure? You can't unlearn this shit," said Blue.

"Yeah, let her do it," said Luke.

"This bitch isn't doing shit," said Blue. "She can't even do it herself. She's like a fuckin sewing machine," he looked at her, "You're stupid," Blue said. She threw her hands up and looked away. Blue held the syringe and looked at it in the light. "Take this crap off. You won't need it," Blue pointed at rubber band on Luke's arm. "Now gimme your arm." Blue knelt on the ground. Luke looked away.

He coughed. His vision went black. He rested on the couch. His vision came back. It was bright. His heart raced and he was sweating. "Holy smokes." He felt like he would explode with energy.

"How was it?" said Kimmy.

"Freakin crazy."

"I told you it was awesome," she said.

Luke got up and started pacing, "I gotta move. We need to do something. Gotta go outside!" Luke went out and lit a cigarette. He started to walk down the driveway then turned back. "I don't know what to do," he said as he came back in the tent and sat on the couch. "Can't sit down," he stood back up, almost walking in place, he could not stand still. Kimmy was smiling. Blue was sorting out screws and messing with tools in the cluttered corner of the room.

"Hey Blue, I'm gonna need a half gram." Luke set two twenties on the desk. Blue gave him the bag. Luke sat back on the couch. He checked his phone as he finished the cigarette. *Homework!* "Gotta go you guys. Later Blue, I freakin love ya cousin."

Luke drove home feeling powerful. He was listening to Rammstein. *Stacy would really hate me now. I wonder how she's doing. Doesn't matter, she's fucked. It was her choice. Now, I got no one holding me back. I can be a freakin crack Ninja if I want, as long as I graduate.*

Luke pulled into his driveway; both of his parents were home. He looked at himself in the rearview mirror. *I guess I look alright, Not too obvious. As soon as I get out of the sun light my pupils will turn to saucers; that will be obvious. How long can I get away with the Adderall cover up? Do they already suspect? As long as I'm busy doing homework they won't worry. Meth users don't do homework, right?* Luke braced himself, grabbed his backpack and went inside.

His parents were talking in the kitchen. "Hey Luke," said Alice. "How was your day?"

"Homework," said Luke. He went to his room. Luke sat at his desk and pulled out his binder and textbooks. *Alright, lets get started.* Luke worked mostly undisturbed until 2am. He had some music playing, so he didn't hear anyone coming up the stairs. The door opened. He looked at Alice with guilty eyes. "Hey mom... what's going on?"

"I had a horrible dream. I just wanted to see if you were okay."

"Well, everything is fine," he tried to avoid eye contact.

"You weren't exaggerating about the homework, were you?" she said.

"Nope, It's definitely crunch time," he looked at her briefly.

"Your eyes," she came closer and looked into his eyes. "There's no blue in your eyes, it's all black. Have you seen?"

"Yeah, I know. I ate the last of my Adderall today."

"Have you eaten anything besides Adderall?" she said.

"Yeah, I had Subway for lunch."

"Is it hard to eat on Adderall?" she asked.

"Yeah, it is for me because I don't do it very often."

"Do you need anything? I can make you a smoothie or something."

"A smoothie would be great." Luke meant it. He had been running full speed on empty for too long.

Alice came back five minutes later with a tall glass of strawberry smoothie. "Here you go, sweetie."

"Thanks mom, you're awesome."

"You're welcome. I'm going back to sleep. Good job on your homework, get some sleep if you can," she said.

"Will do, Goodnight." Luke drank whiskey and smoked cigarettes while doing homework the rest of the night.

~~~

When he got to Dave's, Jack was sleeping on the couch. Luke walked to the bedroom and knocked on the door. The door opened, "Ah, Luke. I'm glad you came," said Dave.

"Yep, said I would," said Luke.

"Wow, you smell like whiskey. Are you drunk?" said Dave.
~~~

"Not drunk. Definitely intoxicated though," said Luke.

"That's cool, did you get that stuff?" said Dave.

"Yeah, I got it. Have you eaten yet? You won't be able to eat after this," said Luke.

"I'm fine, let's just get high," said Dave.

Luke sat on the bed. Dave closed the door and sat down next to him. Luke pulled out the glass meth pipe. It didn't make much difference for Luke; he was high to begin with. Dave went from zero to a hundred after the first hit. "You really scored on this stuff," said Dave as he took his second hit.

"Yeah. It's some of the best I've ever done. Usually I gotta go to Portland for shit this good. I can get as much as you want. Eighty dollars a gram. Most people around here pay one twenty a gram for weak shit."

"Very nice, I might have to get some while it's around," said Dave.

"Right? School is gonna be weird today." *Holy smokes*, Luke thought, *is it really Friday? When did I sleep last? Sunday night? School is sure gonna be weird today. It was weird the past couple of days; now that I've thrown alcohol in with the mix it's almost risky. That might not be good. Maybe I should skip today... Absolutely not! I'm fine. Even better than fine, I am superior. Super human! I will walk amongst the sober people and succeed!*

"I imagine it would be weird. So where has that girl of yours been?" said Dave.

"She's been in Whitefish. We aren't together anymore."

"I hate to say it, but I've had a bad feeling about her. Not that she's bad right now, but she has some bad potential. I've seen girls just like her turn into complete dope whores. Your better off without her," said Dave.

"I don't know about all that. I hope you're wrong, anyway," said Luke.

"Me too," said Dave.

~~~

Luke walked into school. It didn't feel right or natural. He wished he could be invisible. Instead he felt like a pulsating beacon, all he could do was hope people didn't notice. Sober people. Could he even have a conversation with one of them? Did they even speak the same language? All the students looked so natural in their environment, standing in groups, chatting by their lockers. They belonged; Luke did not. One of Luke's ex-girlfriends walked passed without looking at him. They dated in junior high for almost a year. She broke up with him for smoking too much weed. *If only she knew.*

He made it to art class and sat next to Natalie. Luke was safe for now. "Hi Natalie, how are you doing?"

"Pretty good. Talked to my dad yesterday. I think he's gonna give up on his
~~~

anger strike pretty soon. It's Friday; you got any exciting plans for the weekend?"

"No exciting plans. Just homework. Maybe quit my job," Luke laughed. It was a joke, but it actually sounded like a good idea.

"What did you do last night?" she looked at him suspiciously? "You smell like alcohol," she whispered.

"Is it that bad?" he asked.

"It's not horrible, but I can tell from here. What were you doing last night?" she said.

"Homework," he said.

"And drinking?" she said.

"A little," he said.

"You're weird."

What is moral is what you feel good after
and what is immoral is what you feel bad after.
-Ernest Hemmingway

Chapter 5: Crunch Time

Tuesday 5-28-2010

"Done," said Luke. He finished the last of his homework at 4:30am. *All I need to worry about now is finals. Just a few more days, then I can sleep. Actually, I can sleep today. I could come home right after school. I'll just get high one more time so I can make it through school. I'll eat when I get home and go to sleep early. Then I will strategically dose myself before each day of finals.*

Luke had slept once since he started his homework mission on the 12th. It happened on a Monday, and it was by accident. He was living in a dream world that was starting to feel normal. After a while he began to suffer from confusion. It was affecting his progress until he discovered a cure: Nutrition. Eating food was difficult so he invested in Ensure. When he started feeling deprived he would drink a couple Ensures. The downside was that the Ensure cost almost as much as the meth. Luke was all out of Ensure and he needed something. He went down to the fridge; the half and half looked appealing. He grabbed the Costco-size carton and chugged the entire thing.

It was time to go for a drive. His parents would be up soon and he wanted to get high. He got in his Chrysler and looked for a nice spot to park a few blocks from the school. The windows in his Chrysler were tinted, but he still liked to be free of prying eyes. When he found his spot he unlocked the glove box. His supplies consisted of three syringes, Q-tips, one spoon, and his bag of crystal. All this was enclosed in a sunglass case. He learned the procedure out of necessity. IV use got him higher with less and lasted longer. It was economical. Blue couldn't always be around to get him high so he learned to do it himself.

Luke went through the process and took his shot. He coughed and experienced the energizing rush. When that was over he lit a cigarette and went for a walk. It was still dark out; only 5am. The walk was refreshing. He had been stiff from sitting at his desk all night and it felt good to loosen up. It made him nervous when cars drove by. *Teachers,* he thought, *what if teachers see me walking around at this hour? This is not normal behavior.* He walked back to his car through alleys. When he got there he played Tetris on his phone until school started.

~~~

"Hey Luke," said Natalie.

"What's goin on?" he asked.

"What's goin on with you? Your eyes look crazy, and you're pale. Is everything okay?"

"Yeah. I'm okay. Homework has just been killing me. All done now, though. I finished just in time," he said.

"Well, I'm glad. Cause you really do look terrible, and you've been acting strange," she said.

"Everything's gonna get better now. I'll be back to my old self in no time."

"Good, I know we've only really hung out that one time, but I hope we can spirit quest again sometime this summer," she said.

"As soon as schools over I'm gonna unleash. There will be more craziness than you've ever dreamed of, and you're invited anytime."

"Awesome. Can't wait," she said.

When Luke got to history he put the last of his homework in the make-up-work box. He sat at his usual desk in the back corner and tried not to draw attention. Luke had no friends in this class. He hated everything about this class, especially the false representation of historic events. Luke was a conspiracy nut and believed that school history books were made to deceive. Today they were just reviewing material for the test; the three day long test; the test that determined their graduation.

The next class was psychology. Luke did well in psychology. He enjoyed the subject and retained the material effortlessly. Through the semester he finished most of his homework in class. There was no need for notes. He prepared for his
~~~

presentations with one sleepless night with Adderall or crystal.

Math was Luke's most dreadful class. It was painfully difficult for him. He had to rely on note taking; trying to memorize the formulas was pointless. Luckily for Luke, his teacher allowed students to have one notecard filled with as many notes as they could fit on it. Luke's notecard was filled with writing too small for most people to read.

Luke didn't turn his math homework in until after class. That's when he got an unwanted talk with his teacher. "Luke, I want to speak with you for a moment." Luke was following the last of the class out the door when he turned around. He approached his teacher and made the eye contact he was hoping to avoid. "I just wanted to tell you how impressed I am with your effort these past few weeks. A month ago I was ready to tell you to just quit and try again next year. I thought you were hopelessly behind, but you proved me wrong."

"Well, thank you sir."

"Tell me, Luke, where did you get all this motivation?"

Luke's heart raced, "Guess I just really needed to graduate."

"Hmm... very well. We'll see you tomorrow for finals then."

"Sure will. See you then." Luke left the class paranoid. *Does he know? Maybe I'm just being paranoid. There doesn't have to be hidden meaning in what he said. He could have been sincere. I don't need to be around to find out.*

Luke's car was still parked a few blocks away since the morning. He got there fast while looking over his shoulders on the way. Soon as he started his car he relocated to another place. He parked and pulled out his phone. *People need weed. Good, because I need money.* Luke lit a cigarette and headed for his first stop at the Blue and White Motel. He made three stops altogether. During his last sale he got a text.

(From Stacy): Where are u?

(From Luke): Foys Lake. Why?

(From Stacy): I'm coming. Need to see u :/

Luke felt some anxiety. *Is this a good idea? It's been so long since I've even talked to her. She will probably just see that I'm high and leave. What could she possibly want? Maybe she just misses me. Who's driving her?* He waited five minutes, and then lit a cigarette. He was still high, but was tempted to take a couple hits from the meth pipe. *Don't need that; gotta go to sleep tonight, remember?*

A few minutes later a new Pontiac G6 pulled up next to Luke. Stacy got out of the driver side and got into the Chrysler. She gave Luke a long hug. "Whose car is that?" asked Luke.

"Mine. Well, technically Logan's, but he got it for me."

"Wow, looks like he's really taking care of you," he said.

"Yeah. I guess he is," she said as she kept hugging him. "God, your skinny. What happened to all your muscles?"

"Been spending all my time on homework. Finished it all today. Just got three days of finals left."

She let go of him and looked at his face, "Oh Luke, you look terrible. When was the last time you slept?" Her voice was mellow and her eyes looked droopy. She was on opiates. Luke knew it and didn't care at the moment.

"It's been a little while," he looked down at his hands. She grabbed his hand and gave him a kiss. He kissed her back. It felt great. It made him realize how much he missed her. They made out; she grabbed his thigh and eventually his crotch.

"We should go somewhere," she said. Luke drove to a different secret spot close to the lake. The sex was just as passionate as it had always been; only this time they got dressed more quickly afterward. Luke didn't have to ask; he knew they weren't getting back together. She was getting spoiled by Logan in Whitefish; no way was she going to ruin that.

"So is this the reason you wanted to see me?" said Luke.

"No, I just missed you. When I'm around you I just can't help myself, even if I am mad at you for being a tweaker. I still love you, ya know."

"Yeah. I still love you too."

Stacy had a big jar of pot. She loaded a fancy glass pipe and took a hit before handing it to Luke. It tasted like hay and didn't burn quite right. He handed it back without saying anything. When they finished smoking she lit two cigarettes and gave one to Luke. It was a Camel Crush. Stacy preferred hers menthol. Her filter popped as she bit down on it with her front teeth. "Do you want me to pop yours?" she asked with a smile.

"Sure, go for it," he handed the cigarette back to her.

They went back to the lake. Next thing he knew, their visit was over and she was driving away. *At least we're on good enough terms for her to use me as a booty call. That's good enough for now, it will be good for me to be single through the summer. Don't need anyone to hold me down.*

~~~

Luke went home after the lake. It was 6:30pm; a good time for him to go to sleep and rest up for the test. The only problem was that he was still wide awake. He was still high from the shot he took thirteen hours before. Luke tried to sleep anyway. *I should be able to sleep. It's been eight freakin days without a blink of sleep. Finals tomorrow; don't need to be retarded.*
~~~

He lay in the bed for hours, shooing away his parents when they tried to talk with him. He kept looking at the clock: 7 o'clock; 8 o'clock; 9 o'clock. Time was creeping by with no sleepiness in sight. At 10 o'clock he began to worry, *If I fall asleep now I might not wake up tomorrow. I can't be late for my tests. If I miss it, all my efforts have been wasted. I'll take a shot at midnight; that way I can come home and fall asleep right after school. Need Ensure. Better stop by Walmart tomorrow morning. Need nourishment...*

~~~

Luke made it through the night and made it to school. The multiple choice questions were terrible. He had always been slow at multiple choice, or any tests for that matter. He put himself on autopilot and managed to make it through the first day of finals.

Luke never did fall asleep, but he did finish all of his finals. They went by in a blur so he couldn't be sure how well he had done. It was Friday at 3:20pm and he had to be at work at 4:30. When he got to his car he felt he deserved a victory smoke. He turned on some mellow music and took his first hit of weed since he was with Stacy. The effect was strong; physically and mentally sedating. He had been out of meth for 18 hours and was now feeling a comfortable wave of relaxation. After two more hits he put the pipe away and settled into his seat. *Just a few moments of rest; maybe close my eyes for a minute. Time to give them a rest... just for a moment.*
~~~

Why fit in when you were born to stand out?
-Dr. Seuss

Chapter 6: The Love Drug

Luke woke up with his phone vibrating in his pocket. The call didn't matter; the time did. It was almost six, *Fuck; I'm an hour and a half late for work!* He panicked and raced off to work.

"Sorry I'm late," he yelled as he ran through the back door. When he tried to clock in on the computer there was a problem, "This things fuckin broken," he said.

"What the hell are you doing?" said the assistant manager, "You don't work here anymore. Didn't you get any of the messages?"

"No, I didn't. What happened?"

"You no-call no-showed yesterday."

"What do you mean? I don't work on Thursdays," said Luke.

"Sober up man, yesterday was Friday. You never showed up and you never called."

Luke pulled out his phone; it was Saturday. *What the hell? Did I really just sleep for 26 hours?*

"Wow. Sorry guys. I guess a day just disappeared for me." Luke went back to change out of his work clothes. On his way out he waved "goodbye" to everyone. They waved back and said they would see him later. No one was mad at him. And most of them would see him later since almost everyone bought weed from him. Luke felt stupid walking out of the restaurant. He also felt a strange sense of relief. This didn't have to be a disaster; the summer had just begun and it was full of opportunity. Money could be an issue, but he always trusted that the universe would provide. For Luke, the universe always worked in his favor.

When he got in his car he checked his phone. There were 38 new messages and 23 missed calls. He sighed and decided to worry about it later. Luke was hungry and thirsty. He grabbed a water bottle and downed it all. He smoked a cigarette on the way home. It was satisfying and gave him a head rush. Once he got home he went to the fridge. He went to the fridge and consumed for a half hour straight. The pit was never ending. It was the hungriest hunger he ever had. Luke was cleaning up after himself when Alice came out of the bedroom. She looked like she had just woken from a nap. "Hey Luke, how was your celebration?"

"Celebration?" he said.

Allan came in through the sliding glass back door. "My son!" he said as he gave Luke a hug and rubbed his almost bearded face against Luke's cheek.

"Stop it! What's going on?" said Luke.

"You graduated. Didn't you see?"

"No. I haven't checked yet."

"Come see," said Alice, "All the grades just got posted this morning."

They took Luke to their bedroom where the grades were all posted on the school website. He had mostly D's and C's; an A in art class; a B in psychology. "Hey Luke, don't you work today?" said Allan.

"Nope, I got fired."

"What happened?"

"Didn't show up yesterday, said Luke.

"What, you decided to party instead?" said Alice.

"No, I actually fell asleep in my car. Ate a couple pot cookies," he lied. "They put me out for a whole day."

"Oh Luke, that's terrible," said Alice.

"Where'd you get those cookies?" asked Allan.

"It's not terrible. I think I lost that job for a reason. It was holding me back and I've been there for way too long " he said.

"Cookies?" said Allan.

"Cookies from my weed guy. There's no more."

"What about money?" she said, "You're not just gonna be a bum like your buddy 'brain fry," are you?"

"No, mom, for now I'll make my money with weed and enjoy a bit of my summer. Then I'll find a real job; a better way to make money. The low-class restaurant work is not for me," said Luke.

"He will be just fine," assured Allan, "Luke will be successful. I have no doubt about it."

When Luke got away from his parents he checked his phone again. The text from Shawn was most important; Luke still owed him $800 for weed. He counted up his money and found $347. This was a problem because he only had $120 worth of weed left to sell. He would have to violate his self-imposed rule and go to the bank. There was only $1,100 in his bank account, and that money was for emergency. Drug money was supposed to be self-sufficient, but this was the price he had to pay to graduate. He could be back on his feet in no time. It was time to call Shawn.

"Hello?" said Shawn.

"Hey man, sorry I missed your calls. I got your cash whenever you need it."

"Cool. I'm at the gym. Be here at 8:30."

"Alright, see you then."

Luke got rid of the last of his pot and stopped by the bank. He got $400 from the ATM and made it to the gym right on time. There was an empty cop car parked in the parking lot. *Is Shawn* okay? *Holy shit.* Luke waited a few minutes until he saw Shawn come out of the gym. Shawn walked up to Luke's window, "Come park next to my truck and get in." Luke did so without question.

He got in the truck, "What's that cop doing here?" Luke asked.

"Don't worry. I know him," he said.

"How can I not worry? He's a cop. Isn't he our enemy?" said Luke.

"He buys shit from me."

"What kind of shit would a *cop* want from you?" said Luke.

"Steroids, sometimes weed or coke."

"Wow, alright then. Here's your cash." Luke handed over $800.

"Thanks bro. How you been doin? I see you're not tweakin out no more," said Shawn.

"Doin good. I graduated. Also got fired, and I'm single now."

"Should I congratulate you?" said Shawn.

"Yeah. it's all good," said Luke.

"Hell yeah, buddy. It's summertime. Time to stop that tweakn shit; it makes you weak. Take some steroids. Get strong and get some bitches."

"I'm good on the steroids."

"Oh. Well, you can do more business for me now that you don't work anymore, right?" said Shawn.

"Yeah I can. I'll actually be relying completely on our business now that it's my only source of income," said Luke

"Good, because I've got some serious shit I need you to dump," said Shawn.

"Nice, man. What chu got?"

"Can you handle an ounce of molly? You can have it on front for two grand."

"Wow, that's a lot, but I can do it."

"You sure? You can make money off it?"

"If it's good shit. Is it good?" said Luke.

"Hell yeah, bro. The best. Pure fuckin MDMA. Have I ever let you down?" said Shawn.

"Ha, I can definitely make bank off it then," said Luke.

"Good. Can you take a half pound of bud, too?"

"Naw man. I'd better stick with the QP," said Luke.

"Okay." Shawn threw everything together in a brown paper sack.

Luke pulled out the bag of molly and shoved it into a secret pocket on the inside of his pants. *Just in case.* "Thanks man."

"Have fun, bro," said Shawn.

~~~

Luke got out of the truck and into his car. He was still paranoid about the cop. In his excitement, he drove to Dave's. He had been missing out on his friends for too long. Tonight would make up for his weeks of solitude.

Luke ran into Dave's apartment in a frenzy. "Let's go! To my house, everyone." It was only Jared and Jack. Dave was in the kitchen.

"Count me out on this one," said Dave. "I've been trying to get these bums out of here all day. Time for some peace and quiet."

"Alright. Well, Jared, Jack, let's go." They were zoning out on video games. Luke unplugged it. "Time to go."

"Okay, okay," said Jared. They both followed Luke to his car. Luke started texting all his other friends. He let Jared and Jack smoke a bowl while he spent fifteen minutes texting all his people and replying to old messages. On the way home he picked up a pack of Parliament cigarettes. The Parliaments had a hollowed out filter that could measure .1 gram of MDMA; an easy way to sell stuff when there's no time to pre-weigh capsules.

When he got home he sent Jared and Jack to the backyard to start a fire. He took this time to stash his drugs and weigh up a smaller bag to sell out of for the night. He also snorted .1 gram of MDMA.

Luke went inside to talk to his parents. He told them he would be having
~~~

people over. They told him that it was a good idea and that he deserved a celebration. At the end of their conversation he began to feel the ecstasy. By the time he got outside to the fire his clothes were silk. "Get over here you guys," Luke gave both of his friends a hug, "I freakin love you. You're such beautiful people."

"Okay, what's going on?" asked Jared.

"I'll show you what's going on. You guys can try it for free, but don't tell anyone; I gotta sell this shit for fifteen a point," said Luke. He gave each of them a .1 gram sample off a cigarette butt.

The first to show up was Tim in an SUV full of friends. Luke greeted everyone with love. Another car pulled up minutes after them. Luke took Tim to his car so they could talk in private. "You gotta try this shit, man. This is the best molly I've ever done, and I got lots of it." Luke gave Tim a sample just as another car came into the already full driveway. Luke went over to the car and told them to just drive around the house and park in the back yard.

When Luke got back to his party there was music playing and cases of beer scattered around the fire. Luke went around to each group and advertised his product with his behavior. Fat Jared was already loving on everyone. "Luke!" shouted Jared, "These people want some molly." He was with three people Luke vaguely recognized.

The word spread quickly. Soon Luke's yard was full of cars and over fifty people. Everybody was buying molly and everybody was feeling better than they ever had in their whole lives. People were singing and dancing. There were group hugs full of love. Even Luke's parents came out to socialize and absorb the atmosphere. They were sober and figured out everyone was on ecstasy. People Luke didn't even know would offer his parents some of the "Love Drug."

Tim took Luke in private, "Bro, there's a huge party going on out in West Valley. We could make bank if you let me take some of that molly to sell there."

They went to Luke's car. Luke weighed up a 1/8 ounce bag of MDMA and handed it to Tim. "Sell it for twenty a hit. Bring me back four hundred. If you do it right you should be able to make three hundred profit."

" Damn, thanks bro," said Tim. "The only problem is that I don't got a ride."

"What about those people you came with?" said Luke.

"They want to stay here," said Tim.

"Alright, take the Suburban." Luke took the key off his key ring and handed it to Tim. "You'll also need this." Luke gave him an extra scale, a handful of tiny square baggies, and a couple Parliament cigarettes.

"All these accessories," said Tim.

"Accessories are essential," said Luke.

Tim looked at Luke with dilated pupils, "Thanks a lot man. You're the shit like doody."

"Ahhh! Cause I'm sick like yuck!" said Luke. They both laughed and gave each other a hug. "Now go fulfill your destiny. Those people at that party need molly."

"Alright bro, I won't let you down." They both got out of the car. Tim got in the Suburban and Luke went back to his party.

"Luke," said Alice, "Luke, there you are."

"Hey mom, what's going on?"

"Your friends are so much fun! I've never met such nice people. Look at them," she said.

He looked. Sure enough, people were still hugging, dancing, and even rolling around in the grass. Glow sticks were being circulated around the fascinated crowd. Electronic music was being played out of a nice car with an excellent sound system. "Yeah. My friends are awesome," Luke agreed.

Luke's phone vibrated. He pulled it out of his pocket and tried to read the screen. Reading it was difficult with his eyeballs rolling around in his head. He could still text with muscle memory, so he just told them to come over, whoever they were. Luke grabbed his own glow sticks and came dancing back into the crowd.

Around midnight two more cars came driving into Luke's backyard. They were people from his work; a few waitresses and their friends. Some of the cooks came as well. Luke was so excited he ran up and hugged every one of them, "You guys made it. How did you find me?"

"You told us to come here," said one of the waitresses.

"Great. Awesome. There's molly everywhere, you need to get some."

They all got some. Those who couldn't afford were given some for free. Luke felt generous and wanted everyone to share the experience.

~~~

By 2am Luke had taken another dose of MDMA and drank ten beers. His parents had gone inside to sleep. Their only request was that no one drive drunk. People could sleep in Luke's room if they needed.

Of course that didn't happen. People drove drunk. Some people left; some people came back. New people even showed up looking for more fun after a dying party; looking for molly. Luke's party was not even close to dying. His pockets were filling with cash; so much cash he had to stash a bunch of it in the house.
~~~

Luke took a good look at what he had created. People loved him for it. He was included in every smoke circle because it was his house and people were grateful. Luke staggered and danced around as he was appreciated by everyone. He was on top of the world. At some point he even felt compelled to send Shawn a text:

(From Luke): I freakin love you man

Luke knew Shawn was probably not awake right then, but he hoped he would get the message in the morning and be happy about it. A while later he did get a reply:

(From Shawn): I know bro. im thizzin my fukin brainz out

Around 4am Luke rallied the remaining people up to his room. A lot of people had re-dosed and were still high as ever on MDMA and alcohol. They turned on music and started playing quarters on Luke's coffee table. People got comfortable; beer and bong water was spilt; the already broken railing was broken the rest of the way off the wall; a girl was lying on Luke's floor getting a tattoo on her back. It was good fun. Eventually people started passing out. Luke slipped into a blackout and fell asleep sitting on his couch.

~~~

Luke woke up at noon in the same position he fell asleep in. There were less people in his room; eighteen including himself. There were five people sleeping on his bed. The sheets were on the floor being shared by three other people. Luke must have grabbed all the blankets in the house because they were scattered all over his room like a giant slumber party.

Luke's head hurt and his body felt weak. Beer would be the quickest remedy so he downed a couple half empty cans and lit a cigarette. He wasn't supposed to smoke in the house, but since everyone had smoked in it all night, one more wouldn't make a difference.

He needed to assess the aftermath. He checked the backyard first. There were three cars still parked out there. He didn't find anything except beer cans, glow sticks, and a few empty bags of weed. One of the cars still had two people sleeping in the back seat.

Luke didn't think anyone had gone into his garage but he decided to check anyway. He went in the side door and took a quick scan. Everything looked fine except an unfamiliar pipe on the workbench. He was on his way inside when he saw a foot sticking out from behind Alice's car. It was his friend Andy from The Sizzle Steakhouse, lying on his back in a bloody pile of blankets. Blood was all over his face and shirt.

"Andy!" Luke grabbed him by the shoulders and started shaking, "Wake up,
~~~

dude."

Andy's eyes opened; he didn't look bruised or swollen. "What... what is it?" he said.

"What happened to you?" said Luke.

"Oh shit, man. I did something bad."

"Did you hurt somebody? You got blood all over your face."

"What? No, I think I had sex with Brittany."

Disgusting, thought Luke. Brittany was an ugly busser at The Sizzle Steakhouse. "What else did you do with her?"

"I don't know. We started making out and I think I blacked out."

"Oh shit, check your dick, dude," said Luke.

"My dick?" He unbuttoned his pants and looked under his boxers, "Oh no," he went pale then puked on the floor.

Luke was horrified. It was the most disgusting thing he'd ever seen. He couldn't imagine how terrible this must have been for Andy. "It's gonna be alright. Just get in the shower and I'll get you some clothes. No one has to know about this."

Andy followed Luke to the bathroom. He walked like he had a turd in his pants; he would have preferred it to be a turd. At least then it would be his, having sex with Brittany was bad enough; this was revolting.

When Andy came out of the bathroom he still had a sad look on his face. Sure, he was clean and had fresh clothes, but no shower could wash away the shame he felt, even if it was only Luke who knew. He didn't even know if Brittany knew. It had been dark in the garage and he had no idea what time she might have left. Seeing her again would be awkward. Working with her would be torture.

"Don't look so sad," said Luke, "it could've happened to anyone. Let's go smoke a bowl and forget about it." Weed was always good after a night of ecstasy. It can even make people feel like they are rolling again. Luke and Andy went upstairs and filled up the bong. Some people were already awake; others woke up to the smell of weed. They all smoked and reminisced about their awesome night; everyone except for Andy. People offered to help clean the house. Luke assigned everyone a task and they cleaned the place in good time.

Luke's parents came home. They had gone to church with some of their friends. Alice was pleased to come home to a clean house. She offered to make pancakes; most people declined but she made them anyway. Everyone ended up eating pancakes.

Luke realized that he had not taken a shower in a few days. Instead of taking a shower, he announced that he was going to the lake. It was sunny out with no clouds. Also it was Luke's first full day of summer. At this point, people decided whether to go with Luke or part ways. Some people chose to go to their places to grab swimsuits and get ready before meeting at the at the lake.

When Luke went out to the driveway he was reminded that Tim still had his Suburban, he called Tim right away. Ringing... no answer. He tried again, same thing. Luke got in the Chrysler. Jack got into the shotgun seat. Jared and the other people got in the back. "Jared, you gotta sit up front. Jack, get in the back" said Luke.

"Why do I gotta get in the back?" asked Jack.

"Because my suspension is shitty. Fat ass has gotta get up front."

"Fuck you," said Jared.

"It's true! With you back there, I can't even go over a speed bump without scraping the road," said Luke. They drove to the lake with three vehicles following. One was Andy in his eighties Mustang with two of his buddies.

They went to the most secluded beach access. It was still more occupied than Luke would have liked. They found a quiet spot to drink and smoke before getting into the water. It was relaxing. They enjoyed the MDMA after-effects while soaking up the sun. Luke had fun flirting with a girl he had met the night before. It was strange for Luke; he had not flirted with girls for a long time. He had been with Stacy for so long, and since they broke up he had been neglecting his social life. At this point he realized his opportunity. He was single and every girl was fair game. No more holding back. The stress of relationship was no more.

More of Luke's friends showed up an hour later. They were prepared with inflatable rafts and coolers of beer. Everyone gathered the motivation to make a voyage to the island. It took twenty minutes to swim there while pulling the rafts along. Once they were there, they could drink swim and smoke weed in peace.

Luke was alerted by the sound of reggae music. He went to the edge of the tree covered island and saw his parents out on their boat. It was an old boat; yellow with an open bow.

"Luke!" yelled his mother, "Get your friends out here, we brought the tubes." Tim was on the boat as well. They floated as close to the island as they dared. Luke and some friends swam to the boat. There were two triangular double person tubes. Luke got on one tube with the girl he liked and found out her name was Shianne. Alice pressured two other girls to get on the other tube.

Allan was a good driver. He could make people fly without going too fast. It was guaranteed fun with him at the wheel. Luke was a good tuber. He taught

Shianne how to keep it stable and they only flipped once. The other tube sent the girls flying three times before they gave up and got back on the boat.

Luke got off the tube and went back to the island so everyone else could get a chance to ride. He sat on the shore drinking beer and smoking cigarettes while Tim described his successful night. The Suburban was safe and all the MDMA got sold as planned. He did admit that he got laid and also slept in the Suburban. When Tim woke up he drove to Luke's. Allan and Alice decided it would be fun to take the old boat out with Luke's old Suburban.

Luke sat on that beach with his cigarette and appreciated his life to the fullest. He watched his friends laughing and playing out on the boat with the best parents he could ever hope for. The night had been a complete success, and this was a moment of bliss that promised a magical summer.

All that is comes from the mind;
it is based on the mind,
it is fashioned by the mind.
-The Pali Canon 500-250B.C.

Chapter 7: 10161

Thursday 6-6-2010

It was less than a week since school had ended. Luke spent every night at bonfires or house parties. The MDMA was selling like crazy. Someone started a rumor that the molly was running out, so the price went up.

Luke was experiencing some of the bad side effects of MDMA. He was E-tarded, but he also carried the positive afterglow attributed to MDMA. Luke understood the neurotoxicity of the chemical and knew it was time to give it a break.

Shianne turned out to be a nice girl; only she was not as innocent as Luke first perceived. It turned out she had a boyfriend. Luke even knew her boyfriend; he bought weed from Luke and lived in Whitefish. He was big, black, and his name was Otis. Luke had sex with Shianne twice before making this connection. It was even worse that Luke liked Otis. He was friendly and good humored. Luke didn't like hooking up with other people's girlfriends; especially a big black man in his thirties. He had no choice but to keep the dirty secret.

Luke was in the K-mart parking lot waiting for Shawn. Tim found molly for

$100 a gram, so Luke was hesitant on getting any more from Shawn. Shawn had a big ego and Luke wanted to tell him without questioning his honesty. They had done good business together for a few years and Luke would feel cheated if Shawn gave someone else a better deal. Luke could sell his stuff for $100 a gram, but that would hardly be worth his time. MDMA was worth much more than that in Montana.

Luke got nervous when Shawn finally showed up. He double checked his money and got in the truck with Shawn.

"Hey buddy, how'd your week go?" said Shawn.

"It went good. Got all your money and I'll need another QP."

"Good. So you sold everything?" said Shawn.

"Not everything, but enough to pay you off," said Luke.

"Are you gonna want more molly?" said Shawn.

"Well, I'm not sure. I heard a vicious rumor that someone is selling some for $100 a gram. I can't compete with that," said Luke.

"Hmm... I don't know about that. It can't be any good. I get my shit straight from the chemist. If there is good shit out there for that cheap, I'm sorry," said Shawn.

"Are you selling to anyone else around here?" said Luke.

"You're the only guy I sell to in this town. If I did sell to anyone else, they wouldn't be getting it as cheap as you are. You get rock bottom price. We got history. You take care of me, I take care of you."

"Alright man, I guess I'll do another half O. If worse comes to worse I can just sell it cheap. That other shit is probably no good anyway," said Luke.

"Cool, bro." Shawn weighed the product and handed it to Luke in a paper sack. "Good luck, buddy. I'll be back in town in a week or so."

Luke ignored phone calls on the way home. He was exhausted and wanted to relax for the night. Luke always felt guilty when he spent too much time away from his parents. He loved them so much and hated when they felt neglected.

~~~

When he got home that evening, his parents were watching a movie. It was called "Yes Man" with Jim Carey. Luke's family rarely watched movies, so Alice was quick to convince him to join. Luke pressured Alice to smoke some weed before the movie. They made some tea and snacks before restarting the movie.

It was the best movie they ever saw; inspirational and hysterical. They hadn't laughed so hard in ages. They sat on the back patio while Luke smoked a cig. Work had been going good for Luke's parents. Allan got more employees at the health food store, so he only needed to work a couple days a week.
~~~

Alice was still teaching yoga classes in Whitefish two days a week. She loved her job because it wasn't work to her; she did yoga anyway, so teaching a class wasn't much different from her regular routine.

That Thursday night felt good for Luke and his parents. Bonding time was needed. Luke liked having a close relationship with his parents. So many of his friends had no relationships with their families and it broke his heart. Luke knew he was lucky. His parents were the coolest.

After a long talk on the patio Luke brushed his teeth and got ready for bed. He went up to his room and lay on his bed. The desk reminded him of all the sleepless nights of homework. It already seemed so long ago to Luke. So much had happened since school ended and it had only been a week. If he still had his job he would have worked that day. He usually worked six days a week during the summer; it had been like that since he was a freshman. This was his first summer of total freedom. His only job was to sell drugs.

Luke fell into a dreamless sleep; the first real sleep he'd had for a while. The past week he had mostly passed out from alcohol.

~~~

Luke woke up around noon. The sun was shining and the house was quiet. He went downstairs. The coffee pot was hot but the house was empty. He ate some toast with peanut butter and drank some coffee. He finished his coffee on the back patio with a cigarette. The fields behind the house waved in the breeze. It was one of those days where nothing could go wrong.

The peaceful moment was interrupted by his cellphone.

(From Shianne): Luke! Where r u

(From Luke): My house. Why?

(From Shianne): Im in town grumpy pants. Wanna smoke a bowl?

(From Luke): Sure

Luke went upstairs to find some clothes to wear. It was hot so he put on his brown Dickies shorts, Marlboro T-shirt, and brown Nike fitted hat. He saw Shianne pull into the driveway in Otis's Oldsmobile. Luke went to greet her at the front door. "Hi, Luke!" she gave him a hug.

"Hey, how have you been?" he said.

"Good. Been shopping. I got the car until Otis gets off work. Oh yeah, I keep forgetting to get that pipe from you. It's Otis's and he keeps asking about it " she said.

"Yeah, it's in the Chrysler. It should be in the center console. I'll go heat up the vaporizer."

She went to the Chrysler while Luke went to the garage. A few minutes later
~~~

she came in through the side door with a sneaky smile. "What?" Luke asked.

"I found something," she showed him the sunglass case.

"Gimme that!" Luke tried to grab it.

"No way," she held it away, still smiling, "We're gonna do something really fun."

"What? You don't do that stuff, do you?" he said.

"It's been a few years," she said.

"Well, I don't have anything," he said.

"Yes you do. Have you ever tried shooting molly?" she said.

"Are you serious? Can you even do that?"

"Of course you can. I've done it before, let's do it," she said.

"I guess we can give it a shot," he had nervous butterflies in his stomach. The thought of it made his palms sweaty.

They forgot about the weed and went up to Luke's room. He opened a capsule of MDMA and looked at Shianne. "You won't need much," she said. He poured some powder on the spoon. He looked at her again for approval. He filled up a new syringe for her and an old one for himself.

"You better do mine first," she said.

"You can't do it?" he said.

"I'm not very good. It takes me a while," she said.

"Kay," he put his rig down and uncapped hers. Luke was nervous. *What if this goes wrong? What if she dies? I should have done some research. She seems confident; I guess we'll take our chances.*

He poked her, flagged it, and depressed the plunger. She laid back on the couch with a gasp. He looked at her; she nodded, urging him to do his. *So much for my nerve endings*, he injected quickly and lost his breath and vision. He was lying next to her on the couch when his vision came back. Silk was flowing through his blood stream, giving him a fuzzy hug of happiness.

He tried looking at Shianne; it was hard to keep his eyes in one place. She was beautiful; absolutely irresistible. Shianne had always been cute, but now she was glowing with beauty. He ran his fingers through her hair and stroked her down the neck. He looked into her brown eyes and smiling face with vision so crisp. She was soft and silky; the prettiest thing he had ever seen. She took off his hat and ran her fingers through his hair in a messaging motion. It was pure ecstasy for both of them.

They couldn't resist any longer. She pulled him close and they started kissing. It was sensational as they felt each other all over. Her hands went down his pants. He couldn't take his hands from her silky beautiful hair. They were both the most beautiful people in the world.

She took off his shirt and unbuttoned his pants before pushing him onto his back. The overwhelming surge of drugs kept him from becoming erect, but she persisted with some playful tricks with her mouth. Soon he overcame the debilitating effects of the drugs and she was relentless. The magic of the scene left him mystified.

Luke tried to warn her, but she kept going. He reached the climax, but never came. His system was overloaded and didn't know what to do. The point of climax lasted longer than naturally possible, leaving him to squirm helplessly in shock.

Finally it happened. She took it with grace and kept going. After a few helpless moments he regained himself. It was his turn. She deserved the best after what she had done. He took off her shirt and tasted her breast while unbuttoning her pants. The pants came off. He used his mouth on her until she was gushing, then turned her around and took her from behind.

He went into her and she moaned with pleasure. They started slow, savoring the unbelievable ecstasy of the moment. He gripped her and went faster. Her cries became louder as she backed into him with aggression. Soon they both reached the never ending climax.

Their systems were broken, glitching out. They became uncoordinated and tense through the overwhelming sensation. They changed positions and attempted to continue their impulsive 'love drug' experiment.

~~~

They lay naked sharing a cigarette after the exhausting episode. "We're not supposed to smoke in here, are we?" she asked.

"Who cares. That shit was crazy."

"I agree," she said.

They had been at it for almost an hour. The MDMA had worn off, but they were still enjoying the after effects. The cigarette was extremely satisfying as they shared an American Spirit. Luke thought about what he had done. It was wrong, but he couldn't regret it as long as he could keep it a secret. "So... we're not gonna tell anybody about this, right?" he said.

"Nope, this will be our little secret," she said.

"Don't you feel bad about Otis? Because I do kinda," said Luke.

"Don't you worry. We've dated for almost three years and I've never done anything like this. It's been the same thing for so long, I really think I needed this. As long as he doesn't find out, there's no harm done," she said.

"Yeah, I guess you're right."
~~~

They heard the garage door opening. "Better get some clothes on," said Luke. He got dressed and put the drugs away. Shianne was fixing her hair when the door opened, "Luke? Oh, sorry," said Allan.

"It's fine. What's going on dad?"

"Not too much. Just had to check some things at the store. Thought you might still be sleeping and was gonna see if you wanted to do a wake-n-bake."

"Cool. Yeah. We should definitely smoke some weed," said Luke.

"Nice. You left your bag in the garage; I'll go get the vaporizer ready."

Shianne took this time to fix her hair and do her makeup. "Your dad totally knows," she said.

"Yeah, maybe. I think he just feels bad for not knocking first. He might feel like a cock blocker." She laughed, "Your dad is pretty cool, you know that?"

"I know. And I'm grateful for that."

"You should be. I'm not close to my family at all. They're still in Polson drinking pretty much all the time. I moved here when I was seventeen and have only seen them twice since I been here," she said.

"That really sucks. Don't they ever call?" he said.

"Maybe twice a year. It's really no big deal to me anymore," she said.

"That's crazy. Maybe I'm just a momma's boy, but I feel terrible if I go even a week without seeing my parents."

"If I had parents like yours I would wanna see them all the time too. Just don't ever take it for granted, because you're one lucky kid," she said. "All done. Let's go get high." She put her makeup away and headed down the stairs.

Allan was already smoking. He had a guilty look and handed Luke the hose. Luke took a hit and passed it to Shianne. The smoke brought back the ecstasy feeling. *Such goodness*, Luke wondered how there could be so many people suffering in the world when life was so easy for him.

They smoked until the vaporizer stopped vaporizing. It was their first smoke of the day and they were stoned. They went to the back porch to smoke another cigarette. Allan came along for the company. Allan proposed places to go for camping trips. He was just as excited about summer as anyone. "Peak a week this summer. We'll go on Google maps and just find a place to hike. We'll hit a new mountain peak every week. Are you in?" he said.

"I'm totally in," said Luke. He got his enthusiastic social skills from his parents. They got along with people and everyone loved them. They were also ambitious. They came from nothing and made something of themselves. Luke knew he would become successful as well. He had to. His opportunistic view of life would make it inevitable. Luke was the opposite of paranoid. He operated as if everyone was part of a plot to enhance his well-being.

Finally Shianne announced that she had to leave. She had errands to run before she picked up Otis. Luke and Allan sat in silence for a few minutes after she left. "So... what's going on with you and Shianne?"

"Nothing. Well, she's not my girlfriend or anything. Just a friend," said Luke.

"With benefits?"

"No! And if we were messing around I wouldn't tell you because she has a boyfriend."

"Ah, I get it. How old is she anyway? She seems more mature than most of your friends."

"Twenty-four, I think," said Luke.

"Wow. You're a lot crazier than I was at your age. You'll be fine though. I believe in you."

"Yeah. I'm gonna do something awesome with my life. I promise."

Luke knew his phone was filling up with missed calls and messages. He needed a shower; it was time to get his day going. After the shower he put on the same clothes with different boxers. He started the truck and checked his phone.

(From Tim): Need you. Answer your fone. Im at daves

He scanned his other messages. Dave's was the best place to start. Luke lit a cigarette, turned up the music, and headed out.

When he walked into Dave's, Jared and Jack were playing video games in the living room. "Where's Tim?" said Luke.

"In the bedroom," said Jared. "I have some money for you also. People need weed."

"Kay. I'll take care of you in a bit," said Luke as he walked to the bedroom. He knocked on the door, "Dave, it's me."

"Come in," said Dave.

Luke went in. There was a mirror with lines of methadone on the night stand. "I found that cheap stuff," said Tim. He held five capsules. "She tried to tell me I had to get ten for $100, but I got her to give me five for $50."

Luke weighed the capsules. Next, he poured some of the powder onto a plastic tray. The powder was finer than his stuff and had a strong smell. It tasted like molly. He snorted what was on the tray and ate another capsule. If it was any good he would be rolling hard. "Who did you get this from?" he said.

"Some girl named Zuri. I guess she's got two other friends who are selling the same shit for the same price, sometimes more."

Dave offered some of the methadone; Luke declined. They smoked weed. Luke was anxious for the cheap molly to kick in when Jared knocked on the door, "I need weed."

Luke opened the door, "How much?"

"Half ounce," said Jared.

"Okay, we'll have to go out to the truck for that," said Luke.

They went out to the Suburban. Luke was in the process of weighing up the bags when he started feeling the molly. He got the entactogenic fuzzy feeling, but there was no empathogenic effect. They finished their business and went back inside.

"Are you feeling anything?" said Tim.

"Yeah. I'm feeling something, but it's not the same. It's missing the magic love ingredient," said Luke.

Dave looked at Luke, "The love ingredient?"

"Yeah," said Luke, "I think you'd better try this stuff. My receptors might just be too fried to feel the love anymore." Luke feared that he might have ruined himself by shooting the MDMA with Shianne. *What if MDMA never works the same for me again? Will I ever feel the love again? I fucked up; now my nerve endings are toast.*

Tim gave Dave two of the capsules. "I have to take these?" said Dave.

"Yes," said Luke, "We need someone to try these who hasn't been doing molly every day."

"Well, I suppose I'll be your guinea pig."

Dave ate the capsules. Now they would wait. Luke was still worried that he only felt the physical effects. The physical effects were strong, but the magical emotions weren't happening.

Fat Jared knocked on the door again. "Luke, I need a ride to the skate park."

"Hold on! Important experiment. You'll have to wait," said Luke. Luke answered text messages. He prepared people to meet at Super 1; much easier to get everyone at once.

Dave's pupils got bigger. "Do you feel anything?" said Luke.

"Yeah, I'm feeling strange. My skin feels silky."

"Is it the best feeling you've ever had in your life? Do you feel the love?" said Luke

"Umm... I don't know; should I be having the best feeling of my life?" said Dave.

"No. My stuff makes you the happiest you can ever possibly be; it's scientifically proven. This stuff you did is some funky imitation. I don't understand it," said Luke.

"Why don't you give me the scientifically proven stuff?" said Dave.

"I have. You had an awesome time, but you didn't remember it. You were drinking and took some pills; didn't remember anything. I'll give you a sample of the good stuff if you want."

"Of course I want the good stuff. Why would you give me the bad stuff to begin with?" said Dave.

"Damn it Dave, I told you it was an experiment and you were the best test subject. You're kinda slow sometimes." Luke pulled out a bag of MDMA and scraped out a line for Dave. "No more alcohol for you," Luke took Dave's mixed drink and examined it before taking a drink.

"Hey, give me that," said Dave.

"You gotta trust me on this. If you're doing that molly you won't need any of this. Christ, this is strong. There's more alcohol in here than soda," said Luke.

"Well, fine," Dave snorted the line.

Tim asked if Luke could front him some more MDMA for the weekend. Luke agreed. He weighed 1/8 ounce for Tim. "I gotta get out of here. Dave, call if you need anything. I'll probably be back later anyway," Luke finished the mixed drink on the way out.

He was about to drive away when Jared came running after him. "You were gonna leave without me! I told you I needed a ride."

"Well, I'll have to drop you off at Super 1. I got people waiting for me right now."

"Fine. That's fine, let's go," said Jared.

~~~

Luke was at Super 1 for 45 minutes while he got everyone taken care of. There was one more stop: the Sizzle Steakhouse. A few of his ex-coworkers needed some weed. He got a call from Kimmy.

"Hello?" he answered.

"Hey dude, where are you?" she said.

"Heading to the Sizzle Steakhouse."

"Can I meet you there?" she said.

"Sure."

"See you soon," she hung up.

Luke got to the restaurant around seven. They were in the middle of the evening rush. He would have to be patient. Kimmy arrived quickly. She was driving a Geo Metro and was alone. She got in the Suburban and pulled out a wad of cash. "How much for a ball of that molly?"

"Gotta do four hundred," he said.

"C'mon, you can do three fifty," she said.

"No, I can't. I know where you can get some for that cheap, but it's crappy. If
~~~

you want the good shit, the price is set," he said.
"Three seventy-five," she said. He hesitated, "Fine."
"Awesome. Thank you Luke."
Luke took the money and counted it. He weighed up another 1/8 ounce. "Make sure you don't sell that stuff any less than twenty a point," he said.
"Ha, I sell this shit for thirty all day," she said.
"Right on. That's cool. I tried shooting it and it was the craziest shit ever," he said.
"Wow. That's fuckin nuts. I'll have to try it. Oh! There's a rave going on out past Big Fork. It's actually almost halfway to Missoula, but you have to go," she said.
"Who's all goin?" he said.
"Well, Blue's the one who told me about it. He has a buddy who's got a bunch of acid and is gonna be there. I've told a bunch of people about it. Everyone is going. It's gonna be sick," she said.
"Nice, you should come to Blue's in a couple hours. I think it would be better if we all just take your truck. Blue wants to take his car but it's not insured and he doesn't have a license. I would drive this, but it's not mine and my license is suspended," she said.
"That's fine. I don't mind driving. I'll take as many people as I can fit," he said.
"Right on dude, you're awesome. You don't need any crystal by any chance? I got some I'm trying to get rid of," she said.
"No, not really," he said.
"Damn. How about ten bucks and you can do a fat shot with me?" she said.
"Sure, I will take you up on that. Do you have any clean ones?" he said.
"Yep," she opened her purse and handed one to Luke. He took the cap off the plunger so she could drop some crystal into it. He mixed it up in the plunger cap; he didn't want to risk using her dirty spoon. He was already rushing from his shot while she was trying to find a vein. The syringe was full of blood and she had poked herself six times before Luke offered to help. She handed it to him and he asked for a new rig. He squirted the bloody liquid into the new one and poked her once.
It never failed; Luke loved being high. He was ready for anything. He enjoyed another one of those extra satisfying cigarettes. Kimmy stayed in the truck for a few minutes until she saw a waitress walking toward the truck. "I'm outta here. See you tonight," she got back into her Geo and drove off.
Sarah got in the truck with Luke, "Hi Luke! I miss you," she gave him a hug,

"How has it been being unemployed?" she lit a cigarette.

"It's been great. Absolute craziness. Financially, it's the best thing I've ever done. I've got the best MDMA in the freakin world and I'm one hundred percent single. Can't get much better than that," he said.

"Well aren't you just a little stud. When are you gonna come party with all your work buddies? Or are you too good to kick it with us anymore?" she said.

"We'll keep hangin out. I love you people. We got history. Tonight I'm going to a rave way past Big Fork. You're welcome to come."

"Can't do nothing tonight. I got the kids. Tomorrow I might have some people over. You're always the life of the party. I want you to come. We'll drink some Jaeger and Red Bull just like old times," she said.

"I am totally down for that. I will be there." Luke had her bag of weed ready. He pulled it out from under his seat and handed it to her.

"I freakin love you Luke," she said as she looked at the big bag of beautiful weed.

"Yeah, I know," he said.

"Time for me to get back in there. Thank you so much. I'll see you tomorrow," she put her cigarette in his ash tray and went back to work.

~~~

Luke arrived at Dave's. Dave greeted him with excitement, "I've been tryin to call you but I couldn't get this phone to work," he said as he caressed the cellphone, "You were right. No one could possibly feel any better than this. I love you man. I feel the love!"

"Pretty amazing stuff isn't it?" said Luke.

"It's a miracle! How did you get this stuff and why haven't I done it before?" said Dave.

"Man I told you, I already gave it to you before. You were drunk and faded. Didn't remember anything," said Luke.

"I couldn't have forgotten something like this. This is incredible, how long will it last?" said Dave.

"Like three or four hours, unless you take more," said Luke.

"Wow, Luke. I can't begin to explain how good I feel. I didn't know humans were allowed to feel this good. We have to do something. We need to go share this feeling with people. Tell me you have something planned. You always have something planned," said Dave.

"First, we're definitely not allowed to have this much fun. It's illegal. Really super schedule one illegal. Second, I do have something awesome planned for tonight. Big rave way out past Big Fork. Lots of LSD and ecstasy. We'll be able
~~~

to read minds and shit. It's gonna be like Jesus shit," said Luke.

"You're the best. I love you, man."

"Yeah, I love you too. Where did everyone go? Are you here all by yourself?" said Luke.

"Yeah, I actually got so excited I went for a walk and talked with some amazing people. I also made friends with one of the neighbors I've never talked to before. This stuff really makes you social. I just want to meet people and be friends with everybody. Can we go for a drive? That sounds like incredible fun right now," said Dave.

"That would be the best! You need to hear music. Let's go," said Luke.

They got into Luke's truck. Dave lit a cigarette and handed one to Luke. Luke found a song and turned up the stereo. Dave braced himself when they started moving. He had the most genuine smile. Like a child on a roller coaster. Luke felt it too; the happiness was contagious.

The drive was crazy. Dave hung out the window and waved at everyone he saw, telling them he loved them. Luke got a call from Natalie.

"Hello?" he answered.

"Hi Luke, what's going on? Are you busy?" she said.

"No. Not busy. Just driving around. Why? What's up?" he said.

"Can you pick me up? I need a ride into town," she sounded distressed.

"Of course I will. Where are you?" he said.

"In Kila, " she said.

"Okay, I'm on my way. I'll call when I'm close," he hung up. "Sounds like we gotta rescue someone," he said to Dave.

"Who? What happened?" said Dave.

"It was Natalie. Remember that girl I brought on the spirit quest? I think she's having some family trouble again."

"Oh no. Poor girl. We need to cheer her up. Are you gonna give her any of that stuff you gave me?"

"No. Not unless she asks for it. I'm not trying to corrupt the poor girl," said Luke.

It was a magical drive for Dave. The music had so much meaning and vibrated through his body.

An SPM song came on and the chorus spoke to him deeply:

I know that I

Must be high

So that I can function…

It was his favorite song even though he hated Mexican gangster rap. It was the best song in the world, just like every other song that played on the stereo. Every song was his favorite song. "We're having fun right now, aren't we? We're best friends. It doesn't get any better than this, does it?" Dave said as he stroked the silky seat.

"Yeah, we're definitely havin fun." Luke called Natalie when he was close to Kila.

"Hey, I'm at the German bed and breakfast place," she said.

"Cool, almost there. I'll see you in a sec." He slowed down and turned off the highway into a gravel parking lot.

She got up from a log bench and got in the truck. "Thank you so much. My dad is such a prick."

"What happened this time?" said Luke. He drove back onto the highway.

"Well, everything was supposed to be cool when I came back home. My dad said he was gonna lighten up and let me have a social life. Instead he twisted things around and said that I need to pay rent if I'm gonna come and go when I please. How am I supposed to get a job when I don't have a car and I live in the middle of nowhere? So I told him I would find a job. I guess that's what I'm gonna try to do. What are you guys doing? I haven't done anything fun in forever and kinda want to hang out," she said.

"We're going to a rave," said Dave, "You're gonna come and it's gonna be awesome. Luke has stuff that will make you feel like Jesus. Right, Luke? Tell her she can feel like Jesus."

"Well, I don't know. You're welcome to go with us. What are you tryin to do, Natalie?" said Luke.

"Can I go with you guys? I thought you had to be eighteen to go to raves," she said.

"Not this one. It's in the woods in the middle of nowhere. There's gonna be hundreds of people and it's going all night," said Luke.

"Are you guys doing mushrooms again?"

"No. I'm gonna do acid and maybe eat some ecstasy. No one really knows. You could do mushrooms if you'd like. Someone could find them, I'm sure," he said.

"I'm not sure what I want to do. Acid sounds a little extreme," she said.

"I'll tell you now that acid isn't nearly as extreme as mushrooms. It's more of a stable trip. None of the crazy peaks that you get from shrooms. When you mix LSD with ecstasy you really do feel like Jesus," said Luke.

"You need to do the molly," said Dave, "It's amazing; the best drug in the world!"

"What's molly?" she said.

"It's the pure powder form of MDMA; otherwise known as ecstasy. It makes your brain the happiest it can ever possibly be," Luke explained.

"And that's what Dave took?" she said. "Yeah. He took it a couple hours ago."

"Wow. It just seems so crazy. I guess I'm just new to all this," she said.

"Don't feel pressured to do anything. You can do whatever you want," said Luke. "Doesn't all this stuff cost money? Because I don't have anything," she said.

"If you're coming with me everything is free. I can lead you through the land. You're in good hands, I promise."

"Alright, I want the molly stuff," she held her hand between Luke and Dave.

"What? Right now?" said Luke. She waved her hand around. Luke grabbed a crown royal bag from under his seat and handed it to Dave, "Grab a capsule out of the zip-lock bag in there." Dave found one and gave it to Natalie.

"Water?" she said.

Dave picked up a water bottle that was rolling around on the floorboard and gave it to her. "You're gonna love it," he said. This is gonna be the best day of your life."

"Ha, we will see." She chased down the capsule, "Where are we going right now?"

"Well, I guess we can go to my cousin's place unless anyone objects. Does anyone need to stop somewhere first? What happened to Mike?" he asked Natalie.

"We didn't work out. He's with some skanky girl from that alternative school. So yeah, I've been having a pretty bad time lately," she said.

"Well, Natalie," said Dave, "Life is about to get a whole lot better for you. In approximately," he looked at his wrist, "twenty minutes."

"I really hope so," she said.

Twenty minutes later they were in West Valley approaching Lore Lake Road. Dave was like a little kid, "Are you feeling it yet? How bout now?" She was starting to feel it. She had the butterflies; the music was becoming more vivid; her hands were getting sweaty.

Luke turned off the highway onto a gravel road. They were about ten minutes away from Blue's tent. Natalie's clothes turned to silk; everything was so fresh and clean. "You guys, I feel really weird."

Dave turned around. "It's good, isn't it?"

"Wow, yes. This is like... magic. I get why they call it ecstasy now," she said with a smile. "Are you gonna do this stuff, Luke? You need to. You should do it right now."

"I might later. Not right now. We still have a long night ahead of us," he said.

"We're here," said Luke, "This is Blue's tweaker tent." Dave had never been here, so it was just as strange for him as it was for Natalie. They got out of the truck and followed Luke around to the entrance of the tent. There were a lot of people considering the two vehicles parked out front.

"Hey cousin!" said Blue. He gave him a hug and exchanged some small talk. Natalie and Dave introduced themselves. Natalie recognized the two girls she went on the spirit quest with and was excited to see them.

Blue showed Luke a big bag of ecstasy pills. "What are those?" said Luke.

"Got some Green Transformers that I think are mescaline base; got Blue Smurfs, super speedy; and there's the red Mitsubishis, which I believe are heroin base. Wanna try one? Or two? One of each?" said Blue.

"Gimme a couple green ones," said Luke.

Natalie came over, "Wow, those look yummy," she said.

"They don't taste as good as they look," said Blue.

She looked at Luke. He shrugged. "Can I have a blue one?" she said. He gave her one. She examined it for a few moments, "A Smurf pill, huh." Blue handed her a beer to chase it down. "By the way Blue, this place is super cool. And you're awesome," she said.

"I'm glad you think so." Natalie was distracted by a joint across the room. "Good talk," Blue said to himself as she walked away.

They all drank beer and socialized for an hour before deciding to leave. Everyone was high on everything. Dave took the red pill soon as he found out it contained opiates. Luke drank a few beers, but the meth was still strong in his system and kept him focused.

The drive was loud and belligerent. There were twelve people in the truck after they picked up Jack and Jared. People were drinking, smoking, and lying on top of one another in a vehicle filled with drugs and alcohol. They broke every law and no one cared.

The sun began to set after forty-five minutes of driving. Blue pointed to a gravel road off the highway, "There's some sweet jumps over there." Luke turned onto the gravel road and kept his speed at 45 mph. They approached a cattle guard, "Keep going, don't slow down," said Blue from the passenger seat.

Everyone in the vehicle was oblivious. They hit the cattle guard and lifted off. Blue, Luke, and Dave were in the front with their seat belts on. Everyone in the back flew up and bounced off the ceiling with a scream. It was only a foot of clearance and the landing was bouncy. Another cattle guard; they hit it and caught air. The mangled bunch of people let out a yell as they were tossed again. He turned down the music and heard the sound of pain. Jack was upside down with his face pressed to the floorboard. Fat Jared was about to cry. Everyone was on the verge of either tears or laughter.

"That was awesome!" said one person. "Do it again!" said another.

Luke drove further down the dirt road so he could hit the cattle guards on the way back. Everyone had time to brace themselves this time, but a few of them still hit the ceiling. After the jumps they all cheered as they re-lit their broken cigarettes and finished their beers.

Natalie sat in the center of the middle row of seats between Jared and Kimmy. Jack had the worst spot lying across all of their laps. He had hit the ceiling on all four of the jumps. Natalie couldn't believe how much fun she was having. *I love these people, she thought, the party hasn't even started and we're already having so much fun.*

The rest of the drive was great. Every twenty minutes or so, Blue would hand out ecstasy pills to everyone, "Bomb time," he would say. Luke shared his MDMA capsules as well.

It was dark when they got to the rave. Blue's pills gave everyone a tweaky, jaw clenching, trippy feeling. The rave was hidden from the highway. Blue saw an old wooden sign that said, "10161" and knew it was the place. They drove down a narrow dirt road through the forest. One guy told Luke to stop so he could puke. "Too much beer and pills; not enough food," he said as he climbed back into the truck.

They made it. The road opened up to a big open grass area with clusters of vehicles and campfires set up. There were lots of people crowded around a giant half-tent with a stage and DJ equipment set up. One guy manned the equipment while colorful strobe lights projected all around. More trees were behind the big tent.

Blue instructed Luke to keep driving through the crowds of people. They creped through while people cleared out of the way. They went past the tent into the trees. They kept driving until Blue recognized his friend's green Ford Explorer.

Blue got out and greeted a heavyset guy with a goatee, "Rob! Fuckin miss you buddy."

"My boy, Blue. Glad you made it. I see you brought some friends," he looked at all the people getting out of the Suburban. "Are they high yet?" said Rob.

"I been feeding them bombs the whole way here. My cousins got some molly we been taking too," said Blue.

"Time for everyone to *really* get high." Rob held a Visine dropper, "Line em up."

Blue gathered everyone up and told them to hold out their hands. One by one he dropped a hit of LSD on each of their hands.

"One for you," said Rob, "One for you. Oops that might have been two. Ha-ha, sorry Blue."

"Two? Gimme three," said Blue.

"You don't want three. That guy took two," Dave pointed at a long haired hippie who was lying in the dirt playing with a pile of twigs.

Natalie looked at her hand, "What do I do?"

"Lick it," said Luke. She licked it, not understanding why.

They made their way to the music and started splitting up and blending with the crowd. Everyone was in total party mode, it was so easy for them to get right into the scene and just start dancing like fools. No one cared; there was no such thing as embarrassment. Even Natalie got lost in the crowd and danced like she had done it all her life.

Luke danced around to the rave music while advertising his MDMA. He wanted to sell as much as he could before the LSD kicked in. Dealing with money on psychedelics created potential for lost profits. He could sell on ecstasy, and the meth made math simple. But he was experiencing some visual effects from the weird ecstasy pills. The lights were vibrant; people had crazy faces. It didn't matter what drugs were in those pills. The fun thing about E-Bombs was that they were always a surprise. *Life is like a bag of bombs,* he thought, *you never know what you're gonna get.*

Fat Jared had lost all of his friends. He was hanging out with a group of hippies at their campsite. Two people were playing bongo drums and everyone was on LSD. Jared was so high on ecstasy he couldn't stop talking. The hippies were quiet, but he knew they were listening. "My friend Luke has the best molly in the world," he said, "Luke is my best friend ever and he never trusts me with anything. If he did trust me he would front me some of his molly so I could sell it to awesome people like you. I should probably go find him, but I don't want to leave you guys. I feel like we have a connection, like you guys understand me. We do have a connection, don't we?" He looked at them with hopeful eyes.

"We are connected just as the fabric of the universe," said one guy.

"We are all one," said a filthy girl playing with the fire.

"I fuckin love you people, I'll be honest. You need to try this molly my buddy's got. Do you guys want some? I can go find him."

"We will accept your gift," said a hippie with dreadlocks.

"Well, it's not really a gift, because you gotta pay for it. But it's worth every penny, I promise," said Jared.

"Your paper money is no good here," said the dirty girl.

"No, it is good. It has to be good," said Jared. "My buddy needs money to make his living. He sells drugs. He wouldn't be very happy with me if I brought him over here to give out free molly."

"Bring this love drug you speak of," said the dreadlocked man, "We will make trade. If it is green paper money you need, then green paper money is what you will get."

"Good. Awesome. I will return with plenty of love drug. If I don't make it back it means I got lost. So in that case I need you guys to use your universal connectedness to locate me. Peace out hippie dudes."

~~~

Luke was Jesus. He had taken a large dose of his MDMA and the LSD had kicked in. He could read minds and infuse people with his energy. Everything would switch from crystal clear to vibrating. He could see sound and hear colors. He now had the ability to amplify the party on a cosmic level.

Luke felt bad for the drunk people. They were so unaware, unconscious of their surroundings. Luke could feel their shallow state of mind. He could feel every fiber of his surroundings. He could see the color of people's souls, and could feel the energy of their intentions.

Luke was entertaining a group of people when Jared found him, "Luke, I need you."

"What's up buddy? How are you feeling?" said Luke.

"Trippin hard, bro. I was on a mission to find you; I don't remember why. Oh, hippies! The hippies need the love drug. You should come with. They got a sweet fire and bongo drums. And they're trippin just like us. Well, not exactly like us, but they will be when you give them that molly."

"Yeah, we can do that. But we gotta be back soon. The vibrations in this scene are outrageous! You need to join it, and savor it. Those trippin hippies will be there all night; the music won't," said Luke.

They walked away from the big party and made their way through the forest. "Do you even know where we're going? It seems like we're going in circles," said Luke.

"Yeah, I'm not sure. I don't recognize any of this " said Jared. Many people wandered around aimlessly. It was easy to get lost. There were many camps and cars were parked in disarray.

Luke saw someone coming out of the bushes. The person was paranoid.
~~~

"Blue! Where you been? There's a good party going on back there."

"Shh," Blue looked around nervously, "I gotta go somewhere. I'll meet you back at the truck in a bit."

"What about the party? You're missing out, man." Luke could feel the fear radiating from Blue.

"Is everything okay?"

"It's good. I'm good. Gotta go." He disappeared into the trees. "That was weird " said Jared.

"Yeah. I feel bad letting him go like that," said Luke.

~~~

They never did find the hippies, but they did stop by the Suburban. Luke needed water. There was only one old guy sitting by the fire.

"I'm gonna go look for those hippies," said Jared, "Can you give me some molly and I'll bring you the money?"

"Sure," Luke reached into his secret pocket grabbed his capsules, "How many?"

"I don't know. Ten maybe?" said Jared.

Luke counted and re-counted ten capsules. "Make sure you get at least twenty for each one. Are you sure you can handle this?" said Luke.

"Yeah. I can do it. I won't let you down." Jared walked off alone.

Luke had an urge to go talk with the lonely old man by the fire. He sat down on the lawn chair next to the man and noticed he was rolling a cigarette. "Would you like a real cigarette?" said Luke.

"Sure," the old man said in a quiet voice.

"What brings you to a place like this?" said Luke.

"Well, I've been living with Rob. So I just go wherever he goes."

"Did you take the LSD?" Luke was sure he'd taken LSD. He could feel it.

"Oh no, I have no use for that stuff anymore."

~~~

Jared found the hippies. They were pleased to see him. "The love child has returned," said the dirty hippie girl. The music stopped, they all focused on Jared.

"Yeah… I'm back. And I've got the love drug," said Jared.

"So your friend trusted you after all?"

"He did, and he gave me ten capsules and told me to sell em for twenty a piece." Jared understood why the hippies hated the paper money; it seemed such an evil thing in this state of mind.

"I sense your intentions are good. How much money do you need?" said the dreadlocked hippie. They gathered around and made the difficult transaction. Another hippie arrived with a guitar.

He began strumming and the camp came to life. The bongo drums came into play and the dirty hippie girl started singing. Jared was entranced by the girl's voice. The lyrics were improvised. There was no hesitation, no thought; the words just flowed from her mouth in the most beautiful pattern. The forest, the earth, the universe was speaking through her. Jared was witnessing something supernatural.

~~~

By the time Luke got back to the music he was in dance mode again. The electronic music had a darker vibe; the people were more belligerent. There were drunk people with crazy faces. The DJ was a wicked puppet master, controlling the crowd with sound waves. Luke joined in and embraced the energy.

Someone tugged at his shirt, "Luke," it was Natalie.

"Hey, where have you been?" They got away from the music so they could hear each other.

"This is so crazy!" she said, "Are you feeling the same way I am?"

"Yeah I am. It's pretty freakin spectacular, isn't it?" he said.

"It is! I'm completely aware of everything around me. I've met so many awesome people and the dancing comes so naturally. You were right about the acid; about the Jesus feeling."

"Right? Do you want to help me find my cousin? I saw him earlier and something was wrong," said Luke.

~~~

Dave was having his own unique experience. He had been wandering aimlessly for hours. There were no worries and he enjoyed every minute. Sometimes he would just laugh at all the crazy people. An acid trip was his happy place, and the assortment of ecstasy pills gave it an exhilarating twist.

Dave didn't join the rave dancing, but he enjoyed the music and the people. He also went against Luke's advice to stay away from alcohol. Beer was easy to come by and he drank more than anyone should be able to tolerate. He suspected that people were sneaking drinks out of his beer cans because they went empty so quickly.

He left a group of newfound friends to enjoy the sights. The rave was dying down. Drunk people had become wasted. He walked past a girl who was trying to pull her drunk boyfriend up off the grass. A man with blood all over his shirt and face walked past like a zombie. Dave took a drink off his beer. The alcohol didn't make him drunk; it only made him higher. He felt he could drink and party until noon.

Dave left to seek new adventure in the forest. It seemed all the people had continued the party at their own campsites. Each camp spot had its own music; its own vibe. He was contented to just walk and greet the funny people as he passed. The forest was mostly dark, but to him it was vivid with colors. Hieroglyphics of an ancient language appeared on the trunks of trees, spelling out the secrets of the universe.

He was staring up into the trees when his universe shattered into an explosion of light. A glittery girl was waving glow sticks in his face. He burst into laughter while spilling his beer all over the place.

The glittery girl moved on.

"Dave?" it was Luke, "Holy smokes, I thought you were a crazy person. Get it together; we gotta get to the Suburban."

Dave followed, trying not to spill any more beer, "What's going on?"

"Helicopters man! Don't you see the spotlights?" said Luke.

"Helicopters? Look over there," Dave pointed to a camp, "is that Jared?"

"It sure looks like it. Let's go see."

It was Jared, swaying to the music with a smile on his face. "Luke, Dave!" he ran up and hugged them. "These are the awesome hippies I was telling you about."

The bongo drumming stopped and the guitar played a mellow tune. The hippies looked at Luke with wonder. "We've been expecting you," said the dirty hippie girl.

"Yes," said another hippie girl. "We thank you for providing the wonderful love drug." She got up and touched his face, "You are adorable," she took his hat off to feel his hair.

"That's totally groovy," Luke said with a jittery jaw, "I'm glad to share the experience."

The music resumed and the dirty hippie girl started singing. She had a smoldering twig in her hand that she waved around.

Dave and Luke felt the magic. Their environment came alive in a new and special way. The dirty hippie girl sang of the trees and the stars and their new found friends. She sang of Luke, Dave and Jared; she sang of love and the inter-connectedness of all living things. Each word flowed with deep and magical meaning.

Luke stared at the dirty hippie girl in wonder, *this is how the Beatles must have happened; A night on LSD and the steady flow of unfiltered cosmic consciousness.* She paused for a few beats. The tempo changed; the guy with the guitar started to sing. It picked up right where she left off in perfect harmony. It came straight from the soul; the thinking brain could only get in the way. They engaged in a psychedelic freestyle duet on epic proportions. It was supernatural; a gift from God.

~~~

Jack was sitting by the fire with the old man Luke had encountered. They could relate as if they were both on LSD, but the old man had taken nothing. Just then Rob came up and sat on a log right next to them. "Ha, I see you met Billy. He's nuttier than squirrel shit, isn't he?" said Rob.

"Aren't we all kinda nutty right now?" said Jack.

"Well, yeah, because were high. He's not high. Billy can't do drugs no more. He done fried that potato a long time ago," said Rob.

"Potato?"

"You see, back in the nineties, this poor soul was a guinea pig for a new batch of LSD. Turns out the stuff wasn't made right, and this here is what you got. Billy's pretty much stuck in a permanent acid trip. He'll go weeks without sleepin if he don't take his meds, which I don't think he has been. Have you Billy?"

"A person could get stuck in an acid trip? Is it fun? At least you don't have to pay for drugs anymore, right?" Jack laughed, not sure about his joke.

Billy kept looking at the fire and shrugged. He looked like he was about to speak, but didn't. "Billy don't talk much," said Rob, "but we love him. Poor perma-fried fella."

Jack eventually made his way to the Suburban. There were people with glow sticks waving around. He opened the door, "Hellooo fellows."

"Get in!" said Kimmy, "Hurry up and close the door. Our brainwaves are escaping." He closed the door and climbed to the back. There was laughter and glow sticks; this was a good place.

~~~

Luke had enjoyed his time with the hippies. The dirty hippie girl was giving him seductive looks and ambiguous comments, so he decided it was time to leave. Dave went with Luke, but Jared was too mesmerized by the dirty hippie girl to go anywhere.

They made it to the Suburban. There was a group of people laughing around the fire. Luke only recognized Rob and the crazy old guy. "Happy trails," said Rob.

"Totally," said Luke. He walked around to the driver side of the Suburban and opened the door. "Get in, get in!" said Jack from the back. Natalie was the only one in the front seat, Luke and Dave got in the front with her in the middle.

"Wow, looks like everyone survived," said Luke.

"Not Blue," said one of the guys in the back, "No one's seen him."

"Or Jared," said Jack, "Haven't seen him either."

"Jared's totally fine. He's with some hippies. Me and Dave were just with him." Luke turned on some electronic music.

"Is there any more beer back there?" said Dave.

"Helicopters!" said Luke. Beers were passed up. Luke cracked one open and took a drink. Soon three pipes were sent into rotation. Imaginary lights flashed all around the vehicle.

~~~

The sun was beginning to rise when Jared joined them in the Suburban. "I'm so disgusted with myself," he said.

"What's wrong, Jared?" said Luke.

"I don't want to talk about it. It's weird," said Jared.

"Oh c'mon. We're all friends here. You can tell us," said Luke.

"I had sex with the hippie girl," said Jared.

"Which one?" said Luke.

"The dirty one."

"Well that's good, isn't it? You should be proud of yourself," said Luke.

"Yeah, that's what I thought, until afterward," said Jared.

"What happened?"

"You know how she does her singing all trippy like? With all her subliminal messages and hidden meanings? She kinda started singing about us having sex in the forest and stuff. That was cool, but then she started singing about all the other people she had sex with tonight. It was freakin weird. Shit got weird. The other guys seemed all cool with it; they just kept smiling with their acid faces. I'm pretty sure every single one of those hippies had sex with that girl tonight. I've got everyone's sloppy, dirty, hippie juice all over me. It's really fucking with me right now."

"That's pretty gross man," said Jack.

"Oh settle down," said Luke. "A little dirty hippie sex never hurt no one. You'll be fine."

"I need a cigarette," said Jared. Luke gave him one.

"Well, what's the plan?" said Luke. He sipped his beer, "What should we do about Blue?"

"Blue's fine," said Kimmy. "He knows how to take care of himself. We should head back to town."
~~~

"Very well then. I guess we'll get this show on the road." Luke chugged the last of his beer and started the engine.

"Are you seriously good to drive?" said Natalie.

"Of course. Always. Do you question my judgment?"

"Well, I don't know if you're still as messed up as me, but I would not want to be in control of any vehicle right now," she said.

"You have a point. I realize all of your lives are in my hands. If things start getting weird I'll pull over." Luke began his systems check. "Headlights? Check. Paraphernalia in the glove box? Check. Beer? We need more beer up here. Alright, check."

Luke put the truck into gear and coasted out of their campsite. "I'll take the long way out of here so we can make one more sweep for Blue. Everyone keep your eyes peeled." Luke drove around through the trees. They yelled for Blue out the open windows. "Blinker," Luke yelled,"Don't forget to use the blinker, ha-ha." He used his blinker as they turned through the trees. "I give up, let's get out of here." He made it back to the highway and headed for Kalispell.

The drive went smoothly. They smoked weed and drank beer while listening to some rap by Atmosphere and Hilltop Hoods. Luke was low on gas and stopped at a station in Big Fork. He sent Natalie in to pay because she was the soberest one. She came out with Vitamin Water as well; everyone was thankful.

It was 8:30am when they got to Kalispell. Luke pictured Blue being lost somewhere in the forest, completely out of his mind: *Hello? Where am I? Why isn't anyone searching for me? I'm lost in the forest with nothing but a bag of ecstasy pills to eat.*

They went to Blue's. It's where everyone left their vehicles. They pulled into the driveway and got out of the truck. There was music playing from the tent. They ran around to the entrance and saw Blue sitting on the couch, drinking a beer and smoking a cigarette. "Cousin!" said Luke, "What happened?"

"I had to get outta there. Wasn't feeling right about the situation," said Blue. "How'd you get here?"

"Walked. Hitchhiked. It was fun. I rode in the back of a pickup for hours. We were going like seventy. There were deer everywhere and I was trippin balls. Hitchhiked with like three different vehicles to get here. Still got this," he held up his bag of ecstasy pills, "Want some?"

"I'm totally good on that, bro. Lemme get one of those beers though," said Luke.

The party came back to life. Everybody was happy to see Blue alive and well. Whatever was in those ecstasy pills was still working. No one was even close to being sleepy. The party went on until they started drinking themselves into blackouts around noon.

When our pleasures have exhausted us,
we think that we have exhausted pleasure.
-Vauvenargues

Chapter 8: New Friend

Monday 7-15-2010

Luke gripped the steering wheel of his Chrysler with sweaty palms. It had been an exhausting twelve hour drive from Portland, Oregon. Luke and Tim hadn't slept in almost two full weeks. It was almost two months since school had been out. Those two months had gone by in a blur for Luke.

The objective had been to go to the hippie festival in Eugene; also to see his old friends and family in Portland. Luke invested in an ounce of crystal while he was in Portland. It would pay for their trip while also giving them the energy to do everything they needed to do in Oregon.

Luke would go to Oregon at least once a year and stimulant drugs had always been a part of the tradition. There were too many people to see; too much to do. There was no time for sleep. This was the first time Tim had gone with him. He brought Stacy on his previous visit.

Luke pushed himself further than he had ever gone before. He was thirty minutes from Kalispell and was clinging to reality like a roller coaster with no seat belts. He was on the verge of disaster. Vertigo had become a constant threat. Tim was on rear-view duty. They suspected they were being followed.

A week prior, they had a narrow escape in Oregon City. It had almost been the end of the line for Luke. There was a bag of ecstasy pills in a camera case on the back seat. The cop asked to see it. Luke told him no. The cop asked why. Luke told him he knew his rights and that he will not give any permission to search anything. The cop lied, threatened, and interrogated each of Luke's passengers. They all said nothing. Luke had prepared all of them for the hypothetical situation. They handled it as instructed. There was ecstasy, acid, weed, Adderall, Oxycontin, heroin, coke, and an ounce of methamphetamine in the car. Only Tim and Luke knew about the meth. It had to remain a secret around Luke's friends.

It was the final stretch. Luke had trouble staying within the lines. He was running on fumes; his brain was trying to dream while he was awake.

The first stop in Kalispell would be Dave's. They were in Kalispell when a cop got behind them. He stopped at an intersection. The cop was right behind. Luke was gripping his steering wheel with white knuckles. *One right turn,* he thought, *only a few blocks to Dave's.* He turned on his blinker and pulled into the intersection.

Lights flash, sirens on. Tim had been dozing off, but was now horrified. They pulled into a gas station parking lot. The cop sped past them. They made it to Dave's without incident.

Dave answered the door. Tim went straight to the couch and fell asleep. Luke went to Dave's room. Dave smoked some of the crystal and was shocked that Luke didn't want any. "Why don't you want any?"

"Are you serious? My parents expect me home today. I need to get normal, like... quick. My phone is still off and I know they're worried sick. I should at least text them... no, fuck it. I need to sleep," he said.

"Well in that case, take some methadone," Dave pointed at the mirror.

"How bout we smoke some chiba. I picked some up in Portland." Luke reached into his secret pocket and pulled out a small bag of heroin. He put some on a piece of foil and took one hit before handing it off to Dave. "I gotta go right now; I'll come by soon as I can."

~~~

Luke barely made it to Blue's. Blue had been drinking beer and rushed out to the driveway to meet Luke. "Damn it cousin, the whole world's been waiting on you," said Blue.

Luke grabbed a half ounce of meth out of the glove box and handed it to Blue. Blue was back in the tent before Luke could say another word. Blue was in already in the process of taking a shot when Luke came in. He coughed and laid
~~~

back onto the couch. "Wow!" said Blue, "Good job cousin. You really came through this time. No way I'm sellin this shit pure. People will get stupid if I sell it like this." Blue got up and started pacing, "You gonna do any?"

"Naw man, I'm fixin on crashin out. I feel stupid. Been up for too long. Do you care if I kick it here?" said Luke.

"Oh for sure. You want me to set up the air mattress?" he was already unrolling it and plugging in the air pump. "There's food in the fridge, help yourself to whatever."

"Appreciate it." Luke opened the fridge and found orange juice. He guzzled the whole carton.

"There's blankets over there if you need. I've gotta get outta here; stay as long as you like. Do whatever you want. I'll be in and out all day, and all night."

"Cool man. I'm just gonna go ahead and lay down now." Luke was fast asleep within seconds.

~~~

Luke woke up on a deflated air mattress. His shoes were still on and he felt stiff. Kimmy was texting on the couch, "Hey dude. Get enough sleep?" she said.

"I think so. What day is it?" he said.

"Thursday," she said.

"Holy crap, I'm freakin hungry," Luke went to the fridge and grabbed another orange juice. There was a bag of trail mix next to the fridge. He took it to the couch and started munching down.

"So how was your trip?" she asked.

"It was extreme. Met some crazy people and did some weird drugs. The hippie festival was the highlight for sure; it's pretty much my favorite place in the world."

"Was it like that ten-one-six-one we went to?" she said.

"Not really; a lot more hippies. There's thousands of people and it goes on for four days. No cops allowed," he said.

"Right on. What else did you do?"

"I hit up some house parties in Portland; kicked it at the coast with a bunch of friends; ate ecstasy and had a bonfire on the beach; mostly just hung out with all my old friends."

"That's tight, dude. Wanna get high?" she held up a meth pipe.

"No thanks. I'm actually trying to be sober so I can go see my parents. I'll smoke some weed with you though." Luke pulled out his pipe. The first hit had tremendous effect; it always did after a three day nap. Kimmy only took a couple hits, but Luke kept smoking until he was toasted. His eyes were squinty
~~~

and bloodshot. This made him feel better about going home to see his parents. As long as he's stoned, he's not doing anything bad.

"I'd better get outta here. Tell Blue I'll call when I get my phone charged up," said Luke.

The Chrysler felt like home. He had spent so many sleepless nights behind the wheel. There were very few Chrysler Imperials left on the road. For him to be able to take it on such epic adventures was spectacular. Luke liked having old vehicles. He's had many. The Chrysler was the newest one he'd ever owned even though it was made in 1991; the same year he was born.

Luke smoked a satisfying cigarette. He got a head rush. It tasted strange after not smoking for so long. The drive was nice. He listened to Bob Marley. His body felt good, but there was something missing in his life. He felt bad about neglecting his parents. His relationships with friends seemed shallow. The only time friendships seemed real was when he was on MDMA. The only time he felt connected to the universe was when he was on LSD or mushrooms. Luke wanted something real; not something imitated by drugs. Cheating happiness had to come with a price. Every action had to have an equal and opposite reaction. Ecstasy did some noticeable short-term damage. It showed in his speech and cognitive abilities. The short-term problems didn't worry him; it was the long-term stuff that was troubling.

In junior high he overdosed on cold medicine. It gave him a permanent stutter. This was no ordinary speech impediment, it was a brain glitch. At least once a day his brain would lock up and his face would twitch. It felt like a shockwave. His pupils would dilate when it happened. As far as he knew, there was no name for his condition. So, he called it the Triple-C Stutter.

Luke had a dilemma. Life without drugs seemed dull and boring. Luke couldn't stand sober people. He envied their ability to enjoy the simple things in life. He wished he could enjoy something as simple as fishing with his dad.

Luke pulled into the driveway. Alice was out front watering flowers. She looked up with excitement. Luke got out and gave her a long hug while she kissed him on the cheek. "So good to see you," she said between kisses, "My sweet, sweet boy, I've missed you so much!"

"I missed you too, mom."

"Oh come talk with me. Should we have a glass of wine? I want to hear everything."

They went to the back patio. It was a nice afternoon. The Beatles were playing. They had wine and crackers. "You look stoned," said Alice.

"I am. Very. Where's dad?" he said.

"He's out doing some errands; Picking up some paint and other things. Tell me, how was your trip? Did you have fun with your friends? Did Tim have a good time?"

"Yeah, it was great. So much happened," Luke went on to describe every detail of the trip.

"Are you ever gonna get a job?" she finally asked, "You must be running out of money."

"Money's not really an issue right now. I don't know what my plans are."

"You know you can't just sell drugs forever. It's time you start thinking of a career; something you can work towards. Maybe college. You know the government is giving out student grants. I'm sure you would be eligible for something like that," she said.

"I know, you're probably right. I just want to keep this freedom I've got. This should be the funnest time of my life, and I don't want to cut it short."

"Oh I know sweetie. You should have fun after making it through high school. Just try to think about what you might want to do in the future. Keep moving forward. You can't be a drug dealer forever."

They sat together and talked until they finished their drinks. Luke thought about all the people who needed him for weed. He was sure his phone would be exploding with messages. "I need that weed I left with you," he told Alice.

"Oh, of course. Thank you for not taking it with you. Way too much; I would have been worried sick," she went to retrieve his stash. *Good thing she doesn't know about all the other stuff.* She came back with a brown paper sack.

Luke went up to his room. The phone was charged. He had an incoming call from Brittany. She wasn't a priority customer. She always wanted to buy small bags of weed. He answered the call, "Hello?"

"Hey Luke. It's Brittany. I'm sorry to bug you, but I desperately need some bud. No one has any, I've looked everywhere. You're my only hope."

"How much do you need?" he said.

"Well, I only have twenty bucks. But I have something else you might like to trade," she said.

"What can you trade?" he said.

"I got some molly. I can get you a bunch for pretty cheap if you're interested."

Luke wasn't interested. He was about to make an excuse, then he remembered that movie, "Yes Man" with Jim Carey. "Alright, where you at?"

"My place. You remember where it's at?" she said.

"I'll call when I'm close."

He saw that there were 36 unread messages. He didn't read any of them.

Today he would do things one at a time. He had been going full speed for too long; it was time to take things slow.

~~~

The truck felt loud and rumbly compared to the Chrysler. He felt some depression. He thought of Stacy; a painful thought.

He made it to the trailer park. The park was big. He called Brittany and she instructed him the rest of the way. She was waiting with her friends on the porch while smoking a cigarette. One girl he recognized; the other he had never seen before. Brittany gave him a hug when he got out of the Suburban, "Thanks for coming, Luke. Long time no see."

"Sure. How you been?" he said.

"Been good. Not much has changed with me. I like your truck by the way. I swear, every time I see you, you've got a new vehicle," she said.

They walked up to the porch. He said hello to Lisa and introduced himself to the other girl, "Hey there. I'm Luke."

"Hi, I'm Zuri." They went to Brittany's messy bedroom. There was a small desk with an old computer on it. Luke sat on the broken chair at the desk. Brittany and Lisa sat on the bed and Zuri fell onto a bean bag chair. Luke asked the girls about what they have been up to. Brittany talked the most about how she got her GED and had been staying away from the party crowd. Luke loaded a pipe and passed it around. Lisa talked about how she got her own place and was living with Zuri. They were both 17 years old. Luke used to go to school with Lisa, but she dropped out. Zuri didn't talk much, but she seemed nice. Luke thought she might be emo.

Brittany asked Luke about what he had been up to. He explained the trip to Oregon, censoring much of it. He told her about getting fired and graduating high school. She asked about Stacy. He told her that they had been split up for a while; that they had trust issues they could never settle. Brittany was glad to hear they broke up, "No offense, but that bitch was a fuckin psycho. You can do so much better. She's a controlling, stuck up bitch who thinks she's better than everyone. You're a good guy and don't deserve that crap," she said.

"Well, thanks," he said.

"This weed is amazing," said Lisa.

Luke made eye contact with Zuri. She looked away quickly. "Glad you think so," said Luke, "What's the deal with this molly you speak of?" he asked Brittany.

"I've only got two capsules. But if you can, I was hoping you could give me another couple grams for both of them. I can get you a bunch if you'd like; a hundred dollars a gram."
~~~

"I don't think I could do anything with that, but I'll give you an extra couple grams for what you got. And I'm doing it as a favor. Try to have real money for me next time," he said.

"Thanks Luke, you're fuckin awesome." She handed him two grimy capsules that looked like they had been in someone's pocket for too long. Zuri gave him twenty-five dollars for the sixteenth of an ounce.

"Oh no, it's only twenty," he handed five back.

"Cool thanks," said Zuri.

Luke used his scale to weigh out the two bags. He handed one to Brittany and one to Zuri. Brittany and Zuri went halves on a massive bowl. Halfway through the bowl they reached the limit but kept smoking until it was gone. Conversation became a struggle, but they were having fun. They laughed at every stupid thing. Luke was glad he came.

They were outside smoking when Luke tried to check his phone. He was overwhelmed and gave up. There was a strange connection between Luke and Zuri. She was not his type at all. Zuri was unpretentious and introverted. She was plain looking and had a punk rocker image; straight dark hair, pale skin but no makeup. Luke liked her. He wanted to be her friend; wanted to brighten her world. There was a sadness about her and he wanted to fix it.

"I gotta go. People are waiting for me.We'll have to do this again sometime," he said.

"Thanks again for the hookup. See you next time," said Brittany.

They all said their goodbyes and Luke went to his truck. "Hey Luke," it was Zuri, "I forgot I was gonna ask if I could get your number. You know, in case I need to get some weed or something."

"Yeah. That's fine." She opened her phone and he told her his number. "Call whenever. I'll be around."

"Kay. I'll see you later then," she said.

~~~

Luke arrived at his next stop. He was in another trailer park to see his friend Debora. She was an older woman. Luke had known her since he started doing meth. Before Blue was around she was his hookup. They had been friends ever since. She answered the door, "Hey honey, come in. How are you?"

"I've been good," he walked in and sat on the couch. "Got back from Oregon the other day."

"Oh good, how was the trip? Did you bring any of that good stuff?" she said.

"The trip was freakin nuts. I was gone for two weeks and didn't sleep the entire time. Ate lots of acid, ecstasy, shrooms, and yes, I've got the stuff," he said.
~~~

"Oh that's perfect. I haven't been high in a few days and the stuff around here is not so good right now. You can leave some with me, can't you? You know I'm good for it," she said.

"Heck yeah, I can float you a ball. Just get me three hundred," he said.

"Bless your heart. Can we do some?" she said.

They mixed some up. Luke took his shot. Debora took longer to do hers. Her veins were damaged from the years of abuse. She had the same reaction as Luke, "Wow, I forgot how good that Oregon crystal is. Do you have a cigarette? I'm broke, don't get paid till Friday," she said.

"Yeah. I do," he pulled out half of his pack and set the cigarettes on the table, "You can have these."

"Thank you honey," she lit one and Luke did the same. "So, really, tell me how you've been."

"I've been busy, havin lots of fun. The summer has been rough. No more Stacy. No more work. Just been slingin and partying non-stop."

"Well aren't you the wild child. So, Stacy's finally out of the picture? How do you feel about that?" she said.

"Good, actually. I'm seeing that I've got a lot more potential without her."

"You have so much potential. That girl was holding you back. Just after seeing her those couple times I knew how controlling she was. I've seen her type before; she'll use her little bikini body and smooth talking to get what she wants. You don't need that kind of girl."

"You know what's funny? I met this girl today who is like the polar opposite of Stacy. She's not the type of girl I would usually go for; totally shy, not eager to impress. Anyways, we had this crazy connection and it's interesting to picture myself with a girl like that. It might just be all in my head, but for some reason I just care about the girl."

"She sounds sweet. If it turns into something you'll have to let me meet her."

"I will for sure. The thing is, I still don't know nothing about her. I know she smokes weed and maybe does ecstasy, but I have no idea what she would think if she knew about everything else I do. Like I said, she has this innocence about her. The drugs are getting out of control for me. Maybe this girl could be what it takes for me to slow down. She might be the excuse I need to get my life together. Am I talking too fast? Is it too much?" he said.

"It's cute," she smiled, "I think you're funny. As long as you stay away from those manipulating barbi doll girls you'll do fine. I used to get outta control when I was young. That kind of life can get dangerous and I would hate to see you get hurt. It's also no good to get stuck doing drugs your whole life. Look where it's got me. You have got such a strong young body and I would hate to see you ruin it."

"Yeah. I do want to stop. At least before I'm twenty-one. Because the frontal lobe stops developing at age twenty-four, and I want to give it a few years to develop without drugs," he said.

"You're a smart kid. When you first found me, I couldn't believe you were into all this stuff. You'll do good to get out of this kind of life. I think you'll do big things." They talked and smoked cigarettes until Luke decided to put his energy to good use. Phone calls and text messages continued to pile up.

He got into his truck and scrolled through his messages. He decided to just go home. Everyone who needed stuff could come there. He wrote one text and sent it to everyone who had been trying to get ahold of him.

The drive was exhilarating; the music was loud. He blasted Rob Zombie and felt like a badass. Times like this made him feel like he was superior to other humans; smarter, stronger, and faster than the rest. His muscles were tense as dopamine and norepinephrine flooded through his body. *Quit drugs? All drugs? Never.*

~~~

Allan was painting the fence when Luke got home. Luke would have to remind himself to not talk too fast. Allan was already walking to the truck with a smile. Luke got out and gave him a big hug. "My son! How was your trip?"

"It was pretty sweet. I had fun," said Luke.

"Good. I'm glad. You're here just in time to help me out with the fence."

"I am totally ready to paint some fence, but I do got some weed to sell. I kinda told everyone to come here."

"Oh did ya now? In that case, I think you'd better get your ol' dad stoned," he grinned and gave Luke a jab in the shoulder.

"Yeah. I think we'd better do that."

"Vaporizer? It's been a while, I bet you miss it," said Allan.

"Sure," Luke hesitated. *In the garage? With almost no sunlight? My pupils will dilate to the brim!* "Actually, we should just smoke in the truck. I've got a cool song I want you to hear."

"Sounds good to me," said Allan. They got in the truck.

Luke pulled out his variety of weed and handed it to Allan. Pipes in the glove box. "Go ahead and load whatever you want." Luke scrolled through his I-pod while Allan prepared the pipe. Luke played a song by MGMT and the smoking began.
~~~

It was good quality time until the first of Luke's clients pulled into the driveway. "Here they come," said Allan, "is this where you get distracted and forget to help me with the fence?"

"No, I'll make it quick. If they try to linger I'll tell them they can help with the fence," said Luke.

"Cool. Do your business. I'll get back to work." Allan got out and went back to work on the fence.

Luke stuck his head out the window and waved the person over to his truck. When the guy got in, Luke was startled, "Do I know you?"

"What? It's me, Justin."

"Justin?" said Luke.

"From Whitefish. Are you serious? I've bought from you before. You texted saying I could swing by," said Justin.

"Oh wow, I'm sorry. I remember. Your hair is shorter or something," said Luke.

"That's never happened to me before."

"Sorry man. My memory can be unreliable sometimes. I see a lot of faces. What do you need? I gotta make this quick," said Luke.

Within minutes he had Justin on his way. Luke thought about the awkward situation. This wasn't the first time he forgot who someone was. It had been happening more often. There were too many people and his memory was getting worse. Two more cars pulled in at almost the same time. He talked and moved with precision.

Luke got out of the truck so he could paint for few minutes. He barely closed the door before another car was pulling in. It was Otis, in the same car his girlfriend drove to visit Luke weeks before. Luke waved nervously as Otis approached. "Hey lil homey," said Otis.

"Hey what's happenin?" They both got in the Suburban.

"You got a half O my brotha?" said Otis.

Luke grabbed his weed from under the seat and made the transaction. They made friendly small talk. Luke felt guilty.

Luke made a few more back to back deals before helping on the fence. It was only 5:30. Allan was surprised by Luke's ambition. Luke worked with efficiency despite the effects of the weed. Allan moved slowly, overanalyzing every detail. "Your attention span seems to be improving," said Allan, "glad you didn't completely fry yourself in Oregon."

"Yeah. I guess I'm trying to get over the brainfryness. Don't want to end up like Jared."

The rest of the day went well. Luke ran out of weed and the visits stopped. They finished the fence at 8:30 and celebrated with beers on the back patio. The sun was beginning to set and Luke knew his pupils would soon begin to dilate. The solution was heroin. *Just one hit and I'll look as normal as anyone.*

Luke went to his truck to,"Grab more cigarettes," and found the small black glob. He went back to the patio to smoke the cigarette and finish his beer. After the beer he went to the bathroom to "drop a deuce," and grabbed a square of foil on the way. He took one hit. It was soothing and tasted good. He wanted to take another but knew better; two would make him sick.

He grabbed another beer and joined his parents again on the patio. Now he could relax and enjoy the sunset while he pretended to be sober.

Another obstacle presented itself when Alice went inside to make snacks. Food was repulsive. He would have to keep his beer close so he could wash down each bite. While Alice was gone Allan asked Luke about his plans for the future.

"No plans," said Luke, "I intend to enjoy this part of my life as much as possible."

"It must be fun. Do you think you're getting the most out of your life? Are you appreciating everything?"

"Well, I do believe that's exactly what I'm trying to do," Luke was unsure. "I am having fun. All the time. Every day. I think I'm having the best time of my life."

"Are you having the best time of your life? Do you still have fun when you're not partying? When you're not high?"

Do I have fun when I'm sober? When was the last time I was completely sober? Months? Years?Since the last time I went to juvy? How can I know if I have fun when I'm sober? I'm never sober.

"Just something for you to think about," said Allan.

"Yeah... I guess I'll have to think about that," said Luke. He meant it.

Alice came out with a silver platter full of food, "I hope you boys are hungry."

"Oh, wow," Luke tried to sound grateful, "Thank you mom," he took the sandwich and pretended to admire it for a moment. Luke took a bite. He chewed and chewed but could not produce saliva. He wanted to spit it out. A sip of beer and the food went down. He repeated this process; chew sip-swallow until the sandwich was gone.

Allan finished two before Luke finished his first. Alice picked up the trey and held it in front of Luke, "There's more, take another. You're so skinny."

"Oh no, no no no. I'm totally good. I'm stuffed. It was delicious," said Luke.

"Oh Luke, you need it," she said.

"Naw, I ate a lot earlier," he said.

Luke lit a cigarette and soon it was dark. His parents went inside and he went to clean his cars. He asked his parents if he could borrow the garage. In there he cleaned each vehicle one at a time. He finished at midnight and went to his room. Sleep was not an option so he got on his phone. The rest of the night was spent with friends.

My imperfections and failures are as much a blessing from God as my successes and my talents, and I lay them both at his feet.
-Mahatma Gandhi

Chapter 9: Sleep Over

Saturday 7-20-2010

Luke had just gotten home from making some deliveries. His phone vibrated. It was an unfamiliar number. He answered the call. "Hello?"

"Hey Luke, it's me Zuri. Are you around right now?"

"Um, yeah. Definitely. I'm at my house. You can swing by here if you'd like."

"Sure, that would be great," she said.

Luke gave her directions and ended the call. He cleaned his room and changed his clothes and ran down to the bathroom to brush his teeth. Luke felt stupid for his sudden impulse to be impressive. She wasn't that kind of girl, after all.

Luke lit a cigarette on the front porch. She would be there any moment. He tried to make himself look cool somehow. He felt stupid. He barely knew her. He wanted her to think he was the guy who had his shit together. But she was the one who had her shit together.

His cigarette was almost gone when she pulled into the driveway. He walked up to her car. It was an early 80's Oldsmobile with dents, scratches, and peeling paint. Even the wind shield had a huge crack running through it.

He greeted her. She commented on the nice house. He admitted that it was his parent's. "Do you want to check out my vaporizer? It'll be good fun," she said.

"That sounds great." They went into the garage.

"So where are you working at now?" said Luke.

"TeleTech. It's pretty lame," she said.

"That would be tough. I've heard bad things about those jobs. Don't some people kill themselves right there in the cubicle?"

"Well, I haven't seen it happen, but I wouldn't doubt it. What happened with your job? You said you got fired?"

"Yeah. I missed a couple days... Because of homework I guess. But I worked there for a really long time, it was time for me to be done."

"So, what are you gonna do? Don't you like the stability of having a job?" she said.

"I don't know. I kinda thrive off instability. I love not knowing what's going to happen tomorrow. For now, I don't think I'm going to do anything. At least not get a job. I'm having too much fun doing what I'm doing now. And believe it or not, it's actually harder for me to make money when I do have a job."

"That sounds nice, I guess. What do your parents do? Are they cool with all of this?" she said.

"My parents are super cool. I freakin love em. They're kind of hippies I guess. My mom is a yoga instructor and my dad owns a health food and herbal shop."

"That's good. That sounds awesome. My parents and I don't get along too well. We don't fight or anything, but it's not a close relationship at all," she said.

"That's too bad."

They started smoking once the vaporizer was ready. Allan came in the garage, "What is going on in here?" he said with a goofy smile. "Illegal activity. I do not approve," he grabbed the hose and took a monster hit.

"Yeah," said Luke, "This is my dad. Dad, this is Zuri."

"Very nice to meet you. You can call me Allan."

"Hi Allan, it's nice to meet you too."

"Good, good. So, Zuri. Are you gonna be Luke's new girly friend?"

"Dad! You're out of your freakin mind. She's my friend. She just came here to buy weed I only met her the other day. Don't be such a weirdo."

"Sorry Luke. Sorry Zuri. I'm a weirdo, I apologize." He took another hit from the vaporizer before he let anyone else get a chance. "Alright, have fun. I'll get out of here."

"Sorry you had to go through that. My dad can be a nut, but I gotta love him."

"You're lucky."

"I know, I am. He's a fun, loving, spiritual guy." Luke took another hit and handed it to Zuri. "So what do you do on the weekends? Do you like to party? Hallucinogens? What's your thing?" he said.

"I'm not really into drugs. I like the natural stuff; weed, mushrooms sometimes. Molly's all right. Lately I've been doing that quite a bit."

"Is that the same stuff I got from Brittany?" he said.

"Yeah, pretty much. I think it's all the same anyway. Molly is molly right?"

"Well, not really. There's MDA, MDMA; both can be sold as molly. I don't think that stuff you've been getting is either. Maybe it's a new drug. Maybe it was just made wrong. There's definitely something funky about it and I can't figure it out," he said.

"That's weird. I don't really know anything about that. It's the only molly I've ever done."

"Oh wow, I wish you could have tried this stuff I had a while ago. Pure MDMA; the best it can get," he said.

"That sounds pretty cool. Can I smoke in here?"

"Absolutely. Do you need your weed right now? Are you in a hurry or anything?" he said.

"No, take your time. I'm not in any hurry," she said.

"Cool. Right on. You wanna do something fun? Go for a drive maybe? That Suburban might not look like much, but it's a lot of fun on the dirt roads. Plus, you can smoke all the weed you want. It could be fun."

"That sounds really nice. Lets do it," she said.

They went to the truck. Luke made sure he had everything he needed out of the Chrysler. Luke started the truck and let it warm up for a few minutes. "You know Patrick Creek road?" he said.

"Yeah."

"Have you ever taken it all the way to Kila?" he said.

"No."

"Should we try it? I never done it before either but I want to try it."

"Sure," she said.

They headed for Patrick Creek road. Luke plugged in his I-pod and turned on some Rob Zombie. Once they got to the dirt road he handed her his personal bag, "I'll let you be in charge of all this. There should be a pipe in the glove box if you don't got one."

An hour went by. Luke thought they had to be getting close. They were on the top of the world in the middle of nowhere. Luke stopped to enjoy the scenery. "This is freakin awesome," he said.

"Yeah, it is." She got out and lit a cigarette.

"Why have I not been out here before? I bet there's a perfect place around here for a spirit quest. You know, a little mushroom gathering?" Luke saw a trail, "I have to go check this out. I'll be right back," he ran down the trail.

This kid is crazy, thought Zuri, *Maybe he likes me. It's unlikely. If I did somehow get together with Luke, my life would become chaos. He's a drug dealer. Could be problems. I'm sure he's got pretty girls coming at him from all directions. He's probably not interested anyway. Why would he be?*

"Nothing that way," Luke said as he emerged from the trees. "Definitely no good for spirit questing. Too treacherous."

"That's a bummer," she said.

"Yep. I suppose we'd better go if we ever want to make it off this mountain. I still have no idea where we are," he said.

"Yeah, probably," *Though I wouldn't mind getting stuck out here with you...*

They got back in the truck and continued down the endless dirt road. They smoked weed for the rest of the drive. It took thirty minutes before they were in the backroads of Kila. Zuri knew where they were because she had grown up in the area. "Where's your house at?" said Luke, "You know, in case I ever need to make a delivery."

"I'm not letting you see my place," she said.

"Oh. Why not?"

"You've got a really nice place. My place sucks," she said.

"First of all, I can't take any credit for my place. It's my parent's. And I won't judge. I think we're gonna become good friends so you'll have to show me eventually."

"Maybe someday. Not today," she said.

"Alright, that's cool."

They drove back to Luke's. It didn't take long on the highway. Luke was hungry and thought Zuri would be too. "You wanna come raid the fridge with me? I know you got the munchies," he said.

"Sure," she followed him in through the front door.

Alice was cooking Chinese food. "Luke? Is that you?" she said from the kitchen. Zuri felt intrusive until Alice greeted them with enthusiasm. "Oh good, you brought a friend. I hope you're hungry, because I made lots."

"Thanks mom, we're totally hungry. This is my new friend Zuri."

"Hi Zuri, I'm Alice. It's good to meet you."

The food was great. Alice was social as ever, bombarding Zuri with questions. She was easy for anyone to get along with. Zuri couldn't picture a more perfect family.

After dinner they went to the back patio. Alice had wine while Luke and Zuri smoked cigarettes. She offered wine. Luke accepted while Zuri declined. Alice was telling a funny story about one of her yoga classes when Zuri got a text. She announced that she had to leave. She had to go pick up Lisa.

"Good to meet you Zuri. Come by anytime," said Alice.

"Yeah," said Luke, "I don't know whats going on tonight, but you're welcome to join. We could go party, hang out, do whatever."

"Alright. I'll see what's going on. Thank you again for the dinner, I've had a really good time." They said their goodbyes and she left.

Luke had been so content with Zuri that he hadn't replied to any of his texts. When he checked his phone he found that there were parties going on. People wanted party favors. Luke was sad to inform them that he had nothing special. He gave an affirmative on the party text. Luke was always a valuable attribute to any party, no matter what resources they had. The only problem was that Luke wasn't feeling the party scene; he was worn out physically, burnt out mentally. It was his job though. He had to maintain public relations.

What was he really going to do? Was it business, or was he just going to get drunk and smoke weed? Would it just be another wasted night being wasted? Would he get too wasted, then get high so he could keep from getting too drunk? Then he would be up all night which could lead to anything. But that's how it goes, and that's how it's been for Luke.

~~~

Luke pulled out of his driveway in the Suburban. He was all prepared for the party. He got a call, "Hello?" he answered.

"Hi Luke!" she said.

"Who's this?"

"It's Lisa. What are you doing? Can me and Zuri come hang out?"

"Umm... yeah. Definitely," he said.

"Alright, we'll be over in a few minutes."

He was in his driveway when they showed up. Zuri insisted they smoke the twenty sack she bought from him earlier. Luke told them that there was a party down by Flathead Lake. Lisa was excited; Zuri was not. "C'mon," said Lisa, "Let's go have fun and get wasted!"

"I'm good on that, but don't let me stop you. You guys should go if you want," said Zuri.
~~~

"I don't really want to party either. We can do whatever. I've been doing too much partying lately anyway," said Luke.

"Can we just hang out here?" said Lisa, "Would your parents care?"

"They wouldn't care. They'd be glad that I had some friends hang out here for a change."

"Nice!" said Lisa, "Do they care if we drink?"

"No. There's very little my parents will object to. Have you ever watched *The Doors ?* It's one of my favorite movies ever, and I think everyone needs to watch it. Does that sound good?"

"Sounds awesome. Can you get any alcohol?" said Lisa.

"I have some whiskey and beer up in my room. The beer is warm though, I like it that way," said Luke.

"That's really weird, but it will work," said Lisa.

They went into the house. Luke introduced Lisa to his parents before going up to his room. "Wow, this is awesome," said Lisa, "your room is sweet."

"Yeah? Thanks. Beer's in the closet; help yourself."

Zuri wasn't interested in the alcohol so Luke refrained from it as well. It was almost 11:00 and plenty dark out. Luke's friends would be wondering where he was at. He texted, telling them that something came up.

Luke sat on the middle of his couch with the girls on each side. Lisa was drinking Pabst with a strange look, "You are sooo weird for liking this."

"Yeah, okay, get ready," said Luke. He set up the DVD player, "This is the sweetest movie ever." Luke was excited. He loved to show people this movie. It had been his favorite since he watched it over and over with Stacy and Blue. They had been on acid, ecstasy, or both every time they watched it.

Out of nowhere, Lisa asked Zuri, "Hey, don't you have some of that molly still?"

"Yeah, I've got four capsules," said Zuri.

"Well, lets do it! I don't want to sit here and drink while you two are just stoned," said Lisa.

"I kinda wanted to sell them," said Zuri.

"I'll buy em," said Luke, "or give you weed for em like I did last time. I've still got those two. That way we can all take two. It would be sweet. I've never watched this movie sober and I don't want to start now," he said.

"Well, alright. But I don't want you to pay for it though. I'd feel bad about that," said Zuri.

"Okay, well how about I just keep us stoned all night?"

"Okay," she said with a smile.

Zuri dug in her purse to find the four capsules. She took two and gave two to Lisa. Luke had to go to his car to get the dirty capsules he had received from Brittany. When he came back up to his room he chased them down with Lisa's beer. It was her second beer. The beer tasted good. Luke wanted to crack one open for himself. He decided he would, but only one. He could show Zuri that he knew how to drink like a gentleman; even if it's cheap, warm beer.

"You really do like that stuff, don't you?" said Zuri.

"Yeah, on occasion, when the time is right. It feels like a good time, so I figured I'd enjoy myself. You sure you don't want nothing?" he said.

"No, I'm good. Thank you," she said.

They decided to wait until the molly kicked in to start the movie. In the meantime they looked up music and videos on YouTube. Luke blew their minds with a music video by Die Antwoord; disgusting tweaked out South African rappers.

Soon the molly began to take effect. Same as last time, they were rolling without the love. Their eyeballs were googley and their skin was silky. They were listening to music when Alice knocked on the door. "Yeah?" said Luke.

Alice came in looking happy and social as ever. "Hey guys, how's everything going up here? Do you need anything?"

"Everything is awesome, mom. I don't think we need anything," said Luke.

"Well, how about the girls? Are you hungry or anything?" she said.

"Oh Alice, no thankyou," said Lisa.

"Okay then," she paused and looked at Luke, "Oh geez, look at your pupils." Luke's pupils were dilated to the brim. Both of the girls had dark brown eyes that blended with their pupils.

"Yeah. We ate some molly. We're gonna watch The Doors," said Luke.

"I see. Just don't be taking that Adderall. I don't like how you get all wigged out," she said.

"Sure thing, mom."

Zuri noticed a glass bong in the corner of the room. She went to examine it. "This is so cool! Can we use this? I really want to try."

"Can we smoke up here?" said Luke, "It's kind of a special occasion. I'll set up the fan to create a wind tunnel."

"Oh, I suppose," said Alice.

When the bong was loaded he gave it to Zuri. Lisa was talking to Alice, complimenting her good looks and awesomeness. Lisa offered the bong to Alice. She declined, but Lisa persisted. "I don't like these things. I don't even know how to use it," said Alice. Luke intervened; he took the bong, filled it with smoke, pulled out the stem, and handed it to Alice. "What do I do with this?" she said.

"Just inhale it," said Luke.

"Oh, okay then. So much peer pressure," Alice did it. "Too much," she said between coughs. "Way too much. I'm done. You kids are crazy."

Allan was surprised at what he saw when he came up the stairs. He saw them laughing with Alice as she spoke nonsense. "The kids are out of control," she said.

"What is going on up here?" Allan said in his goofy smiley way, "This is unacceptable. Smoking in the house is unallowed."

He picked up the bong and took a huge hit for himself. "What have you done to your mother?"

"Lots of peer pressure," said Luke.

"I guess so. She hardly ever smokes with me."

"I think I have the munchies," said Alice, "Who else has the munchies?"

"We can't get the munchies, remember?" said Lisa.

"I've got the munchies so bad. I'm gonna get so fat," said Alice.

"You'll never get fat," said Lisa, "You're so beautiful, like supermodel pretty."

"Oh, you're so sweet. This is fun. It's been lots of fun. I'd better go now. Those munchies are serious." She walked over to Allan, "Come help me make something."

"Sure thing, girly. Goodnight kids. Behave yourselves, whatever that means," he laughed and followed Alice down the stairs.

"Yeah," said Lisa, "If I had your parents, I wouldn't want to move out either. And what's this Adderall your mom mentioned. Do you get wigged out often?"

"They're just these ADD pills; pretty much legal speed. I used it a lot for school and road trips, and sometimes just for fun."

Lisa was excited, "Do you have any?"

"Well, maybe. Why? You want some?"

"Bust it out you stinge!" she said.

"Damn, I didn't know. Do you both want some?" he said.

"I don't know," said Zuri, "is it okay to mix with molly?"

"You can mix it with anything. I do, anyway," he said.

"Alright, I guess I'll try it."

"Kay, I'll be right back." Luke got up to get the pills out of his car. The girls were on his computer watching more videos by Die Antwoord. "I can't believe these people," said Lisa, "They're fuckin psycho. I love em!"

Luke walked over to the desk and set six pills in front of them. "I'm taking three. You only need one, but take more if you want." Luke swallowed his down with beer.

"What happens if we each take three?" said Lisa.

"You'll be really high. All night. And tomorrow. It'll be fun. Go for it."

"I have to work tomorrow," said Zuri.

"That's fine. It's good actually. Why do you think they call it speed? Because it makes you fast, efficient, and awesome. All the time," he said.

"Okay, I'm trusting you. I'd better not feel bad tomorrow. Is this water any good?" she held up a glass that had been sitting on the desk.

"Yeah. It's the best," he said. She laughed and took the pills.

~~~

The molly began to wear off around 3am. So far all they had done was listen to music, talk and goof off. The Adderall had kicked in strong. Even Luke was high from the three amphetamine pills. "This is fucking cool," said Lisa, "you were right when you said it makes you talk a lot. Am I really going to be high like this all day tomorrow? Because that's fuckin awesome."

The movie was playing on repeat, but it only served as back ground noise. They sat on Luke's bed and talked while smoking weed and cigarettes. For a moment Luke thought about his parents. They had such simple rules: No Adderall, and no cigarettes in the house. What if Alice saw them all wigged out in the morning. That would be a problem; he couldn't let that happen. Luke hated seeing his mother sad. He felt so guilty about his graduation binge; or binge to graduate; whatever it was, he saw her sadness at his condition. He didn't want her to have the fear that it would happen again.

No matter what Luke's consciousness told him, his primitive instincts drove him to get higher. Luke was high. The girls were *really* high. Luke wanted to be like them. "I'm gonna go get another Adderall. Anyone else want one?" he said.

"I would," said Zuri, "but I don't think I could possibly get any higher. I'm maxed out. Already have more energy than I could possibly know what to do with."

"Me too," said Lisa.

"Alright, I'll grab a couple for you to save for later then." Luke went out to his car.

He moved with efficiency as he prepared some crystal for injection. There was no time to filter the drugs; instead he dropped some crystal in the back of the rig and hoped for the best. It went smoothly. The rush was powerful. He put everything away and went back to his room.

Now it was his turn to talk. He gave an animated description of the Oregon Country Fair; the most epic psychedelic paradise he had ever known. Luke was
~~~

motivated. He didn't want to be home when his parents woke up. They would know he'd been up all night.

Luke needed to find a solution. "We should go on an adventure," he announced.

"Adventure where?" said Zuri.

"How bout Lone Pine. If we leave now, we could be at the top in time to see the sunrise."

"Should we take my car?" said Zuri.

"Sure, I'll take mine too. You know… just in case," he said.

"In case?"

"In case if something happens? I don't know. It just makes me feel better."

"Okay then. I hope you're not scared of my ugly car," she said.

"It's not that. I'm sure your car is fine. It's just that I have to be on call. Sometimes I have to go certain places at strange hours. And with certain people I have to go alone."

"Oh, I see," said Zuri. *So many secrets.*

~~~

It was a ten minute drive. Luke took the Chrysler because the Chevy was loud. He would rather his parents not know he left at 5am. They parked at the trail head. Luke rolled a couple joints; best to have disposable paraphernalia in a state park. It was still dark when they began their hike up the mountain.

They made it just in time. The clouds were pink and orange. The view was amazing. "This was a good idea," said Lisa.

"Should we celebrate with a joint?" he pulled a joint from his hat.

"Absolutely," said Lisa.

Zuri was mystified. There was something strange and magical about Luke. At that moment, everything was right.

They were almost to the parking lot when he announced that he had somewhere he needed to be.

"Well, thanks for hanging out with us," said Lisa.

"Sure thing. I had fun. I'll see you both sometime soon," he gave both of them a hug and got in his car.

And there he goes, thought Zuri, *off to whatever could possibly be important this early in the morning.*

~~~

Luke arrived at the apartments. Dave was always awake early. The door opened, "Hey Luke, come on in. What are you doing this early in the morning?"

"I'm high. Just felt like coming over." Luke followed Dave into the kitchen and saw a bottle of whiskey on the counter. "What are *you* doing this early in the morning?"

"I'm grieving... or celebrating. Not really sure," said Dave.

"What happened?" said Luke.

"Almost beat up my boss' son. Ended up getting fired. The owner wanted to keep me because I was their best body man, but I refused to apologize to his son. Instead I called his son a spoiled little bitch. And that was it."

"Wow. That's nuts. It might be a good thing if you see it as an opportunity. A free vacation. You'll get unemployment, right?"

"Yeah. I will. But that's not the point. I've never been fired before. It's a pride thing, I guess. You bring any drugs over?" said Dave.

"Drugs? Are you suggesting we smoke some drugs?" said Luke.

"Yeah Luke, and the crystal too. Are we gonna party or what?"

"Party? Yeah, I guess it's a good time to party," said Luke.

That Sunday they partied; or partook in a two man drug fest under the excuse of celebration. They drank. They smoked. The day was a blur.

He that maketh haste to be rich shall not be innocent.
-Proverbs 28:20

Chapter 10: Discovery

Tuesday 7-23-2010

Luke was sitting on Debora's couch when he received a phone call. It was Zuri. "Hey," he answered.

"Luke, what are you doing?" she said.

"Kickin it with a friend. What's up?"

"My molly buddy needs some weed. He wants to meet you. Can you come by?" she said.

"Sure." Zuri gave Luke directions and they hung up.

"Sorry Debora, I've gotta get outta here," he said.

"Alright honey. Have fun now. Thanks for everything."

Luke felt some anxiety. He still hadn't slept since that day he found out Dave got fired. He didn't want Zuri to see him like this, but it was too important for him to meet this "molly buddy." He was already feeling guilty. Zuri wanted to hang out the previous day, but he was high and avoided it.

For some reason Luke cared about this girl, not in any lustful way, but for her wellbeing. She seemed like she had too many let downs in her life. Luke didn't want to be another let down. Zuri represented stability. With her, he would never have girl problems. She would be trustworthy and easy to please. Unlike with Stacy, he would have no need to worry; no need for jealousy.

~~~

Zuri was standing next to her car. It was the same trailer park that Brittany lived in. Luke got out of the car and gave her a hug. "Sorry I couldn't hang out yesterday. I feel bad about that," he said.

"Oh, it's okay. I understand you're a busy guy."

He followed her inside where they were greeted by a barking Pitbull. The dog sounded angry, but he was only trying to smother the newcomer with love.

"Satan! Get over here," said the goofy guy at the kitchen table. Lisa was sitting there too. Brittany was attempting to clean a massive pile of dishes. The place was messy. Dubstep music was playing in the living room.

Luke introduced himself, "Hey, I'm Luke."

"Steve," the nerdy guy shook Luke's hand.

There were blankets covering every window. Luke could feel his pupils dilate. He wished he had taken opiates. Luke sat down next to Zuri. He observed the mirrors with piles of powder scattered on the table. "What's going on here?" Luke asked as he pulled out his weed.

"Do you like molly?" Steve slid one of the mirrors over to Luke.

"Totally. May I?"

Steve nodded. Luke snorted the line, "Ouch." He took some weed out of a bag and handed it to Zuri, "Can you load this for me?" She loaded a bubbler and started the rotation.

"Go ahead and check it out," Luke handed the weed to Steve. Each bag was labeled with the strain and quantity.

"Damn, this shit is crazy," said Steve. He was looking at the Afgan Goo through a magnifying glass. "Can you do a sample package? I want to get an eighth of each."

"Yeah, sure. Whatever you want." Luke started weighing bags.

They talked and smoked weed. The molly started kicking in, which gave Luke an excuse for his dilated pupils. His eyes were googley. His mouth was raw from biting on his cheeks constantly. It was a terrible habit he had on stimulant drugs. Lack of sleep would keep him from healing. He would keep chewing even though his mouth would bleed. It was a nervous habit, impossible to overcome.

Steve was cautious about who he meets; his paranoid mannerisms showed it. "Hey Steve," said Brittany from the kitchen, "you should let Luke try that THC stuff."

"You want to get really stoned?" Steve asked.

"Definitely," said Luke.
~~~

"This is different. Go ahead and load a fresh bowl and I'll sprinkle some on top."

Zuri loaded another bowl and handed it to Steve. Steve pulled a small zip-lock out of his pocket and dusted the bowl with white powder. Luke noticed a few letters on the bag. *JWH? Did I see that correctly? What the hell does it mean? What kind of funky shit has this guy got us smokin?*

Steve took a small hit and passed it to Lisa. Zuri skipped and handed it to Luke. Luke did too much. In a few seconds he was uncomfortably retarded. "Holy bubbly brain. That stuff's freakin weird."

The drugs were still kicking in stronger, making it hard for him to think or speak. Lisa had the same feeling. She made a few attempts to speak, but only muttered an inaudible stutter. Luke was panicking. He felt like there was a bubble in his chest, making it hard for his heart to beat. There were other smaller bubbles in his brain. He felt like an aneurism or stroke was imminent. "I think I'd better go," he managed to say.

"You want any molly?" Steve asked. "Umm... sure," said Luke.

"Well it's..." Luke lost concentration as Steve explained prices. It didn't matter, Luke just wanted out. He grabbed a wad of money and threw it on the table.

Steve was talking as he facilitated the deal. Luke just stood there feeling stupid. What Steve was saying didn't matter; Luke was dying, and he didn't want it to happen in front of these people. Steve handed over the bag of powder. Luke mumbled something and left. He drove off quickly to find a place to die.

~~~

"He's not normally like that," said Zuri.

"He just got too high off that shit. I shoulda told him to go small," said Steve.

"Holding it in was his other mistake," said Brittany. "Isn't that right, Lisa?" Lisa didn't know what was going on.

"Does Luke do meth?" said Steve. Zuri was shocked by the question.

"No way," said Brittany, "I've known him for a long time. He would never do something like that. Luke's a good kid. He even finished high school; normal high school, with all the normal kids."

"He does pills sometimes," said Zuri.

"What kind of pills?" said Steve.

"Adderall. Me and Lisa tried them. They were a lot of fun, actually."

"You know what's in those pills, right?" he said.

"No, not really," she said.

"Meth."

"What?" she said in disbelief.
~~~

"Look it up on Wikipedia. It contains dextroamphetamine and methamphetamine; two other stimulants as well," he explained.

"I don't believe it," she said.

"Come, I'll show you." Steve grabbed his lap top. Zuri saw that it was true. He pointed at the screen, "Prescribed for obesity and ADD/ADHD."

"I thought meth was illegal. What about all those commercials?" she said.

"It's a schedule two drug; meaning it has medical uses, same as cocaine and some opiates," he said.

"Do people know about this? Do you think Luke knows he's basically doing meth?"

"I have a feeling he knows what he's doing," said Steve.

Zuri texted him.

(From Zuri): Are you ok?

"Do you think he's gonna be alright?" she asked.

"Yeah. He'll be fine. Might not make it out of the trailer park, but he will live. Probably just had a panic attack."

"Hope so."

"You like him, don't you?" he said.

"No. I told you, I'm not trying to have any boyfriends." This caught her by surprise. Her usual tactic was to seem uninterested until people came after her. She had never been the initiator. Relationships never lasted long for Zuri. She would get bored of people easily. So far, Luke was the only person she ever felt the need to pursue. It gave her anxiety. She liked to have the upper hand. With Luke, it seemed she would be the vulnerable one.

~~~

Luke sat on a rock and stared at the river. He was still struggling with the bubbly brains. He had driven to the Old Steel Bridge. It was only a few minutes away from the trailer park, but the drive had still been reckless. It had been two hours since he did the funky shit. The high was intense and showed no signs of stopping. *What the hell was that shit? Hopefully Zuri doesn't think I hate her. I'm starting to look like a real jerk. First, I avoid her. Then, I run off all crazy without saying nothing.*

Luke looked at his phone for the first time in hours. He had missed calls from Kimmy, Stacy, Andrew, Zuri, Fat Jared, Blue.

Holy crap, my brain must have been vibrating too hard for me to notice. The text messages were from the same people. He was angry about the one from Stacy. She hadn't even tried to talk to him for a long time. The text was simple:

(From Stacy): Luke??

A one word text that stirred up so many emotions. Thinking of Zuri made
~~~

him feel better. In Luke's mind, Stacy was an overly seductive, deceitful woman who was used to getting whatever she wanted. She didn't deserve the attention.

The phone vibrated. It was Stacy. "Hello," he answered.

"Luke, where are you?" she said.

"I don't know? Why?"

"I'm coming to see you. Just tell me where you are."

Luke heard a familiar voice in the background. "Where are you?" he said.

"I'm at your house. Your mom's right here. Please just tell me where you are." Stacy sounded emotional.

"Fine. I'm at the Old Steel."

"Okay, stay there. I'm coming," she hung up.

Oh, I'll stay here alright. Definitely in no condition to drive; probably the best condition to have to see you.

A few minutes went by. He was zoning out when he received another call. It was Zuri.

"Hello?"

"Hey, is everything okay?" she said.

"Yeah, I'm good. Just had a little freak out I guess."

"Well, you can come back if you want."

"I'd really like to, but I can't right now."

"Okay. Just call if you want to hang out or anything," she said.

"I will. Sorry for bailing out on you again. I really am."

"It's fine. I'll let you go now," she said.

"Kay, I'll talk to you later."

Luke felt bad. *Fuck, I'm a dirt bag. That sweet girl wants to hang out and I'm going to hang out with my rotten ex.*

Luke was spacing out when he heard someone coming up behind him. "What's that look for?" she said as she sat next to him. "Can I have a hug? Or are you just gonna look at me like I'm crazy?" He hugged her. It felt good. The familiar smell; the soft pretty hair; it was a relapse. "I miss you," she said.

Luke was having trouble finding words. Of course, he missed her, but he didn't know if he should tell her that. The hug finally ended.

"Luke? Is everything okay? You seem out of it."

"Yeah. I am," he said.

"On what?"

"I'm not totally sure," he said.

"How can you not be sure?"

"I smoked some funky stuff. Supposedly some kind of synthetic THC."

"So you're stoned?"

"I guess I am. It's like a really trippy mushroom stoned. I felt pretty horrible for a while," he said.

"Is that why you're here all alone?"

"Pretty much."

"Your mom's worried about you. Says you haven't been home much lately. Is everything okay?"

"Yeah. I'm fine. Just been busy."

"Busy? Your mom told me you went to Oregon. How was that?"

"Good," he said.

"You can talk to me, you know."

"Sorry. I'm still really messed up. And it's been a while," he said.

"I'm sorry for not trying to talk more. It was fucked up of me and I want to fix it. We've shared too many good memories. I want to at least be your friend no matter what. I love you and I love your family. Will you please be my friend again?" she said.

"Yeah. We can be friends," he said. She hugged him again, he couldn't resist.

"Oh Luke, how'd you get so skinny? What happened to all those muscles?"

"Not sure."

"We should go for a drive," she said.

"I can't drive," he said.

"I'll drive. We can take my car."

"Why should we go for a drive?" he said.

"So I can rape you. Just kidding! Kinda. Not really. Unless you want me to."

"My brain can't handle whatever you just did right now, but I'll go for a drive. Just a drive," he said.

"Ha-ha, sounds good. Lets do it," she grabbed him by the hand and led him up to her Pontiac G6.

"Wow. It's like a freakin spaceship," he said as he got in.

"It's pretty nice. I like your truck better though. I'm a country girl, remember?"

"Yeah... country girl."

She turned on some music and they drove off. Gorilla Zoe was playing. "Everybody was talking about that molly you had."

"Everybody?" he said.

"Pretty much. I tried some, you know?"

"Yeah?"

"Yeah. It reminded me of the pistols. Remember when we took the pistols and ate that acid? We had sex for like seven hours straight. That was the best ever." She grabbed his leg.

"Yeah, it was the best," *I'm getting raped.*

~~~

An hour later they were back at the Old Steel Bridge. "Why do you do this?" he asked.

"Do what?"

"Cheat on your boyfriend. I mean, you're obviously still together, right?"

"Yeah, we are, but he cheats on me too."

"That sounds awesome," he said.

"It's not. I fuckin hate him."

"You hate him?"

"Most of the time," she said.

"Then why are you with him?"

"He's got his shit together. Has his own place. And believe it or not, he used to be a really nice guy."

"Yeah. I guess that would be a plus." There were a few moments of silence as they sat in the parking lot. "I guess I'll see you later," he said.

She hugged him again, not wanting to let go. "I love you," she said.

"I love you too. Always will." He let go of her, knowing she would try to kiss him, "Gotta go."

He got in his car. She left. They loved each other; there was no denying it. But Luke knew he couldn't have a relationship with her again. It was too destructive. The thought of being friends sounded good in theory, but in practice didn't seem possible. *Can't we just hang out without getting all emotional and sexual?* They were each other's favorite drug that they couldn't use in moderation.

Luke was finally feeling sober enough to drive. The sex seemed to clear his system Luke was sick of being high. *I'm done. So fucking done. Time to sober up. Time to clean house.*

Luke opened his phone and called Blue.

"Yo. Where the fuck you been?" said Blue.

"I don't know, man. I'm tryin to dump the rest of my shit. Can you help me out?"

"Yeah. Hurry up and get to my place," said Blue.

Luke hung up and was on his way. He wanted to get there before he changed his mind. At one point he stopped at a green light and was freaked out when people started honking at him. *Sober up, Luke!*

He made it to Blue's tent. He brought all his meth and all his molly. When
~~~

Luke went inside he saw Kimmy was there too. "Hey guys. Sorry I've been out of reach," said Luke.

"It's cool. Kimmy, I need you out. Gotta talk to my cousin alone."

Kimmy lit a cigarette as she walked out of the tent. "What chu got for me, bro?"

"Got a quarter left. Pure shit," said Luke.

"I'll take it all. Can pay you tomorrow," said Blue.

"Deal." Luke handed over the crystal. "I also got some molly."

"Talk to Kimmy about that. She's been on my ass for weeks lookin for that shit."

Luke didn't know how much molly he had gotten from Steve. The powder weighed out to three grams. He fronted it to her for 300 dollars.

~~~

It was dark when Luke headed home. He kept a quarter gram of crystal for emergency. It was 10:30 pm. He looked in the mirror and noticed his enormous pupils. He pulled over on a side street and took a hit of heroin. *That should fix it.* Luke could have gotten rid of the heroin that night. His small glob was worthless in Oregon, but in Montana it was worth hundreds. It could wait. He would sell it tomorrow.

Luke arrived home and greeted his parents. They were in their room watching the news. He didn't want to talk long because they looked tired.

"Are you gonna be here in the morning?" said Alice.

"Yeah. I will. Goodnight," he closed the door and went up to his room. He sat at his desk and opened his laptop. *JWH?* He typed the three letters and did a Google search. There was a Wikipedia for JWH-18. He clicked on it. He read about the chemical and learned that it was a synthetic cannabinoid; not THC. The effects were consistent with what he had experienced. What confused him was that the chemical had recently been banned. His eyelids got droopy as he read the pharmacology section. It was time to sleep. Luke laid down and twiddled his eyelids for a half hour before falling asleep.

~~~

Luke woke up at noon and felt weak. His stomach hurt with hunger. He made a bowl of cereal and guzzled a carton of half and half. Alice came in from the patio while he was cleaning dishes. She hugged him, "Hi my boy. So glad you're home."

"Yeah, me too," he said.

"How did things go with Stacy?"

"Pretty good, I guess."

"I love that girl. Do you think you two will ever get back together?"

"I don't know. Probably not. I'll always love her, but I don't think it would be a good idea. We're each doin our own thing right now. Maybe someday we could try it again."

"You're still gonna be friends, right?"

"Gonna try. It's tough. It's physically tough for us to be just friends."

"I can imagine. She's a beautiful girl, and you're a very handsome boy. You two always seemed so perfect for each other."

They talked while Luke smoked a cigarette. After that, he went back up to his room and got on his computer. This time he Googled *designer drug supplier.* He researched and cross-referenced for hours. The more he learned, the more excited he became.

Finally, after all the research, Luke had a notepad filled with notes. He learned about three chemicals and found a lab supply company that would sell them. Luke decided the powder Steve had been selling as molly was a chemical called methylone. This chemical was a structural analog of MDMA with similar effects. All he needed was a credit card. Asking his parents was out of the question. He tried to think of someone he trusted; someone he could share this precious secret with; someone with a credit card.

~~~

"Dave!" he yelled, "Wake up!" Luke slapped him in the face. Dave was passed out sitting on the couch. His breathing was barely noticeable. Luke checked his pulse; it was faint and slow.

The man was drunk and had taken a dangerous dose of opiates. "Wake up, wake up, wake up!"

Luke sat for a while, wondering what to do. *Fuck. He could be out for days. What was it? A four day runner? He'll be slow to recover; extra slow because he's old. I don't have days to wait. I need him functional. I need him now! Ice cubes are supposed to wake people up from heroin overdose. Maybe that will work.*

Luke went to the kitchen and grabbed a handful of ice cubes from the freezer. He started by pressing a cube to Dave's fore head and rubbing it around. That didn't work so he splashed a glass of water in his face. That didn't work either.

Luke was running out of options. He looked at his soaking friend and had a guilty feeling. *Maybe I should have just let him rest peacefully.*

Luke went to his car and came back with his junkie kit and emergency stash of meth. He prepared a small dose into an unused syringe. *He would still be awake if I had left him with more drugs anyway. Easily justifiable. No reason to feel bad for what I'm about to do.*
~~~

Dave remained motionless while Luke inserted the needle. He depressed the plunger, extracted the needle, and hid the paraphernalia.

Dave gasped, "What the fuck?"

"You okay?" said Luke, "You were barely breathing."

Dave looked around, obviously confused. His eyes were wide. "You dumped water on me?"

"Well, yeah. Isn't that what you're supposed to do when you think someone's overdosing? I decided I'd try that before sticking ice cubes up your butt."

"I wasn't breathing?"

"Barely. And your pulse was freakin scary too. I seriously thought you were dead for a minute."

"Wow. Sorry, I guess," said Dave.

"Just lay off the freakin opiates, man."

"Okay." Dave was high and didn't know what to think of it. He didn't suspect Luke of anything; just figured that's what it's like to get splashed with water when you still have meth in your system. No reason he couldn't be high from the night before. Just took too many methadone; maybe drank too much as well.

"Are you feeling okay? Because I have something important to talk to you about," said Luke.

"Yeah. I feel fine. You scared the crap out of me, but I feel good now."

"Good. Where's your lap top. We're gonna be freakin rich. I'll show you."

Dave went to his room and came back with the lap top. Luke opened Wikipedia pages for each of his chemicals. He explained the methylone, and how it was being sold as molly. He explained JWH-122, the synthetic cannabinoid that had been discovered after the ban of JWH-18.

"This all sounds good," said Dave, "but can we really get high from shit off the internet?"

"Only one way to find out. I'll pay; just need to use your credit card."

"It's legal?" said Dave.

"Yeah man, I showed you. Most of this stuff is only illegal in a few states. Here in Montana, we're good to go."

"You know, this reminds me of something I saw on CNN the other day. People were getting high off bath salt. Guess it was supposed to feel like cocaine," said Dave.

"That sounds pretty retarded, but lets check it out." Luke made a new search. He scrolled through the results and found a news article. The article described bath salts being sold in head shops. They found traces of methylonedioxypyrovalerone in some of these bath salts which produced a cocaine or amphetamine effect. This was only happening in a few southern states.

Luke made a new search for methylonedioxypyrovalerone. They couldn't believe this stuff was legal. Luke read it aloud: "It acts as a norepinephrine-dopamine re-uptake inhibitor... MDPV has been shown to produce robust reinforcing effects and compulsive self-administration in rats... MDPV has been distinguished by some for it's powers as an aphrodisiac. It also has been repeatedly noted for inducing strong cravings to re-administer. Users have reported a compulsive desire to continuously re-dose, even following onset of the unpleasant side effects induced by prolonged use and higher doses. You hear that, Dave? We're gonna be rich! All these junkies around here are gonna get hooked on our shit!"

"Are you sure you can buy it?" said Dave.

"Well, lets see. I'll just check my nifty web site. Product search... MDPV... there it is! $28.99 per gram if you buy ten grams or more." Luke typed in ten grams and clicked purchase.

"Now hold on," said Dave, "That's $290. What if it's no good?"

"Then it's my problem. I'm payin you up front. All the risk is on me. Now let me finish my order." Luke ordered smaller amounts of some other chemicals. They were nearly the same price as the MDPV.

The order ended up being about $450. Luke counted out $500 and set it on the coffee table. "For the fastest shipping." He went and smoked a cigarette while Dave filled out the credit card info, He smoked on the back patio while pacing excitedly. There was a natural high. *This must be what Einstein felt like when he came up with the theory of relativity.* Something big was happening. Luke could feel that his life was about to change dramatically.

All life is an experiment.
The more experiments you make, the better.
-Ralph Waldo Emerson

Chapter 11: The Spirit Molecule

Wednesday 7-25-2010

"Hi, you've reached Bank of America technical support..." Zuri said through her headset. She felt like a robot. She remembered Luke's comment about people killing themselves in their cubicles.

Her cellphone vibrated. There was a strict rule about cell phones at Teletech. She opened her phone; it was Luke. *How lame. He finally wants to hang out and I'm stuck in this horrible place. He probably just wants to get ahold of Steve; that would be more likely.*

She thought of that phone call for hours and couldn't do any thing about it; not until she got off work at 9pm.

~~~

9 o'clock came around. She rushed out of the building and made the call as fast as she could.

"Hello?" said Luke.

"Hey, sorry. I was at work when you called."

"That's cool. What do you got goin on?" he said.

"Nothing really."
~~~

"We should hang out. What do you say?" he said.

"Yeah. Definitely. What do you wanna do?" she said.

"I don't care. Whatever you wanna do. Just come pick me up or something."

~~~

She was at Luke's in twenty minutes. He was outside smoking a cigarette, wearing a blue New Era hat and a black shirt that said, "I Love Haters." Luke got in Zuri's Oldsmobile and she noticed he looked better than usual. His eyes were brighter; his skin had more color.

"Hey Zuri, sorry I been such a bad friend lately."

"No worries. Where should we go?" she said.

"Not sure. We'd better get stoned first. I've been stupidly sober all freakin day," he said.

They got stoned. Really stoned. And eventually decided on Taco Bell. Lisa would be working the drive through. The drive was fun. They listened to Hollywood Undead and acted stupid. It was encouraging that Luke could have so much fun without being on drugs. Weed didn't count; not for Luke. It was just an everyday herbal remedy that made life better. Whenever it was time to take a break from drugs, weed was always there to fall back on.

"Lisa!" said Luke, "What's going on you little Mexican?"

"Hey guys! What's going on?" said Lisa.

"Not much," said Zuri, "just got the munchies. What are you doing tonight?"

"I'm goin to hang out with Brian. He's got alcohol and a hotel room or some shit. You?"

"I don't know. Just hangin out with Luke for now," said Zuri.

Cars were lining up so they took their food. "Fire Roasted sauce!" said Luke. "More Fire Roasted!" Finally Lisa just threw two big handfuls of sauce packets at Zuri's car. Only half of them made it in. "Thank you." They were all laughing when Zuri drove away.

Instead of taking the food to-go, they just ate in the parking lot while music blasted from the crappy speakers.

After the food they each lit a cigarette. His were American Spirits; her's were Camel 99s. "We should watch that movie. For real this time. All the way through. It's my favorite movie and I've never watched it all the way through," he said.

"Sure, that sounds good," she said.

"Sweet. Your house?" he said.

"No way."

"Yes way!"
~~~

"Uh-uh," she shook her head.

"Oh c'mon. We're friends now. Besides, I've hung out in some trashy rundown places. There's now way your place is gonna scare me off," he said.

"I don't know."

"What if I let you in on a really important secret?" he said. "What secret?" she said.

"A really important secret. And I don't know if I should tell that secret. If I can't then I'll tell you another secret."

"Geez, how many secrets do you have?" she said.

"Only a few big ones. One's awesome. The others aren't so awesome. But I think we're gonna have to learn to trust each other. Know what I mean?"

"Alright. We can go to my house," she said.

~~~

Luke had almost fallen asleep on the way to his house. *Not good, not good. Guess my dopamine levels are a little effed up. Just a little pick-me-up would make the night much better.*

Zuri stayed in the car while Luke grabbed the movie from his room. On his way back he stopped by his Chrysler. He opened the glove box and looked at the sunglass case. There was a tiny bag of meth in there. He opened the case and grabbed the bag. For a few conflicting moments he squeezed the bag in his fist. He forced himself to make a decision, *Fuck that shit,* he threw the bag into the glove box, *not tonight. I'm gonna tough it out.*

"Tired?" said Zuri.

"Shit, sorry," he woke up with a startle. *Yep. Already regretting it. Should have brought the dope.*

"We're here," she said.

"Oh, wow. Right on." They got out of the car and went to the front door. It was a single wide trailer in terrible shape.

Zuri stopped after she unlocked the door, "Alright, promise you won't judge. Lisa lives here too, and she's kind of a slob."

"Hey, don't worry. At least it's yours. You should be proud, he said."

She opened the door, he followed her inside. When she turned on the light he understood why she was self-conscious. There were alcohol containers everywhere; some spilt on the floor. Luke usually took his shoes off when he entered a home, but this was not the place. Zuri wasn't a drinker. Luke had figured that out but didn't understand why. The disaster was Lisa's doing. Lisa had been there first; it was her natural habitat. Luke admired Zuri. She was only seventeen and making it on her own. She was a good girl. Things had been so
~~~

bad with her family that she was driven to this place.

"I gotta get out of these clothes," she said, "You can set up the movie if you want."

"Sure thing."

When she came back, the movie was ready and Luke was sitting on the couch. She was wearing a baggy T-shirt and sweat pants, "My lazy clothes," she said.

"Right on, looks good. Now get over here and watch this movie with me." She sat next to him. He put his arm around her and pulled her close, "Is this okay?"

"It's perfect," she rested her head on his chest.

Luke started the movie with the remote. "This is the best. I love Jim Morrison. My favorite movie by far."

"Sounds pretty cool. You think you can make it through the whole thing?" she said.

"I sure hope so. Why wouldn't I?"

"What if you pass out on me again?"

"I'll try my absolute hardest?" he said.

"No more Adderall?" she said.

"To be honest, I'm trying to stop doing Adderall. Or at least do it less often. Why? You wanted some? I would have brought some if you asked."

"No! No. I think it's a good thing you're trying to cut down. Do you think you have a problem with Adderall?"

"Sometimes. I mean... I do a lot of them sometimes. Too often, anyway. My parents don't like it. It's kind of a problem."

"You know what else helps you stay awake?" she said.

"What?"

"Mountain Dew! Want some? I got lots."

"Yes, I do. I freakin love Mountain Dew."

She went to the refrigerator and came back with two tall glasses. They sat comfortably together and enjoyed the movie. Luke made comments on how much he loved LSD.

"I've never done LSD," she said, "but I really like mushrooms."

"If you like mushrooms you'll love LSD. We'll do it together sometime. It'll be epic fun," he said.

"Kay, sounds awesome."

~~~

"Luke?"

"Shit. I'm sorry," he said.
~~~

"It's okay. You can go to sleep if you want," she said.

"I want to watch this movie. My dopamines are all effed up. All that freakin Adderall."

"You can crash out in my room if you want," she said.

"Alright. Lets try that," he said. He followed her to the tiny bedroom. He was amazed by how clean it was compared to the rest of the house. "Nice," he kicked off his shoes and fell onto the bed. "Very nice." He held his arms open. She was happy to accept his embrace.

They enjoyed it for a few moments before he finally kissed her. It felt natural. Perfectly natural. The kissing turned into making out. Soon they were under the covers. They made love.

They were cuddling together, naked and sweaty, when Zuri asked him to tell her a secret.

"I'm gonna be rich," he paused for dramatic effect, "I've made a very important discovery."

"What did you discover?" she said.

"I'll tell you, but first I need to know what you know about that molly Steve's got."

"Well... he doesn't really talk about where it comes from, but he says it's ninety-eight percent pure. Something like that."

"What about the THC stuff?" he said.

"I don't know anything about it, really."

"Well, I think I do. And I think I can get all that stuff for really cheap on the internet."

"That's pretty cool," she said. There was silence.

"That's it? You're not excited?" he said.

"Not really. I'm not a hustler, and I'm not really into any of those drugs that Steve has."

"Your way too innocent," he said.

"Sorry?"

"No, I think it's adorable. I love that about you," he said. There were a few more minutes of pleasant silence. Luke was trying to think of what to say and how to say it. "So... I don't know if you want to be my girlfriend or not-"

"I do," she interrupted.

"Well, there's a few things you would have to know first. If we do this thing, I want us to have a completely honest relationship. Me and my ex had so many secrets and I don't want it to be like that with us."

"Okay... what is it?" she said.

"Promise you won't freak out, or tell anyone?" he said.

"Kay."

"I do meth a little bit sometimes."

"I know," she said.

"You do?"

"Yeah. Adderall has meth in it. I saw it on the internet the other day."

"Oh. Well, I'm talking about crystal meth," he said.

"Hmm..."

"And I use a needle."

She was quiet for a few moments. He thought she might just tell him to fuck off right then. "You're trying to quit though, right?"

"Kinda. I'm trying to slow down. I don't think I could ever actually quit. Sorry, but I'm just trying to be honest. I really care about you, and I'd totally understand if you don't want to be any part of it. I have to warn you that my life could get stupid crazy here soon. I have a destiny to fulfill. It would be selfish of me not to warn you. But I will try my best to be a good boyfriend if you want me to."

"I don't care. I'm keeping you," she squeezed him harder.

"Can I be really honest?" he said.

"Of course," she said.

"I think I love you."

"I think I love you too," she kissed him again. Luke felt so much emotion. He cherished this girl. At that point he wanted nothing more than to make her happy.

~~~

Zuri woke up at 9am. She moved around and squeezed Luke thinking he might wake up. He didn't. She savored the moment as she snuggled next to her new boyfriend. This was different than previous relationships. She wanted this to last.

Luke didn't have the ego problems that most guys have. He was honest, and said exactly what was on his mind. There was no shallowness to him. She was sure he could get any pretty girl he wanted; why would he choose her? How could she be so lucky?

Zuri had her own secrets; secrets she had never even thought of telling a boyfriend. She felt Luke loved her as a person. She had other boyfriends that said they loved her, but it wasn't the same.

She squeezed him one more time. Part of her wanted him awake because she knew he would kiss her and say something sweet. But he needed the sleep, and
~~~

he looked happy the way he was. She got out of the bed, grabbed some clothes, and went to the shower.

~~~

Luke woke up at ten. Zuri was on top of him, "Wake up sleepy."

"Hey there, cutie. Good morning," he kissed her.

"I made pancakes," she said.

"That's badass."

"Hurry up. Everything's ready," she left the room. He got out of the bed and felt well rested.

Everything was perfect when he got to the kitchen. No more beer bottles; no more dirty dishes; no more trash laying around. "Are you sure you don't have your own secret supply of Adderall?" he joked.

"I have to clean up after Lisa all the time. If I could afford it, I would get a place of my own," she said.

"Well, if I get rich off my chemicals I'll make sure that happens."

"Don't start thinking I'm gonna let you spend a bunch of money on me. Even if you do get rich, I don't like being spoiled. It drives me nuts," she said.

"That's crazy. I can try not to, but don't even try to buy weed from me. Smoking weed is free for me, so it's gonna be free for you too."

"I guess I can deal with that," she said.

"Ha-ha, but seriously, I think I'm gonna be rich. I didn't tell you about the special secret chemical. It's new. Hardly anyone knows about it, especially in America. From what I've read it's gonna be like that old school crank. If it turns out to be good, I'm gonna get all the tweakers hooked on it." Luke went on to describe MDPV.

"Sounds pretty awesome," she said.

"Aw, can't you just pretend to be super excited? I can hardly contain myself," he said.

"Ooooh, yay. My boyfriend is gonna be super rich and buy me everything. Yippe, drugs, money, awesome."

"Wow. That was a perfect impression of my ex," he joked.

"She was like that? What a bitch. I can't stand spoiled rich girls."

"Then you would definitely hate her."

"Are you still friends with her?" she said.

"I try to be. I'm friends with most all my exes. It's kinda tough with her though. She's nuts. Manipulative. Vicious heroin addict. Lets not talk about her. Shouldn't have brought it up," he said.

"Touchy subject?" she said.
~~~

"No. A little bit maybe. The heroin part, anyway. That shit's the devil. It makes me sad to see people hooked on that crap," he said.

"Yeah. My ex was addicted to opiates too. He would eat lots of Loretabs and smoke those oxy's," she said.

"Did you break up over that?"

"No. We didn't date very long. He was obsessive. Had to know where I was at all times and got jealous really easy. It was totally stupid, because I've never cheated on anyone. I've had it happen to me, it sucks, and I would never want to put someone through that," she said.

"I don't know if I've ever been cheated on. Actually, yes I have. Once in junior high, my girlfriend kissed another guy. Broke my heart."

"Ha, I bet that was terrible."

"Yeah. Those days were awesome. But I've never cheated on anyone either. It's mean. I don't like it," he said.

"That's good."

Zuri's phone rang. Luke was lost in his thoughts. "Hey Luke, can you sell any weed to Steve?"

"Umm… yeah. Sure can," he said.

"Yeah he can. I'll see you in a few," she hung up. "Steve wants us to come smoke with him. You wanna come?" she said.

"Yeah. I've gotta stop by my place to grab more weed. Do you have to work today?"

"At one," she said.

"Then I'd better just take my car. That way you won't have to drive me home."

"Sounds like a plan," she took his dishes to the sink.

"Hey now, you gotta work all day. At least let me do the dishes," he came up behind her.

"No way," she said.

"Alright sweetie," he hugged her and kissed her on the neck. She giggled and turned around to kiss him. The kissing turned to making out and soon they were back in the bedroom.

~~~

Steve was getting impatient when they made it to the car. They were running late, but it was well worth it. Nothing started off the day like passionate morning sex. They held hands and shared a cigarette on the way to Luke's house. When they got there, Luke told Zuri he would take a quick shower before going to Steve's.

"Okay. Be fast, I'll meet you there," she said.

"I sure will," he kissed her.

"I love you," she said.

"I love you too, sweetie," he kissed her again, " see you soon"

~~~

"My sweet boy, you're home!" said Alice.

"Yep. Not for long though, I gotta go."

"You look really good." She hugged him, "You smell like a girl."

"I stayed at Zuri's last night."

"Which one is that?" she said.

"You met her a week ago, remember? You got really stoned."

"Oh yes. Was that the little native girl?"

"No, that was Lisa. Is she native? I thought she was Mexican. Same thing though, right? Mexicans are just natives that got raped by Spaniards, right?"

"I don't know, she's your friend. But talk to me, are you dating Zuri?"

"Yeah. I am. She's a really nice girl. Responsible too. Totally completely opposite of Stacy," he said.

"Tell me more about her. Do her parents like you? Were they okay with you staying over?"

"She doesn't live with her parents. She's got her own place, and works a lot."

"She has her own place? But she looks like she's still in high school. She looks a lot younger than Stacy."

"She's seventeen and has her GED. I gotta jump in the shower and get out of here. I'll be home later."

~~~

Luke was in a hurry. It was only 11:30; an hour and a half until Zuri had to be at work. The old Chrysler felt modern compared to the Oldsmobile. Luke was sitting at a stoplight when he glanced at the glovebox. It triggered a series of thoughts through his head.

Might as well finish it off. That way I won't have to think about it anymore.

Luke turned onto a side street and opened his glove box. There was an old water bottle on the floor with just enough water. He poured it into the cap, sucked it up, and squirted it into the spoon with the last of his meth. He was seconds away from taking the shot when his phone vibrated. He was going to ignore it, but decided to see who it was first. It was Zuri. He answered it; the phone in one hand and a needle in the other.

"Hello?" he said.

"Hey Luke, are you on your way yet?"

"Yeah. A few minutes away," he said.

"Okay. Steve's really excited and wanted to know."

"Alright," Luke said as he stared at the syringe, "I'll see you in a sec."

"See ya."

Guilty feelings started to overpower the cravings. *Fuck this shit*, he rolled down the window and squirted the meth into the street.

~~~

Luke knocked on the door. Zuri answered. She gave him a hug and kiss. He was glad he hadn't taken the shot.

Steve was sitting in the same spot at the kitchen table. Drugs and paraphernalia covered the table. "What's going on Luke?" said Steve, "Please tell me you've got more of that Afgan Goo."

"Got about an eighth or so. Is that all you want?"

"I'll need a half ounce at least. I shared some with my buddy and he loves it. I'm gonna be needing your shit on the regular. Can you do any special deals for ounces or anything?"

"I can do two fifty an ounce, but I'll need one forty for a half."

"I'll just get a half for now, but I'll need an OZ in a few days." Steve loaded his bong and passed it around. "So, Luke. What did you think of that molly?"

"Well, when I tried it the other day it just blended into the whole mix of shit I was on. That cannabinoid shit really messed me up. That's why I left in a panic like I did. I sold all the molly though. All at once. No complaints."

"You gonna be wanting anymore?" said Steve.

"Actually, I did a little research on the internet. Found an interesting chemical called methylone. From what I've read, it's almost the same as MDMA. I ordered some and it should be here any day," said Luke.

Steve didn't know what to say. This was a secret that nobody was supposed to know about. Designer drugs were his way of making a living, and Luke had the power to take it away. Or worse, he could expose it. Soon everyone would buy their drugs online.

"I'm not gonna tell no one," said Luke. "It's gotta stay a secret for us to make the most money out of it. And I don't want to steal none of your clients. I've got another chemical thats meant for an entirely different crowd."

"What about Zuri?" Steve asked.

"I'm not saying anything," she said, "You know I don't care about the chemicals or selling drugs. I don't want any part of it."

"Alright, then," said Steve, "What's this other chemical you discovered?"

"I gotta keep that one a secret, at least until I find out if it's any good. It's not
~~~

a rave drug though. More like speed," said Luke.

"Like speed?"

"Yeah. I'll let you check it out when it comes around if you want."

"Sure. That sounds interesting."

The tension was going away. They each took turns with the bong. Steve offered Luke a beer and the three of them made good conversation about chemicals.

"Can you get anymore 2C-B?" said Steve.

"Not right now, but I could bug my guy about it. If I bug him enough, he might make it happen. He has a chemist who makes the shit, but he makes other stuff too."

"That's cool. I've got a chemist buddy of my own. He doesn't like to mess around with the illegal stuff anymore. Once in a while he will do a batch of DMT, but it's been a while."

"DMT? I did that once at a barter fair. I was on ecstasy, mushrooms, 2C-B, and LSD, so I don't remember much of the experience. Kind of blacked out for a few minutes it seemed like."

"You got black-boxed," said Steve.

"Huh?"

"Black-boxed. If you're not in the proper mental state, your brain will protect you from the experience."

"What's the proper mental state?" said Luke.

"Preferably not on any drugs. And it's good to mentally prepare yourself to let go," said Steve.

"Let go?"

"Of your self; the world; that chair you're sitting in; any sort of attachments. You don't want to be occupied with materialistic thoughts."

"So it's supposed to be a spiritual experience?"

"Some people think so. I think it's just another drug; a way to get high. It's just a better experience if you have the right mind-set," said Steve.

"I wish I could try it again. I definitely wasn't ready for it last time," said Luke.

Steve got up from his chair and went to the freezer. He dug around for a minute and pulled out a metal pipe and small bag of yellow crystalline powder. "Think you're ready for it now?"

"Seriously? Yeah. I'm ready. I've drank half a beer though. And smoked weed. Is that okay?" said Luke.

"Should be fine, as long as you're not on any anti-depressants," said Steve.

"Why not anti-depressants?"

"Certain SSRI's combined with DMT can cause serotonin syndrome."

"Seretonin syndrome?" said Luke.

"It's not good. Serious problems. It can kill you." Steve sprinkled DMT into the pipe. He held a lighter to melt the DMT into the steel Brillo pad before handing it to Luke,

"You smoke it like crack?" said Luke.

"Yeah. That's the best way to do it."

Luke looked at Zuri, "Have you tried this stuff?"

"Yeah. I did it once. It's pretty neat. It made me feel really good for the next week or so," she said.

"Wow. Alright. I think I'd better do this on the couch." Luke went to the couch in the living room Dubstep music was playing.

"Now, you're gonna want to torch the shit out of it. And it's gonna taste like you're smokin straight garbage."

"Alright, good to know." Luke was nervous about the unfamiliar drug. *Just let go*, he told himself, *Leave the world behind.*

"Letting go now," he said before taking the hit.

He held it in. The music turned to static, vibrating out of the audible realm. There was a humming noise as everything began to vibrate. Suddenly he went spiraling into a colorful, geometric wormhole.

He disappeared into an atom. A universe exploded. He disappeared into another atom inside that universe. The wormhole continued into infinite smallness.

Everything stopped. Luke was in space, surrounded by stars. Not outer space, but inner space. He was floating between galaxies inside of a universe, inside of a universe times ten. He had gone too far. His soul was jerked back through the geometric wormhole.

The travel back was brief. Soon he was back in the confines of his physical body.

Steve was still watching him, "How was your trip?"

"That was crazy. I saw a universe inside of an atom. It makes so much sense!"

"Well, that's DMT for ya," said Steve.

"You can't sell any of that stuff can you?" said Luke.

"Can't. This is all I got, and I don't know how long until more gets made."

"Let me know when you get more. That shit could like... start a religion! That way I might be able to understand it better. I want to share it with people!"

"I'll let you know. Try to get some of that 2C-B for me, too."

Zuri got up from the table and walked into the living room. "Hey Luke, I gotta head to work."

"Oh, right. I'll walk you to the car."

"Bye Steve. Thanks for smokin a bowl with me," she said.

"Yep. See ya," said Steve.

Luke opened the door and they walked to the Oldsmobile. "What are you doing tonight?" she asked.

"I'll probably be home. I feel like having a peaceful day after that stuff I just did. Call me. Stop by if you want."

"Alright, I will," she kissed him, "I love you."

"I love you, too. Have a good day at work."

Luke went back to the trailer. Steve was back at the kitchen table drinking his beer. Luke decided he might as well finish his too. There was a few moments of silence after Luke sat at the table. "I've got to tell you Luke, I really care about Zuri. It's cool you two are dating, just don't you ever break her heart. If anything bad happens to her because of you, I'm fuckin you up."

"Whoa man, nothings gonna happen to her, and I'm not gonna break her heart. I care about her too. I'm not perfect, but I'm gonna try to be the best I can for her."

"I'm just sayin. I know you're into some bad shit, and I don't want her to be any part of it."

"Are you talking about the Adderall?" said Luke.

"I'm talking about whatever you were on the last time you were over here."

Luke was silent for a moment. Steve was smarter than he expected. "Look man, I was completely honest with her about my problems. I told her I'm tryin to get better and that I don't want her to get into any of my bad habits."

"Just be careful," said Steve.

Luke took a drink of his beer. His intentions were good. He didn't know how to say it any more clear. "I will. I gotta bounce," he finished his beer and stood up. "Thanks for the DMT session. Good talk. No hard feelings. I know you care about Zuri, she's a sweet girl."

"Alright Luke, take it easy."

Luke drove home feeling peaceful. He reflected upon his DMT experience. *Everything is infinite. Every thing contains just as much everything as every thing.*

~~~

Allan and Alice were on the back patio when Luke got home. He was happy to see them. "Luke, you're home!" said Alice. She gave him a hug and kiss on the cheek.

"You look extra sober today," said Allan, "What's going on? I want to hear
~~~

about this new girlfriend."

"Yeah, I don't know. She's pretty cool. I like her a lot."

"Your mother said she looked like a punk rocker. Is she one of those emo girls?"

"No, she's not emo! Maybe she's emo. I don't think so. She likes me a lot though."

"Of course she does," said Alice, "you're a handsome outgoing boy. You could get any girl you want. You don't have to jump right into a relationship. Being single for a while wouldn't be so bad."

"No. I really do like this girl; for good reasons. She's got her shit together. I'm taking a break from the high-maintenance crazy girls," said Luke.

"So, Zuri doesn't do drugs?" she said.

"She smokes weed. Doesn't like drugs, or even alcohol. I think she actually hates alcohol. Like I said, she's way opposite of Stacy."

"Stacy seemed sober last time she came over. More sober than you've been lately," she said.

"She does opiates. Opiates are easy to hide. You don't really want me to get back together with her, do you?"

"I just like having her around. We have fun. I love her," said Alice.

"I love her too, but I can't date her anymore. You can be friends with her either way. I don't mind. I'll try and be friends with her too. You'll like Zuri. I promise. She's a lovable person."

"Zuri sounds great," said Allan. "Stacy definitely had her problems. I'm glad you're moving on. You're looking really good. You're glowing. Gotta be doing something right."

"Yeah. I'm doing good things," said Luke.

"Are you thinking about getting a job yet?" said Alice.

"Not really. Not until I need one."

"What about college? Have you thought about that at all? You can't just sell drugs forever," she said.

"You could do a business major. Do what I did. Maybe you would like to open a dispensary. That way you could sell weed legally," said Allan.

"Plus, you could get a student grant. It would be free," said Alice. "Might as well do something. At least get the paperwork going. That way you'll be able to jump right in and start at the end of summer."

"I'll look into it. I don't want to talk about that right now."

"Sorry. You just don't want to procrastinate this too long. The state could run out of funding," she said.

"Kay. I'll check it out tomorrow."

They changed subjects; talked about camping trips. It was time to go camping, or at least go to the lake. Luke was always gone and his parents didn't like to go without him. He felt bad about that; he wanted to spend more time with his parents. Zuri didn't have much of a family it seemed. Luke was excited to share his family with her.

Drugs were the last thing on Luke's mind. All he wanted was to make things better; for him and his parents. Maybe it was time to do some college. Time to come back to reality. He got a phone call. It was Dave. Luke got up and went inside. "Hey," he answered.

"Got that package, man. You should get over here," said Dave.

Anyone who has never made a mistake has never tried anything new.
-Albert Einstein

Chapter 12: First Time's Free

Friday 7-26-2010

Can't wait till work is over. Hopefully I get to spend another awesome night with Luke. Zuri sat in her cubicle, not wanting to get her hopes up. Luke was unpredictable. She liked stability, but couldn't help it; some unstoppable force of nature brought them together. All she wanted was to be in his arms.

Nine o'clock came around. She smoked a cigarette, waiting for him to text back. *I wonder what he's been doing all day.*

Luke was smoking on the front porch when she pulled into the driveway. He greeted her with kisses, "Hi sweetie. How was work?"

"It was okay. How was your day?" she said.

"My day was badass. That stuff finally came in the mail," he said.

"Oh, yeah? How is it?" she said.

"It's good! Really good! I only tried a tiny bit way earlier. Not feeling it much anymore. It's kinda like coke, almost like Adderall, but it doesn't last as long as most amphetamines. I've been waiting for you to get off work to do any more."

"Oh. That's cool."

"We're gonna have fun. You're gonna like it," he said. "Okay. Sounds like fun. I really need to get stoned," she said.

"Yes, you do! C'mon," he grabbed her hand and took her to the garage.

"So," said Zuri, "What are all your friends doing tonight? Don't you usually party on Fridays?"

"There's stuff goin on. We can go if you want," he said.

"No, that's not what I mean. I just don't want you to miss out on any fun because of me."

"I told you, we are gonna have fun. This stuff I got is awesome. You're gonna love it. I just wanna spend this night with you. I been looking forward to it all day."

"Alright, good. I've been looking forward to it, too."

Allan came in, "What's going on in here?" he took the hose,

"Don't you be smokin without your daddy."

"You're nuts," said Luke.

"How are things going with the girly friend?" he asked.

"It's good. Just been working a lot," she said.

"Well, some people have to be responsible. Luke's a problem child, you need to straighten him out," he said.

"Yeah. I know. I'll try," she said.

"I want to get a camping trip going. It's been too long. You should come too. How about that?" said Allan.

"Yeah, camping sounds good. I haven't done it for a really long time," she said.

"Next weekend, then. How about Hungry Horse? We'll take the boat and everything."

"Sundays are my only day off. I can come out Saturday night and stay Sunday night."

"You work six days a week? That's terrible! Luke, get a job so this poor girl doesn't have to work so much."

They kept smoking. Alice came out a few minutes later, "Hello Zuri, it's good to see you."

"It's good to see you too."

"Are you keeping Luke out of trouble? Tell him to get a job," said Alice.

"Zuri works six days a week!" said Allan.

"You're kidding," said Alice, "Luke, it's time for you to do something with your life. Look at your responsible girlfriend."

"Alright, fine! I didn't want to say anything yet, but I found a way to make lots of money," said Luke.

"Selling drugs is illegal. You can't-"

"It's nothing illegal! But I don't want to say anymore about it because I don't understand it all the way."

"Well, what is it? You can tell us," said Alice.

"I might be a kind of sales man. Might even be able to start my own internet business. But I'm not sayin any more. Not yet."

"Oh Luke, don't get involved with that Amway crap," she said.

"It's not Amway."

"Vacuum cleaners?"

"No."

"Mary Kay?"

"No!"

"Well, give us a hint," she said.

"I gave you one, and that's it. I'm sayin no more."

"Alright. Just don't be a part of any of those pyramid schemes."

"I won't."

Alice looked at Allan, "Did you ask them about camping next weekend?"

"Yes, they're coming. Zuri can only stay one night because she has to work."

"Oh, can't you take a day off? We're going to have so much fun," said Alice.

"I'll try. Can't promise anything though. TeleTech really likes to fire people. Especially for calling in without a ridiculous amount of notice. I'll ask tomorrow. Hopefully they will let me have Saturday off."

"Oh, I sure hope so. I can't believe they have you working so much," said Alice.

"It's actually hard to get so many hours. They don't like giving out overtime."

"Luke isn't usually so lazy," said Allan, "He had a job for almost four years. He's just taking a break."

Alice didn't smoke that night. She just talked and watched, being her social self. She asked Zuri questions about her family. Zuri gave vague answers. She didn't have much good to say about them, but she didn't want to make them sound bad.

After an hour or so, it was time for the parents to go to bed. "Goodnight, and be safe," said Allan.

Luke and Zuri stayed in the garage and smoked a cigarette.

"So… are you gonna stay the night?" said Luke.

"If that's okay," she said.

"Yep. I already asked, ha-ha. That's pretty lame isn't it? I should probably move out soon. Maybe we could get a house together?"

"You would do that?" she said.

"Hell yeah. It would be fun, don't you think?"

"Yeah. It would. Are you sure you won't get sick of me? I am pretty boring, after all."

"True. I don't know if I could handle that too well... kidding! Cut it out with that crap. You're freakin awesome, and I love you," he kissed her.

"Mmm, I love you too," she said.

They finished their cigarettes and went upstairs. Luke grabbed a few metallic zip-lock bags. They were slightly transparent with a label on each of them. One labeled MDPV, another methylone, and another called JWH-122.

"This is the good shit," he held up the bag labeled MDPV. "Wanna try some?"

"Sure."

They sat on the couch while Luke scooped two small specks of powder onto the coffee table.

"That's it?" she said.

"Yeah. That's all you need. I did less than that earlier and felt it good."

"Is it going to burn?" she said.

"Not at all."

She snorted the powder and he snorted his. "It should take about twenty minutes. What do you want to do?" he said.

"You should come here." She was laying on her side of the couch with arms open.

~~~

"I can feel that stuff," she said with her head resting on his chest.

"Do you like it?"

"I think so. It's weird. It feels like I've got really bad butterflies in my stomach."

"Are you getting energized at all?" he said.

"Yeah. I don't want to move though. I like it right here," she said. They started kissing. Soon they were naked on the floor.

That went on for a while. They still had plenty of energy afterward. Zuri wanted to play on the internet. They watched videos on Youtube for a couple hours; things were going good. Luke was excited about his new drug and hoped Zuri liked it. If she liked it, everyone would like it. If everyone liked it, he would be rich.

Zuri got quiet. "How are you feeling?" Luke asked.

"I don't know," she said.

"Should we do some more? I kinda want to."

"I don't want to do any more. I think that stuff is evil."
~~~

"Evil? In a good way, right?"

"No. Not in a good way. That stuff is bad news," she said. Luke was quiet for a minute. "Do you think other people will like it?" he said.

"Probably. Yeah."

"But it didn't feel good to you?"

"It did. I liked it... at first. It's hard to explain. I just have this feeling. This stuff is going to do weird things to people. It's evil. I can feel it."

"Alright, maybe. I'm not totally sure though. Maybe I need to try a little more to see the evilness," he said.

"Can we just go to bed. I have a bad feeling ," she said.

"Of course, sweetie. Sorry," he kissed her on the cheek.

~~~

Zuri woke up in a good mood. She rolled over to find Luke, but he wasn't there. She sat up and saw him at the coffee table putting a twenty back into his wallet. "What are you doing?" she said.

Luke looked at her with a guilty smile, "Experimenting. I needed to do another test on that stuff."

"Oh whatever. You didn't need to test it anymore," she said.

"I did, though. I wouldn't feel comfortable selling it if I didn't give it a thorough test," he said.

"Will you just get back over here?"

Luke went back to the bed. He was still wearing his boxer shorts. "I'm sorry. I shouldn't have done that," he said.

"I"m not mad at you. That stuff just scares me. There's something wrong with it."

"I just want to test it out today. That's it. So that way I know what I'm selling to people."

"Just don't get addicted to that stuff. It's evil. I'm telling you," she said.

Luke's parents were gone. They smoked a joint and had some morning lovemaking before Zuri went to work.

~~~

Luke arrived at Blue's. "Man, I've got this new connect who sold me some weird shit. But it's awesome, I want you to check it out," said Luke.

"Alright bro. Bust it out." Blue was already getting his needles and spoon ready. Luke pulled out his bag. He used a plunger from a syringe to scoop out a small amount of powder onto the spoon. Then he sealed the bag up again.

"That's it? Don't be a stinge. How am I supposed to get high off that?" said Blue.

"That's for both of us. I'm telling you, it's good shit," said Luke.

Blue squirted water into the spoon and prepared the syringes. He took the shot.

"What's going on?" Luke held his needle, waiting for Blue's reaction.

"It's good. Way good."

Luke took his shot. The rush was intense. It was satisfying. His product was a success.

"Can you get more?" said Blue.

"Yeah. For a hundred a gram, or three hundred a ball."

"Who else knows about this?" said Blue.

"No one. My girlfriend, but she's not sayin nothin."

"Don't sell it to anyone like that. It's too strong. We need to cut it. We need as much of this stuff as you can get. Damn, cousin. I'm so fuckin proud of you right now." Blue got up and walked in a few circles before going to his safe. He pulled out a wad of cash and handed it to Luke. "Here's six hundred. It's all I got, but I can make it back double in a day if you can get me a quarter ounce."

~~~

First stop was Tim. Tim hadn't been into the speed for long, but he knew lots of people all over the place. Luke trusted him completely and wanted him to make some money too.

Tim was at a friends on the East side of town, so he just picked him up. Tim got in the truck, "So, what's goin on man? Long time no see."

"I got some shit. It's really good, but I gotta charge full price."

"I don't got much money right now-"

"I know. I don't care. I want you to try it. Then I'm gonna give you some to sample out to people. I'll be able to get you better deals sometime soon, but only you. I don't want everyone knowing it's coming from me, either," said Luke.

"You're bein serious, aren't you? You're goin full time meth dealer."

"It's not meth, dude."

"What is it?" said Tim.

"Here, I'll show you." Luke pulled into a parking lot. "Snort that," he held a key in front of Tim's nose.

Tim snorted it, "What is this stuff?"

"It's some kind of crank. Like old fashioned speed," said Luke.

"It's speed?"

"It's a lot better than meth," said Luke.

"Better than meth? And you can get lots of this stuff?"

"Yep. I'll be able to get it to you cheaper here soon. There's a lot of money to
~~~

be made. I want you to help me sell this shit."

"Alright, man. Hell yeah! Am I gonna make money too?" asked Tim.

"You're gonna make a shit load, bro."

"That's fuckin awesome! Who else is helping you sell this stuff?"

"Only Blue so far. I only want a few people selling it for me. And I'm only selling to people who won't be stepping on each others toes. Know what I mean? I won't sell to anyone else in your crowd of people," said Luke.

"I get it. That's cool."

"I am gonna be sampling it out for a little while so people can get a taste for it. If they're people you know, I'll tell em I got it from you. I don't want anyone knowing this stuff is coming from me, got it?"

"Yeah. I got it. That's smart shit man."

Luke checked his phone. He had a text. Jared was at the skate park and needed weed. Luke pulled out his scale and weighed up a gram of 50% MDPV and gave it to Tim. "This is yours. It's for sampling to people or whatever."

~~~

Luke made many stops. He met with Fat Jared and other friends. He met with Debora. He met with Steve. Luke needed more MDPV, so he went to Dave's.

"Come on in, buddy. How's it goin?" said Dave.

"It's been good, man. People are goin crazy over that shit. I'm gonna have no problem making money with it."

"I believe it. Why don't you bust some out?"

They went to Dave's room. Luke scraped out a couple lines on Dave's mirror. "The big one's for you," said Luke, "I've been doing too much."

Dave snorted the line. "That was a lot more than I did the first time, wasn't it?"

"I had to cut it down quite a bit in order to make it a realistic potency; a safe potency," said Luke.

"Cool. How about some weed? You want a drink? Let's make it a party," said Dave.

"Sure, but we should wait to smoke. Zuri's almost off work. Can she come over?" said Luke.

"Of course. I'll go make you a drink," said Dave.

"Alright. I'll get this order set up." Luke logged onto the computer.

~~~

Zuri pulled into the Appleway apartments. Before she got out of the car she saw Luke come into the covered parking space. He made a suspicious glance over his shoulder before smiling at her.

He opened the door, "Hey girly. How was work?"

"I missed you."

"I missed you too, sweetie," he gave her a kiss. She looked him in the eyes, "You look crazy."

"It's just the lighting out here," he said.

"Are you high?" she said.

"Very."

"Let's go inside. I wanna get stoned," she said.

~~~

"All done," Dave said halfway through their smoke session. "What do I do now?"

"There should be a button that says order somewhere," said Luke.

"Oh, I see." He clicked the button.

"You're getting more?" said Zuri.

"Yep. Twenty-five grams this time instead of ten. Now that I've sampled it out to people I'll be able to start makin money," said Luke.

"And you're gonna stop doing it, right?"

"Yep, I'm stopping after tonight."

"You're stopping?" said Dave. "You're not gonna get high no more?"

"Nope. Can't be getting high on my own supply. I'm just tryin to make money here," said Luke.

~~~

"Bonfire out at the Kila cliffs tonight. It's a really sweet spot. You need four wheel drive to get there. You're gonna love it," said Luke.

"It sounds like fun," said Zuri.

"Yep. I'd better start texting; make sure every one knows what's going on. Before we go, does anyone want to get high? I've got that molly, remember?"

"You mean that stuff you got from the internet," Zuri clarified.

"Yep. The same stuff Steve had."

"I'll do some," she said.

"I probably don't need any," said Dave, "but I'll trust your judgement."

"Alright! That's what I like to hear." Luke poured a pile of powder on Dave's mirror.

~~~

"Alright!" said Luke, "We're ready. Let's go swervin in the Suburban," he finished his drink. "Just joking about the swervin part. Here's my sober face," he gave Zuri a serious stare.

"You're out of your mind," she said, "and you're not fooling anyone."
~~~

"Damn. Well, hopefully I don't need the sober face. Lets go!"

They left the apartments and got into Luke's truck. Luke licked his lips and twiddled his fingers. They headed off once he found a good playlist.

The first and closest stop was to pick up Jack and his new girlfriend. They parked by the elementary school that Jack told them to meet at. Jack and a girl came out of a house across the street. As they got closer, Luke recognized the girl. He got out of the truck, "Alison!"

"Oh my god, Luke!" she ran up and hugged him.

"I thought you were in Washington," he said.

"I'm back. Got here a month ago. Kind of lost touch with all my old friends."

"Well, you'll probably get in touch with some people tonight."

"You guys know each other?" said Jack.

"Yeah, we used to party hard together," said Luke.

"Like everyday!" she added.

"We gotta go," said Luke. "We can talk later. Time to go, go, go!"

~~~

They arrived at Steve's. Lisa came out first, asking if they wanted to come in.

"There's no time!" said Luke. "We gotta go!" he jumped around in his seat.

"Alright, alright. I'll tell him to hurry up," said Lisa.

"At this rate I'll be sober before we get there. Is anyone in this vehicle sober?" he looked back. Alison and Jack raised their hands. They were both given lines of MDMC. "One for the doctor," Luke said before snorting his own.

"What about that other stuff," Dave asked.

"What other stuff?" said Alison.

"You'll see," said Jack. "He's got some funky kind of speed. It's like a fake, synthetic coke."

"That sounds fun. I love coke," she said.

"Evil," said Zuri.

"Not evil. Good, innocent fun," said Luke.

"It's evil," Zuri lit a cigarette. "I'm telling you. I've got special spidey senses and I can tell."

~~~

They drove out past Kila to pick up Natalie. She was with her friend at the same place he had picked her up at before. The two girls climbed in the middle row next to Alison.

"Natalie! How are you?" said Luke.

"I'm good," she yelled over the music, "This is my friend Molly. Molly, this is Luke. He's freakin awesome."

"You're freakin awesome!" he pointed at Natalie. Luke peeled out in the gravel and got back on the highway. Zuri was in charge of keeping pipes in rotation.

They made it to the meeting spot. It was a gas station in the middle of nowhere. A gravel parking lot behind a closed gas station. Luke's Sizzle Steakhouse friends were there. Kenny was in a 90's Mustang. Tim was in an SUV full of familiar people.

Luke got out of the truck and made his rounds talking to everyone; people he hadn't seen for some time. Sara, the waitress from the Sizzle Steakhouse hopped out of Andy's truck and hugged Luke. "Luke, I freakin miss you! We never hang out anymore."

"I know it. I'm sorry. We're gonna have fun tonight though," he said.

"Hell yeah! I brought some Jager and Red Bull. We're gonna get shit-faced, just like old times."

They all got back in their vehicles and followed Luke. It was a 45 minute drive into the middle of nowhere. They turned onto an ancient, grass covered, dirt road. They scaled their way up the mountain through the trees, passing old logging trails on the way.

They found the turnoff. It was a steep trail. Luke drove up it without hesitation. The other two trucks followed.

The Suburban dipped and shifted from side to side. "Everyone lean to the right so we don't fall into the jungle," Luke said, successfully scaring everyone in the vehicle.

They made it to the top. There were other trucks parked around the fire. The clearing was bordered by a 70 foot cliff. Luke recognized most of the people; the usual party crowd.

Tim pulled Luke to the side, "Dude! Jared has people who want to buy that shit you got. You still want people thinking it's coming from me, right?"

"Yeah, yeah. Come with me," Luke took Tim to the truck. They weighed some bags for Tim to sell. Luke kept some to use and share with people throughout the night.

Luke did some Jager bombs with his old restaurant friends. The music was loud, playing Gorilla Zoe. Time went by. Luke found Zuri and hugged her. "Hey girly. Are you drinking anything?"

"No," she said.

"Will you be the designated driver. I'm gonna be pretty smashed by the end of the night."

"Sure. Can we do some more of that molly?" She was with Brittany and

Steve.

"Absolutely!" said Luke, "Let's do it." The four of them went to the Suburban.

They snorted MDMC(methylone). "You don't mind if I sell molly to these people, do you?" said Steve.

"Please do," said Luke, "I don't have much and I want to consume it myself."

"What about that speed stuff you said you were getting?" said Steve.

Luke brought out the MDPV. He gave a bump to Brittany and Steve before taking one for himself.

"Aren't you gonna do some?" Brittany asked Zuri.

"No. I don't like it. I'm just smoking weed and doing molly."

Steve and Brittany got out of the truck. Luke did another bump of MDPV. "Sorry," he said, "I'm done after tonight."

"Are you sure?" said Zuri.

"Yes. Absolutely. I don't want to get addicted to the stuff. I promise." He gave her a kiss, "I love you."

"I love you too."

~~~

Zuri came out of her bubble. The molly was doing its job. She felt good. Her skin and clothes were silky and her voice was fuzzy. She was with Lisa and Brittany, talking with a couple guys she had just met. Lisa was stupid drunk already. Zuri wasn't usually into meeting new people, but this was fun.

She looked around for Luke. He was on the other side of the fire, jumping around, telling an exciting story to a bunch of people she didn't know.

"Zuri," said Brittany.

"Huh?"

"You're spacing out. Can we smoke a bowl?"

"Yeah. Sure."

~~~

As the night progressed, people got higher. Luke had just finished a Jager bomb when someone came up behind him, "Hey Luke."

Luke turned around, it was Blue. He was with Kimmy. "Blue!" Luke gave him a hug, "How'd you find me?"

"We been here with you before, remember?"

"Oh yeah. What's happenin?" said Luke.

"Kimmy needs molly."

"That guy." Luke pointed to Steve. Kimmy went after him.

"Bro!" Blue whispered, "I banked out on that shit! It sold like that," he snapped his finger, "and everyone wants more."

"Is it all gone?" said Luke.

"No. Why? You're getting more, right?"

"Yeah. In a couple days. But I'm almost out, and this night is still young," said Luke.

"I can give you a gram. Just get me back, alright?" said Blue.

"Yeah, of course."

"Alright, it's down in the car. I couldn't drive all the way so we'll have to walk."

They made their way down the trail. Blue had been driving an 80's Pontiac; A highly conspicuous coupe that fit his profile with perfection.

"You sure keep it classy," said Luke as they entered the rusted-out vehicle. The smell was musky from decades of cigarette smoke and semi-homeless inhabitants. Of course Blue's resourcefulness ensured a decent sound system with excessive bass.

Blue prepared the solution as vicious gangster rap enhanced the profound drama of the situation.

Then I went to college,
Basketball was my dream.
Quit the team,
Cause I'd rather shoot rock with the fiends...

There was euphoric tingling sensation as the anticipation built; the self importance; the disbelief; the surreal sensation of plunging into the abyss. Everything was shiny. The windows were black. This velvety bubble of bass and burgundy was the only thing that existed.

A syringe was handed to Luke. He examined it for a moment. "Will you get this on for me? My head's fucked up. Like, meltdown status."

Blue took the syringe and held Luke's arm. Luke watched the plunger depress. Blood vessels constricted, eyes widened, and heart raced. The music grew loud and chaotic. Hands went cold and pale as his underarms began to sweat.

Blue took his own shot and continued to move frantically about. Luke continued to stare at the ceiling while paying attention to what was happening in his body. The song lyrics narrated the scene with chilling accuracy.

I'm feelin strange in the night,
I met myself, I feel I'm thrown into a fight.
Nowhere to run, nowhere to hide, nothing's right.
My skin is burnin and my heart begins to speed,
There's somthin goin wrong with me.

I am changing mentally,

I'm feelin stronger more alert, I'm on the move.

The ego had reached its limit. Luke had reached the realm he had come to this earth to explore. He lifted his shirt and saw his heart thudding unnaturally at his solar plexus. The rush refused to let up and the tightness in his chest persisted. There was the slight discomfort of not being able to get a large enough breath; a shortness of breath. Even the painful and filthy aspects added to his sense of self-importance. The music was made for him. Everything in the world revolved around Luke.

~~~

Zuri saw Luke come back to the party with Blue. She ran up to him with a smile and hugged him. "Where'd you go?"

"For a walk," he said.

"You did more of that PV stuff, didn't you?" she said.

"Shh!" he looked around to make sure no one had heard.

"Sorry. No one heard. You did some and now you're not having fun. I told you it was bad stuff, didn't I?"

"I'm fine. I think I just did a little too much," he said.

"Well, no more. Eat some molly. I want you to feel like I do. That way we can go home and have some fun later," she kissed him.

"Okay. I'll go eat some right now."

Zuri went back to the fire. Lisa was out of control, making out with random guys. The tiny girl could drink a lot of alcohol.

Steve pulled Zuri to the side, "Can you tell me what that stuff is that Luke's got?"

"Why?" she asked.

"Because it's good, and I want to get some," said Steve. "You'll have to ask him," she said.

"Where is he?"

"I don't know. Let's look."

They circled around the fire and went to the truck. Luke was in there all alone. Zuri pulled on the passenger side door handle. It was locked. Luke unlocked it and she got in. Steve got in the back. "What are you doing? Did you eat that molly yet?"

"No," said Luke.

"Why did you lock the door," said Zuri.

"I got scared," he said.

"Scared of what?" she said.
~~~

"I have no idea. I'm fucked up," he said.

"I told you that stuff was no good. You're all weirded out. You should smoke some weed," she insisted.

"Did you have a freakout?" said Steve.

"It's not good to do too much of that stuff," said Luke.

"It's not good to do any," said Zuri. "You're camping."

"Huh?" he looked at the pipe in his hand. "Oh." He took a hit and passed it.

"You should eat these." Steve handed Luke two capsules of methylone. Luke ate them and smoked some more weed.

"Are you ready to get back to the party?" said Zuri.

"Yeah."

Luke went back to drinking, deciding he wouldn't do any more MDPV until he started getting tired. If he drank himself to sleep the experiment was over. He had to pace himself to see if MDPV could keep him awake like crystal did.

~~~

"Luke, we need to go. Lisa's passed out in the forest. We need to get her out of here," said Brittany.

"Seriously? Can't we just put her in the truck?"

"Please Luke? It's almost four, anyway," she said.

"Oh fine. Where's she at?" He followed Brittany away from the fire. They found Zuri crouched next to a slurring, babbling drunk girl.

"Lisa, get up," said Zuri.

"Nooo..."

"C'mon. You're not sleeping out here," said Zuri. "Luke, can you help me?"

"As long as she doesn't puke on me." Luke helped Zuri pick her up and carry her to the Suburban.

Once she was in the truck, Luke went around the party to gather his people. No one wanted to go; everyone was high on molly, some were high on MDPV.

They were all loaded up when someone knocked on the door. It was Fat Jared. Jack opened the door. "I need a ride! My people already left without me," said Jared.

"That would exceed our capacity," said Luke.

"Ha, like that mattered when you were up in the driver seat," Jared started climbing in.

"Sorry guys," Luke climbed over the seat to the very back seat next to Steve and Natalie.

Once they were all settled, Zuri started driving and Brittany found some music.
~~~

~~~

It took over an hour to drop everyone off. Finally Zuri, Luke, and Lisa made it to the trailer in Kila. Lisa was still passed out. Luke and Zuri got her to bed.

They were in the kitchen drinking orange juice and smoking a cigarette. "I think I'm gonna stay up all night," said Luke.

"Why would you want to do that?" said Zuri.

"I need to put that MDPV to the test. You know... research purposes."

"Will you at least come to bed with me until *I* fall asleep?"

"I will definitely do that," he said.

~~~

Luke woke up. He was unhappy. The sex had put him to sleep. Luke found his pants on the floor and grabbed the MDPV out of the pocket. He wanted an IV dose, but insufflation would have to do. Luke snorted the powder off Zuri's night stand.

"What are you doing?" Zuri had woken up. "I need to finish testing," he said.

"Luuuke," she whined, "will you just come back to bed."

He went back to bed. Zuri fell asleep, but Luke stayed wide awake. He didn't dare move; not when she was wrapped around him so comfortably. The MDPV had helped him. It was scary to see how addictive this stuff was. *I should probably stop doing this. Further use could lead to some serious problems. Should I even be selling this stuff to people? It could be bad Karma. What if I ruin people's lives? Turn people into slaves?*

They would all be doing meth anyway; most of them, at least. All I'm trying to do is replace the meth market. If anything, I'm just helping people stay out of jail. People on parole won't fail drug tests because of me.

~~~

Zuri woke up around noon. She squeeze him tight and they started kissing. The kissing turned to morning sex. Around one o'clock they smoked some weed and contemplated the day.

"We should do something fun today," said Zuri, "Like hang out with your family."

"That would be fun. We can make it happen. I need to call a dude. I'm about out of weed." He texted Shawn.

A few minutes later Shawn texted back:

(From Shawn): Albertsons. 45 minutes

"Gotta go." Luke put out his cigarette and started getting dressed.

"Where do you have to go?" said Zuri.

"My guy's in town. Need to meet him at Albertsons," he said.

"Are you coming back?"
~~~

"Of course," he kissed her on the cheek, "I won't take long."

"Okay, I love you," she said.

"I love you too," he walked out the door.

~~~

He made it to Albertsons early. *I gotta get some rigs. Can't keep snorting the stupid shit. If I'm gonna do it I might as well have fun with it.* He went to the pharmacy.

"How may I help you?" said the overweight pharmacy lady.

"I need a ten pack of hypodermic needles."

On his way out he grabbed a box of Q-tips and a small bottle of Fiji water. He saw Shawn was parked next to his car. Luke climbed into Shawn's truck.

"What's up, bro?" said Shawn.

"Research chemicals, man. Found some fake coke shit that's freakin bomb."

"I can get some real coke if you're interested."

"Naw man. The shit I got is much better," said Luke.

"Fake coke is better than real coke? What the hell is it?"

"It's called MDPV and it's not even illegal yet."

"Yet?" said Shawn.

"Well, it's illegal in some places. Not Montana though. Don't tell people about it. It's kinda my secret discovery. The only reason I'm telling you is because you don't deal with anyone that I know of."

"Alright buddy, I keep it a secret. Do you got any with you?"

"A little. I'm getting more in a few days though."

"You have enough to give me a sample?"

"Not really. I kinda want to make this last until I get more," said Luke.

"Wow, must be pretty good shit then. I'd like to get a little sample when you've got enough. Here's some more groceries for you." Shawn handed Luke a brown paper bag.

"Is it okay if I get this one on front? I've got my money invested for the moment."

"That's fine, bro. It's always fine. What did you need from the pharmacy?"

"Oh, that… had to get some needles."

"For what? They'd better be for steroids," said Shawn.

"No! I'm diabetic."

"Oh shit. You are?" said Shawn.

"No. They're for the MDPV," said Luke.

"You're shooting that shit?"

"Yeah. It's a lot of fun."

"You're fuckin crazy. Be careful with that shit. Seriously."
~~~

"I'm stopping after I run out of what I got," said Luke.

"Good. I'm gonna get out of here. Stay out of trouble," said Shawn.

"Alright, take it easy," said Luke.

"And if it's easy, take it twice."

~~~

Luke parked in an abandoned Skippers parking lot. There was no spoon, so he mixed up the MDPV in the plunger cap. *Better not do too much. Need to make it back to Zuri without having another freakout.*

The rush had the perfect amount of fear in it. That's what made it so exciting. It's the same reason people like to watch scary movies. They do it for the rush; they do it for the fear.

Luke made a few nervous glances around his vehicle before starting the truck. He felt like he was in a movie; like every thing in the world revolved around him. The music was blasting an electronic beat with rap lyrics. His eyes shifted to the rear view mirror. Cops could be on him at any moment. His senses were sharpened to precision.

He made it to Zuri's. He walked in and saw Zuri in the kitchen. She was cooking. "I hope you're hungry," she said.

"Actually, I'm not the slightest bit hungry."

She knew what he had done. "Well, you have to eat something."

"I appreciate what you've done, but I can't eat right now. I'm sorry."

"I wish you would stop doing that stuff," she said.

"I'll stop." Luke meant what he said, but his brain signaled otherwise. As long as MDPV kept going into his bloodstream, Luke was doing good and would be rewarded with pleasure. The mid-brain was taking over.

Zuri was sad. She fought back tears. Luke was beginning to feel like a jerk. "Please don't cry. I was being stupid and I won't do it again," he meant every word.

"I don't want to lose you," she said.

"You won't lose me no matter what. I love you."

"If you get addicted to that stuff I won't matter to you anymore," she said.

"That's not true. And I'm not getting addicted to anything."

~~~

They pulled into Luke's driveway. Luke had taken a small puff of chiba to bring his pupils down to size. Zuri looked stoned; Luke did not. He didn't look high, stoned, or even sober. Just a cloudy state of funkiness.

They walked in the front door, "Hey mom." She was on her lap top in the living room.

"Luke, my sweet boy. You're home." She got up and hugged him.

"What are you doing today? Are you hungry?"

"Not hungry. We want to go to the lake. Maybe you and dad could bring the boat?"

"My son, how have you been?" said Allan.

"Good. Do you want to take the boat out?"

"Sure, we can do that. Did you get my messages yesterday?"

"Yeah, sorry, I got distracted and forgot. But I'm not too busy today and Zuri has the day off."

"Very cool. Let's do it."

~~~

They made it to the lake. Tim had been bugging Luke about the MDPV, but Luke couldn't help him. All he had was weed, synthetic cannabinoids, and some methylone.

Luke opened the glove box in the Chrysler, and pulled out a piece of foil and the metallic bag of JWH-122. "Be careful. Don't do too much. You remember what happened last time," said Zuri.

"Well, here we go." With a pen tube in his mouth he held a flame under the foil and inhaled the smoke. He blew it out quickly. It was a nasty cloud. "Holy shit."

"What?" she said.

He paused a few moments to let the feeling sink in. There was a tightness in his chest and his brain felt like it was in a microwave, "I think I'm dying."

"Why? What's wrong?" she said.

Luke didn't respond, he only stared out the window. Zuri grabbed the foil out of his hand and threw it in the glove box. "Breathe, Luke," she said. He hadn't been breathing, but started once she reminded him. "Will you say something?"

"Huh?"

"Are you okay?"

"I don't know," he spaced off into the trees again. "Don't just tell me that! Do I need to take you to the hospital?"

"No, don't do that," he said.

"What are you feeling?"

"Painful," he said.

"Painful?"

"My brain feels like it's dying and my chest… my heart is bubbly and clogged up feeling. It's hard to breathe."

"That's scary, Luke!"
~~~

Ten minutes went by. "Maybe you should get out of the car. Do you wanna go for a walk?" she said.

She grabbed his hand and took him for a walk. She felt like she was taking care of a mentally retarded kid. He couldn't make conversation and his motor skills were off.

~~~

Luke and Zuri made it to the loading ramp and saw Luke's parents. Luke was still toasted and was trying to think of an excuse for it. "If they ask why I'm so retarded, we tell em I smoked some incense I got from a head shop."

"Sure, that's not too far from the truth, anyway."

"Good, because I hate lying to my parents," he said.

They walked down to the dock. Alice was in the boat and Allan was backing it into the water. "Hey guys!" Alice yelled from the boat.

Once the boat was in, Alice parked the boat next to the dock. Luke and Zuri got in and they waited for Allan to park the truck.

"Are you going to do some wakeboarding, Luke?"

"I don't know. I'm feeling a little retarded from this stuff I bought at the head shop."

"Oh, weird. You're gonna do some tubing though, right? You too, Zuri."

"Sure," said Luke.

"I don't know," said Zuri.

"Oh you have to," said Alice, "It's so much fun. Allan is a really safe driver."

"I guess I'll give it a try," she said.

"Is it just you two coming? No other friends?"

"I told a few other people. They might show up."

Allan made it back to the dock and got in the boat. They turned on some reggae music and floated away.
~~~

Human desires are endless.
It is like the thirst of a person who drinks salt water:
one gets no satisfaction
and one's thirst is only increased.
-Vaipulya-Sutra

Chapter 13: Hungry Horse

Thursday 8-1-2010

"I found a couple places in C-Falls for really cheap," said Zuri.

"Right on," said Luke. He was weighing out bags of MDPV on Zuri's bed. There had been twenty grams of pure MDPV. Blue used the same method to cut it down to fifty percent. Blue got 14 grams out of the 40 grams at the same cost as before.

"I wish your door had a lock on it," said Luke. Lisa was home and Luke didn't want her to see the chemicals.

"She won't come in without knocking. Don't weigh your drugs here if you're scared."

"Shhh!"

"Oh my god. Don't be so paranoid," she said.

"This is exactly why we need to get our own place. We need to get into a place, like tomorrow."

"Probably not gonna happen. You know we're supposed to go camping with your parents tomorrow. Remember?"

"Shit, I forgot about that. Are you sure you want to go?" he said.

"Of course I want to go! We have to go. I already took the time off work."

"I really need to sell this stuff. I want to make another order as soon as I can."

"We're going camping. You're not bailing out on your parents like that. Your parents would blame it on me, and I already think they don't trust me," she said.

"Of course they do. They love you," he said.

"Your dad loves everyone, but I don't think your mom likes me."

"Why would you say that?"

"I just get that feeling. She still hangs out with your ex all the time. That's kinda weird, isn't it?"

"They're friends. It has nothing to do with me or you," he said.

"I just think your mom would rather you be with her instead of me."

They each went on to do their own activities. Zuri was looking for a rental. Luke continued to weigh chemicals.

"I have to go to work." Zuri closed her laptop and stood up.

"Already?"

"Yep. You can stay here as long as you want. Gimme a kiss," she said. "Don't do too much of that stuff. We need to go to sleep early so we can meet your parents in the morning."

"Or we could just stay up all night. I have Adderall. Brand new bottle," he said.

"Not funny, Luke."

"Joking. Just joking," he wasn't joking.

"Okay, bye. Be safe. I love you," she said.

"I love you too, sweetie. Have a good day."

She left and Luke tried to organize his thoughts and chemicals. He needed to get out of the house; he needed a shot.

~~~

Luke was in his Chrysler, driving down the country road. He found a gravel turnoff. He accidentally poured too much MDPV into the spoon. *Oh well, I'll just do seventy units of water and save half for later.*

The seventy units turned to eighty-five once it was sucked up through the cotton; almost a full syringe. He squirted forty-five units into the back of another syringe and saved it for later.

The forty units he was about to consume looked more yellow than usual. It was hard to get the powder to dissolve.

He stuck the needle, flagged it, and depressed the plunger down ten units,
~~~

good . Another ten, good. Every thing was getting brighter. Sound amplified. He heard a vehicle approaching. *Fuck it,* he injected the rest, capped the needle with shaky hands, and threw the junkie kit back into the glove box.

His heart fluttered way too fast; he wasn't getting enough oxygen; his chest hurt; he was terrified. There was a vehicle approaching with flashing lights. Luke panicked. He got out of the car and locked the doors. He watched the vehicle approach. It wasn't slowing down. It wasn't a cop. Not even close.

Luke paced around nervously after the vehicle passed. He had shortness of breath; his keys were locked in his car. There was a hide-a-key stashed under the car, but he didn't dare grab it until he was sure he was safe. He was in danger. Someone was watching him. He could be attacked at any moment. He wished he had a weapon.

~~~

Luke made it into town. He picked Tim up at a friend's house. "Dude, people love that shit!" said Tim. "I hope you got the same stuff."

"It's the same, and I can front you a lot more for much cheaper."

"How cheap?" said Tim.

"225 a ball. I'm goin out to Hungry Horse for the weekend. Can you handle two?"

"Hell yeah, I can! I fuckin love you, bro."

"Good." Luke reached into the glove box, "You should be able to make at least two hundred dollars profit and have a half gram just for fun. Just make sure I get four fifty and we can keep this going." Luke handed over two bags, each weighing 3.5 grams.

"Thanks a lot, bro. I won't let you down," said Tim.

"Be careful with that stuff. I'm pretty sure it could kill you if you do too much. But you'll probably be fine if you're not shooting it."

"You're shooting it up?" said Tim.

"Yeah man. It's freakin nuts."

"That's crazy. Be careful, bro."

~~~

Luke headed to Debora's after dropping Tim off. He knew she could sell the stuff. Luke decided he would give her the same price as Tim. Luke was making almost 500% profit. He finally felt like he was doing something important with his life; he was creating history.

"Hi hunny, come on in." Debora was excited to see Luke. Luke had 18 grams of MDPV left. He sat down on the couch next with Debora.

"I can do 225 for 3.5. Same stuff I let you try last time."

"How much can you front me?" she said.

"A half ounce."

"So nine hundred dollars?"

"Yep, when will you have the money?" he said.

"Probably before Monday."

"Perfect. Because I've got debts and the quicker I get money, the quicker we can keep it pushin."

"So you're gonna keep getting this same stuff?" she said.

"Yeah. I don't see it stopping any time soon. I've got a reliable connect."

"You're awesome, Luke."

Luke gave her four bags, each containing 3.5 grams. That left him with four grams. There were many uncertain variables. He still owed Shawn for the weed. He needed to move into a place with Zuri. If any of these deals went bad, he would be screwed. "You wanna get high?" she asked.

"Let's do it."

She prepared the solution. She respected the power of the drug. He had a lot of money invested in her and it was good to know she wouldn't go losing her mind on the stuff. She was injecting responsibly, if there was such a thing.

"I'm not trying to do a bell ringer," she said.

"I like where your head's at. Big shots of this stuff are terrifying."

"Ha, I believe it. You need to be careful with this stuff, Luke."

"I will. I figured it's just best to do less," he said.

"Alright, here you go," she handed him two syringes, "Will you do mine for me?"

"Oh… sure. I've never done it for anyone else before," he said.

"It's just hard for me to get the one on my forearm," she said.

"Why don't you just do the same one I do?"

"All those veins are collapsed. I don't think blood even goes through them any more," she said.

"What? That's really bad isn't it?" he took a closer look at her arm.

"It's what happens if you use dull needles a lot."

"Jesus. Alright, I'll try and get that other one for you."

"Thanks Luke."

He made it work and did his own shortly after. So satisfying; so energizing.

~~~

Luke sold a few bags of weed before going to Dave's. He had done all he needed to do; now was his last chance to really get messed up before going camping.
~~~

"Do you have any more of that black stuff?" Dave asked.

"Just a little. We might as well finish it off." Luke went out to his car. He wanted to take a shot. Luke went back inside with the bag of H and his sunglass case. Luke handed the small glob of heroin to Dave. "Hey Dave, can I ask you a question?"

"Sure, Luke. What's up?"

"Well... for a while now, I've been using a needle to get high," he paused to read Dave's reaction, "Can I take a shot in your bathroom?"

"Are you being serious? What are you shooting up?"

"I been shooting that MDPV," said Luke.

"You sure that's safe? You know what you're doing?" said Dave.

"Yeah, it's safe. And I'm a pro. Nothing can go wrong," Luke assured.

"Well, since you're already doing it, I guess it's okay."

"Okay, I'll be right back." Luke went to the bathroom. He still had the 45 units already in a syringe. He squirted half of that into another syringe and injected it. In two minutes he went back to Dave's room and sat on the bed.

"What do you need?" said Dave.

"Nothing."

"You did it already?"

"Yeah." Luke was rushing and didn't want to talk.

"You've got to be kidding. You were barely in there a minute."

"Nope, not kidding." Luke stood up, putting his hands behind his head.

"Are you okay?" said Dave.

"Yeah, yeah. I'm good."

"Smoke some of this with me. Maybe it will calm you down." Dave already had the heroin on a piece of foil.

"Sure, just gimme a minute."

~~~

Zuri got off work and was on her way to Dave's. She hoped Luke wasn't too messed up. The higher he was, the more apprehensive he would be towards camping. She was sure Luke's parents would blame her if Luke didn't go camping.

She knocked on the door. Luke opened it, "Hey girly! How ya been?" He gave her a kiss. He smelt like alcohol. They went into Dave's bedroom to smoke some weed.

"Did you do everything you needed to do today?" she asked Luke.

"Yeah. Basically. I pretty much fronted everything out, so I won't have the money for a few days."
~~~

"Good. So we can go camping and you won't have to worry about anything."

"Yeah. I guess so," he said.

"How long are you going to be camping? Will you need me to order you any more of those chemicals?" said Dave.

"We'll be back Monday. You probably shouldn't make another order until I get paid for all the shit I borrowed out."

"Do you trust the people you loaned out to?" said Dave.

"Absolutely. I just don't want to take any chances not being able to pay you back," said Luke.

"Well, let's put in an order. If you can't pay I'll just keep it myself. Just help me sell it."

"You got it man. Let me see your computer."

~~~

"Wake up, Luke. C'mon wake up." Luke woke up in Zuri's bed. "Are you awake?" she kissed him on the cheek.

"Nooo… fuck that," he barely had the energy to roll over away from her.

"You have to get up. We need to go to your parent's," she said.

"Awww man." Luke got up and walked out of the room. Zuri followed, knowing what he was going to do. Luke was trying to get to his car.

"You need to eat first. I already made breakfast," she said.

Luke stopped and looked at the food in the kitchen. He was torn. His body and mind screamed that he needed a shot.

"You can do your thing right after you eat," she said.

"Kay… I guess I'll eat first," he sat down at the kitchen counter and chewed his food lethargically. He was hungry enough; starving actually. Eating food felt unfamiliar and took too much energy.

After eating, Luke went to the car and finished the 20 units he had prepared the day before. Within seconds he was revitalized and feeling great; ready for camping; ready for anything. He got out of the car and walked a few circles. He had his hands behind his head and was still only wearing boxers.

He went back inside, "Thanks for the food, sweetie. That was a good call."

"You're welcome. Now get dressed so we can get out of here."

~~~

They made it to Luke's parent's house at 8:30am. Allan greeted them at the front door, "Children! You made it. I had my doubts."

"Doubts? How could I miss it?" said Luke.

"You're not the most punctual person in the world. I'll give the credit to the responsible girlfriend."

"Well, yeah. I guess she does deserve most of the credit," said Luke.

They went inside. Alice was in the kitchen organizing all of the food they would need for the trip. "Hey kids. Do you need anything to eat?"

"No thanks," said Luke, "Zuri made breakfast this morning."

"Good. Then you can help your father pack the boat."

"The boat's already here?" he asked.

"Yeah. He's been using your truck."

"Oh. Alright then." Luke and Zuri went to the garage to help Allan.

~~~

Once they were all ready to go, Luke gave Alice some money for whiskey. "We're taking the Chrysler too."

"There's no need to," said Alice. "We should all go as a family."

"We need the Chrysler. You know, just in case the truck craps out. And we also need to stop a few places on the way back to Kalispell."

"Okay then. It's your gas money, and I know you're probably runnin low these days," said Alice.

"I'll get by."

"And you'd better not be spending all of Zuri's hard earned money," she looked at Zuri, "Don't let Luke be a bum."

"He's not. He makes money, kinda," said Zuri.

"Alright," said Luke, "Let's get outta here. Are we going to the old abandoned campground we like?" "That's the plan," said Alice.

They headed out. Luke let Zuri drive. "Why am I driving?" she asked.

"Oh, just because. Is that okay?"

"I guess so."

Luke rolled up a joint 45 minutes into the drive. It was a diversion, meant to distract her. Once they were stoned, Luke grabbed his sunglass case out of the glove box and climbed to the back seat.

"What are you doing?" said Zuri.

"Something a little unorthadox. Don't worry about me," he said.

"Well I still know what you're doing. Do you really need to do it right now?"

"If I do it now, I won't have to do it later," he said.

"You're gonna do it later anyway," she said.

"Not when my parents are around."

"I really hope you don't. They're not dumb, you know." She knew there was no hope of talking him out of getting high, but hopefully he didn't get too high and freak out around his parents.

Luke crawled frantically to the front seat. He looked at Zuri with wide eyes,
~~~

"Did that look suspicious?"

"We're in the middle of nowhere. Will you just relax?" she said.

"I know. Sorry." He forced himself to look forward and act normal.

"Why do you even do that if it makes you freak out?" she said.

"I don't know. I like it... for some reason."

"You're not going to stop, are you?"

"Yeah, I am. Not right now, but probably soon. It's probably gonna be illegal soon anyway and I won't be able to get it any more," he said.

"So you're just gonna keep doing it until you run out for good?"

"I don't know Zuri. I think I'm just gonna try taking this as far as it will go."

"So you're gonna keep doing that crap until you run out or die?" She was trying to hide the emotion in her voice.

"I don't know. Yeah. I really just don't care any more. I'm done trying to restrain myself. I warned you in the beginning. You don't have to be with me, you know."

"Don't say that!" she stopped the car and started crying. They were on a dirt road. Luke looked around nervously.

"I'm sorry," he said, "but I think life is about to get crazy for me. You need to decide if you really want to be a part of it. I wouldn't blame you if you decided to bail out."

"You want me to leave you?" she said.

"No Zuri, I love you. But I also don't want to drag you into something bad. If you wanna stay I'll do my best to make you happy."

She cried some more in his arms. Leaving him was not an option. "I don't care what you do. I'm not letting you go."

~~~

They made it to their abandoned campground; as close as they could get to it, anyway, since the road into it was blocked off. "How are your parents going to bring everything in here?"

"They'll bring everything on the boat and park it right at our camp spot."

"Do you know where our camp spot is going to be?" she said.

"Not really. I guess we can just walk around until they show up. You wanna smoke a joint? I'll roll a fat one."

"Yeah, that would be nice," she squeezed his hand.

They found a mossy picnic bench where Luke rolled the joint before going on the nature walk. Luke felt bad about making Zuri cry. It was obvious that she would do anything to keep their relationship together. Stacy had been different. If she was pissed at Luke she would just leave and make him do the work. Now
~~~

he had a girl who really cared; who wouldn't give up on him.

"I think I hear your truck," said Zuri.

"Oh snap! My mom's probably at the shore with the boat, then." They walked along the shore until they found the boat. It was parked right up on the sand.

"Hey kids. Help me unload this stuff."

Allan came walking down to the camp a few minutes later. Once everything was unloaded, they opened beers and started setting up camp.

"There's still lots of daylight," said Allan, "We should get out on the boat. You're ready to do some wake boarding, aren't you, Luke?"

"Yeah, sure. Let's do it."

~~~

Luke was getting agitated by the time they got back to camp. His parents didn't see, but Zuri knew he needed a shot. She only hoped it wasn't too big of one.

"Can you set up the fire for us, Luke?" said Allan.

"Yeah, sure." Luke made the fire and disappeared, "Need to throw my phone on the charger. Be right back."

Luke walked blindly through the trees to find his car. Every cell in his body screamed out for MDPV. There was no way he was going through the night without it.

He made it to the Chrysler and prepared the solution. Luke took the shot and realized he had underestimated it. It suddenly felt like there were dangerous animals lurking around his car; just waiting for him to get out.

Luke opened his knife and gathered the courage to get out of the car. The trip back to camp was terrifying. He was so concerned with what could have been following him that he'd almost gotten lost.

"It's about time," said Alice, "dinner's almost done."

"Sorry, I kinda got lost," said Luke.

Zuri looked at him with concern, "Did everything go okay?"

"Yep, it's good. Just needed charging. Who wants to smoke? Can I borrow a pipe?"

Zuri dug in her purse and gave him a pipe. He loaded it, fighting every instinct to look around the woods for whatever might be stalking him. *It's probably watching, waiting for a time to attack. Probably one of those vicious mountain tigers.* Luke made himself a strong mixed drink with whiskey and squirt, hoping to calm himself. He also needed to regain his appetite. Food was important. If he stopped eating food he'd run out of energy.
~~~

He tried to pay attention to the conversation going on between Zuri and Alice. They were talking about some of the houses Zuri had been looking to move into.

"Yeah. I think we're going to stop by a place in C-Falls when we leave here," said Zuri. "Isn't that right, Luke?"

"Yeah, yeah. That's the plan. Rent is really cheap there."

Luke soon realized that his fear of the woods was ridiculous. The alcohol and weed were helping. Soon he felt intoxicated and socialized properly. The night became more enjoyable for Luke. Quality family time with his girlfriend.

Luke was a good storyteller, and soon he was giving an animated description of an experience at the Oregon Country Fair.

"The first time I tried 2C-B, I bought it from some naked chick at the Country Fair. I was with Blue when the naked girl asked us if we wanted any 2C-B. I said, '2C-what?'

"She said, '2C-B, it's like acid and ecstasy mixed together.'

"I said, 'That's exactly what I'm looking for!' so she gave us each a capsule and charged us ten dollars a piece. There was hardly any powder in the capsule, I almost thought we were getting ripped off.

"We ate the capsules and about forty minutes later I could feel those butterflies that tells you it's about to hit you really hard really fast."

Me and Blue were just walking around. I wasn't paying much attention until Blue pulled me to the side of the trail and told me to hold out my hand. Some acid fried lookin guy with shaky hands was holding a visine bottle. I held out my hand and asked Blue if we should be doing that since we just ate the funky shit.

"The crazy guy dropped some into my hand and said, 'Oh shit, that might have been too much.'

I was worried. I licked the LSD off my hand and hoped for the best. Right after that, Blue handed me another capsule; this one was full of MDMA. Since I had already gone this far, I figured it couldn't hurt to go a little further. I ate the capsule and within five minutes the 2C-B kicked in. Almost immediately I lost Blue and wandered around admiring the trippy scene.

Once the LSD kicked in I completely lost it! I felt like I was climbing through a jungle of colorful branches and ferns that were growing all around me. It was late at night, but to me it felt like a cartoon in broad daylight.

Some guy walked next to me for a while. I asked him what was going on. 'Just watchin you trip out, man,' was all he said.

Pretty soon I could hear bongo drums. The beat was escalating; getting louder and louder. Boom-bada-boom-bada-boom! It felt like it was heading towards some sort of climax. I was walking, or climbing through the colorful branches that were growing in front of me.

It kept escalating, Boom-bada-boom-bada-BADA-BOOM! then it stopped. There was a horrifying silence. I stopped and looked around. I was surrounded by Native Americans. There was a huge circle of them, all wearing loin clothes and the tribal shit. I walked right into their sacred ritual. I looked around and said, 'I am so sorry.'

They just looked at me and laughed. One of them said it was okay. A few of them came up and hugged me.

I tripped so hard that night, it even lasted well into the next day. Every night there is like the craziest night of your life. I don't think you could be sober there, even if you didn't take any drugs. There's so many people, and everything that happens there is so trippy; like Alice in wonderland shit.

"That sounds pretty crazy, Luke," said Alice. "That sounds dangerous. You need to be more careful."

"There's no need to be careful. No one dies in places like that. There's even little kids running around during the day time. Little kids! Playing with bubbles and glow sticks. Freakin trippy stuff. Nothing can go wrong there. No fights, no stealing, all good vibes. Zuri's gonna see next year, isn't that right?"

"I guess so." She was smoking a cigarette by the fire.

"You're not so much into drugs as Luke is, are you?" Allan asked.

"Not so much," she confirmed.

"What do you think about all of that crazy nonsense?" he said.

"I like the natural stuff. Like weed and mushrooms."

~~~

It got late. Luke's parents were drunk and went to sleep. Zuri was tired and almost sober. Luke was drunk and coming down from his high. He wanted to go and take another shot, but decided he'd better go to the tent with Zuri. It was hard, but he knew it would make her happy.

They went to the tent and zipped their two sleeping bags together. After some kissing and loving on each other they went to sleep.
~~~

The descent to hell is easy;
the gates stand open night and day;
but to reclimb the slope,
and escape to the upper air, this is labor.
-Vergil: Aeneid VI

Chapter 14: MDPPP

Monday 8-5-2010

Luke helped load all of the gear into the boat before heading to the Chrysler. "Bye mom. Bye dad."

Alice gave Luke a hug, "I love you my sweet boy."

"I love you too, mom."

"If you need any help looking for a house, let me know," she said.

"Sure. We'd better get outta here so Zuri's not late for work."

"Okay sweetie, see you later. Bye Zuri. Have a good day at work."

"Bye Alice, thank you," said Zuri.

Luke and Zuri left camp and headed to the Chrysler. They held hands as they walked through the woods. "I've had a lot of fun this weekend," said Zuri, "Your parents are so nice."

"It's been a good time, that's for sure. I'm glad you made sure I didn't bail out," he said.

"It was a lot better than running around selling drugs all day every day, huh?"

"Definitely better. I needed a break from all that," he said. They made it to the car and Luke handed Zuri the keys. "You wanna drive?"

"Why do you want me to drive?" She knew the answer, but asked anyway.

"Because I've got things to do, and phone calls to make," he said.

"Can't you just go one day without that crap?"

"I don't know, but I really don't want to."

She took the keys and sat in the driver seat. She turned on the car and shifted into drive.

"Let it warm up a few minutes," said Luke. He started to prepare an MDPV solution in a spoon.

"Why can't it just warm up while we're driving?" she said.

"Because it would warm up too fast, and that can cause problems."

"What kind of problems?"

"Well, when metal heats up it expands. If shit expands too fast, gaskets could crack and cause leaks. I don't know, but anyone who knows about cars would tell you that."

Zuri started driving after a few minutes. Luke took his time to prepare a couple syringes full of liquid; enough to last all day. He had come to favor making a bunch at once. It saved time in the long run. Taking a shot every few hours was time consuming when he had to make new solution each time.

He took the shot and scrambled to put all of his paraphernelia into the glove box. Luke was terrified even though he felt safe only moments before. "Drive normal!" he said.

"I am driving normal! Why are you freaking out?"

"Is there a sheriff behind us? Wait, I can't see him anymore. He'll be coming around the bend." They were on a winding dirt road going around the lake.

"Oh my god, you're insane. There's no one behind us," she said.

There was no one, but Luke kept his eyes glued to that mirror. His heart was racing and he started to sweat. He instantly developed a horrible body odor. Still, he stared into the rear view mirror.

"You have a serious problem," said Zuri. "How can you even want to keep doing that crap when it makes you scared of every thing? And I can smell it coming out of your skin." She lit a cigarette and cracked the window.

~~~

Forty minutes later they were approaching Columbia Falls. "Okay, you seriously need to smoke some weed. Please, Luke."

Luke pried his eyes from the mirror and forced himself to smoke weed. He took a hit and handed it to Zuri. They each took three hits before Luke put it
~~~

away.

Zuri was driving down an unfamiliar residential street. Luke had never been sober in C-Falls, so everything was vaguely familiar. It was a trashy little town where rent was always cheap.

"Here it is," she said. They pulled over in front of a one story duplex with paint peeling off the ancient siding. "You want to check it out?"

"A duplex?" said Luke.

"Yeah, it's only $350 a month."

"I don't think that's a good idea. We're going to need some more privacy than that," he said.

"Well, there's a couple others around here." She drove down a few blocks and stopped in front of another dumpy looking house. There was no one living in it. "It looks condemned," said Luke.

"It's C-Falls. This one's $400 a month," she said.

"Let's check it out," Luke got out of the car and walked past the weathered, white picket fence. It was a one story house with an unfinished basement.

"I like the basement," said Luke.

Zuri looked through the same window, "It's pretty messy down there."

"That don't mean nothin. I could have it cleaned up in no time." He went around the house looking through any window he could, then decided it was good.

"You like it?" she said.

"Yeah, I think it's perfect. For now, anyway."

"You don't mind being so far from Kalispell?" she asked.

"Kalispell is like twenty minutes away. In big cities most people have to drive at least forty minutes just to get to work."

"Well, there's one more place in C-Falls. Then there's a couple places in Kalispell, but they're way smaller for pretty much the same price. And since you don't want to do a duplex, I'm sure you won't want to live in an apartment either."

"No, I really like this right here," said Luke.

"It's eight hundred for the first month including the security deposit. Can we afford that right now?" she said.

"How much money do you have?" he said.

"Not even close to that much. I just paid rent for last month," she said.

"Well, let's just wait and see if I can get all my money for those chemicals I borrowed out."

"I guess we'll see. I'll keep looking around," she said.

~~~

Luke pulled into Zuri's driveway and gave her a kiss. "Have a good day at work, sweetie. I love you."

"I love you too," she kissed him some more before getting out of the car.

Luke drove off with a purpose. He had money to collect. If everything went as planned, he would be moved into his own house in no time.

First thing's first; need to take a shot. He was still high, but because of the nature of the drug, he wanted more. He had the liquid already prepared so it didn't take long. The car was only pulled over for a couple minutes while he took the shot. It was a small one, so he was able to drive off after the injection.

Tim was the first person he called. "Hey, bro," Tim answered. "What's up, man? I'm back from Hungry Horse," said Luke.

"I'm down in Evergreen. Same place you dropped me off at last time. You wanna come get me?"

"Be there in twenty." Luke hung up the phone.

Tim was waiting outside, right where Luke had dropped him off a few days before. He got in the car, "Dude!"

"What's up, man?" said Luke.

"I been sellin that shit for $120 a gram. Everyone fucking loves it!"

"That's awesome, dude."

"I got your money. Can I get any more? Same deal?" said Tim.

"I only got a little right now. Should have more today or tomorrow."

"Alright. Well, here's your money." Tim counted out $450. "Let me know as soon as you get more. Oh yeah, I've got someone who has a pistol he wants to trade for some shit."

"What kind of pistol? How much does he want for it?" said Luke.

"It's a Walther PPK. I looked it up. It's worth like $700 bucks. He was hoping to get a ball out of it," said Tim.

"Well, I barely got three grams on me now. I don't want to get rid of it all in case it takes a couple of days to get more," said Luke.

"I can probably get it to you for three. Could you give me a half g when you have enough?" said Tim.

"Sure, dude. That will work."

"Cool, man. We can go get it now if you want. He lives over by the college."

"Let's do it," said Luke. Tim made a text on his phone and gave directions.

Luke parked in a cul-de-sac while Tim went into an apartment complex with the three grams. *Less than fifty bucks worth of research chemicals for a $700 gun? Didn't James Bond use a Walther?* This was the protection Luke had been craving. Every-
~~~

thing was falling into place.

Tim got back in the car, "Got it."

They left the cul-de-sac. Tim pulled the gun out of his waistband. "Dude, that's like James bond status!" said Luke. "What size bullets does it take? Is it loaded?"

"It's not loaded. It says .38 on the side here."

"Right on. Thanks for getting that for me. You really came through on this one."

"You're welcome, bro. You want me to keep an eye out for shit people want to trade? I've met a new crowd of tweakers who steal a lot of shit," said Tim.

"Yeah man, especially guns. I can get rid of them in Portland really easy for top dollar," said Luke.

"Alright. It shouldn't take long for me to come across some more shit."

~~~

Debora was home when Luke got there. Luke sat down and she handed him his $900. "Can we do the same thing again? I've already got money lined up for people who want more," she said.

"Wow. That fast?"

"Everyone loves it. No one knows what it is, but everyone wants more. I hope you can keep getting this stuff, because we could make a lot of money."

"I'm cleaned out right now, but I'll get more as soon as I can. We can keep doing the same deal for as long as you want. I don't see it stopping any time soon," Luke assured.

"Alright then, good. Do you wanna get high real quick?" she said.

"I'd better not. I get so distracted after I do a shot. I gotta go meet someone and see if I can get some more shit," he said.

"Nice. Make sure you let me know as soon as you can get more of that stuff."

"I will for sure."

"How was your camping trip, by the way?" she asked.

Luke went on to explain the camping trip and the house he might be moving into.

~~~

Tim climbed back into Luke's Chrysler, ready to do something fun. "Man, what should we do? We gotta do something cool, cause we hardly ever kick it anymore it feels like," said Tim.

"I agree, man. What do you wanna do? I'm down for whatever," said Luke.

"I don't know, but we should get high first."

"I am totally down for that," said Luke.

"I kinda want to try it your way," said Tim.

"Are you sure? You won't want to do it any other way after you try it."

"Dude, I saw a fucking twelve year old shooting up the other day. It can't be so bad," said Tim.

"A twelve year old?" Luke was shocked. "What kind of people are you hanging out with? That's not cool at all."

"It's fucking weird. I don't understand it either. I met these people in a camper behind someone's house. That little kid was there. It felt weird even selling drugs in front of him. Once they had the shit, he pulled out the needle and spoon and did the whole thing himself. It was fucked up, I can't even explain... he's the one who found that gun of yours."

"That's some weird shit, man."

"It is fucking weird. I've ran into some pretty strange people since I started selling this stuff for you."

They talked for fifteen minutes while Luke drove to an unfinished neighborhood. There were streets, but no houses. Luke parked in a secluded cul-de-sac. "Are you sure you want to do this?"

"Yeah, I'm sure. I would have tried the other day with those kids, but they were all sharing the same dirty needle."

"That's no good. I got a clean one for you." Luke grabbed the Junkie kit out of the glove box. He used a clean rig and plunger cap to make the solution for Tim.

"What's that other stuff for?" Tim pointed at the other syringe full of liquid.

"That's for me; it's not clean. It's easier to just make it ahead of time. That way I don't have to fuck with it all the time."

"It looks yellow," said Tim.

"That's cause it's really strong. So I only need like fifteen units."

Luke finished preparing Tim's shot. It was thirty units of liquid. "Just to let you know," said Tim, "I'm terrified of needles."

"You won't be after this. Just look away." Luke grabbed Tim's arm and rested it over the arm rest. Tim's veins were deep, narrow; not easy to hit. But Luke found it, flagged it, then depressed the plunger.

"Did you do it yet? Oh shit..." He looked at Luke who was capping the needle and marking it with a knife.

"How do you feel?" Luke asked.

Tim didn't answer; his expression made it clear. "Are we safe right here?"

"We're safe, I promise. The paranoia can be pretty vicious sometimes, but we're totally safe." Luke took a shot for himself and threw everything in the glove box before locking it shut. "Now we're not safe," he looked around and checked his mirrors. "Kidding. Totally kidding." *Not kidding.* Luke felt the same danger Tim felt. To the brain, it was real, authentic danger.

"Alright, let's bounce." Luke put the car in gear and drove off.

They stopped at a stop sign. Both of them kept glancing in the mirrors. They both looked at each other and laughed, realizing they were wigging out over nothing. "What the fuck is going on?" said Tim.

"We are definitely doing some bizarre chemicals here," said Luke.

Luke got a text. "Someone needs an oscar. You don't mind if we go drop it off, do you?" said Luke.

"Naw man. I don't really care what we do. How is Dave, by the way? Have you seen him lately?" said Tim.

"Yeah, actually. Me and him kick it quite a bit."

"I wanna go see Dave. Has he tried this new stuff yet?"

"Yeah. I've shared some with him," said Luke.

"Can we go kick it with him after you sell your weed?"

Luke hesitated, "Sure," Luke was beginning to see how insane it was to try and keep this chemical secret from his best friend. *Do I tell Tim now, or wait until Dave's drunk ass spills the secret? I'll just take my chances with Dave. If Tim finds out that way it will be a fun surprise.*

~~~

Luke sold his bag of weed; another couple hundred bucks in his pocket.

"So, how is Dave?" said Tim, "I don't think I've talked to him since he lost his job."

"He's alright. He drinks a lot, but he makes pretty good with unemployment."

They parked in front of Dave's apartments. Luke brought his gun and the last of his MDPV. Dave answered the door, "Hey boys, come on in." He had been drinking. "You've got some mail, Luke."

And my cover is blown. "Right on, thanks Dave."

Tim had a confused look on his face. Dave realized his slip, "I mean... aww crap. Sorry Luke."

"It's fine, I was thinking about telling him, anyway."

"Tell me what?" Tim asked.

"The chemicals, man. The funky dope. I've been ordering it online."

"No way, dude. How can you do that without getting in trouble?" said Tim.

"It's a new drug. It's not even illegal yet," said Luke.

"How can it not be illegal? It feels completely illegal."

"It's illegal in some countries, and only like seven states."
~~~

Dave handed Luke his package, "Here you go."

"Let's go try it out," said Luke, "I ordered from a different company. This shit is supposed to be from Sweden or some shit."

"Dude, you're a fuckin genius!" said Tim, "Are you like the first person to figure this shit out?" said Tim.

"I don't know, man, but I was the first person I know of to try this shit. I know someone else who orders different chemicals online, but nothing like this stuff."

"Like what different chemicals?" said Tim.

"You know that cheap molly? Someone ordered it online. It's called methylone, or MDMC, and it's not even illegal yet."

Luke opened the package as soon as they were in Dave's room. Tim watched in anticipation. Luke held the metallic zip-lock bag with a disappointed look.

"So the stuff we've been doing is called MDPPP?" Tim asked.

"No. This is the wrong shit. I was supposed to get MDPV," said Luke.

"What does this mean? Are we fucked?" said Tim.

"I don't know. I hope not, cause I spent a good chunk of money on it," said Luke.

"Let's just try it. Maybe it's just as good," said Tim.

"I don't want to open it in case I can get a refund." Luke grabbed Dave's laptop and logged onto the internet. "I'll look up MDPPP on Wikipedia, so at least I know what it is."

Dave and Tim were leaning in to watch. "I think this stuff is just an ether base form of MDPV. The chemical structure is almost exactly the same," said Luke.

"That's good, right?" said Dave.

"Yeah. Except this stuff is illegal. It's been around since the late 90's and has been used as an ingredient in imitation ecstasy pills."

"How can that be? Didn't this stuff have to come through customs? It came from Europe, right? I sure hope I don't get in trouble for this," said Dave.

"I think this was a big mistake, so no one could really know we have this stuff. Anything they could find on the computer would show that we ordered MDPV; an unscheduled research chemical."

"Well, if everything is good to go, let's try this shit," said Dave.

"Alright, let's do it! Do you mind if I do mine my way?"

"How does Tim feel about that?" Dave looked at Tim.

"I've tried it that way too, and I kinda want to do it again," said Tim.

"Jesus, you kids are crazy."

"I'll go grab the supplies," Luke ran out to his car and came back with the junkie kit.

"You guys should do it in here," said Dave. "I want to see. You know, to make sure you're being safe and all."

"Alright then. Tim, can you grab me a glass of water?"

Dave was watching curiously. "None of this looks very sanitary," he said.

"That's the way we like it. Make's our immune system strong," said Luke.

"No, no, no. At least go wash your hands first," he saw Luke rolling up a piece of cotton between his dirty fingers.

Luke washed his hands; not for himself, but for Dave. He had two shots ready; one for himself and one for Tim. "I guess I'll go ahead and be the lab monkey," he held the syringe upright and flicked it so the bubbles went to the top. When he pushed all the air out of the syringe there was a drop of liquid at the tip of the needle. Dave freaked when Luke stuck the needle in his mouth to wipe off the droplet of MDPPP.

"Why the hell would you do that? Didn't you know that your mouth is the dirtiest part of your body?"

"Oh whatever," said Luke.

"I hope you're at least going to use an alcohol swab on your arm before you do that," said Dave.

"No way, dude," Luke had the point of the needle inches from his arm.

"Now just hold on! I've got alcohol swabs in the bathroom." Dave got up, went to his bathroom, and returned with a handful of individually packaged alcohol wipes. "Will you please do it? There's a reason they do it in hospitals. You should do it too."

"Oh god, fine." Luke took a wipe and cleaned off the injection site. "Okay, here we go," he took the shot.

"Is everything good?" Dave asked.

"Yeah, whoa," he almost puked. "Just gimme a minute."

After a minute Tim had to ask, "Dude, how is it?"

"Fuckin crazy! I could like… taste the chemicals fuming out of my mouth."

"Is it better than the other stuff?"

"Way better. The rush is, anyway."

"Hurry up and give me one. I wanna try," said Tim.

Luke sat up and tried to gather his senses. "This might be a little difficult since I just got my bell rung. You'd better tie off with something."

Dave went to his closet and came back with a shoe lace, "Will this work?"

"Sure," They tied up Tim's arm so his veins would show. "Alright, here we go." This time Tim didn't look away.

It hit Tim the same as it had for Luke. As he exhaled, he felt the ether fumes.

It seemed as if he could blow it into a balloon and save it for later. The rush was warmer, more comfortable than the MDPV.

Tim laid back on the bed in bliss. Dave gave an envious look, "Is it really that good?" said Tim. His eyes focused wide on the ceiling.

"Just give me a line already. I wanna get high too," he said.

Luke knelt down by the nightstand and scooped a small amount of powder onto the mirror, "What the hell?" the powder didn't lay out on the mirror like it should. He tried to scrape it into a line, but couldn't. "It's like some sort of reverse magnetism. It won't stay together." The pile kept pushing itself apart as Luke tried to keep it together.

"Isn't that strange," Dave looked close with his glasses.

Tim sat up, "What's doing reverse magnetism?"

"This powder, man. I can't make a good line out of it. It just separates from itself," said Luke.

"Why is it pink?" said Tim.

"I don't know, but it's fuckin cool." Luke fixed up a line as best as he could and told Dave to give it a try.

Dave snorted the line and ended in a zig-zag motion to get all the leftovers. "That stuff sure goes down nicely. Gives an interesting sensation to the nasal passage. I think you both should try."

"I don't see the point," said Luke, "but why not?" Luke went back to the mirror and tried to lay out a couple more lines.

"I think we need some drinks. You boys want a drink?"

"Sure," They both accepted.

~~~

Zuri got off work and texted Luke. She got a reply right away. *Of course he's at Daves. I wonder how fucked up he'll be this time.*

She sat in her car smoking a cigarette. She knew Luke would be high, but was still excited to see him. That was his business and she chose to accept it.

She made it to Dave's. Luke greeted her with affection. He'd been drinking. He was always drinking when he was with Dave. "How was your day?" he asked.

"Pretty good, I guess."

"Guess who raked in fifteen hundred bucks today? I did! We're moving into that house as soon as possible. I need you to arrange that. I want it in your name, not mine."

"Awesome. I'll call the guy tomorrow morning." This brightened her day. She hadn't expected Luke to get all the money he had been hoping for.

"I got more chemicals today, but they sent the wrong ones."
~~~

"So you're gonna stop getting high for a while?"

"No, this stuff is even better!"

"And by 'better' you mean worse?" she said.

"This stuff is totally awesome and completely illegal. I have no idea why they sent it to me!"

"Great," she said with sarcasm.

"It's weed smoking time, isn't it? Why don't we go smoke some weed?" They went to Dave's room and loaded Zuri's glass pipe.

Pretty soon Zuri was tired and ready to go home. She wasn't willing to try Luke's new drug.

"Do you need a ride anywhere, Tim?" said Luke.

"Naw, thanks man. I'm probably just gonna kick it here. Will you leave me a small bit of that stuff?"

"Yeah man. I owe you a half gram, remember?"

"Awesome, bro. Thanks," said Tim.

Luke weighed out a half gram of MDPPP before saying goodbye. "I'm outta here, guys. Talk to you tomorrow."

On the drive to Zuri's, Luke thought about his crazy day. He wasn't ready to sleep, but he was ready to spend some alone time with Zuri. *Life is good. Things are working out. The universe is conspiring to my success.* Luke's destiny was unfolding perfectly, and he wouldn't want it any other way.

Pleasure is very seldom found where it is sought.
-Samuel Johnson

Chapter 15: Nosey Neighbors

Wednesday 8-7-2010

"Should we unload this shit now?" asked Tim.

"No," said Luke, "I think we should try to clean this place up first."

"I think it's about time we get high," said Dave.

"No doubt." Luke, Tim, and Dave went into the house. They gathered in the filthy bathroom. Luke tried to be sanitary. It made Dave feel better. Luke prepared two clean syringes with MDPPP. He gave the first one to Tim.

Luke took his shot after injecting Tim. He stood up, paced a few circles and peeked out the window. Dave watched with envy as his friends enjoyed their energizing blast of chemicals. "Is it really that good you guys?"

"It is definitely that good," said Luke.

"The best," Tim confirmed.

"Do you have another clean one? I'd like to try it once myself," said Dave.

"There's plenty of clean ones, but there's no just trying it once. I'll tell you that right now," said Luke.

"Whatever. Just fix one up for me."

"You got it." Luke prepared another shot with shaky hands. Dave wiped off his arm with a fresh alcohol swab. "Ready?"

"Umm... yeah. Are you sure you can do this? Do I need to tie off with anything?"

"You're good. Just gimme your arm and look away if you're scared," said Luke.

"I'm not scared," Dave still looked away. Moments later, Dave experienced the first time rush he would remember for the rest of his life. Now he understood why Tim and Luke liked it so much. His brain recorded the message that this was goood; no need to fear the needle.

"You good?" Luke asked.

"Oh yeah... wow." He looked at his arm where Luke had injected.

They walked around the house trying to figure our what needed to be done. "This place is pretty fucked up," said Luke, "Look at this carpet."

"It can be cleaned up good," said Dave. "All of this can look good in no time. Especially with those drugs of yours."

"Well, lets get started. What do we do?"

"Do you have a shampooer? You'll need a shop vac too," said Dave.

"I don't got none of that," said Luke.

"Let's take a run back to town. I've got all the cleaning supplies you're gonna need."

~~~

Luke and Dave returned with a truck full of supplies. Tim had been appointed to watch over the house. "You guys took forever," said Tim.

"Sorry. Dave is having serious attention deficit problems," said Luke.

They brought the equipment inside and Dave assigned them jobs. "Tim, why don't you start clearing out the basement. Throw all the garbage in the dumpster. Organize everything that might be useful. Luke, start vacuuming the bedroom. I'll get the shampooer set up."

They got to work; sweat pouring and vacuums blaring. Tim was confused and distracted all by himself in the basement. There were so many boxes and random pieces of scrap wood. Dirt was layered so thick he could hardly see the concrete. People had used this basement to grow pot.

Three hours of hard work went by. No one drank a drop of water; no one was thirsty. The chemicals took away any desire for food or water, no matter how badly the body needed it.

Tim had the hardest job, carrying garbage up the stairs and out to the alley. Once he started getting drained from dehydration, he decided he needed more drugs. He went upstairs, "Luke, can we go do another one?"

"Yes we can." Luke turned off the vacuum cleaner and came out from behind
~~~

the refrigerator. He got Dave's attention and they went to the bathroom.

Luke made up three shots and gave the first two to his friends. Just as he finished injecting his own, there was a knock at the door. "Fuck!" Luke dropped the syringe on accident and knocked the spoon off the back of the toilet.

The front door opened, "Luke?" it was Alice. "Where are you?" In a panic, Luke grabbed the paraphernalia and crammed it into his pockets. He held back a scream when one of the dirty needles jammed into his thigh.

"I'll go distract them," said Dave. He knew Luke was still too overwhelmed to have conversation. The surge of drugs was too strong.

There were two exits to the bathroom; one to the kitchen, and one to the basement. Luke went down to the basement. Tim followed since he had taken his shot after Dave. Luke needed a few minutes to calm down and overcome his panic attack. He also took the time to stash all the illegal paraphernalia that was bulging out of his pockets.

When Luke was ready, he went upstairs to greet his parents. Tim stayed to fulfill his duties in the basement. "Luke, my sweet boy! I love your house," said Alice.

"You do?"

"Yeah. It's cute. Dave says you guys are gonna fix it up nice."

"Yeah. We'll get it cleaned up good."

"Are you going to show us around?" said Allan. He looked eager to help.

"Well, the carpets are all wet in the living room and the bedroom. I don't want any shoes on the carpet so that will have to wait. You can see most of it from here anyway. There's a nice walk-in closet in the bedroom."

Luke's parents leaned into the living room and peeked into the bedroom door. "Very nice," said Alice, "It's just you and Zuri living here?"

"Yep. She's at work right now. I'm trying to get this place clean before she gets home. The basement's a mess. Here, I'll show you." Luke gave them the tour of the bathroom and basement. Tim was down there smoking a cigarette and looking clueless.

"Hey Alice. Hi Allan."

"How's it goin, Tim?" said Allan.

"Pretty good. Just trying to figure out what to do with all this crap. I think someone used to grow weed down here. I even found some trimmings over in that corner."

"Speaking of weed," said Allan, "Have you smoked yet in the new house."

"No, actually we haven't," said Luke.

"Well, what do you say? Should we burn one?"

"Yeah, let's do it. We needed a break anyway." Luke ran out to his truck to grab a pipe.

When he came back down, Dave was hauling a stack of five gallon buckets. "Look what I found. These are useful." He set them down in a circle so everyone had a seat.

They smoked while having a stimulating conversation about plans for the house. Dave was a talkative person to begin with; Luke could tell he felt like a million bucks. Luke's parents were energetic people so their enthusiasm matched everyone else's.

Luke was fighting paranoia. He glanced at the windows to make sure no one was watching. He hoped it wasn't obvious; he hoped his parents didn't suspect.

They smoked an excessive amount of weed. Luke announced that it was time to get back to cleaning.

"We want to help," said Allan, "What do you need help with?"

"Well, the kitchen and bathroom are filthy. There's cleaning supplies in the kitchen."

"Alright, let's get to it!" said Allan. They all went upstairs; even Tim. He couldn't handle the lack of supervision in the basement. Instead, he helped Allan disinfect and clean the bathroom. Luke and Alice went to work on the kitchen. Dave went around oiling hinges and door knobs while making a list of things that needed fixed or replaced.

~~~

Zuri arrived around 9:30. She was amazed at all the work that was being done. *Is everyone here on drugs?*

"Hey girlfriend!" Luke greeted her at the door and gave her a kiss. "We been cleaning the crap out of this place."

"I can see that. It's looking good. Where's all my stuff at?"

"Still in the trailer. I wanted to do most of the cleaning before I brought everything in."

"Oh. Well, can I have some weed? I'm ready to get stoned."

"You certainly can. In fact, I think we all need to get stoned." Luke announced a smoke break and they all went to the basement.

"Why are we smoking in the basement? It's dirty and cold," she said.

"This basement is gonna be totally awesome." Luke put up an extra bucket for Zuri. "I love it down here; and you're gonna too when I get done with it."

"We'll see."

As they were smoking, Luke could tell Zuri was exhausted and wanted to relax in peace. Luke's parents decided it was time to leave.
~~~

Luke found his stash and they all raced up to the bathroom, leaving Zuri behind. *Wow, right on guys. Looks like he got his friends hooked on the evil crap too.* She took one more hit before heading up the stairs.

She grabbed the bathroom door handle at the top of the stairs. It was locked. "Luke, will you let me through?"

Luke opened it and re-locked it behind her, "Sorry."

"Why are you locking it anyway?" she said.

"It's a psychological thing. It makes me feel safe."

Zuri noticed three syringes on the back of the toilet, "You got your friends doing that shit too?" She unlocked the other door and went into the kitchen to search for the thermostat. Luke locked the door behind her.

Dave was giving Luke a puzzled look.

"I don't understand your situation here. She doesn't do drugs or even drink. You do *everything* and take it way beyond the extreme. Why is she with you?"

"Dude, I have no freakin idea. I warned her that I'm out of control. She insisted that it was fine. I guess she just loves me."

"That's a very strange relationship. I don't see how it can work," Dave said.

"It is pretty odd, but I love her. We don't got any secrets. She's so much different than Stacy, and I think that's why I like her so much. I trust her completely, and there's no weird mind games."

"Well, as long as you're happy," said Dave.

"Alright, who's first?" Luke held up one of the syringes.

~~~

Zuri had found the thermostat and cranked it up to eighty. She went into the bedroom and found nothing there. *This sucks.* She could hear Luke and his friends in the basement talking and banging stuff around. *I'm way too exhausted for all this. I need my bed.*

The bathroom door was locked. *Oh my god, stupid tweakers.* "Luke!" she knocked on the door.

Luke ran up the stairs and opened the door, "Hey, sorry."

"Can you help me get the bed and some of my other stuff?"

"Yeah sweetie, of course. Hey guys! Can you help bring stuff inside?"

They went out to the trailer and grabbed what they needed to grab. Luke had them set the boxes in the kitchen so no one had to walk on the carpet.

Tim helped Luke bring the mattress in. They took off shoes before stepping onto the carpet. Once the mattress was in place Luke noticed the dirty footprints going into the bedroom. "What the fuck! Who the hell walked on the clean carpet?"
~~~

Zuri was standing in the kitchen, "Sorry, I think I did."

Luke came out into the kitchen. "We spent a lot of time cleaning that carpet. I don't want any shoes in there. Once we get settled in, there will be no shoes anywhere in this house. It's gonna be like a Chinese persons house. It's gonna be nice, and we're going to keep it nice," he said.

"I'm really sorry. I'll clean it if you want."

"No, it's fine. I just want us to be on the same page here."

"Okay."

Luke felt bad about his freak out. This was Zuri's house too, and she looked like she just wanted to relax for the night. "I'll go ahead and take these guys home. When I get back I'll help set up the bedroom."

"Kay," she said.

"C'mon guys, let's bounce. You can come back and help tomorrow if you want."

"You're sleeping tonight?" asked Tim. "I don't know. Yeah. I'm gonna try."

"Can I buy a little bit of that stuff you got?" said Tim,

"No way! This shit is extinct. It's exclusive; a miracle, I even got it. I'm hangin onto it as long as I can."

"Oh Luke, don't be a stinge," said Dave.

"I'm not bein stingy. I'll share, but I'm not giving it away."

"I said I would pay for it," said Tim.

"It's not about the money. If it was anything but this PPP shit I would and you know it. Just come by tomorrow, we'll do as much as you want."

"Alright bro. I'm down," said Tim. They went out to the Suburban and took off.

~~~

Luke made it back as fast as he could. It took all of his effort to avoid distractions. Distractions had become a major obstacle since MDPV. "I'm home," he said as he walked through the door.

"Hi hunny. I got the bed all set up."

"That's awesome," he gave her a kiss, "the first night in our own house."

"Yep. Can we go to the bed now please?"

~~~

Forty minutes later it was cigarette time. Zuri lit her own; Luke didn't bother, he just took a few drags off hers. "Can we smoke a bowl?" she asked.

"We certainly can. I'm just gonna roll a quick joint."

After the joint, Luke threw on a pair of boxers and went to the bathroom. Zuri wanted him to hurry up and come back so they could fall asleep together.

It's been like ten minutes. There's no way he's getting high right now. Not right before bed; that would be stupid.

She couldn't take the suspense. She got up to look for him. She could see the light on under the bathroom door. "Luke? What are you doing?"

"Nothing. I'll be out in a minute."

She tried to open the door. It was locked. "Will you please open the door?"

"Shhh, hold on a minute," he said.

"You're not seriously getting high right now, are you?"

Luke opened the door, "Shhh! You don't need to say that so loud."

"Oh my god. You're out of your mind. So you're gonna stay up all night now?"

"No. Not all night, but there's some stuff I should get done before I go to sleep."

"You can get things done in the morning. I just want you to come to bed with me. Will you, please?"

Luke looked around at all the boxes; all the stuff that needed to be sorted out. Then he looked at Zuri. All she wanted was him, more than anything. "Yeah... let's go to bed," he said.

They went back to the bedroom and took off clothes before crawling into bed. "Are you sure you're gonna be able to go to sleep?" she asked.

"Yeah, I only did a small one. It might take me a while, but I'll fall asleep." He wasn't convinced of that, but he knew it's what Zuri wanted to hear.

She held him tight, "Mmmh, I love you."

"I love you too," he kissed her on the forehead.

~~~

Zuri woke up in an empty bed. There were voices coming from the kitchen. It sounded like Luke and Dave. She grabbed her phone and looked at the time. It was 8:30am. *What is Dave doing here so early? Probably just fiening out for those stupid chemicals.*

She got out of bed and put on some sweats and T-shirt before going to the kitchen. "What are you guys doing?"

Luke was standing in the entry while Dave was spreading some kind of chemical all over the floor with a mop. "Sealing the floor," said Dave. "It's gonna look real nice and will be much easier to keep clean."

"Why so early?" she said.

"Luke called me this morning. I'm always up early."

"Why are you up so early?" she looked at Luke, "I thought you were gonna go to sleep."
~~~

"I did go to sleep," he lied, "but I woke up way early. Someone decided to turn the thermostat up to eighty. I woke up sweating and couldn't go back to sleep."

"Oh. I think that was my bad. Sorry," she said:

"It's fine. We've been getting shit done this morning. Dave found us a lawn mower. Tim's out there about to get it started right now."

"Oh, wow. What are we doing for breakfast?" she said.

"I don't know. If you want anything, you'll have to drive somewhere. The kitchen is gonna be off limits for a few hours."

"Hmm, okay." She went back to the bedroom and lit up a cigarette. After a couple hits of weed she laid back down and fell asleep.

~~~

Dave had brought Luke his thirty grams of MDPV. "Once it gets to be a reasonable hour, I'm gonna have to make a run to Kalispell to sell some shit," said Luke.

"Well, I can stay here if you'd like. There's an endless amount of things that need to be done."

"Cool, that would be fine with me. I shouldn't take too long."

"The floor is all done. Now we just need to let it dry," said Dave.

"Time for a smoke break?" said Luke.

"Yeah, I think so." They went out the entry and sat on the concrete steps. Tim was texting and making phone calls. Luke had sampled the new batch of PV with his two friends, but wasn't going to sell it or front it out until he had it cut down to 50%.

Luke was surprised at the support from Tim. Even though Tim knew Luke was getting the chemicals cheap and diluting it down he didn't complain about the price. Tim was just happy to be a part of the operation. As long as Luke gave him the best price, he would be happy.

"So, are you sure this PV stuff is any good?" said Dave.

"Shh!" Luke looked around to make sure no one was listening.

"Oh c'mon. Even if people heard, they would have no idea what it means. It might as well be a foreign language, all these crazy acronyms; I can hardly remember any of it," said Dave.

"Yeah, I guess. You can never be too cautious though. But I do know what you mean about the PV. The rush isn't nearly the same; not as euphoric. No mouth vapors either. It is good though; the same as before. You've been talking a million miles an hour all morning. It's definitely working, but I do wish I could get more of the pink stuff," said Luke.
~~~

"The pink stuff is incredible. I don't see how it could get any better than that," said Dave.

"I gotta bounce," Luke closed his phone, "Tim, you coming with?"

"Yeah. When can I get some of that stuff?"

"I'm gonna go get it taken care of right now. I'll bring you with me."

They took off, leaving Dave to clean things up around the house.

~~~

Luke pulled up to Blue's tent, "Will you wait in the truck? I'm gonna try and get this done quick." He got out and went into the tent, leaving Tim in the Suburban.

"What's up, cuz? Bout time you came around," said Blue. "How much you got this time?"

"Got thirty grams."

"Why the multiples of ten? We don't use metric around here. We use that old English shit," said Blue.

"I don't know. My supplier gets his shit out of the country, I guess,"

"Hmm, and you're also gonna need to start getting more. Lots more. People want this shit bad, and no one's getting enough."

"I know it. I need to step it up, for sure," said Luke.

"And you're gonna have to come watch how I cut this shit. It should be your job, not mine," said Blue.

"Is it okay if I go in to your landlord's house?"

"Yeah, he's not around right now. Let's go," said Blue.

Luke came out to his truck $800 richer and with 32 grams of MDPV cut to perfection. They headed back to Kalispell, ready to do some business. "How much did you give him?" Tim asked.

"An ounce of the cut shit. I got thirty-two grams left. How much are you gonna want? I'm doin forty a gram for this shit," said Luke.

"That's exactly fifty percent pure?"

"Exactly. I helped do it myself."

"And you can front it to me?"

"Yep," said Luke.

"I guess I'll do ten grams if that's cool."

"Totally cool. We can get this situated right now." Luke turned off on a gravel road. He parked in a tall grassy spot.

"We should do a shot first," said Tim.

"We should do a shot after. I can't be weighing out chemicals when I'm looking for fake police," said Luke.
~~~

"Or we could just do the pink stuff. That stuff doesn't make me as paranoid."

"I'm saving the pink stuff. Someday you're gonna miss it, and I'm gonna have it," said Luke.

"Dude, I already miss it," said Tim.

"You'll thank me later." Luke got started weighing and bagging Tim's MDPV.

"Can you just weigh it out one gram at a time? Like... individually?" said Tim.

"Damn, dude. You're really gonna make me work for this shit?"

"Sorry. I want to get maximum profit. If people see I got more, they'll wanna buy more and expect a better price."

"I hear ya. It's no problem. I like where your head's at."

Luke took his time weighing each small bag to perfection, "Now you should be able to double your money, at least, and keep a gram or two to consume."

"Hell yeah, bro. That's awesome," said Tim.

"This is a good system we got. I'm doubling my money; you're doubling yours; and people below you could make money too. It's like the trickle down effect. Opportunity for everyone," said Luke.

~~~

Zuri woke up to the sound of a vacuum cleaner. *Oh what are they doing now?* She lit a cigarette and went to check it out. After walking through the bathroom, she found Dave in the back entry, digging around in an old cabinet. "Hey, Dave," she said over the sound of the vacuum.

Dave turned around and switched off the vacuum. "Hi Zuri, what's up?"

"Where's Luke?" she said.

"He had to make a run to Kalispell; said he would be back soon."

"Kay." She went back to the bedroom and picked up her cell phone. The vacuum switched back on as she left. *What is going on here? Why is Dave cleaning my house? Can't Luke hang out with me for just a couple hours before I go to work? He could have made his run to Kalispell after I left.* She dialed his number.

"Hello?" he answered.

"Hey, what are you doing?" she said.

"Just runnin some errands, trying to make some money."

"You know Dave is still here, don't you?"

"Yeah. He wanted to help. Is that okay?"

"I guess. It's just weird. I kinda hoped we could set up the house together."

"We can. I'll be home in an hour or two."

"It's already eleven. I have to be to work in a few hours."

"Just quit your job. Fuck it. Then we can spend the whole day together."
~~~

"I can't just quit. Not without a two week notice. What if I need to get a job again? And what if, for some reason, you stop making money."

"That's not gonna happen. We're in the business. I promise."

"Will you please just come home soon?"

"Yeah. I'll get there as soon as I can."

"I love you," she said.

"I love you too. See you soon."

She hung up the phone. *It would sure be nice to quit my stupid job. But life isn't that easy. You can't just live for free. What Luke's doing can't possibly last forever. That shit is gonna be illegal soon. It has to. Then Luke's gonna have to get a real job and we can live normal lives.*

~~~

Luke made it home at 1:00, way behind schedule. He walked through the front door. Zuri was in the kitchen stocking the cupboards with old plates and silverware that Luke's parents had given them. "Hey girly, sorry I took so long."

"Geez Luke, you can't just tell people you're busy?"

"It's a demanding job I've got. I need to maintain public relations, you see? It's an important part of the business."

"Well, I have to head to work in a half hour," she said.

"Oh please, will you just call in sick at least? It's our first full day in our new house," he said.

"Yeah, I guess I could."

"Good!" He grabbed her and gave a few kisses on the cheek. "We're gonna have so much fun today!"

"You look really high right now," she said.

"I'm high on life! Well... I have done an excessive amount of drugs today. That's part of the business as well," he said.

"It really doesn't have to be a part of your business. You could sell it without doing it."

"Well, don't you think the owner of Budweiser probably drinks Budweiser? I can almost guarantee he does. I need to endorse my product. It's just good salesmanship."

"Sure. Whatever you say. Now will you help me with this stuff? There's pots and pans and stuff in those boxes."

"Alright, let's get started here." Just then Dave came up from the basement.

"Hey Luke, you've got a problem with your ventilation. You should come check it out."

~~~

Twenty minutes went by and Zuri was beginning to wonder what had distracted Luke so badly. She walked down the stairs and saw Dave putting the furnace back together. Luke was in a dark corner of the basement on his tippy toes looking out a dirty window. "What are you doing?" she asked.

"Just checkin things out. We've got some very suspicious looking people around here. The same two strange guys and a little kid walked through the alley twice now. The guys were both bald with matching sunglasses. The kid looked out of place with them. It doesn't add up."

Zuri walked back up the stairs. *He's losing his mind. My boyfriend is going crazy. I might as well forget spending any time with Luke today.*

Twenty more minutes of window peeking went by before Luke went upstairs. He found Zuri in the bedroom and sat down next to her. "Can I get a couple drags?" he grabbed the cigarette from her hand, "Thanks." He took a drag and stared at his shaky hands.

Zuri grabbed his free hand and held it. "You're hands are freezing," she said.

"I'm not crazy," he looked at her with dilated pupils. "There seriously was two suspicious looking guys with a little kid. It didn't make sense, and they walked by twice. One of them looked right at me."

"You said they were wearing sunglasses. How would you know if he was looking at you," she asked?

"It looked like he was looking right at me. Or he was scoping out the property. Either way it's weird. Isn't it weird?"

"I don't know, probably not," she said.

"Two bald guys with matching sunglasses. With a kid, do you at least believe that I saw what I saw?"

"Sure, I believe you, but I don't think it's anything to be paranoid about. Probably just an ordinary kid with his dad and uncle or something."

"But they walked by twice," he pleaded.

"Maybe they were just going to the bank."

"Then why were they staring at me?"

"Maybe because they saw some weirdo staring at them through a basement window. Now they probably think some creeps moved into their neighborhood."

Luke tried to see it from her perspective; a sober person's perspective. "Alright. Maybe you're right. But if I see them again, I'm showing you. You wouldn't think I was over reacting if you saw it yourself."

"Okay, it's a deal. If you're not gonna smoke that can I have it back?"

"Oh, oops." He looked at the cigarette that was about to ash on the floor and handed it back.

She finished her cigarette. "Let's go get this house put together, shall we?" she said.

"Let's do it."

~~~

Around 5pm they had all their possessions organized in the house. "I'm so glad I didn't go to work today."

"Me too," said Luke. They sat at their makeshift kitchen table and passed the pipe around with Dave.

Zuri was texting between hits from the pipe. "Is it okay if Brittany, Lisa, and Steve come over?"

"Of course it is. It's time to celebrate! Tell Steve to bring some beer or something."

"Okay."

"I'm gonna go throw on some music." Luke plugged an I-pod into the boombox in the living room. *Let's see if I can piss off the neighbors.* "Tell Steve to bring some of that molly." Luke turned on a Dubstep mix at full volume. While he was in the living room he took a few glances out the window. *Where you at now, sunglass dudes? Using a child as a prop for disguise. Not foolin me. You'll have to do better than that.*

Luke went to the bedroom and found a blanket. He brought it to the kitchen, "Someone hold this for a second." Zuri held it, not knowing why. Luke ran to the basement and came back with a hammer and some nails.

"What are you doing?" Zuri asked.

"We need to put this blanket over the window."

"Why?"

"Because we don't have any blinds, and we will be doing lots of illegal shit in here."

Zuri reluctantly helped Luke. The blanket shut out all of the natural light in the kitchen. "Now it feels like we're in a cave," she said as she turned on the light.

"Caves are good. Caves are safe." Luke pulled out his pistol.

"Oh my god! Why was that thing in your pants?" she said.

"I don't know. Just forgot about it," said Luke.

"And why do you have it out now? Is this still about those two guys?"

"I'm just admiring it, damn. And it's definitely not about those two guys. I've totally forgotten about them," he went to the bedroom to stash the gun.

"Where'd you put that thing?" she said.

"In the closet," said Luke.
~~~

"Can you just sit still for a few minutes and smoke some weed? You're driving me nuts," she said.

"Sure." Luke sat down and picked up the pipe. "Is Steve and them on their way right now?"

"Yep," she said.

"I'd better go do one more shot. I don't want to have to do one when they get here."

"But you just did one! Just smoke some weed like a normal person," she said.

"I'll be just a minute. Dave, you want to join?"

"Sure do." They both retreated to the bathroom.

"Right on, guys," she said. "That's just awesome."

~~~

Zuri opened the bathroom door, "Hey guys, they're here." Luke was peeking out the bathroom window.

"Who's here?" said Dave.

"They're friends," said Luke, "It's cool. Just don't mention shooting up or MDPV. They don't know what it is and we want to keep it that way." Luke left the bathroom and Dave followed.

"Hey Luke!" Brittany gave Luke a hug. "I'm so happy you and Zuri got your own place together."

"Yeah, it is pretty awesome. Will you take your shoes off, please? I don't mean to be a Nazi, but I need you guys to take off your shoes. Thanks. I'll go grab some extra chairs." Luke came back with a couple lawn chairs from the living room. "Yeah. I know. It's white trash, but it's only temporary."

"Right on, bro," said Steve, "I think it's sweet." They all sat around the kitchen table with electronic music blasting from the living room. "Who does this song? It's fuckin sick."

"This would be Flux Pavilion. Tell me you brought the molly," said Luke

"Sure did. Do you got any more of that synthetic coke stuff?"

"Hell yeah! Let's do some freakin research, shall we?" said Luke.

"Yep. Research time. Does anyone have a nice mirror we could bring to the table?" said Steve.

"I found a good one in the basement," said Dave. "I'll be right back."

Dave came back up from the basement with a couple small rectangular mirrors. He wiped them off with a microfiber rag before setting them on the table.

Steve pulled out a bag of methylone and another bag of a more crystalline substance. "What's 4-MEC?" said Luke.
~~~

"It's that M-CAT shit you find at raves and shit. It's also called mephedrone. Speaking of raves, there's some going on in Missoula tomorrow. I was wondering if you would want to go."

"Yeah, sure. I'd go. Who's all going?" said Luke.

"Well, my best friend's girlfriend wants to go. I wanted to see if I could find us a ride."

"That's cool. I'll drive. Is it just you two?"

"Might have a couple other people with us also," said Steve.

"Right on. Bring as many people as you want. As long as there's room for Zuri. You're coming too, aren't you?" he asked, Zuri.

"Umm… I'm not sure," she said.

"What's not to be sure about? It's gonna be lots of fun. Eat some drugs, do some dancing?"

"Yeah, I'm not really into all that. But I don't care if you go. Don't let me stop you."

Steve busted up some shards of 4-MEC and Luke lined up some MDPV. They smoked, drank, and snorted as much as they desired. Zuri was a good sport; she talked and had fun even though all she did was weed.

The drugs kicked in and the music escalated. For Luke, this represented complete freedom. *My own house*, he thought, *I can do whatever I want. Easy money; unlimited drugs; I hope it lasts forever!*

~~~

Time flew by. Luke felt great even though he hadn't consumed MDPV for many hours. He was about to swallow another capsule of methylone, "Luke, haven't you had enough of that stuff?" said Zuri.

"I don't know. Why?" he said. The music was still loud and everyone was still engaged in conversation.

"You're going to sleep tonight, aren't you?"

"Should I?" he said.

"I wish you would. You're gonna be gone tomorrow night. I want some time with you tonight; without you being high."

"Okay. We can do that. When should we get everyone outta here?"

"It's already midnight," she said.

"Crap, that sucks." Luke got up and turned down the music. "Alright everyone, sorry to be the party pooper, but everyone's gotta get outta here," he saw all the dilated pupils and could tell they were in party mode. They got up and took their time saying goodbye.

"You want me to swing by tomorrow?" asked Dave.
~~~

"Sure man. Just gimme a call," said Luke.

"See ya tomorrow, Luke," said Steve.

Brittany hugged Zuri and Luke, "Bye guys; thanks for having us over."

Soon Zuri and Luke had the quiet house all to themselves. "This is nuts," said Luke. "The music is off but I can still hear it playing in my head."

"You've eaten way too many drugs, and that music is probably scrambling your brain."

"It's good to scramble the brains once in a while," he said.

"Yeah, but you scramble your brains every single day," she said.

He shrugged, "Oh well."

"Let's go to bed already," she grabbed his hand and took him to the bedroom.

"Okay, but don't expect me to fall asleep anytime soon."

"That's fine, because I'm going to need you for a while." She started kissing him and they fell onto the bed together.

I've learned that people will forget what you said, people will forget what you did, but people will never forget how you made them feel.
-Mark Twain

Chapter 16: Zoo Town

Friday 8-9-2010

Zuri woke up. Luke was in a dead sleep and had not moved an inch. They were tangled together in a comfortable knot. She didn't want to move; didn't want to risk waking him up. He needed sleep. *He also needs food,* she noticed how skinny he was getting. *He must have lost at least ten pounds since we've been together, and he was skinny to begin with. I need to make sure I have breakfast ready before he gets up. Can't have him getting high before he eats.*

At 11:30 she decided to try and wiggle her way out of Luke's arms. It wasn't what she wanted to do. She would stay right there forever if she could. It seemed like it was becoming more and more rare to have Luke in one spot for any length of time. The most important thing was to make sure he had food before he started getting crazy.

~~~

Luke woke up to the smell of bacon and weed. "Here you go, hunny," she handed him a plate.

"Oh, wow," he said as he sat up out of his coma-like sleep. "Thank you," He wasted no time. Luke felt like a starving Ethiopian. Each bite felt like it was full
~~~

of life. Zuri sat next to him and continued smoking weed. She tried to hand him the pipe. "I think I'm good for right now," he set the pipe down and started to get out of bed.

"Will you please smoke with me?" she said.

"I really don't feel up to it. I need to do something first, then I can smoke," he went to the closet and closed the door behind him.

Zuri took the dishes to the kitchen and finished smoking weed. She looked at the closet with disgust.

"I'm dying!" Luke ran out of the closet holding his chest and jumped into the bed next to Zuri.

"What do I do? Should I take you to the hospital?"

"I'm having a heart attack! I'm dying for sure. I love you. I'm sorry."

Zuri ran to the bathroom with tears. She grabbed some aspirin and ran back to the room. "Eat these! Chew em up!"

Luke started chewing. She handed him a glass of water. He swallowed it down. He laid there hyperventilating, feeling an incredible amount of regret. *I'm going to hell. I should have been a better person. What are my parents going to think?*

"You're gonna be fine, just control your breathing," said Zuri.

"Look at my fucking heart! Why is it doing that?"

Zuri could see his heart beating through his shirt. "Just take deep breaths," she said.

"It hurts. If I breathe too deep it feels like my heart is gonna explode!" he said.

"The aspirin is gonna get into your system any minute. People survive heart attacks all the time because of aspirin."

"Are you sure?" he said.

"Yes, I'm sure. You're gonna be fine."

"I'm done doing that stuff. I'm stopping for good."

"I hope so," she said.

"Never again. I promise."

~~~

"I should probably get going to work," said Zuri, still laying with Luke on the bed. It had been a couple hours since Luke had taken his reckless injection.

"Alright then," he squeezed her tight, "I love you, sweetie."

"I love you too." She gave him a long kiss. "Be safe." She got up and headed out.

I will be safe. He smoked some weed. *I'm lucky to be alive. Poor Zuri. I almost just died right in front of her. Since I survived, I might as well get up and enjoy the rest of my high.*
~~~

Luke went to the fridge and cracked open a beer and lit a cigarette. The cigarette had no appeal, but he smoked it anyway out of habit. *I should invest in some air filters. There's gonna be a lot of smoking in this house.*

He went back to the closet and sat down in his office chair. His lap top sat on a low shelf that worked as a desk. The drug paraphernelia was on the shelf above it, right where he had left it.

He turned up the music on his lap top and took a drink from his beer. Atmosphere was playing:

Bikers in the basement dirty and nervous,
Tryin measure out the right amount of laundry detergent.

A drag from the cigarette. The needle and spoon were appealing. He looked at his arm; the track marks were looking bad. Any person with a lick of sense would know what he'd been up to.

There's enough residue in that spoon for at least two more shots. I should just quit after I've finished what I've started there.

He put out the cigarette and picked up the syringe. *Just doin a rinse; no biggie.* Luke filled the syringe with thirty units of water and squirted it into the spoon.

Once it was ready, he held the syringe against the light. It was yellow, but not as dark as his previous shot. *With all that aspirin in my system I could probably survive any shot.* He took it with no hesitation.

Pupils dilated; blood vessels constricted; his heart pounded, but not as painfully as before. Something bad was about to happen. He turned the music off and grabbed his gun with safety off. He could hear the refrigerator humming; a clock ticking; a car drove by slowly; too slow; there were voices outside; radio static. Any second the door would be kicked down; Luke was certain of it. He was too scared to go check. He was too scared to move; too scared to breathe, in fear that whoever was after him would hear. All he could do was listen. He crouched in the corner of his closet with the gun pointed at the door.

What if they do come storming in? I've only got seven bullets in this tiny ass clip. I'd probably just fire em all off in a panic, then get fuckin smoked. I wish I had a bigger gun, at least an extra clip.

Something caught his attention. A silhouette of a person went past the bedroom window He adjusted his sights; ready to shoot if they decided to come crashing in through the glass. *Oh fuck, I can't die today; my soul is tainted. I'll go straight to hell! I need to live so I can fix my soul. I'll kill them all! That's my only hope.*

Luke listened closely. He heard more radio static followed by voices: "We've got a ten-eighteen in progress. Requesting backup."

Luke waited in the closet; muscles tense and sweating. His pistol was aimed at the window, ready for the head shot as soon as they came flying in. Every shot would have to count, then he would have to take guns from the dead cops. The whole scenario played out over and over in his head.

I hope they bust in here without a warrant. Just try it you stupid fucks. See what happens.

What if they're not even real cops? Maybe they're the research chemical people, here to check up on their lab monkeys. They might not even have to abide by normal police protocol. They make their own rules, like the CIA or some other kind of secret police; the lab-monkey police. They're trying to keep tabs on whoever is consuming their chemicals.

Hours went by. Luke's phone would vibrate in the bedroom. *Probably a diversion.*

Another hour went by. *They want me to lose focus. Not happening.* Luke was getting fatigued and dehydrated. His ass was numb and his arms were tired from holding the pistol. The pistol was now resting on his knee, still pointed at the window with his finger on the trigger. His vision was blurring from staring down the sights for so long.

What the fuck! When are they gonna make a move? Maybe they're not here to intervene. Maybe they just wanted to observe; maybe set up some bugging devices.

Luke finally gathered the courage to investigate. With the pistol in hand, he came out of the closet and peeked out the window. There was nothing but an empty alley. He checked every other window in the house. Nothing strange.

One more precaution. He threw on a sweater and stuffed the pistol in his waistband before going outside. A walk around the block convinced him that everything was safe. *If anyone was here, they're gone now.*

~~~

Luke pulled up to Steve's in his Chrysler. Dubstep music was blasting as usual. "What's up, bro?" said Steve.

Luke came inside. Two girls were drinking and dancing in the living room. "There he is!" said one of the girls, "We thought you were gonna bail on us."

"Yeah, sorry. I kinda got stuck. Got way too high," said Luke.

"High on what? With who?" she said.

"High on some weird shit. All by myself. It was a bad scene," said Luke.

"I like weird stuff. Do you have any more?" she said.

"Sure," he handed a capsule to each of the girls. "It's a kind of stimulant. A research chemical. An analog of MDPPP," he said.

"Sounds good to me. Can you snort it?" she said.

"Wait," said Steve, "did you just say MDPBP?"

"No. MDPPP," said Luke.
~~~

"Hmm, we used to use MDPBP, PMA and some other shit when I was into pressin ecstasy pills."

"I've got some MDPPP also, but I didn't bring it since it is illegal," said Luke.

"How'd you get that shit?" said Steve.

"I have no idea. Some laboratory supply company in Europe accidentally sent it to me. I can't get anymore. I've tried. No one will give it to me."

"That's crazy, bro. Can I get one of those?" said Steve.

"Sure man." Luke handed him a capsule. The girls were already snorting theirs. Steve did the same. Luke figured he might as well do one, too.

One girl introduced herself, "Hey, my name's Jaime by the way."

"And I'm Erica," said the other.

"Right on. I'm Luke." Steve handed him a beer. "Thanks dude." Luke cracked it open and chased down a capsule of MDPV. "Should we smoke a bowl?"

"Yes please!" said Erica, "Steve says you have the best weed. I tried some of that Afgan Goo. That shit was bomb!"

"Nice. Yeah. I only brought the New York Diesel with me this time." Luke grabbed a bubbler from the table and loaded a fresh bowl. He took the first hit and passed it around.

"You want to eat some more of that M-CAT?" said Steve.

"I would totally like to eat some of that," said Luke.

~~~

Soon they were entering Missoula. Erica helped Luke navigate to a secluded parking lot in the city. "We'll be able to walk from here," she said.

They took their time in the parking lot. "Everyone should take another one of these." Steve held out his hand; everyone took a capsule. Luke guzzled some water and took a capsule.

It was a ten minute walk. The party had just started and the line was long. Erica was already being greeted by people who knew her. It seemed like her natural environment, except that everyone called her 'Pepper' instead of Erica. After a short conversation with a couple other girls, she whispered to Luke, "So, everyone here thinks my name is Pepper. Don't use my real name."

"Okay sure."

At the front of the line they had to show ID. Green bracelet for 21 and up; red for 18-20. Jaime and Erica were surprised to see Luke with the red one. "You're not 21 yet?" said Jaime.

"No. Only eighteen. Still just a kid."

They entered the club and were overloaded with rave music and crazy lights. Luke lost control and went bouncing into the crowd.
~~~

The place was hot with all the crazy X'd out ravers. Everyone was on drugs and didn't care who was watching. Most people had outfits. Girls wore anything from skimpy fairy costumes to pink spandex. Guys could be found wearing similar garb, including Hello Kitty backpacks and tutus.

Luke was pulled out of his trance by Erica. She grabbed his hand and dropped something into his palm and closed it. Luke took a peek. There were three pills; red, blue, and purple. He made his way to the nearest water fountain and swallowed his pills. He had the familiar empty butterfly feeling in his stomach that would happen when he ate excessive amounts of drugs.

Luke realized how shifty his vision was. Even though he was all sweaty, he still felt cool and silky. He made his way back into the crowd, not wanting to waste a minute.

~~~

An hour of non-stop bliss went by before Luke was interrupted. Erica found him bouncing with his hands in the air by a set of speakers. She grabbed his hand and pulled him away so he could hear her. "There's an afterparty later. Are you down?" she said.

"Hell yeah I'm down!" he said.

"Cool. We probably won't get back to Kalispell till really late," she said.

"That's cool. I can stay up all night and I'll be good to drive, no problem."

"Awesome! You're awesome, Luke."

"You're freakin awesome!"

~~~

The time flew by. Before long, some party pooper came up to the DJ and told him it was time to shut down. The dancing stopped as soon as the music cut out. People were disappointed.

Everyone was herded out of the club. Some went out the front and some went out the back. Luke saw Jaime and followed her out the back. There was a large crowed of people who were forced out but did not know where to go. Luke found his crew socializing with people.

Luke lit a cigarette; the first he had smoked since arriving in Missoula. It was completely satisfying; the first cigarette he actually craved since MDPV. He felt good, relaxed, and free. "Hey guys," said Erica, "This is my friend Luke. He drove us here."

"Hey man! It's good to meet you. I'm Jimmy," one of the guys shook Luke's hand vigorously.

"Right on, dude. It's good to meet you, too," said Luke.

"You're all coming to the party? That's awesome! I think we're gonna be heading out any minute." Something caught Jimmy's attention and he walked off.

Luke talked with Jaime and Steve while smoking his cigarette.

Everyone seemed to know Erica, but no one called her by her real name.

"Alright, guys, we're following these people," said Erica. A chunk of the crowd was breaking off and heading out of the alley. Luke and his friends went with them.

Two friendly guys started talking to Luke. They asked him where he was from since they hadn't seen him around before. Luke asked them about their life in Missoula; they were doing college like many other young people in the area. "So, do you guys do these raves every weekend?"

"Pretty much, yeah," said one of the guys.

"That's freakin sweet, dude. We don't got these kind of raves in Kalispell. This place is awesome, I should live here."

"It's a lot of fun. And there's lots of good drugs."

"Man, that's sick. Not a lot of good shit comes through Kalispell. There's too many tweakers, not enough of the hippie raver type. That's kinda what I am, if I could be classified. At least that's what I thought I was. Lately it feels like I been slipping off the deep end into something else," said Luke.

A small girl, decked out in glowing accessories, handed a joint to the guy. He took a hit, then handed it to Luke. "You look really familiar," Luke said to the glowy girl.

"Yeah, I think we went to school together," she said.

"We did, but I don't think we've ever really talked to each other. I'm Luke, anyway."

"I'm Alley," she took the joint and went over to a different part of the group.

"That's nuts," said Luke. "I totally went to school with her. I wish I would have made more friends in school. I never paid any attention to people in school. School was a trip for me."

The two guys were still walking on each side of Luke. They were rolling hard on ecstasy. Luke could feel the love radiating from them. "Man, this is a lot of fun," Luke told them, "I love you guys. We're going to remember this for the rest of our lives, aren't we?"

"It is one of those nights."

The rest of the walk went great. Cops passed suspiciously, but didn't get crazy. Erica introduced Luke to more of her friends. Steve was quiet with Jaime flirting around with all the guys, including Luke.

They made it to the house. Luke squeezed between people on the couch and loaded a bong. "Is this cool? Is it alright if I do this?" No one objected, so he lit the bong and sent it into rotation.

Two beautiful girls were singing and dancing to the music. Vicks vapor rubs were a common item. Luke had them shoved in his face multiple times throughout the night.

Erica's loud voice could be heard from the kitchen. Luke got up to explore. "Hey buddy!" Erica gave Luke a hug and handed him a pipe. "My new buddy Luke, he's way cool," she announced.

Luke sat down next to one of the guys he'd walked with. He noticed a line of white powder on the kitchen table.

"Do you want it?" the guy asked.

"I totally want it. What is it?" said Luke.

"MDA."

"I freakin love you, man." Luke snorted the line and felt the pain.

"You want another?" the guy asked.

"Seriously?" said Luke.

"Hell yeah, man."

"Well, it would be a sin to turn it down," said Luke. The guy scraped out another line and handed a rolled up twenty to Luke. "You're very generous," Luke said before snorting the line.

When Luke looked up he saw the other kid he had walked with earlier. He was standing behind the kid with all the MDA. They looked at each other, then leaned in and started kissing. "Holy smokes," Luke said quietly.

The kissing became passionate. The kid grabbed the other's hand and pulled him out of the chair. They started to leave the kitchen with a purpose.

Now that was weird, Luke thought as he stared at the rolled up twenty in his hand. "Oh shit!" Luke got up to follow them.

The two guys were almost into a bedroom when Luke caught their attention. "Hey dude," Luke held out the twenty.

One kid smiled at the other, "Do you care if he joins us?"

"Whoa," said Luke, "What? No, man. Here's your twenty."

"You can join if you want," said the other kid.

"I'm good. Thanks though." The kid took the twenty and went into the bedroom with his friend.

Luke made his way to the front entry where cigarette smoking was acceptable. He opened the door, "Whoah, hey Pepper. Do you mind if I smoke?"

Erica was straddling and making out with some guy on a futon.

"Oh Luke, I'm doing bad. I shouldn't be doing this right now."

"I don't know what to say. Should I leave?" said Luke.

"No! I need you to talk some sense into me," said Erica.

"I don't know what to say. I hardly know you. I mean, I know you have a boyfriend, right?"

"I do have a boyfriend, and I have two kids with him."

"But I love you, Pepper," said the stranger on the futon. "I've always loved you. I promise he doesn't love you like I do."

"I'm just gonna go outside," said Luke. Luke went and sat on the front steps. He waved his cigarette around and noticed the tracers. His hands looked like they were vibrating; jaw muscles tensed and stomach tightened. *Wow, what a beautiful place.* The street lights sparkled with a magical light. Electronic music still bounced around in his head along with flashy lights.

That cigarette was the most enjoyable cigarette he'd ever had. He paid full attention to each drag. He had an intense desire to socialize.

A car turned onto the street. The shiny piece of technology started to resemble a cop car. It creeped by suspiciously. *Nothing to fear,* thought Luke, *probably just another beautiful human being in there. A beautiful human being with a twisted desire to subjugate people. That's your thing, I have no room to judge.* Luke stared at the technological miracle as it passed. *Amazing. Look at what our species has created.*

Luke stood up and went inside. Erica was not in the entry, but an abandoned bra was on the futon where she had been. Luke walked into the house and was engulfed by an ocean of positive energy. He felt so silky and perfect; everyone was perfect.

Two gorgeous girls were making out on the couch. *Now that is sweet.*

There was an inviting weed session happening at the same time. Jaime made room for him and he sat down next to her. "Luke, how are you?" She gave him a hug and kissed him on the cheek.

"I'm totally awesome. This is like the best time of my life right now," he said.

"Isn't it? I freakin love you," she said.

"I freakin love you too!" Luke noticed Steve on the other side of Jaime. He looked angry. "What's up, man? Is everything okay?"

"No. Everything is not okay," said Steve.

"What's wrong?" said Luke.

"I need to get Erica out of here."

"Why? What's happening?"

"She's in one of these bedrooms with some guy. Her boyfriend is my best friend and I promised him I would take care of her. I'm fucked. He's gonna be so fuckin pissed at me," said Steve.

"Damn, dude. That's no good. What are we gonna do?" said Luke.

"We need to get her out of there and leave."

A bong was handed to Luke. He took a big hit and held it as long as he could. "Well, let me know when it's time to bounce. I'll be ready whenever." Luke got up to find other people to mingle with. He didn't want to leave. The night was still young. *What time is it anyway?* Luke pulled out his phone to check, but the screen was overwhelmed with missed calls and unread messages.

(From Zuri): Hey how it goin?

(From Zuri): Did you make it to missoola yet?

(From Zuri): Why won't you answer my calls?

(From Zuri): Im worried. Plz call back.

(From Zuri): I hope everything is okay. I guess I'm gonna try and sleep now. Call as soon as u get this. I love you.

Poor girl. How could I not feel my phone vibrate? I guess my whole body has been kinda vibrating all night. He called her.

"Hey," she whispered as if she had been sleeping.

"Sorry, I have no idea how I missed your calls."

"Where are you?" she said.

"Still in Zoo town. We're at some afterparty."

"When are you coming home?"

"As soon as I can. We're trying to find Steve's friend. As soon as we find her we're leaving."

"I love you," she said.

"I love you too, sweetie. So much. Do you want me to wake you up when I get home?"

"Yeah," she said.

"Okay, I'll see you then."

Luke hung up the phone and felt relief. Before long, Luke was distracted into a conversation with a group of strangers.

~~~

"Hey bro, let's get outta here," said Steve.

"Oh wow. Okay." Luke had been having a spiritual conversation over beer and weed in the kitchen. "Well guys, good talk. It's been a pleasure," Luke told his new friends.

"Later bro. Hope to see you around."

They left the house and walked down the quiet street. Luke lit a cigarette, "I hope you guys know where we're going because I have no idea where we are."

"I know where we are," said Steve.
~~~

"Me too," said Jaime.

There were some bad feelings and Luke could feel it. "Hey guys, I think we had a great night. Even though Erica-can I call you Erica?"

"Yeah. My name's Erica," she said.

"Even though Erica made some bad choices, I think we all had a good experience here. And Steve, you can't blame yourself for what happened. Your buddy trusted you to bring Erica to Missoula and keep her safe. You couldn't stop her from doing what she did."

"Yeah. I don't know, man," said Steve.

"Well did you guys know that the Chinese use the same character for disaster as they do for opportunity? It's the same freakin word! Every disaster is also an opportunity. Maybe we could learn something from the experience." Luke put his arms around Steve and Erica as they walked. "Did you learn anything from what happened tonight, Erica?"

"I don't know. I feel like shit. I might have just thrown away my family for what I did tonight. Steve's gonna tell Dan what happened and my whole life's gonna be screwed up," she said.

"You're gonna tell?" Luke asked Steve.

"I don't know, man. He's my best friend. Someone's gotta tell him," said Steve.

"I know none of this is really any of my business, but I'll stop prying if you guys want. I just don't like seeing you all bummed out. I like to help if I can."

"You're doing good, Luke," said Steve. "You can't fix the situation, but it helps to talk about it."

"You're a cool kid," said Erica. She rested her head on Luke's shoulder and gave him a hug.

"Can I make one more suggestion? Everyone needs to stop. We need a group hug. Jaime, get over here. It'll be therapeutic."

Steve had not been a part of many group hugs. "Alright, I guess we're doing this," he said.

"I love you guys," said Erica.

"Awesome," said Luke, "I feel the love. This is good." They hugged it out for thirty seconds. "Did it work? Do we all feel better now?"

"I feel better," said Jaime.

"Me too," said Erica.

"Good!" said Luke, "Because I was not about to let us have a sad drive home."

"Can I have a cigarette?" said Erica.

"Sure," said Luke.

"Can I have one too?" said Steve.

"I only got a few left, so we're gonna have to do the community cigarette thing. But it's okay; they're American Spirits, so they last forever."

~~~

They made it to the Chrysler without incident. "Holy smokes!" said Luke. "Is it seriously six already? The cops won't even be prowling at this hour."

"These cops prowl at all hours. Just drive good," said Steve.

"Dude, I always drive good, I systematically obey every traffic law. I'm like a freakin pro at fucked up driving."

"Hope so," said Steve.

"The first precaution we must take is to throw all the illegal shit in the glove box," said Luke.

"Isn't your registration in there? You do have all that stuff, don't you?" said Steve.

"Woah dude, I definitely got all that stuff, and it's definitely not in the glove box. We're squared away, bro."

Steve handed up his bag of capsules. "This stuff is technically illegal if it's in capsules since capsule indicate it's for human consumption."

"Good to know," said Luke, "Any pipes, weed, roaches?" The girls dug through their purses and handed up an assortment of paraphernalia.

Before Luke put away his remaining capsules he asked if anyone else wanted one, "Anti-sleeping chemical?" Everyone wanted one. "One for you; one for you; one for you; and two for me, since I'm driving and need to be super focused. In fact, I'm gonna snort one of these for quick absorption." Luke grabbed a CD case out of the center console and scraped out a line.

They headed out. The ecstasy effects gave Luke great appreciation for his vehicle; his mechanical miracle. *I'm sure happy to have this old, reliable piece of technology.* He admired all the pretty lights and gauges. *All of these pieces of metal; all these moving parts working in perfect harmony, with intelligent creatures maneuvering it all.* Luke felt like he was a part of the vehicle; the vehicle and him were one.

~~~

Once they were safely out of the city, Luke turned up some tunes. Some mellow rap by Atmosphere; a perfect jam for winding down the night.

"Luke, do you have any more weed?" said Erica.

"I've got enough for one more bowl." He handed over the key to the glove box.

They savored their last bowl and reminisced over the night. "Man, what was up with all those Vicks vapor rub things? I got so many of those things shoved in my face," said Luke.

"It's a rave thing. It's supposed to feel really awesome on ecstasy," said Erica.

"Did you guys see Jill fingering that girl in the living room?" said Jaime.

"That was hot!" said Erica.

"Are you serious?" said Luke, "I got stuck seeing dudes make out when that shit was going on?"

~~~

As the drive went on it started getting quiet in the back. Luke and Erica had good conversation up front while sharing cigarettes. "You need to meet my boyfriend. I can tell by the way you talk about all your chemicals, you would get along great. He's kind of a genius when it comes to all that stuff."

"That's way badass. I really had no idea people were into that stuff until recently. It's pretty amazing, really," said Luke.

"It is. There's so many new chemicals coming out these days," she said.

"Yeah I bet. I only know of a few. I've got a lot to learn about it all still."

"You'll definitely learn something if you spend some time with my boyfriend."

Luke turned up the volume. *Someone is definitely doin something sexual in my back seat.* Luke and Erica talked and shared cigarettes for the rest of the drive.

~~~

Luke made it home around eight in the morning. He crawled on all fours over Zuri, "Hey sweetie, I'm home."

Zuri opened her eyes and looked up at Luke. "Oh my god, what time is it?" She noticed the window showing daylight.

"Like eight or something. Sorry I took so long. It was hard to find Steve's friend. She was in some bedroom with some dude and wouldn't come out."

Zuri reached up and pulled Luke down to her. Luke crawled in the sheets and held her tight. "You didn't do anything bad, did you?"

"What do you mean?" he said.

"You smell like girls," she said.

"I danced with some girls, but I definitely didn't do anything else with any girls. I wouldn't do that to you, I promise," he said.

"I hope so. Because that's pretty much the worst thing you could ever do to a person."

"Don't you worry about that. I care about you too much."

"I love you," she said.

"I love you too, sweetie," he gave her a kiss. She kissed back. One thing led to another and the kissing turned to passionate morning love making.

The junk merchant does not sell his product to the consumer, he sells the consumer to his product.
-Terence McKenna

Chapter 17: Out of the Closet

Saturday 8-10-2010

Luke woke up. *Fuck, I wasn't supposed to fall asleep. 6pm? What the fuck?* He went to the closet and closed the door.

He was about to inject when the door flew open. "Hey, what-oh, sorry," said Zuri. The syringe flew out of his hand and stuck in the carpet.

"Thanks for scaring the shit out of me. That was my last clean one," he said.

"Sorry, I just got home. Just got all our laundry done at your mom's house."

"You were at my mom's?"

"Yeah. She stopped by earlier. You were sleeping. She said we could do our laundry over there any time," said Zuri.

"You should have woken me up or something. I had lots of stuff I needed to do today," he said as he examined his ruined needle.

"I took the day off so we can do something fun today," she said.

"I don't know how much time I have to have fun today. People need me. If I would have been up earlier we could have done something fun together." Luke was digging through a bag of old needles trying to find one that wasn't too dull.

"People need sleep, you know. You can't just skip sleep all the time and expect to live," she said.

Luke felt weak and was sore all over. His brain craved the wicked chemical.

"That's disgusting!" she said, "Are you seriously using that thing? It has old nasty blood in it!"

"Well, I don't have a fuckin choice," he sucked up clean water into the dirty rig and squirted it into an old beer can. He repeated the process before filling it with drugs.

"Ew ew ew," Zuri watched as Luke brought the point to his arm.

"You don't have to watch. In fact, you're making me uncomfortable," he said.

"I'm sorry. It's just really weird. I wanna see."

Luke straightened out his arm and took the shot. His skin went hot and he breathed the ethery vapor. He put his hands above his head like he was out of breath. "Are you okay?" she asked.

"Good."

"Why do you do that?"

"If I don't, my armpits will start stinking immediately."

"That's weird. That stuff makes you smell nasty."

"I don't care." Luke stood up with wide eyes and dilated pupils. "I gotta go. I got things to do. I'd better get to it," he left the closet and started checking his phone.

"Can't you just take a day off? Why can't we spend the day together?" she asked.

"Because people have lots of money for me. All I need to do is bring them their shit." Luke texted at lightning speed and licked his lips in concentration while pacing the room. "I need to weigh some bags. Will you help me with that?"

"Yeah." She followed him to the closet. He weighed out piles of powder and dumped them onto pieces of paper for her to funnel into baggies.

"So, how much are each of these baggies worth?" she said.

"One forty. Three point five grams each."

"Oh my god! How much does one of these bags cost you?"

"Like fifty bucks maybe," he said.

"Are you serious? That's crazy. Why don't people buy their own on the internet," she said.

"I have no idea, but I'm gonna keep selling it like this until they figure it out." Luke threw all the bags into a Crown Royal bag. He stuffed the bag into a paper sack with all of his weed. "Alright, I'm gonna bounce."

"Where are you going? Can I come with?" she said.

"No, I don't think that would be good. I like to do this stuff alone."

"Please? I don't have anything to do today. And I took the day off so we could spend some time together," she followed Luke around as he tried to gather everything he needed. *Cellphone; cigarettes; wallet; cellphone; scale; keys; jacket, which jacket? Hat; lighter; knife; gun; keys; we're good to go.*

Luke was about to head out the front door when Zuri grabbed his arm, "Luke, please," she had tears in her eyes. "If you leave, I know I won't see you again tonight. Just take me with you, I won't get in the way."

"Oh Jesus, you need more friends. Don't you have any friends to hang out with?"

"I'll hang out with other people tomorrow if you want. I just want to be with you today," she said.

"Fine. I guess it will be okay. Just don't make things difficult for me," he said.

"I won't," she hugged him and they left the house together.

~~~

After many stops they headed to Debora's. It was 12:30pm. "This is probably gonna be the last stop for the night. This chick doesn't know you, so don't get weird or anything," said Luke.

"I haven't been weird all day, but I can wait in the car if you want," she said.

"No way. That would be weird. I'm probably gonna do a shot with her. She usually wants to, so don't make any fuss about it."

"C'mon Luke. Don't worry."

"Kay." Luke drove into Debora's trailer court. "Can you grab that stuff out of the glove box?"

"Just the Crown Royal bag?" she said.

"Yeah, and throw the triple beam in there too," he said.

"Sure." She gathered everything and put it in her purse. Luke parked in front of Debora's and shut off the car.

They both got out. Luke locked the door and they went to the front door. Debora answered, "Hey kids, c'mon in."

They sat on the couch. Debora sat on a chair across from them."This is Zuri. Zuri, this is Debora."

"Hello sweetie," said Debora, "I've heard so much about you."

"You have?" Zuri was surprised.

"Luke talks about you every time he's over. He told me about you before you were even together."

"Wow." Zuri looked at Luke, "That's pretty cool."

"Luke's a good kid. He's like a grandson to me. It's funny actually; one of my
~~~

neighbors asked if he was my grandson and I just went with it. Now if people see him coming over they just think he's my grandson."

"Nice," said Zuri. She was enjoying the visit. When Luke told her they were going to a girl named Debora's, she pictured a good looking young girl. Seeing who Debora really was made her comfortable that Luke spent so much time with her.

"So, what was your surprise?" Debora asked Luke.

"Yeah," he looked at Zuri, "can you get me that sunglass case?" Zuri reached into her purse and handed Luke the case. Luke opened it and pulled out a small zip-lock with the pinkish powder. "I got some funky stuff called MDPPP. It's an analog of the MDPV, and it's illegal."

"Let's do it. Do you have any clean ones?" she said.

"I do. I just bought a box of a hundred."

Once it was ready there were two syringes with 30 units of liquid. "Aren't you going to make one for your girlfriend?" said Debora.

"No. She doesn't do anything like this," he said.

"Are you okay with us doing this right here," she asked Zuri.

"Oh yeah, it's fine. I see it all the time anyway. Is it okay if I smoke in here?"

"Sure sweetie, go ahead. Luke, can you do this one for me?"

"Yeah. Let me see." Debora bent her elbow so the bottom of her forearm was facing Luke.

It was done quickly. Luke set her syringe on the coffee table and picked up his own. "Oh wow," said Debora. Luke took his own shot and experienced his rush just the same.

It was an awkward feeling for Zuri. She smoked her cigarette and watched one of Debora's cats as it came up to rub against her leg. "Hey kitty," she gave the cat a head massage. *What do you think about all this nonsense, kitty? Are these people doing bad stuff? You don't seem to mind. Maybe it's not so bad that they're doing this. Maybe it just looks bad to me. They're not hurting anyone but themselves, after all. And who doesn't hurt themselves in one way or another?*

~~~

When they made it home Luke went straight to the closet. He had bought a new locking doorknob for the closet. It was meant for a front door to a house. He had also bought an air filter for the closet. Smoking in the small room had become a problem.

Zuri watched him as he got busy with his tools in the closet. "Can't you do that tomorrow? Let's just watch a movie or some thing. I could even take an Adderall so we could stay up together."
~~~

Luke looked at her with surprise. "Yeah... sure," he stopped what he was doing to find his stash of Adderall. It had been a while since anyone had wanted Adderall. Jared's recent prescription had gone to Luke for MDPV.

Luke handed her an entire bottle, "Here you go. I really don't know what to do with these anymore. Eat some, sell some, buy cigarettes with them or something; I don't care."

"Okay, thanks. How much are they worth?" she said.

"Like five bucks a pill. Or ten if you don't really like the person," he said as he went back to modifying his doorknob.

"Nice. I think I know some people who will want these." She asked Luke if he was hungry.

"No thanks," he said.

"How about a milkshake?"

"Sure, I guess," he didn't want it but knew he needed the calories. Zuri took her time eating microwaveable pizza pockets before making milkshakes. She grabbed the finished shakes and went to the bedroom. The closet door was locked. "Luke? Open the door."

"Hold on!"

"Hold on for what? Just unlock it for me please."

Luke opened the door looking wide eyed and greasy faced. His body was trembling and he was sweating. "Gimme a sec," he laid back down on the floor.

Zuri noticed the needle and spoon on the shelf. "Are you okay?" she asked.

"Yeah. I'm good."

"You don't look good," she said.

"I just took a really big one. I don't know why."

"Why can't you just take Adderall? This stuff is really great, you know?"

"Yeah, I know."

"Why do you have to shoot everything? Don't you get just as high when you eat the stuff? It doesn't look like fun. It looks scary. Remember how scared you were when you thought you were having that heart attack?"

"It's a good kind of scary. It's hard to understand," he said.

"You're weird. Take this." Luke grabbed the drink with shaky hands.

"I really wanna smoke a cigarette. Do you wanna come smoke with me? I kinda want to smoke outside," she said.

"Let's smoke in here. I wanna test out this new air purifier thing. It's supposed to filter out 99.9 percent of pollutants or some shit."

She sat next to Luke and lit a Camel 99. Luke set the air purifier on the office chair in front of them and turned it on high. "Close that door. I really want to put this thing to the test."

Zuri closed the door and held the cigarette close to the intake side of the filter. "Remember the last time we did Adderall together? We just stayed up and talked all night. Then we went on that adventure up the mountain."

"Yep. That was pretty sweet," he said.

"You were so sweet. I think that's when I started to fall in love with you."

"I'm not so sweet anymore?" he said.

"You can be an asshole sometimes. I blame it on the PV stuff," she said.

"Sorry. I don't mean to be an ass. I just get so stressed out. This can't last forever, so I've pretty much committed to taking this as far as it can go. I think I was meant to explore this part of reality."

"Maybe you are, and I'm gonna be here for you no matter what you do. I'm pretty much committed to taking *this* as far as it can go," she said.

"You're crazy. I love you," he put his arm around her and held her close.

"I love you more," she kissed him on the cheek and handed him the cigarette. "Cigarettes feel really good right now. I feel awesome. I can't believe you've had all these Adderall this whole time. You don't smoke many cigarettes anymore. Why is that?"

"I think it's these drugs I been doing. They must occupy whatever part of the brain that makes you want cigarettes."

"Then why do I want cigarettes so bad right now?" she said.

"I don't know. I used to smoke like crazy on Adderall too," he said.

"I have like… these really good butterflies or something. Do you feel good right now?"

"I feel pretty good. It's getting hard for me to sit still like this. I feel like I need to get up and do something," he said.

"What do you need to get done tonight?"

"Remember that furnace filter I bought at Walmart? I need to do that. The old one is effed up. Our air is probably filled with mold and nasty shit because of it," he said.

"Okay. I guess I'll get all the laundry folded while you're doing that." She gave him a kiss and put out her cigarette before getting up.

~~~

Luke went back upstairs after the furnace was taken care of. Zuri was reading a book. "You're reading?" he said with disgust.

"Why not?" she asked.

"That's fuckin weird! How can you just sit there and read at a time like this?"

"I don't see what's wrong with reading right now. Lots of people like to read,"
~~~

she said.

"I would rather shoot myself. You couldn't pay me to sit down and read a book right now."

"I like it," she said.

"What are you reading anyway?" he said.

"It's called *Crank*. It's about drugs and stuff, kinda."

"You're nuts." Luke went back down to the basement.

~~~

Thunk! Thunk! Thunk! *Oh my god! What is he doing down there?* She read a few more paragraphs before there was more pounding. She lit a cigarette and went downstairs. Luke was picking up knives from the floor. "What are you doing?" she asked

"Throwing knives," he said.

"It's loud."

"Sorry." He lined himself up and threw again. All three bounced off the board and rattled onto the concrete. "Damnit, I freakin suck."

"Looks like fun," she said with sarcasm.

"It will be fun when I can get it to stick once in a while." He picked the knives back up off the floor and examined the damage.

"Do you want to smoke a bowl with me? It sounds really good right now, doesn't it?" she said.

"Not really, but I guess we could smoke one. I need to do something productive after that though. There's so much to be done and my attention deficit-ness is killing me." Luke opened his phone and replied to a text.

"Who are you texting?" she said.

"It's Blue."

"What does he want?" she said.

"Not sure. He just asked what I was doing."

"Oh. Can we go smoke now? I really wanna smoke," she said.

"Sure." Luke took a long glance around the basement before heading up the stairs.

"Do we seriously have to smoke in the closet?"

"Yeah. C'mon. Close that door."

"Can we use your bong? We haven't used that thing in forever."

"I don't care," he said.

Zuri got up and found the bong in the bedroom. It was a glass vase that had been modified into a bong. She filled it up with water before bringing it into the closet. Luke was fascinated with his air purifier. He blew each hit into the intake
~~~

side of the purifier. "This thing is so awesome."

Luke opened his lap-top when the bowl was done. "You're not gonna stay in the closet all night, are you?" she said.

"I don't know."

"It's weird. It's a closet. Who puts a lock on the inside of a closet anyway?"

"You don't get it. This is my office. I feel safe in here. I have everything I need in here."

"Kay, fine. I guess I'm gonna go read a book or something."

"Okay. I'm gonna educate myself on the internet somehow."

Zuri went to the bedroom, Luke closed the door behind her and turned up some music.

~~~

Zuri checked her phone. It was 4:30am. She had been reading for almost two hours since Luke had shut himself in the closet. There was a knock on the door. She didn't want to answer. "Luke, there's someone at the door," she said after trying to open the closet door.

"It's Blue. Let him in, will you?"

"Sure," she went to the front door and let Blue in.

"Hey Zuri."

"Hi Blue. Luke's in the closet."

"What do you mean?" Blue walked in looking around for Luke.

"In here." Zuri went to the bedroom and tried to open the closet again. "Open the door, he's here."

Luke opened the door, "Hey dude, what's up?"

"I don't know, bro. What's up with you?" Blue examined the doorknob on the closet door.

"Do you like that? This is like… my office. C'mon in," said Luke.

"Are you weirding out in here, or what? This is not normal behavior," said Blue.

"I know, but it's comforting. I got everything I need in here. It will keep people out when I'm not up here, and it's also nice to know that no ones gonna sneak up on me when I'm takin a shot." Luke grabbed a chair from the living room and brought it into the closet.

"Pretty sweet house you got here. You gonna be living here for a while?" said Blue.

"I have no idea how long I'm gonna live here. But here's the shit I was tellin you about," Luke held up his pinkish baggie of MDPPP.

"Alright big spooner, let's give it a shot."
~~~

It is not the man who has little, but he who desires more, that is poor.
-Seneca

Chapter 18: The Mad Scientist

Sunday 8-11-2010

"Luke? Luke!" said Zuri.

He turned off the shop-vac, "What?"

"It's noon. When was the last time you ate anything?"

"It's noon? Holy crap, I need water," he said.

"Yeah. You also need to stop vacuuming. You've been doing it since Blue left, and that was around eight. That's like four hours ago. It's clean. Be done with it," she said.

"It is clean, isn't it? You don't even need shoes down here anymore."

"Yeah, good job. Now come eat something with me."

Luke put down the vacuum and went upstairs with Zuri. "Jesus, I need water," he licked his chapped lips, "and half and half. Where's all the half and half? We need a steady supply at all times."

"Sorry. We have lots of food though. What do you want?" she said.

"I want half and half. I'm going to the store." Luke chugged a glass of water and put on his shoes.

"Wait, hold on! What store? You're going just for half and half?"

"It's like a five minute walk. I'll be back."

"Jeez Luke, hold on. I'll come with." She grabbed her cigarettes and followed him out the door. "Slow down, Luke. What's your problem?"

"Nothin. I just want half and half."

"You're agitated. What's wrong?" she said.

"I don't know. I'm stressin out," he said.

"You should take it easy today. Let's just relax and watch a movie or something. I feel like I never get any time with you. You're so distant and you're always busy."

"I don't think I'll have much time for relaxation today," he said.

"You do have time though. You can do whatever you want. You could just be lazy and hang out with me all day if you wanted."

"But I have responsibilities. People need me. And I have debts I need to pay. I need to pick up more weed. I'm probably gonna have to sell some more of that pink shit, damnit. And I really need to make another order. Fuck, I should have done that friday."

"I don't think you need to do any of that. It's Sunday. I think you should just spend the day with me since I work tomorrow. You'll have all week to do your crazy business."

"We'll see how it goes. I don't want to make any promises, but I'll try," he said.

"Fine. I guess that's as good as it's gonna get," she put her arm around him.

The rest of the walk was quiet. Luke felt out of place in the new town. He didn't know many people in C-falls. The people he did know, he didn't really know. Tim knew lots of people in the area. Tim had also lived in Montana most of his life; he knew everyone.

Luke had spent most of his time in C-falls with Tim, and they had always been on weird drugs. The place had a strange vibe to Luke. He had never seen the place with sober eyes. Most of the people he had met on cough and cold medicine, Dramamine, or alcohol combined with severe sleep deprivation. He often met people in the area who recognized him, but rarely could he recognize them back. They were odd encounters:

"Dude, you're that fucked up kid from that party, aren't you? You were trying to steal the dog; the invisible dog! Do you remember?"

"No, sorry. I'm not sure if I do," Luke would say. It was a small town. Everyone knew each other in some roundabout way.

Luke and Zuri made it to the grocery store. Luke bought a pack of American Spirits and two of the largest cartons of half and half he could find. He chugged one entire carton in the parking lot before lighting a cigarette.

"That is so disgusting," said Zuri. "It's not normal behavior, and it's definitely not healthy. You need normal food."

"My body craves half and half; I think it is healthy. Lots of fat is supposed to be good for the skin. I don't know if you've noticed, but I'm looking very vascular," he held out his veiny arms, "I think that means my skin is lacking in fat. That's probably why I want half and half so bad."

"I don't know, Luke. You treat your body so horribly. I don't know how you expect to live very long at all."

"I'm not gonna do it like this forever. Everyone goes a little hard at this age. I'll mellow out eventually, and live a long and peaceful life. I won't have any regrets either; I'll know I took it as far as it could go."

"I don't even know what you mean by that. I think you're crazy," she said.

Luke received a text. "Who was that?" said Zuri.

"Stacy," he said.

"What?" she said in disbelief. "Are you serious?" she stopped walking, expecting Luke to stop as well. "What the fuck, Luke? Why are you even talking to her?"

"I'm not. You don't need to make a scene," he walked on through the front gate and up to the front door.

Zuri hurried up and followed him inside. "What do you mean you're not? You can't just tell me you're talking with your ex and expect me not to freak out."

"She just wants weed. See look," he showed her the text.

"You're not gonna give her any, are you?"

"Nope," he showed his reply:

(From Luke): outta town

Stacy texted back.

(From Stacy): How far outta town? I can come to u

(From Luke): outta weeed

Zuri watched with anxiety as the conversation continued.

(From Stacy): will u call me if you get more?? I really need some :/

(From Luke): K

(From Stacy): I'm in kalispell. ur mom asked me to come visit

(From Luke): right on

Luke closed his phone. The conversation was over.

"Why does that bitch want to hang out with your mom?" said Zuri.

"I don't know. They're friends I guess."

"You should tell your mom you don't want her to hang out with Stacy."

"No way. She can do what she wants. Stop being so insecure. Jesus Christ."

"I'm not insecure! You shouldn't have anything to do with your slutty ex-girlfriends!"

"You're totally insecure!" Zuri flinched. "What, you think I'm gonna fuckin hit you? If you don't trust me we should just break up."

"No Luke," she said through tears, "I do trust you. I just know she wants to steal you from me. She's gonna get your mom on her side and she's gonna try to take you from me." She grabbed Luke and buried her face in his chest.

Luke stood there for a few moments with no emotion. He was surprised that he felt nothing. Zuri was overflowing with emotion and he felt nothing. He pried himself out of her arms and made a break for the closet. "Luke, what are you doing? Please don't do that, we need to talk." She tried to follow him into the closet.

"Get out. We'll talk later," he pushed her out and locked the door. Zuri lost it. She slumped to the floor and cried.

Luke mixed up a reckless solution with shaky hands. He turned up the music so he didn't have to hear her. Luke took the shot and fell to the floor. The tightness in his chest was so strong he wondered if he would die. His ears rang and the music faded out. *I'm dead. I'm dead. Sorry Zuri, I really fucked it up for us.*

~~~

After two hours, Zuri started knocking on the door. "Luke? Please Luke. Just tell me if you're okay. I'm scared."

Luke was still lying on his back staring at the ceiling. Australian rap music was playing. "I'm good," he said.

"Will you let me in? Please Luke, I can't take it anymore."

Luke sat up, unlocked the door and laid back down. Zuri came in and laid down next to him. She didn't say anything, she just held him close.

A half hour went by in peace. If not for the stimulant drugs, they would have fallen asleep. Luke finally checked his phone to see two hours worth of unread messages and missed calls.

"Shit, I gotta go meet dude."

"Is that it?" she said.

"It looks like a few people are gonna need weed. That girl from the rave needs some. Jared, girl from work... yeah. I'd better get going," he said.

"Kay."

Luke didn't move. He didn't want to leave after treating her so badly. "I'm sorry. Sorry for being such a dick. I'll come home as soon as I can."

"Okay. I forgive you. And I do trust you. I'm sorry for acting like I don't," she said.

Luke took a few more moments to reflect. He wondered how Zuri was so
~~~

worried that he would leave her. He wouldn't. His mind was made. She was the sweetest, most selfless girl he'd ever met. He couldn't help but love her. "I love you Zuri. I don't know whats happening to me."

"I love you too, and I know what's happening to you. It's those horrible chemicals."

"Yeah... it's not good." Luke stood up and tried to organize himself.

~~~

"You look like shit, dude," Shawn set a brown paper bag in Luke's lap.

"For real?" said Luke.

"You look like you quit sleeping and eating. Knock that shit off, man. It's no good."

"Yeah, I'm workin on it. Just been real busy lately. Moved into a new house with my girlfriend; went to a rave in Missoula the other night; been sellin lots of shit; people are demanding." Luke counted out some cash for Shawn.

"I put a half P in there since I'll be out of town for a week or two. Don't worry about payin till I get back," said Shawn.

"Alright dude. Thanks. That helps me out a lot right now," said Luke.

"No problem. I know you're good for it."

"Cool man. I'd better bounce. My phone's been blowin up," said Luke.

"Alright bro, I'll see you later."

Luke hopped out of the truck with his overstuffed paper sack and got into his Chrysler. He looked at his phone and sent each person the same message:

(From Luke): At old steel. hurry up

~~~

One of his old co-workers beat him there. A handful of cars showed up shortly after. Luke took care of his customers as quickly as he could.

Erica had been anticipating Luke's arrival. He kept telling her he was close. He was about to leave when he got a call from Stacy.

"Hello?" he answered.

"Hi Luke. Are you still at the bridge? I'm almost there," she said.

"Yeah, hurry up."

"Kay. I'm like two minutes away."

Luke waited with anxiety. She arrived in the same expensive car. Stacy got in Luke's passenger seat. "Hi," she said, looking at him through large sunglasses.

"What's up?" Luke knew she was judging his sickly appearance. She was beautiful as ever and had the same familiar scent.

"I was just having wine with your mom. How are things?" she said.

"Things are good. Way good, actually. How much weed do you need? I've got to be somewhere right now. It's pretty urgent." He had such a helpless feeling around Stacy. They had been through so much together and it felt wrong to try and blow her off.

Stacy sorted through her purse to find a few large bills. "I guess a half ounce," she said.

Luke sorted through his own bag, "Any preference?"

"Afghan Goo, please." Luke measured out 14 grams. "Your mom wants to see you. You should come over tonight."

"Are you inviting me to come over to my parents house?"

"Yeah. I'm going back over there right after this. She told me to ask you. Plus, it would be nice to talk with you for a while; maybe smoke a bowl together."

"I don't know if I can do anything tonight. I got a lot goin right now."

"I'm sorry for not being a better friend. I do want to be your friend. Even though we haven't been spending much time together you're still the best friend I've ever had. I really miss you, Luke. It's sad not having you in my life anymore. I want my best friend back."

Why is everyone getting so emotional today? "Yeah... I miss you too. It does suck, but it doesn't feel like we can be just friends."

"We can, Luke. I promise I just want to be your friend. Can we just try at least?"

"Sure," he said.

"Good. We should hang out sometime soon. I want to see your house and I want to meet Zuri. I want her to know that we're just friends."

"We'll see. We can talk about it later, I really need to go," he looked at his phone with impatience.

"Okay, can I have a hug?" Luke gave her a hug. It was hard for either of them to let go. "I love you, Luke."

"I love you too."

~~~

Luke called Erica when he knew he was close. It was a dirt driveway. Erica was there to guide him to a strange parking space in the grass between two old cars. Erica gave Luke a hug as he got out of the car. "Hey Luke. How have you been?"

"I been good. How are you?"

"Not bad." Luke followed her to the kitchen.

"Hey dude, I'm Dan."

"Nice to meet you. I'm Luke," he sat at the table with Dan and Erica. "Sorry I took so long. It's been a stressful day."
~~~

"You're cool, man. Erica says you got some killer weed."

"Yeah, for sure. Here's like six strains I got," he unloaded the variety on the table.

"This Afghan Goo smells so good," said Dan. Erica was mesmerized by the Buddha Cheeze.

"You wanna try it? We can have a little sample sesh if you want," said Luke.

"Hell yeah. Hunny will you grab the bubbler," said Dan.

Erica grabbed a glass bubbler out of a kitchen cabinet. Luke took his time breaking up a piece of the Afghan Goo and loaded it into the bubbler. He heard toddlers playing in another room. Once it was loaded, he handed it to Dan, "Tear it up, man."

Luke took a few moments to admire his surroundings. He noticed DJ equipment in the living room. Erica had mentioned research chemicals. Luke was dying to breach the topic.

"That shit's amazing," Dan handed the bubbler to Erica. "Do you have this stuff all the time?" he said as he worked on his laptop.

"Yep, any time."

"That's cool, man. I might just have to make you my new weed guy," said Dan.

"Works for me."

A crying kid came running in from the living room. His older sister came in next. She was four. The boy pointed and babbled something accusingly at the girl. "Lizz, what did you do?" Erica got up to take care of the kids. The commotion left the room. Luke held the bubbler and took another hit.

"So, you're into the research chemicals?" said Dan.

"I am definitely into the research chemz," said Luke.

"Which ones?"

"Well, I'm familiar with the MDMC and the 4-MEC. Also dabbled into the JWH-122. The big one for me is the MDPV," said Luke.

"Yuck. That's some nasty shit, bro."

"You've tried it?" said Luke.

"Yeah. I got a sample of that shit a few months ago. That shit's evil, dude."

Funny you say that. "Well, you see, I got this whole strategy about it. For some reason all the tweakers love the stuff. So I'm just giving it to the people who can sell it to all those guys. Everyone seems to like it better than the crystal methamphetamine, so I see it as a good way to make money from people who are doin the same kind of shit anyway."

"Yeah, I bet. You're probably making bank too," said Dan.

"Oh yeah. These tweakers are up my butt for the shit."

"Do you label everything before you sell it?"

"No, why?"

"You need to have all your shit labeled. It needs to have the name of the chemical and 'Not For Human Consumption' written on it. If you do that it's completely legal."

"I did not know that," said Luke.

"Can you do anything with methylone?" said Dan.

"Yeah, I've got lots of people who love that stuff."

"Well, I've got it for forty dollars a gram if you want some right now."

"That would be good, but I need to put in an order for some MDPV. I'm probably gonna spend everything I got on that," said Luke.

"How much are you paying for it?"

"Like, twenty something a gram."

"Damn. I can order you some right now for… hold on, let me check. How much are you trying to get?" said Dan.

"I don't know. Fifty grams, maybe."

"Alright… I can get it to you for… 12.50 a gram."

"Holy smokes, are you serious?"

"Yep, I can have it here by Tuesday. Just sell some methylone for me and I'll put in an order right now," said Dan.

"Dude, I will sell so much methylone for you! How much do you want me to buy?" Luke started grabbing wads of cash out of his pockets.

"Damn, you need to get organized," said Dan.

"Yeah, I know. I haven't had time to deal with it yet."

"I'll be right back," said Dan. A few minutes later he came back with his own scale and a large bag of white powder.

"Holy crap, dude." Luke stared at the bag of powder. "That could keep a village properly fertilized for weeks."

Dan laughed, "Yep. I've actually got a greenhouse out back where I do my research," he used his fingers to quote "research."

"That's sweet, man. Does that make you a legitiment chemical researcher?"

"It does. We like to keep everything nice and legal around here. If we ever got raided, there would be nothing to worry about," said Dan.

"That's pretty legit, man. I'll make sure not to bring any illegal things around here. That way your whole operation stays legit."

"That would be appreciated. Would you like to do some research before you make your purchase?" said Dan.

"Totally. I'm always down for research."

Dan opened the bag and held it close to Luke, "Take a whiff of that."

Luke's eyes watered and his nostrils burned as he stuck most of his face in the bag. "Oh wow, that's some ferocious stuff there."

Dan used an ID card to scoop out a generous pile of powder. He lined it out on the table and asked Luke for a bill. Luke handed over a hundred. "Now, this stuff is not for human consumption," said Dan, "but we're going to do it anyway at our own risk."

After their research, Luke mentioned how he had accidentally obtained the MDPPP. "That's strange. You're sure that's what they sent you?" said Dan.

"Yeah dude. It was labeled MDPPP and it matches all of the descriptions. It's pink and has some strange static sensitive properties," said Luke.

"I think I know what you're talking about. I'll be right back." Dan left and came back with a mirror and a vial of white powder. He tapped a small sample onto the mirror. Luke was amazed by what it did.

"That's what I'm talking about! That prope stuff does that same thing. What is this stuff?"

"This is AM-2201. It's a nonselective agonist for the cannabinoid receptor. It's even more potent and psychedelic than the JWH which you've probably tried before." Dan sprinkled some AM-2201 onto the half-burnt bowl of weed. "We must exhibit extreme caution as we attempt to injest the substance in it's pure form."

"Extreme caution for sure," said Luke.

Dan took two hits; Luke took one. The effects came strong. Dan continued talking, but Luke could not comprehend. Luke could feel his brain turning inside out.

"Should we do business? How much methylone would you like?" said Dan.

"Oh wow… I suppose we could." Luke looked at his unorganized pile of cash.

"You wanna just start with ten grams? That's only four hundred bucks."

"Sure dude." Luke didn't understand what was happening. He decided to leave the whole transaction up to fate. Luke watched as Dan operated the scale with care and labeled the bag properly. Dan set the zip-lock bag in front of Luke.

"I just… can you help me out here?" Luke was lost and bubbly brained.

"Sure bro," he unrolled the hundred that was still on the table and set it to the side, "There's one hundred." He found another hundred and set it on top of the other, "There's two hundred." He counted the rest and re-counted it for Luke.

"Looks good, man."

"You like Dubstep?" said Dan.

"Totally."

"You should do something with all that cash and come check something out."

Luke stuffed the rest of the cash back into his pockets and followed Dan into the living room. They both sat on the couch.

Dan set up his laptop and DJ equipment on the coffee table. All the dials, buttons and knobs were glittered with trippy lights. Dan made some adjustments on his computer. A baseline came in. He pressed buttons and turned knobs. Twinkling sounds came in. The sounds escalated with the beat, then the dirty drop.

Dan was a mad scientist, smiling, head bobbing while working all the confusing gizmos. It was sensory overload for Luke. The brain drilling sound combined with chemicals had Luke's brains scrambled into a blissful trance.

Some filthy female vocals looped in. Erica came running to the living room, "Dan! Oh my god!" She was disgusted. The music stopped.

"Sorry, I got carried away. I forgot where I was. I didn't realize..."

"None of that when the kids are here! Are you trying to corrupt our children?" said Erica.

"No, it was an accident. Sorry, I'm done." Dan closed his laptop.

"Dude... that was freakin sweet," said Luke. "You're like... a freakin ninja with that shit."

"Thanks bro. I'm gonna need some weed from you. Can we go take care of that?" said Dan.

"We sure can." They went back to the kitchen. Luke weighed out a quarter ounce for Dan with confusion. "Sorry man, I'm not usually this retarded."

"Hey bro, I know how you feel," said Dan.

"I don't think you do. You managed to do that freakin electro-genius-ness back there. My brain has zero tolerance for that cannabinoid stuff," said Luke.

"Believe it or not, you actually build a tolerance to the synthetic cannabinoids the same way you do with pot. This was your first time with AM-2201; I wouldn't expect you to be functional."

The transaction was finished. Luke's phone was filling up with missed calls and messages. "Damn dude, I'd better get outta here. I just re-upped today and everyone is tryin to see me."

"Alright bro. Your fifty grams should be here the day after tomorrow. You're gonna come pick it up for sure, right? Because I would have no use for it. The only thing I could do with it is shut down someone's club."

"I am definitely coming to pick it up. I'll be here as soon as you call no matter where I am or what I'm doing. It's important that I get that shit as soon as possible. You have no idea how bad people will be jonesing by then. I'm all out right now. I made a big mistake by waiting this long to order more."

"Well, at least you got it cheaper this time. If this turns into a regular thing, I'll call up the manufacturer to work out a way better deal. I got some pull with this shit, bro."

"Thats awesome. Alright man, I'm out. See you in a couple days," said Luke.

Luke got in his car with a sense of accomplishment. He made it to a stoplight and called Zuri.

"Hello?" she answered.

"Hey girly, what's up? Sorry I haven't been able to get to the phone."

"Serious? You couldn't get to the phone for two hours?" she said.

"I got extremely high and met with a very important person."

"Who did you meet with?"

"I don't want to talk about it on the phone. I got to meet a couple more people then I'll be home."

"Fine. Please hurry."

"I will," he said.

"Kay. I love you."

"I love you too."

~~~

Luke went inside with excitement. After giving Zuri a hug and kiss he made his way to the closet. "Luke, it's almost nine. Where have you been all day? Why couldn't you answer my calls?"

Luke explained himself while preparing a solution of MDPPP. He displayed the weed, money, and bag of methylone as proof of his success. Zuri was sad. She had been neglected when all she wanted was time with Luke.

Luke came up with a solution, "We'll, eat some Adderall and we could spend the whole night together."

"But last night I stayed up and all you did was clean and throw knives," she said.

"I promise I'll be all yours tonight. There's nothing else I need to do. Plus, I want to make it up to you."

"Can you please not do what you're about to do?" She watched as he got the last of the bubbles out of the syringe.

"That would be… out of the question. There is nothing that could stop me from doing what I'm about to do right now."

"You have a serious problem, Luke."
~~~

"That's fine. I don't care. I'm going along with it for now."

Luke checked his vein and squeezed his fist. He took the shot and laid on the floor.

What is a man profited,
if he shall gain the whole world,
and lose his own soul?
-Matthew 16:26

Chapter 19: Crusty Cotton

Tuesday 8-13-2010

"You're seriously all out?" said Tim, "You have to have a secret stash somewhere?"

"Dude, I am not holding out," said Luke, "I should be getting shit today. Just waiting for a call."

"From who? I thought Dave was ordering the stuff for you."

"I told you I found someone else; an actual chemical researcher person. He's way legit."

"Man, I knew you shouldn't have let Jared and Nick smoke all your shit. It's such a waste," said Tim.

"I got some crusty cottons I been saving up. We can probably rinse em out and get a good shot." Luke dug around his junkie kit to find some old Q-tip ends that were caked with residue. They were in the closet while Jared and Nick threw knives in the basement.

The MDPPP was gone for good. All that was left was encrusted in pieces of dirty cotton all over Luke's house. What used to be garbage was now the object of their obsession.

Luke had been feeling generous since meeting with Dan. The drug supply plummeted while Luke spent two days renovating the basement with his friends; especially since Nick was insistent that he smoke the chemical.

"Can't you get that cotton fever from doing this?" said Tim.

"That's what I've heard, but if I fall asleep today, I'm fucked."

"Found another," Tim picked up another nasty cotton out of the carpet and set it in Luke's pile.

"Nice, dude." Most junkies had to endure the fever at least once during their lives. A bacteria can grow on cotton that can cause a painful sickness.

"Here you go," Luke handed one of the syringes to Tim.

"Can you get this one for me? I always get a better rush when you do it."

Luke looked at his bruised arms, "Dude, that's because you don't even get it in the vein. You're just shootin it into the muscle. That's why your arm is all fucked up. Jesus dude."

"I thought it's supposed to hurt when you miss," said Tim.

"It does with meth; not this stuff for some reason." Luke searched Tim's arm for a decent vein. "Fuck this, dude. Go drink some water. Your veins are so fuckin small right now."

Tim watched with envy as Luke took his own shot and enjoyed the rush. "Serious, man? You can't just do it now? I can tie off or something."

"Water, dude. Your veins will get bigger if you drink some."

Tim went to the kitchen and chugged two glasses of water. He could still hear Jared and Nick throwing knives in the basement. Fifteen minutes of jonesing went by before Luke would give it another try. Luke got in, flagged it, and gave the injection.

Tim was enjoying himself until Jared came bursting into the closet with his loud mouth. Tim and Luke were still hyper sensitive to the noise because of the drugs. "Damnit Jared! Will you shut up?" said Luke.

"I thought you were all out. Why are you guys in here getting high without us?" Nick peeked in behind Jared.

"I am all out. I just rinsed out a couple old pieces of cotton. There's nothing for you unless you want to suck on one."

"Will it do anything? Give me one," said Jared. Luke picked out a piece of cotton and handed it to Jared.

"I want whatever he's having!" said Nick.

"Oh my god, you guys are dope whores." Luke picked out another cotton and gave it to Nick.

"What do I do with this?"

"I don't know, dude. Stick it up your butt. Just get outta here." Luke was flooded with more questions as he pushed them out of the closet and locked the door. "I don't know how much longer I can handle it," he told Tim. "They're so fucking loud."

~~~

Luke got a text from Dan at 3pm. "Gotta go!" Luke closed his laptop and stood up.

"Is your shit ready?" said Tim.

"Yeah. I'ma run and get it. Keep the house under control while I'm gone."

"You got it bro."

Luke drove to Dan's in a hurry. He was hunched over the steering wheel on the edge of his seat. The crappy speakers in his Chrysler rattled with rap music. He pulled into the same strange parking space and walked to the front door. Dan answered, "Hey bro. Come on in."

They went to sit down in the kitchen. An unopened International Postage package sat on the table. "This is for you," said Dan.

"Badass, dude! How much do I owe?" said Luke.

"Six eighty-four and some cents."

Luke counted out $1,085 and handed it to Dan. "There's an extra four hundred for some molly."

"I don't sell molly, bro," said Dan.

"Oh shit, my mistake. I got you four hundred for some methylone. Research went well with the last batch."

"Good deal. I can do another one of those for you. Be right back." Dan got up to grab the methylone.

Luke opened his package and looked at the bag of powder with amazement. *I wonder how many people could get high off this bag. If there's 1000mg in a gram, and it only takes 20mg for a good dose... that means fifty people could get high off one gram.*

Dan came back and set the large bag of methylone on the table. "What's fifty times fifty?" Luke asked.

"That would be twenty-five hundred," he gave Luke a puzzled look.

"Dude, twenty-five hundred people could get high from this bag."

"Doin big things," Dan said as he started measuring methylone for Luke.

"Do you mind if I take a small tester?" Luke was dying to open the bag of MDPV.

"Go for it, bro."
~~~

Luke opened the bag and got a whiff of the distinctive smell of MDPV. He also noticed that this bag was packaged different than his previous orders. The chemical was in a clear plastic zip-lock instead of the metallic static resistant ones he had seen before. The label said:

PV

Not For Human Consumption

"Why does this only say PV? Is the methylonedioxy ring not significant enough to specify? Pyrovalerone is an entirely different chemical without the methylonedioxy ring. PV without the MD is actually illegal, and has been since the sixties. Did you know that Pyrovalerone used to be a pharmaceutical? They made it illegal because it was too addictive and caused really bad weight loss."

"I did not know that," said Dan.

"Yeah man. They used to prescribe it for lethargy and chronic fatigue."

"That's a trip, bro. You really know your shit, don't you."

"I try to. I feel like I should anyway."

"Well, I'm certain that stuff is MDPV. I don't know why they just write PV," said Dan.

"I'm sure it is, too. I don't think your company would send some old school pharmaceutical through customs. But after getting that MDPPP by mistake, it wouldn't surprise me. Where do your chemicals come from anyway?"

"China. It all comes from China. Even the stuff you got out of the US was most likely manufactured in China," said Dan.

"Wow dude. It's like chemical warfare; except they're making us pay! I can just imagine those Chinese people: *Stupid Americans! We kill der brains and dey pay us money*! What's our world coming to?" said Luke.

"I don't know. It's pretty crazy when you look at it that way. You know most of these designer drugs are just byproducts of other chemicals they are trying to make. They have tons of shit that would be destroyed if we wouldn't buy it. Did you know that they give the death penalty if you're caught with any of these chemicals in China? They know how bad some of this shit is. You're probably right; it is chemical warfare. They're attacking the minds of our nation."

"And we're helping them! We're like freakin terrorists, dude!" Luke whispered

"You're nuts." Dan set the bag of methylone in front of Luke. "You wanna try something cool?" He pulled out a small glass vial out of his pocket. It had a dark tint and was half full of liquid.

"It's not chloroform, is it?" Luke joked.

"Naw, man. It's fun. Try it out."

Luke gave a long sniff. It smelt like nail polish remover. His face felt heavy.

Soon his whole body felt the heaviness and was accompanied by a wah-wah-wah noise. "Whoa... dude," the effects started to dissipate as quickly as it came on. "That was weird. Kind of reminds me of huffing air duster."

"Pretty cool, huh?" Dan took a sniff for himself before screwing the cap back on. "I get free samples of weird chemicals pretty much every week."

"That's sweet, dude. I'm totally down with all the weird shit. I'll be your lab monkey anytime," said Luke.

"Well, there's lots of experimenting to be done. You're welcome to participate. Speaking of that, do you have any opiate addicted friends?"

"I do. I know a shit load of opiate junkies. Why?"

"I've got some shit called methoxetamine on the way. It's a derivative of ketamine, but might also act on the opiate receptors. I'll fill you in on the details when I get it."

"Hell yeah, man. That could be good business since heroin is so expensive around here."

"Could be. We'll see," said Dan.

~~~

Luke set his 100 gram bag of 50% MDPV on the table with a thud. His friends were astonished. "Dude, that's a fuckin brick!" said Jared.

"You're like scarface, man," said Nick. Luke weighed out a gram for each of his friends. "Are you serious? I can do whatever I want with this?"

"Yep. Smoke it, sell it, stick it up your butt," said Luke.

"I will never stick drugs up my butt," Nick said in his most serious voice.

"Why not? It's actually pretty popular in some places. It's supposed to give you a rush like shooting up," said Luke.

"Then why don't you try it?" said Nick.

"Because I do shoot up. C'mon dude, I'll give you another gram if you try it."

"No way. I would never degrade myself to such behavior," said Nick.

"I'll do it!" said Jared.

"Why would you want anyone to do that to themselves?" Nick said with disgust.

"Hey dude, these are research chemicals. It's all in the name of research," said Luke.

"Research is supposed to be done with laboratory animals; like guinea pigs or monkeys," said Nick. Dave couldn't believe what Luke was proposing.

"Jared's our lab monkey. He just volunteered. Don't be a freakin buzz kill," said Luke.

Dave had to make it stop. "Why don't we just get high like normal people
~~~

right now. You guys can do your weird stuff on your own time."

"That sounds very reasonable," Nick said as he unfolded a piece of aluminum foil.

"You're right," said Luke, "I'm being selfish. I forgot you guys are almost sober."

Luke went to work preparing a solution for Tim, Dave, and himself to share. He gave each of his friends a shot before taking one himself. The mood changed. Things were suddenly not so funny. There was the unmistakeable feeling of impending doom.

Luke looked at the small windows and realized how exposed they would be if someone were too peek in. "Why don't we go ahead and cover up these windows," said Luke. He went under the stairs and found a piece of cardboard. "Hurry up guys, help me out here!" he tore off a piece that would cover one of the windows. Tim grabbed another piece and covered up another window.

"Is everything cool?" said Nick, looking guilty with a lighter and foil. "Things were fine a few minutes ago. What's changed?"

"I've got a bad feeling. Just let me do this." Luke peeked out of a window with his hand on his pistol that was wedged in his waistband.

Dave took a peek for himself, "We're fine, Luke. Just calm down."

"Yeah, I know. I just needed to make sure." Luke went back to the table and began dividing the MDPV into 5 gram bags. He couldn't shake the feeling that something bad was going to happen. But his friends said things were fine.

Dave noticed Luke glancing at a small slit in one of the windows. Luke expected something to happen; anything. "Do you want me to check the house for you?" Dave asked.

"Would you do that?" said Luke.

"Of course I would," said Dave.

"Okay. Will you lock the door on your way out? Knock three times if the coast is clear. Knock once if there's weird shit happening."

"Are you serious?"

"Yes, please. I've got like five grand wortha shit here. I don't want to take any chances."

"Fine." Dave walked upstairs.

Tim was worried too. Luke's paranoia was contagious. He just had to remind himself that he had nothing to lose; nothing to incriminate him. If shit did go down, it was all on Luke. *But why would anything bad happen?* Tim thought, *There's no reason for any weird shit to happen. Not unless there's some larger conspiracy at work here. Maybe it's an experiment. Someone has to be monitoring this research chemical business.*

Does the government know about these chemicals? They have to! Why would they allow us to even have the chimicals unless it was some sort of experiment? We're all lab monkeys volunteering at our own will.

When will they decide to shut it down? It can't possibly last long. It's gonna start causing danger to the public. If they are watching they will eventually see what it's doing to people. People are gonna get fucked up. The experiment will be too risky.

There were three knocks at the door. Tim opened the door, "All clear?" he asked.

"Yep," said Dave.

"Nothing weird?"

"Nope. There's a black Chevy parked down the street. Just one guy sitting in there. probably nothing, though."

"What kind of Chevy?" said Tim, now peeking out of the kitchen window.

"A newer Silverado. Tinted windows," said Dave.

"And you don't think that's suspicious?"

"No. Why would it be?"

"Feds drive Silverados, dude!"

"Oh, c'mon. Now you're getting paranoid. Lots of people drive Silverados," said Dave.

"Don't you ever wonder about these chemicals? Don't you think someone might want to see what we're doing with them?"

"The stuff isn't even illegal. We should have nothing to worry about."

Tim went downstairs and told Luke what he saw. "I think we should all take the batteries out of our cell phones," said Luke. "Batteries out as long as we're in this house."

"Now that's ridiculous," said Dave. "What difference will that make?"

"Don't you know about the Patriot Act? They can listen through our phones and see out of the cameras even when the phone's turned off."

"No way," said Nick.

"Yes way. I've done the research. I'm absolutely certain," said Luke.

"But you have to be a suspected terrorist for them to actually do any of that," said Nick.

"They can suspect anyone. Don't argue with me. Batteries out."

"No. What if there's an emergency and someone needs to get a hold of me?"

"Let me see your phone," said Luke.

"Why?" said Nick.

"Just let me see it."

"No. You're going to break it."

"I won't, I promise."

Nick handed the phone to Luke. Luke took a sharpie and marked over the camera lense.

"Nooo!" Nick grabbed for the phone, "You asshole! Why would you do that?"

"You were obviously intending to break my rules, so I took the necessary measures to maintain security. I won't tolerate any disobedience."

"Dick! You're such a dick."

~~~

8:00pm came around and Luke had still not checked his phone. "Alright guys, I gotta get outta here. People need me, I gotta stop fuckin around."

"But I still wanna do that booty bump for that free gram," said Jared.

"Another time. I really gotta get going. It's getting late." Luke tried to think of all the people he needed to see. He wasn't about to turn on his phone until he left the house.

Dave had nowhere he needed to be. Tim asked Dave if he would drive him a few places so he could sell PV. Dave accepted, not knowing the strange crowd of young drug addicts he would be exposed to. Nick and Jared hopped in the Suburban with Luke to be dropped off in Kalispell.

~~~

Luke pulled into the Walmart parking lot next to an old rusty Subaru. Blue got out of the Subaru and into the Suburban with Luke. "Hey cousin, what's happenin?" said Blue.

"Same shit. Who's that?" Luke nodded toward a creepy older woman in the Subaru. She was glaring at Luke suspiciously.

"That crazy bitch is Mandy. She's fuckin nuts. Don't ever do any deals with her."

"I'll take your advice on that. Now, how much do you want? I gotta do forty a gram."

"Can you front me twenty? You're not gonna run out again, are you?"

"Naw man. I should be steadily supplied from now on." Luke counted out four 5 gram bags and handed them to Blue. "I'll write you down for eight hundred." Luke pulled out a pocket-size notebook where he kept people's debts recorded. Before the list, he would just forget about the debt and rely on his customers to be honest. There were plenty of people who would just hope for him to forget. It saved him thousands in lost profits.

"What is this? Why does it say, *Not for Human Consumption,"* Blue pointed at Luke's handwritten label on each bag.

"That's MDPV; a research chemical. It's not illegal yet, as long as you don't sell it for human consumption," Luke explained.

"This is the same stuff you've been giving me?"

"Yep. I cut it just the same too. It's fifty percent MDPV, and fifty percent MSM."

"Alright bro. Thanks. I should have your money in a few days," said Blue as he opened the door.

"See ya, dude," said Luke. Blue got back in the Subaru with the creepy lady and drove off.

The next stop for Luke was Kimmy. She was on the East side of town and had asked Luke if he was with molly. Luke responded saying he was indeed with molly.

Luke turned into the alley behind Papa Murphey's as instructed. Kimmy was waiting outside of a small rundown apartment building. She got in the truck. "Hey Luke, how you been?"

"I been good. What's new with you?" Luke drove out of the alley to find a safe place to do business.

"Oh, same shit. You know. I got these raver kids that keep bugging me to find molly for them."

"I got some methylone for eighty a gram."

"What's that?" said Kimmy.

"A newer structural analogue of MDMA. It's not illegal yet, but has the same effects as molly."

"Can you give me five grams for three hundred?" she asked.

"No way! Four hundred. I'm not making much off this stuff," said Luke.

"How about three fifty? That's seventy a gram. I know you can afford that."

Luke thought about it for a few moments, thinking he had waisted his time. From the right people, Luke knew he could get $120 a gram. "Yeah. I guess I'll do that for you."

"Sweet, dude. I got another deal for you, too."

"What's that?"

"I've got a ball of criss I want to trade for some of that Nazi dope."

"That's really not my department. Maybe you should ask Blue," said Luke.

"It is your department. I know Blue gets his shit from you. It would really help me out."

"Is the shit any good? Why would you want to trade?" said Luke.

"It is good, but no one wants crystal when that other shit's around."

Luke found an empty parking lot behind a coffee shop. "Can I check out the shit you got?"

"Sure." Kimmy pulled a dirty glass pipe out of her purse along with the bag of meth. She scooped a small shard into the pipe and handed it to Luke.

Luke melted it down and blew gently into the mouthpiece with his finger above the carb. A white powder film covered his finger as the smoke ran past. Once the cut burned off, he took a hit and blew out a massive cloud.

"There's some cut in there, but I guess that's what we've come to expect around here. How much do you want to trade for?" he said.

"I don't know. How much will you give me?" she asked.

"I'll give you an eighth. Gram for gram," he said firmly.

"Awesome. Thanks dude," she set the bag on his lap.

Luke brought out a scale and an unmarked baggie to put the MDPV in. Since he wasn't taking money for the chemical, he didn't feel obligated to explain that it was a research chemical not meant for consumption.

"Can I try some of it right now?" she said.

"You sure can. I could go for a hit right about now as well." Luke grabbed his junkie kit and prepared a solution. *Better not do too much right now. Need to keep my cool while doin business.*

"Are you making it up for both of us?" she said.

"Yeah. All my stuff is clean. I got a clean one I just use to draw it up."

"Yeah, but that's all we're doing?" she said.

"You think I should throw some more in there? I take pretty small shots of this stuff, but I can give you a big one if you want."

"No, it's fine. I'll try the same as what you're doing. Maybe I've been doing too much. Do you ever feel that tightness in your chest; like you're having a heart attack or something?"

"Yeah, that's happened a few times for me. Big shots of this stuff scare the crap out of me. Chest pain, shortness of breath, the paranoia can make things weird, too," he said.

"Good-I mean, it's not good. I'm just glad I'm not the only one weirding out. A lot of the people I sell to are snorters or smokers. They get the same kind of feelings, but not so suddenly and not so intense. I've seen the most paranoid people I've ever seen on this stuff. It's a trip."

"I believe it. Here you go," he handed her one of the syringes. She took hers without trouble and he took his.

"Oh yeah," she said. "That was a good one. I'm keeping this," she put the needle in her purse. "I've been using the same dull one for like three days."

"Oh my god," Luke said with disgust, "Don't be doing that, I got some you can have." He gave her a handful of unused syringes.

"That's awesome. Thanks man," she said.

Luke finished measuring out and bagging chemicals for her. The shot was perfect. There was a slight anxiety, but the paranoia stayed under control. Luke had his gun; if anything did happen, he was sure he would come out on top. They left the parking lot as soon as everything was squared away.

Luke dropped her off in the same alley where he'd picked her up. Before she got out of the truck, Luke asked, "Just out of curiosity, how much are people paying for that shit?"

"For the dope? It sells for one twenty a gram easily. Sometimes more."

"Wow. Alright, thanks," he said.

"Thank you, Luke. I'll see you later." She got out and Luke drove off.

~~~

Luke made it home by ten. There was an unfamiliar car parked in his driveway. Luke gathered his weed, money, gun, chemicals and paraphernelia and went inside. Zuri was smoking weed in the living room with a young blond kid.

"Hi Luke!" said Zuri as she stood up to give him a kiss,

"This is my friend Kyle."

"What's up, man?" Kyle gave Luke a friendly wave.

"Not much. Let me go unload here. I'll be right back." Luke went to the closet to empty his pockets and stash his drugs. He also put a jug of acetone in the freezer.

Once everything was secure and the closet was locked, he went back to the living room. "How was your day?" said Zuri as she handed him a pipe.

"It was good. Real busy. I saw some good friends." He didn't know if he could trust the kid.

"Well, Kyle was asking where to find molly. I told him I could probably help him," said Zuri.

Zuri trusted Kyle. The kid also looked high; stimulated on something. His pupils were dilated and he was chewing on his lip. "What are you on right now?" Luke asked Kyle.

"Adderall. I took some Adderall," he said.

"I sold him some," said Zuri. "He's cool, I promise."

Luke took a hit from the pipe. "Alright dude. How much do you want?"

"I've got a hundred bucks. I was hoping to get a gram."

"Okay. Hold on a minute." Luke left and came back a few minutes later with a bag of methylone. He threw the bag on the table, "There you go, dude."
~~~

"Awesome, thanks. I've got another fifty if I can get some weed."

Once Kyle had his weed, he loaded another bowl for them to smoke. Halfway through the bowl there was a knock at the door.

Luke looked in the peephole and saw that it was Dave. He opened the door, "Hey man, what chu doin?"

"Not too much. Still goin strong from that stuff you gave me." He took off his shoes and came inside.

They went to the living room and Zuri had an annoyed expression. *Here we go again,* she thought. There was an increasing tension growing between Dave and Zuri. Dave seemed intrusive to her. But Luke didn't care; he had intruded on Dave for years. Dave had always been welcoming, and Luke was going to show him the same respect no matter what Zuri thought about it.

"Here you go," Luke handed the pipe to Dave, "Get some of that. Dave, this is Kyle."

"Nice to meet you," said Kyle.

They passed the pipe around and socialized. Luke became comfortable with Kyle. It turned out that Kyle worked at the Verizon store and made good money doing it. Luke was surprised by that because he looked 16, but was actually 18.

Kyle looked at his phone, "I'd better get outta here. Friends are ready to party."

"Cool, dude. See ya," said Luke.

"Bye," said Zuri.

Dave pulled out two narrow glass vials full of liquid. "What's that?" said Luke, grabbing the vials from Dave. "Epinephrin and Lydocain? What's this stuff do?"

"I don't know. I was hoping you would," said Dave.

"Where'd you find these?" said Luke.

"In my neighbors house. Are they worth anything to you?"

"Yeah, the vials themselves are worth something to me. This is some medical grade shit."

"I know. You're supposed to stick a needle in that end and suck the stuff right up out of there. That little rubber squeegee piece on the other end will move up with the liquid as it comes out."

"I can see that. Should I try shooting it up?" said Luke.

"I think that's what you're supposed to do with it," said Dave.

"Do you want a couple grams for it? Or do you want money?"

"I want some of that good stuff we've been doing."

"Awesome. Step into my office." Luke and Dave went to the closet. Luke showed off the bag of crystal he'd acquired. Dave was not interested; he wanted

PV. Luke measured out a couple grams of PV and gave it to Dave. "Did you know that what I just gave you is worth $240 on the streets?"

"You're kidding," said Dave.

"Nope. People are paying $120 a gram for the shit."

"Wow. Are lots of people doing this stuff?" said Dave.

"Everyone who knows about this stuff is doing it. No one wants meth anymore. And I haven't heard of people getting it from any other sources besides me. But now that I'm doing it legal and labeling shit, someone should figure it out and buy their own.

"Even if people do start ordering their own I don't think it will be much of a problem. I found someone who can get me the same shit for insanely cheap. I could undercut any price other people want to sell the shit for."

"Wow Luke. It sounds like you've got it all figured out," said Dave.

Luke used a fresh needle to stick in the glass tube. After drawing up 10 units, he tasted a drop of the liquid. His tongue went numb, "That's weird, it's kinda like coke."

"Is that the synthacain one? I think it might be like synthetic coke," said Dave.

"That would be sweet. Here we go then..." he took the shot and waited for a rush.

"Anything?" asked Dave.

"Nothing. Maybe I need to do the whole thing." He drew up the rest; it came out to be 90 units. The syringe was almost completely full. He tasted it once more before injecting it all in 10 unit intervals.

"Be careful, Luke. That's a lot of shit in there."

Luke waited a few seconds after he finished. "Nothing dude. I think it's meant to be an inter-muscular injection," said Luke.

"Maybe it's for people with allergic reactions."

"Or maybe when someone dies you're supposed to stick it right in someone's heart to bring them back to life. Ha."

"They do use epinephrin for that, don't they?" said Dave.

"That's what I thought."

"So make sure you keep that other vial with you in case anyone dies from your experimental chemicals," Dave joked.

"For sure. Any responsible chemical researcher would. I'm ready for a real shot after that let down."

"Me too. This one's on me; I want to mix it up for us," said Dave.

~~~

After an hour Zuri went to check on Luke and Dave. "Hey Luke, what's going
~~~

on in there? Will you unlock the door?"

Luke opened the door. They had been on the computer listening to music. "Hey, what's up," he said.

"Nothing. Just missing my boyfriend."

"Sorry sweetie. We're just learning about aliens and the Hollow Earth theory. Come on in, this is good stuff," he said.

Zuri came in and sat on a tote that was under the rail of coat hangers. Luke pushed the clothes out of the way.

"You wanna see how much money I made today?" he asked. Before she could answer he pulled out the stack of cash and counted it out for her. "That was just from today and I still got a lot more PV. Someone even traded me some crystal for PV." He showed her the bag of meth. "I don't know what to do with this stuff. No one wants it anymore now that PV is around."

"I know someone who might want it," she said.

Luke was shocked, "You do?"

"I have an ex who does a lot of that stuff now."

"Could you get a hold of him?"

"Yeah. He still tries to hang out with me once in a while."

"Why don't you wanna hang out with him?"

"Because I don't think you're supposed to hang out with your ex. Especially when you're with someone," she said.

"Well I'm a firm believer in the complete opposite. I think it's good to at least try to stay friends with your exes."

"Well, maybe I will," she tried to threaten.

"You should," he said sincerely.

"You make no sense to me. Let me see that stuff." She took the bag of meth. "So this stuff is pretty much the same thing as Adderall?"

"Well, pretty much. Typically the pharmaceutical stuff is L-methamphetamine. That stuff is probably D-meth or DL-methamphetamine. But it's all pretty much the same shit; I can't tell the difference," said Luke.

She paused for a few moments, thinking hard. "I wanna try it," she said.

"Go for it," he said.

"I wanna do it your way," she said.

"Not happenin."

"Why not?" she said.

"Because you can't unlearn that shit. I don't want to be the one responsible for corrupting you."

"If you don't do it I'll have my ex boyfriend do it," she said.

Oooh that's dirty. I can't have some filthy weirdo poking my girlfriend with some nasty needle. Even worse, some guy would be giving my girlfriend a rush ten times better than sex. "Fine. If you're gonna be doing this shit. I'm gonna clean it first." Luke got up and went to the kitchen.

He came back with a drinking glass, a coffee filter, acetone, and a shot glass. "Let me see that bag," he said.

Zuri gave him the bag of meth. "What are you doing?" she asked.

"Making it pure again." He crushed up the meth in the drinking glass and poured it onto the coffee filter. Then he dumped the acetone on top.

"What are you doing? You're ruining it!" said Dave.

"No I'm not. Just watch."

~~~

Luke measured out 100 milligrams of pure meth and threw it into a clean spoon. He didn't want any PV in the meth solution. Once it was ready he told her to hold out her arm. As soon as Luke got close with the needle she jerked away.

"It's not gonna hurt," he said, "I promise."

"I know, I know. Sorry," she said.

Luke tried again and she jerked away. "Now you're gonna have to look away or something. I need you to stay still," he said.

Zuri turned away and held her arm out. Before Luke even got close she whimpered and pulled her arm away. "Okay, I'm done," Luke capped the syringe and set it down.

"No, you have to! I'm sorry, I'll stay still this time," she said.

Luke tried again and she reacted just the same. "Look, I didn't even want to do this to you in the first place. Maybe you should just smoke it or snort it," he said.

"Nope. I'm doing it this way. I'm ready this time," she said.

~~~

An hour passed. Luke was freaking out; Dave was becoming irritable. "Jesus Christ!" said Dave, "Is it like this every time you go to the doctors?"

"This is your last chance," Luke said for the tenth time. "After this I'm taking the shot myself."

"Kay fine. I won't move, I promise." She held her arm out shaking. Luke came close with the needle; she closed her eyes and squealed. He got in the vein, flagged it, then injected.

She coughed and opened her eyes. The fear was gone, "Whoa..." she leaned back against the wall and stared toward the ceiling.

"Good? I was afraid I'd miss some of it with you shaking like that."

"I think you got it," she said in a weak voice.

"Nice." He looked at Dave, "I think we deserve one after putting up with that."

~~~

At 3:00am Luke received a phone call from Debora. "Hey, what's up?" he answered.

"There's people outside! I don't know who they are. Luke, I'm scared. They keep walking by and staring in here. All my lights are off, I don't know what to do."

"I'm on my way," Luke ran to the closet, grabbed his gun and threw on his shoes.

"What's going on?" said Zuri.

"Deboras in trouble; I need to leave now. Dave, I need you to come with me. My friend is in trouble," said Luke.

"What kind of trouble?"

"Just put on your shoes, let's go! We need to go now."

"I'm coming too!" said Zuri, putting on her shoes and chasing them out the door.
~~~

No man chooses evil because it is evil; he only mistakes it for happiness, the good he seeks.
-Mary Wollstonecraft Shelley

Chapter 20: Rescue Mission

Wednesday 8-14-2010

They creeped into Debora's trailer court in the Chrysler. It had only taken them 15 minutes to get there. Luke stayed over 100mph for most of the drive, not taking Zuri's advice to slow down. "I'm outside," Luke told Debora over the phone. "Everything looks fine from here."

"I think someone's in the backyard. I just saw the fence moving."

"Kay, I'll check it out then come knock on your door when it's clear."

"Okay," she said.

Luke hung up the phone. "Hop in the drivers seat for me," he told Dave. "I'll be right back." Luke wedged the gun in his waistband and got out of the car.

After a thorough search around the trailer, Luke knocked on the front door. Debora opened it looking frightened. "Everything seems fine. Do you wanna get out of here?"

"Yeah. Come inside for a minute." Luke followed her inside.

She hurried around the house looking for things she needed to bring with her. She sorted through things, picked them up, moved them, and set them back down. Finally all she had was a large can of hair spray and a pack of cigarettes. "Okay, I'm ready."

They left the house. Debora got in the back with Zuri while Luke hopped in passenger seat. Dave drove off and asked if everything was okay.

"I'm fine now, thank you guys so much," said Debora, "Somebody was sneaking around my house. I've never been so scared in my life. Luke, you're my hero, thank you so much."

"Not a problem. Debora, this is Dave, a really good friend of mine. Dave, this is my good friend Debora."

Dave looked back and gave a small wave, "Lovely to meet you, Debora."

"Good to meet you too." She looked at Zuri, "Hello sweetheart, how are you?"

"I'm really good. I'm super high right now." She took a drag from her cigarette.

"On what? I thought you didn't do anything."

"Crystal. It's really good. I don't see why everyone switched to that other stuff."

"Have you tired the other stuff?" said Debora.

"I did once. I think it's evil. The stuff I did tonight is perfect. I feel great."

"Ha, I bet you do. Where are we going right now? Do we have a plan?"

"We're going to our house," said Zuri.

"Are you guys okay with that? I'm not imposing, am I?"

"Absolutely not," said Luke, "It's gonna be good fun."

~~~

They were slowing down as they entered C-falls; only a few minutes away from safety. Luke turned down the music, "We've only seen like two cars since Kalispell. Kinda creepy."

"That is creepy," said Zuri.

A cop pulled out of nowhere and was right behind them. "Oh my god it's a cop!" Debora panicked.

"Seriously?" Luke tried not to panic. He threw the gun in the glove box and locked it.

"It's a cop," Zuri confirmed.

"Everyone act cool. No more tweaker peeking. Dave, obey all traffic laws," said Luke.

"Don't worry, guys," said Dave, "they can't pull us over unless we do something wrong."

"Well, we did mob to Kalispell at a buck ten. Someone could have reported us," said Luke.

"He's probably just running the plates. Is everything legal on this car?"
~~~

"Everything is legit, but you should turn up here so we can take the side streets the rest of the way. I don't want this pig knowing what street I live on," said Luke.

Dave used his blinker before parking. The cop creeped past. Luke was thankful for the tinted windows. The cop took a right at the end of the block and sped off. "Okay, everyone out, we're walking the rest of the way," said Luke.

"Oh c'mon," said Dave, "we're only three blocks away."

"Exactly. That cop's trying to pull us over. If we're not in the car he can't do shit. Everyone out, lock the doors, illegal shit stays in the car out of sight."

They walked away after locking up the car. Moments later the cop came creeping up behind them; he had circled the block. Luke had his hoody up and hat facing forward. Dave was wearing his leather jacket and walked with confidence.

The cop creeped up to the end of the block with them and stopped. Luke and his friends kept walking, Debora lit a cigarette and tried to look casual. The cop drove off for the last time.

Luke approached his house with care, paying close attention that they weren't being followed. They all relaxed once they were safely in the house. Luke turned on some uplifting electronic music; something that would suppress the paranoia. Only Debora and Luke seemed to be having the paranoia problems.

The music helped. "Hey Debora, remember the first time we got high together? We stayed up all night playing Yahtzee with that one lady."

"That was a good time. You seemed so young; I felt so weird doing all that stuff with you. So did Linda. But you were so fun to be around, just so cool about everything."

"Pretty trippy. Look at us now! You gotta see my basement." Luke showed off the house and offered a mandatory weed smoking session.

Everyone's nerves were now calm. They were having a good time talking and smoking in the living room. Luke was obsessing over his air purifier, blowing weed and cigarette smoke into the filter. Basshunter was playing on the stereo; Zuri's choice of techno music. The beat was uplifting with some European guy singing something romantic in another language. Zuri was having an awesome time. Everyone else felt the same.

Luke could feel himself starting to jones for MDPV, but he wanted to try something different first. He excused himself to the closet.

Luke came back ten minutes later with the glass epinephrin tube. "You're not trying that stuff again, are you?" said Dave.

"No, I filled it up with 4-MEC! Who want's to try? Me first!" He pulled out a syringe and drew up 15 units. "What is that?" said Debora.

"It's like an analogue of MDMA," he said.

"Be careful, Luke," said Zuri.

Luke took the shot. His eyes went googley as he tried to recap the syringe. He couldn't do it; he dropped the syringe and laid down on the carpet.

"Are you okay?" Zuri grabbed his hand.

"I'm awesome!" Luke's voice came out in a vibration as he melted into the carpet. His bloodstream was flowing with silk. He pulled Zuri's hand to his face and felt the softness. The light was bright, but his eyes wouldn't stop moving; all he saw were shifting colors.

It took fifteen minutes before Luke could fill up another syringe. "Who's next."

"I'll go," said Dave. "That looked like fun."

Luke gave him the shot. Dave melted into the carpet. He laughed to himself. *This must be what heaven feels like. I think I get it now; the crazy music these kids listen to... it all makes sense.*

All I ever wanted, was to see you smilen
All I ever wanted, was to make you mine
I know that I love you
Oh baby why don't you see
That all I ever wanted, was you and me...

What a happy place. How did I end up in such a place? Ooh, I love this carpet. This song is the best.

Zuri's shot was ready. Dave was still laying on the floor feeling the best he'd ever felt. She held out her arm and looked away. There was no jerking this time. She took it and was flooded with the silky ecstasy sensation.

While she was soaking into the floor with pleasure, Luke readied the next shot for Debora. "Your time to shine," he said.

"Are you sure I should? I'm still high from the stuff I did earlier."

"Of course you should," said Luke.

"You really should," said Dave, still smiling on the floor.

"I don't like losing control of myself. I won't lose control, will I?"

"No, it's awesome. Let me see your arm." She held her arm out reluctantly. He examined her damaged veins with care. His eyes were still out of focus, going googley if he didn't concentrate. He settled with the awkward forearm vein as usual with Debora.

The injection went smoothly. The arm that she was leaning on buckled. She fell back onto the carpet, looking scared.

"I can't see! Oh no, I'm dying!" She squirmed on the floor, kicking her legs and grabbing at the carpet.

"You're not dying. I promise you're not dying," said Luke.

Debora moaned in horror, "I still can't see! Way too much, oh this is bad."

"You did the same as us; it's supposed to be intense."

It took five minutes for Debora to calm down. The panicking stopped as soon as her vision started to return. "You guys are crazy," she said. "I've never been so high in my life!"

"I'm gonna do a big one now," said Luke.

"Bigger than what I just did?" said Debora.

"We all did fifteen units. I'm gonna try twenty five."

"Don't do it, Luke! You'll die," said Debora.

"I don't think you can die from this stuff. It doesn't mention any reported deaths on Wikipedia. But then again, it doesn't mention much about this stuff yet. It's still in the experimental stage."

"You want me to grab the actual epinephrin in case you die?" Dave joked. "I'll stick right in the heart!" he mimed a violent jab at Luke's chest with a needle.

"Ha, sure dude." Luke drew up 25 units. He looked at it with the needle still in the vial. It was intimidating. He pushed a few units back into the vial, *Twenty two looks about right.*

Luke took the shot. Debora watched with fear. The silkiness came on followed by a hot tingling feeling in his head; as if his synapses were bursting in his brain. Vision was gone and pupils dilated to the brim. *This cannot be healthy,* he thought.

"Are you okay?" came a distant echoing voice.

"Totally," he managed to say through the rollercoaster of sensory overload.

~~~

At 5:00am Tim pulled up in an old Honda hatchback. Luke had retrieved the Chrysler which was now parked in the driveway. Tim came in. Luke noticed a paranoid vibe about him. "What's up, dude?" said Luke.

"Crazy night, man. I need to talk to you about some stuff."

Dave, Debora, and Zuri were taking turns playing tetris on the X-box in the living room. "Sure man." They went to the closet. Tim barely greeted the people in the living room.

Tim took the battery out of his cellphone. "I think we should do this."

"Absolutely." Luke took his out as well. "Who's car is that?"

"It's mine. I got it for three grams."

"That's badass, dude," said Luke.

"I know, man. Check this out." Tim pulled out a beautiful revolver.
~~~

"Holy smokes!" Luke took the shiny pistol and admired it with care. It was a Colt 357 Trooper MK-II. "How much do you want for it?"

"I don't know. How much will you give me?" said Tim.

"How much did you get it for?"

Tim hesitated, deciding if he should tell the truth. "Two grams."

"Damn dude! Serious?"

"There's some desperate people out there."

"Are you selling it as drugs or research chemical?" said Luke.

"I'm doing it the same way you are. MDPV, not for human consumption."

"And they're still payin up the ass for it?"

"They don't care what it is. They're used to paying shit loads for crystal, so this stuff is easy to sell, especially since no one likes meth anymore."

"Wow. I know what you mean. Someone got me to trade them PV for crystal, gram for gram. Zuri likes it so I guess I'll probably just give it to her," said Luke.

"She's doing that stuff now? I was wondering why she was still awake."

"Yep. She forced me to give her a shot. Now she likes it. I corrupted her." He stared at the gun for a few moments, "I'll give you five grams for this. That way you pretty much got your car for free."

"Alright man. That's cool," said Tim.

Tim asked if they could do a shot. "I don't think you need a shot. Not of PV, anyway. You wanna try some 4-MEC?" Luke held out his cool new vial.

Tim wasn't enthusiastic about it; he wanted to do more PV. Luke knew Tim was plenty high on PV; he just wanted to do another shot for the rush. *If he wants a rush, I'll give him a rush.*

~~~

After a half hour there was a knock on the closet door. Luke opened the door; it was Dave. "What's going on in here?" Luke handed Dave the shiny nickel plated revolver. "Oh, how beautiful. This is incredible. Do you have any idea how much something like this is worth?"

"That's what I'm looking up right now." Luke had the computer open and was staring at the screen. "Seven hundred seems to be the going price."

"You lucky dog! Have you ever shot a 357? This thing is a cannon."

"I've never shot one. I'm gonna need you to buy me some ammo for this if that's cool."

"Of course I will. When are we going shooting? You're gonna need to clean this first. Or better yet, let me do it. Can I clean it now?"

"Sure." Luke found his gun cleaning kit and gave it to Dave.

"You wanna get high first? I think it's time."
~~~

"Oh, we certainly should," said Dave.

~~~

Luke, Dave, and Debora were smoking in the basement. Zuri was in the bedroom putting together a photo album. Luke was playing with his throwing knives while contemplating whether he should buy another air purifier. "Do you think there's mold down here?" he asked.

"Probably is," said Dave. "It's an old house. If there is mold, it's most likely underneath the bathroom. Where would the bathroom be?"

"I think over here by the stairs." They went to inspect. Sure enough, there were moldy spots on the ceiling.

"Oh yeah," said Dave, "See all this?"

"Shit, what are we supposed to do? Is it black mold? Will it make us sick?"

"I don't know. You would have to have someone come in to take a sample."

"What could we do about it now?"

"I suppose you could spray it with bleach. Another air purifier down here wouldn't hurt either."

There was suddenly a bunch of commotion coming from upstairs. Zuri came running in terror, "Someone's outside!"

"Who's outside?" said Luke.

"Some fat creepy weirdo. He was outside the bedroom window."

Luke hoped Zuri wasn't already seeing shadow people. Maybe something was really happening. "I'll be right back." Luke ghost reconned his way up to the closet and grabbed the Walther PPK. He carefully approached the window with gun drawn and safety off. Once he gathered the courage, he peeked out the crack between curtains. *Nothing.*

Luke checked all of the windows as he made his way back to the basement. "It's all good, guys."

"Someone was out there. I promise," she said.

"If someone was out there, they're gone now." Luke went to the far side of the basement to check a window. The pistol still ready at his side. He pulled the cardboard to the side, stood on his tippy toes, and gave a good long tweaker peek. "Yeah, I don't think there's anything to- Oh fuck!" He crouched to the floor with both hands on the pistol.

"What is it?" Debora was hiding behind Dave.

"Someone just walked by!" said Luke.

"What did they look like?" said Dave.

"He walked close to the house. I could only see his legs. He was wearing black pants and black boots. Like the kind of boots only a cop or a psychopath would
~~~

wear."

Debora made a fearful noise. "We're gonna die. It's probably the same people who were at my house."

"No way!" said Luke, "I'll take those fuckers out." There was a knock at the back door at the top of the stairs. "Was that a cop knock?" No one answered.

"What are you gonna do?" said Debora.

"If they don't make a proper entrance I'm gonna shoot em." Everyone except Dave went to the far side of the basement. Luke crouched at the bottom of the stairs with his gun pointed at the door.

Five minutes went by with no movement; no noise. Zuri finally spoke up: "If you don't go check it out I'm gonna."

Luke looked at her and felt insulted. He was the one with the gun; he should have no fear. "Fuck. Fine, I'll go investigate."

He crept up the creaky stairs with his gun fixed on the door. Any second the door could come flying open. Would he be quick enough? Could he take whoever was on the other side?

He made it past the door into the bathroom. With the lights turned off he peeked out the window. That way whoever was outside could not see in, but he could see out. There was a figure sitting on the back steps. It was a fat person. Luke could not recognize the outfit.

Luke figured he could open the back door and interrogate the person at gunpoint. He had every right. This was Montana, and this person was a trespasser; a very strange trespasser.

Here it goes, Luke thought, *I hope he doesn't get crazy. I'll kill him in a heartbeat.* He unlocked the door and pushed it open, but then scurried back into the bathroom with his gun pointed toward the door. He peeked out the bathroom window; the fat person was turned around staring into the opened door. He was still unarmed and looking confused.

Luke charged at the back door and pointed the gun. It was Fat Jared, looking at Luke with a fearful puppy dog face. "Dude, what the fuck are you doing?" Luke put the gun down.

"Oh thank god. I need help, Luke. I didn't even know for sure if I was at the right house."

"Get in here, man. Why didn't you call?"

Jared stood up with a stiff robotic movement and clenched jaws. Luke could see in his eyes; Jared was high on DXM. "I lost my phone," he said through labored breathing.

Jared followed Luke down to the basement. "I found the fat creepy weirdo.

Looks like he's been eating triple C's. Is that what happened, Jared?" Jared nodded, eyes wide and fearful. "Why did you do that? How did you get here? What's up with the boots? Explain yourself." Luke noticed now that the laces were untied on each of Jared's boots.

Jared thought for a few moments before trying to speak. "I think some-" his face twitched mid-sentence as he lost his train of thought. Luke recognized this as the triple C stutter; the same stutter Luke still suffered from years after he quit eating cold medicine.

"How much did you eat, man?" said Luke.

"Two. Two boxes," he said.

That meant 32 pills. The usual dose was 16, though Luke had seen people black out from 8 pills. "Did you black out?"

Jared nodded, "I think something bad happened. I appeared in some house. It was a fake-" *stutter,* "a fake house. There was some furniture, a couch, but no one lived there. I don't know how I got in the-, I don't know how I got in there and I couldn't get out. I thought it was where people go when they die. I thought I was dead."

"I didn't have any shoes and I wasn't wearing a shirt. There was no clothes anywhere in the house. I'm telling you this place was ff- it was fake! Goddamnit. There was no phone either; I didn't have a phone."

"The doors were all locked. I couldn't get out so I threw a vase through a window and crawled out."

Debora stared at him with shock and disbelief. She had never met Fat Jared and was unfamiliar with Coricidin Cough and Cold. Luke, Dave, and Zuri had each done it or seen it done on many occasions.

"You need to take off your boots," said Luke. "There's no shoes allowed in here."

"I don't think that's a good idea," said Jared.

"Do it."

Jared removed one boot, revealing a stinking muddy and bloody sock. Everyone winced; Debora gasped in horror. "Yuck, dude. Put it back on," said Luke.

"Don't put it back on!" said Debora, "You need medical attention. Up to the bathroom, now." She grabbed Jared by the arm and helped him up the stairs. Luke filled up a spray bottle with bleach and cleaned up the bloody footprints.

Debora cleaned and bandaged Jared's feet in the bathroom Jared had never met Debora. He asked her who she was and why she was fixing his feet.

"I'm Luke's friend and I used to be a nurse. These cuts could get infected if we don't clean them properly."

Once his feet were all fixed up they went to the living room. Luke loaded a bowl of weed to smoke while Jared finished his story:

"I found the boots and sweater in some random car. Then I just started walking. I was at some gas station, trying to find ugh- trying to find a cigarette. Some-… someone asked me if I needed a ride. I didn't know where I should go. He told me he was heading to Hungry Horse so I asked him if he would drop me off in Columbia Falls.

"So- ugh, damnit- I couldn't figure out where you lived so he just dropped me off at the gas station. I walked around and eventually found your house."

"Wow, man. I'm glad you made it." Luke passed the pipe to Jared.

"And you say cold medicine did this to you?" said Debora. Jared nodded with the fearful triple C face. "You kids are crazy. Do you guys do this stuff?"

"No," said Luke, "but I used to do it all the time. It gives you pre-death hallucinations; makes you leave your body some times."

"I used to do it when I was in elementary school," said Zuri.

"The first time I met Luke, he was on that stuff," said Dave. "He was all messed up and ended up on my doorstep one night. Kinda freaked me out until I realized he was just lost and harmless, so I took him in for the night."

"Yep, that's how we became friends," said Luke.

"What's the point of being so high? Why would you want to go into blackouts and leave your body?" said Debora.

Luke went into an animated explanation of triple C's and told trippin stories. Some of the stories included Tim since they had eaten cold medicine so many times together.

~~~

The sun came up and everyone except for Zuri was fiending for a shot. Jared wanted to get high too, but Luke said no. "You're still trippin, dude. DXM and MDPV sounds like a deadly combination. You're heart could freakin explode or something."

"Please Luke. I don't wanna go to sleep. My heart will be fine."

"Do you know how to check people's pulses?" Luke asked Debora. She nodded. "Can you check his?"

She took his wrist and watched the clock that was ticking up on the wall. "That's scary. It's over 150 beats per minute."

"See dude! You don't need any speed. You need to be sedated.

Do we have any opiates or benzos around?" Luke looked at Dave.

"I certainly do." Dave went to his car and came back with a bottle of
~~~

methadone. "Do either of you want one?" he asked the girls.

"Nooo thank you," said Zuri.

"I'm fine, thanks," said Debora. "But I wouldn't mind doing a hit of the other stuff."

"For sure, that's exactly what we need to do." Luke went to the closet and came back with the paraphernalia.

Zuri watched with wonder while Luke got everything ready. "Do you guys really need to do more? I got high once and I don't feel like I'm even close to coming down. Are you coming down already?" she asked Luke.

"Well, I'm not tired, but I definitely feel like I should do more. I have plenty; there's no reason not to," said Luke.

"But you guys just did some not even two hours ago. Why do you like it so much? It seems like you have to do more every hour to stay up all night."

"I guess it's more like coke in that sense. It's got a better rush, but doesn't last nearly as long as meth," said Luke.

"So you like coke better than meth?" she asked.

"No way! I'd rather do Adderall than coke."

"If PV is like coke then why don't you just do meth?" she said.

"Would you guys rather do some crystal?" he asked his friends. They both shook their heads. "Why not?"

"I like the stuff we've been doing," said Dave.

"Me too," said Debora.

Zuri was frustrated. "So you guys have a craving specifically for PV?"

"I guess you could say that," said Debora.

"You've done meth for a long time, right? And you're saying you wouldn't do any crystal right now even if it was free?" said Zuri.

"Well, I don't know. Probably not since we have this other stuff. I have no desire for crystal."

Zuri tried hard to wrap her head around the situation. *A lady who's been addicted to meth all her life doesn't want any, all because some evil internet drug is around.*

"Do you want me to take a hit of crystal instead?" said Luke.

"Will you try?" said Zuri.

"I will. I'll do it for the sake of research, just to see what happens." Luke handed two fresh needles full of MDPV to Dave and Debora. The third one he put away for later.

Luke prepared the same dose for himself as he had for Zuri. He took the shot, coughed and experienced a nasty rush. *Strange.*

"How is it?" she said.

"I don't know. I think I need to do more." Luke measured out and drew up another 100 milligrams of meth. *Now this should do the trick.* He took the shot with the same results.

"Are you high yet?" Zuri asked after Luke made it through the rush.

Luke tried to feel what he was supposed to feel. He should have been bouncing off the walls. Instead he was just as tired and still jonesing for PV. "I don't feel shit," he said.

"Your pupils are big though. Bigger than they were before you did any of that stuff."

"That's about all it did, because I'm still jonesing for PV."

"No way," said Zuri. She didn't understand how the same stuff that had her bursting with euphoric energy did nothing for Luke.

"Dead serious. I could probably fall asleep right now if I wanted. I'll try one more shot. If it doesn't do nothing, we can conclude that amphetamines have no stimulating effects to MDPV users."

Luke drew up a quarter gram this time. "Now what we have here is 250 milligrams; an extremely large dose, not including the 200 milligrams I've already done."

"Be careful," said Zuri, she had only done 100 milligrams and couldn't imagine doing 5 times that amount.

"Don't worry. You can't die from this stuff," he said. That didn't make sense, but she was sure he believed it.

Luke took it, coughed, and laid down where he sat to brace himself for the rush. He couldn't see or hear; there was just blackness and a loud ringing.

~~~

Luke woke up to Zuri tugging at his arm. "C'mon and get up. It's time for bed."

"What the fuck? No! I'm not going to bed. How long was I asleep?" Luke got up on his own, feeling a nasty griminess covering his body. Dave and Debora were watching *The Doors.*

"It's nine o'clock. You slept like two hours after that shot," said Zuri.

"Yeah Luke, you scared the crap out of us," said Debora.

Luke was more drowsy and miserable feeling than ever. He went straight to the closet and took the shot of MDPV he should have done hours ago. Instantly he was good to go and full of energy, with some anxiety as a mild side effect. *Holy crap I need a shower.* The sweat that had covered his body stank of chemicals.

"What are you doing?" Zuri asked as Luke raced around the bedroom looking for clothes.
~~~

"Gettin in the shower. I feel disgusting," he said.

"Can I take one with you?"

"Sure," Luke walked into the living room, "Where's Jared?"

"He's sleeping in the basement," said Debora. "We set him up with some blankets and stuff down there."

"Right on." Luke went on to the shower. Zuri came in minutes later.

Rust grows from iron and destroys it; so evil grows from the mind of human and destroys him.
-Dammapada

Chapter 21: Imposter Bitch

Wednesday 11-20-2010

Blue sat at the desk in his cheap motel room. He was messing with a scanner while nervously glancing at the girl sitting on his bed. Dez was sitting on his bed drinking orange juice and texting.

Blue was beginning to hate this girl. She was a face picker, and would mutter things under her breath without realizing it. The muttering was the worst, he confronted her on it a few times; "Are you wearing a fucking wire? Are you speaking into a microphone or are you just a psycho bitch?

She would defend herself, saying that she hadn't made any noise at all. He barely knew her even though they'd been having sex for most of the night before.

"Hey Blue," said Dez, still holding the cellphone, "I've got someone who wants a gram. They said they'll pay 120."

"Okay," Blue made an adjustment on the scanner.

"Do you want me to go deliver it? I can have the person meet me at Taco Bell."

"Sure." Blue pulled out his scale and weighed up a gram of MDPV. "Here you go."

She took the bag and looked at it for a few moments. "Do you think I could have a hit before I go?"

"Sure, gimme your spoon." He tapped a small amount of powder into the spoon and gave it back. She then disappeared into the bathroom for ten minutes.

"I'll be back soon," she said as she headed for the door.

"Hey, grab me a pack of Marbs while your out," he handed her some cash.

"Kay." She took it and left.

Blue watched as she left the parking lot. *Where the fuck are you going? Thought you said you were going to Taco Bell. Dumb whore.* He didn't trust the girl. He had only met her a couple days before and something about her didn't feel right. She was a junkie. He could tell she had been using MDPV long before she'd met him. At one point he suspected her of going through his phone. Since then he kept it safely in his pocket, along with everything else he wanted to keep out of her hands.

Blue was in the bathroom about to take a shot for himself when there was a knock on the door. He went to the door and looked out the peephole. "That was quick," he said as he opened the door.

"Well, that's how drug deals are supposed to go, right?" said the girl who appeared to be Dez.

"I don't know why you would say something so fuckin stupid," he said as he closed the door.

"Oh, my bad. Should I not say that?" she said in an oddly different voice.

Blue started to notice that this girl's features were different than the girl who had left ten minutes before. There were no scabs on her face and she had more meat on her bones.

"Who the fuck are you?" he asked.

"What do you mean? It's me, Dez," she said in the same unfamiliar voice. "And here is your money."

"I don't want your money, you don't owe me shit. We're straight," he said.

"Are you sure? You should really take this, it's yours," she said.

"Fuck you, no it's not." Blue couldn't believe what was happening. He had been through the depths of amphetamine psychosis before, but this was different. This was real. There was no way this was the same girl.

"Why are you being a jerk?" she said.

"Look, I don't know who you are or what kind of games your trying to play, but I think you should leave." He stared her down, absolutely certain his accusations were true. The imposter Dez was starting to look nervous. Blue felt a sickening feeling when she pulled out her phone, not taking her eyes off him.

There was a knock on the door. Blue had two options: He could take the imposter bitch hostage, or he could surrender to the trap he'd fallen into.

The knock persisted, "Bluuue, open up." It was another girl, this one sounding familiar. He stood up, eyes wide, trying to read the imposter Dez's face. He looked out the peephole, "Blue, it's me, Monica. Blue opened the door. "Hey dude," she said as she walked in, "Hi Dez." The imposter Dez gave her a wave. Monica was a skinny white-trash girl.

Blue closed the door. Monica didn't notice anything unusual about Dez. She sat down on the bed. Blue sat down at the desk. Monica looked back and fourth between the two, "what the fuck is wrong with you two?" she asked.

Dez shrugged. Monica looked at Blue, "Nothing's wrong," he said, "You tell me if you feel like something is wrong here."

"Okay, well, I need to talk to you. I got someone who's got some money. They wanna get a ball," she said.

"Their money's no good here. I don't sell shit."

Monica gave another glance at Dez. She could tell Blue was paranoid. "Come talk with me for a minute." She grabbed his hand and took him to the bathroom. "What's goin on dude?"

"That fuckin bitch out there! She's weirdin me out. Don't you notice something different about her?"

"No, not really. What do you mean?" she said.

"I want you to pay close attention to her when we go back out there. Her voice, her features, her entire personality. I don't think that's Dez at all," he said.

"You're losing your mind. It's all in your head, remember?"

"I don't think so. I really don't see how it's not obvious to you. That bitch is different," he said.

"Does that make any sense at all? Why would some girl pretend to be Dez? Cops don't send people in pretending to be other people, that would be retarded. Now, are you gonna be able to help out my friend? Or should I tell him to find it somewhere else?" she said.

"Fuck no. I'm not feelin it."

"C'mon Blue. There's nothing to worry about. Your gettin all stressed out over nothin." She stuck her hand down his pants.

"Give me a ball for 250. I'll suck your dick."

"You're a whore." She unzipped his pants, not about to take no for an answer.

Blue and Monica came out of the bathroom after a half hour. Blue had weighed out the MDPV and they each took a hit. Dez was smoking a cigarette. "You guys were in there forever. I ate a bowl of cereal," said Dez.

"That's cool," said Blue as he sat back down at the desk.

"I'm puttin on some tunes," said Monica,"My buddy is coming in from C-Falls to pick me up."

"I have to ask," said Dez, trying to sound friendly, "Why would someone like you have Lucky Charms? I mean, your like this badass tweaker gangster guy, and you eat Lucky Charms? I think it's pretty cool."

"You bought that shit at Walmart last night. If you were the real Dez you would fucking know that, bitch!"

"Oh. I guess I forgot. Sorry," said imposter Dez, taking a nervous drag from her cigarette.

"Did you at least grab some cigarettes for me. The other Dez said she would come back with some."

"Oh, you want some cigarettes?" she pulled out a pack of Camel 99's. "I can share some."

"You didn't get me a pack of Marbs?"

"No. Was I supposed to?" said the imposter.

"Never mind." Blue laughed to himself, "What the fuck is going on?" he muttered.

Blue opened his phone. He wanted to see Luke. The situation was getting worse, he'd been in the motel room for too long. *I need to relocate. All this confinement is getting to my head.* Twenty minutes went by with no reply. Blue made the call.

"Hello?" Luke answered.

"Hey *Frank*, I need to see you," said Blue.

"Okay, I'll be at Walmart in forty-five minutes."

"Kay bro, I'll see you there." Blue hung up the phone.

The next ten minutes were awkward. Why was the fake Dez still there? Her cover was blown; wasn't it time to abort the mission? It was all starting to seem like a game for Blue. The song lyrics were no coincidence: "*They shoulda nevuh evuh let you out...*" Monica was trying to communicate with Dez.

I see what's going on here, they're both in it together; big joke on Blue. What are they trying to do? Dez still has my 120 dollars. Maybe I should ask for it... No way. Something's wrong. She would have spent it all on heroin already.

The subliminal communication was getting worse. Neither of the girls had spoken to Blue for some time. They only looked at each other, exchanging messages. Blue was sure he'd heard the final message: "*Caught in a trap...*" a shadow passed over the curtain, "*There's no turnin back...*" He was sure a squad of special ops looking guys were about to burst through the window.

"Why don't you just come out and fuckin say it?" he asked the girls. "All of these messages and shit; do you think I'm stupid?

"What are you talking about?" said Monica.

"You two are communicating with the music and shit!"

"No one's said anything. Are you okay?" said Monica.

Danger was coming. Blue left the motel and expected a violent takedown. He made it to his truck, knowing every move was being watched.

~~~

"Is that him?" said the guy in the driver seat.

"Yep. He should be heading to meet his dealer right now," said the lady in the passenger seat. The two people were parked at a restaurant right next to the motel. They watched as Blue walked in paranoid figure eights to his truck.

"You're sure he's going to meet his dealer?" he said.

"He's all out of shit. You think he's just gonna run out? This dude never runs out. He meets his guy at least twice a week," she said.

Blue started driving out of the parking lot. He sat waiting for an opening in traffic. The guy started to follow, "Wait a minute. If Blue sees me following him he'll freak."

"Well, I don't want to lose him!" he said as he circled around to follow. Blue pulled out. They kept a safe distance.

"Be careful. This dude doesn't take his eyes off the rear view mirror." She pulled the visor down to block her face. With her out of view, all he would see was an old guy driving a beat up Buick.

They followed him all the way to the Walmart parking lot. Twenty minutes went by. They could see Blue shifting nervously in his seat. "What the fuck is taking so long?" said the guy.

"Just be patient," she said. A few moments later a low-riding Chrysler came cruising in next to Blue. Blue got in the Chrysler.

"We'll make it look like a coincidence. You're good enough friends with Blue, right?"

~~~

"Hey cousin, how ya been?" said Luke.

"I been trippin, bro. Shit's been gettin weird for me," said Blue.

"I know what you mean, dude. How much do you need this time?"

"I only got enough for ten grams. Shit hasn't been working out lately. I got a lot of shit fronted out."

"Alright man." Luke started to weigh out some MDPV. He was disappointed to have to sell such a small amount. Dan had been helping him get PV much cheaper lately. Now they were getting it for $4.50 a gram; 100 grams at a time. The street price hadn't budged. Luke was greedy and wouldn't sell it any cheaper.

Luke handed over the ten grams-less than twenty five dollars worth of chemical-and Blue gave $400 in exchange. Luke had been selling to more than his small handful of people. Tim had proved himself unreliable. He would flush his drugs down the toilet, or get robbed by his friends. He was too far in debt. Luke had to cut him off and find new people.

Blue usually did well. A couple times a week he would pick up at least thirty grams. Debora was still keeping a whole other hidden piece of society supplied with PV. All of those people went on assuming it was biker speed or Nazi dope; same with Blue's clients, they were oblivious that the drugs were legal. Even the people who knew it was legal would hide and smuggle the stuff around. Nothing about the stuff felt legal. It was the most vicious drug anyone had been addicted to. No wonder it was a death penalty offense if possessed or consumed in China.

"I think I'm gonna take a hit real quick. You wanna do one too?" Luke pulled out his sunglass case. He filled up a syringe out of his glass epinephrine tube.

"Sure, I'll do a small one," said Blue.

"That's cool. Small ones are the only ones I like anymore." He handed Blue a syringe and prepared to take a shot for himself. "Are we safe, dude?" Luke looked around the vehicle, "I have that horrible feeling that someone's watching us. But it's not real, is it? It's our brains being tricked into thinking we're in a constant state of emergency, right?"

"I can hardly be sure anymore. So much weird shit has been happening lately. Honestly I don't really care if anyone is watching. We're not doing anything that illegal really. We're just getting high off some random shit. I don't think we're breaking any laws."

"I guess you're right." Luke took the shot, and suddenly felt that he was in real, imminent danger. Someone was approaching them, for real.

Luke scrambled to throw everything in the glove box before the strangers could see. There was a knock on the passenger window. Blue rolled the window down halfway and gave a menacing glare at the lady.

"Hey Blue, I thought I recognized your Nissan. How are you doing?" Luke recognized the lady to be Mandy. She was in Blue's car during one of their previous meetings. Blue had told Luke that she was not to be trusted.

"I'm busy," said Blue.

Another guy came up after Mandy and introduced himself, "Hey guys, I'm

Wade." The man wore a leather jacket with lots of zippers.

"This is my boyfriend," Mandy told Blue.

"You must be Blue, and you must be Frank. I'm glad to meet you two," said Wade.

"This isn't Frank," said Blue, "and I think you should mind your own fuckin business."

Luke was extremely paranoid, hunched forward with his hand on the pistol under the seat. "Whoa man, that's no way to talk to someone who's been trying to help you make money," said Wade. Wade shifted his view to Luke, "I'm just a decent guy who is tired of dealing with piece of shit middle men. We could really help each other out, man. Your buddy here won't give any bulk deals. He's greedy, and he's holdin you back. Give me a call, or send someone decent to talk to me." Wade tossed a business card through the window, "I only got good intentions for you, brother."

"I don't know who Frank is and I definitely don't have what ever it is you're looking for. I'm afraid you've got the wrong guy. I gotta bounce." Luke put the car in gear.

Blue opened the door, "Who the fuck do you think you are?" he said.

"You wanna get crazy, punk?" Wade whipped out a switch blade.

Luke had the pistol in his lap now, ready to defend his cousin.

"I don't care what chu got, I'll fuck you up old man." They both had a look of pure hatred in their eyes. The staredown lasted a few moments, then Blue got in his Nissan and took off.

Luke followed suit, but didn't drive so recklessly as Blue.

~~~

Luke headed home after a few more stops. The past couple months had been rough. It had been snowing on and off recently. The cold made his bad circulation even worse. He was also beginning to develop a condition called "Athlete's Heart," where it became enlarged and covered in scar tissue from multiple mini heart attacks.

A lot of Luke's time had been spent on the internet. He would find ways to self-diagnose his problems and find natural remedies. His father's herbal shop supplied him with an arsenal of remedies for all his ailments. He used a combination of DMSO, goldenseal root, and vitamin E oil to heal his track marks and prevent scarring. He used valerian root for anxiety; Co-Q10 for heart cell regeneration; ginko for memory; echinacea to prevent infection; grapefruit fiber to unclog arteries; vitamin E and C to open up arteries; grape seed to strengthen blood vessels; kudzu for blood pressure and dilation of blood vessels.
~~~

There were many more remedies and he was always discovering new ones. He would pay his friends to make up capsules for him. He also insisted that his friends use the remedies as well.

Zuri was still using crystal and selling some to her ex-boyfriend in Columbia Falls. Luke had given her an injection almost every day since she tried it the first time. Even doing meth everyday she still looked healthier than Luke. Luke drank lots of V8, Ensure, and other fruit/vegetable drinks. Zuri survived purely on ice cream and pizza bites.

Not all of Luke's friends were hooked on PV. He had some acquaintances who were more interested in other chemicals. Luke was an unreliable test subject. Many chemicals affected him abnormally because of his MDPV addiction. He would still sample any chemical that Dan would put in front of him; all in the name of research.

The love of money is the mother of all evil.
-Phocylides 6th century B.C.

Chapter 22: Asbestos

Tuesday 11-26-2010

Luke was in his closet organizing his gas masks and Nuclear Biological Chemical suits. He had been ordering many things from the internet. There was a web site that sold ex-military gas masks and accessories. He bought an Israeli, a Ukrainian, and two Swiss gas masks. The Russian NBC filters were the cheapest, so he bought a whole crate. All the gas masks were at least twenty years old. The NBC suits were new and expensive.

He checked the delivery tracking on one of his other purchases as he organized his new gear. There were more guns in his arsenal some were reported stolen and had to be hidden in the mountains.

He particularly cherished his Romanian AK-47. The rifle was un-registered and perfectly legal for him to carry wherever he pleased. When he first got it, it was old and worn out. Now it had a polished wood grip and a fold-out synthetic stock.

"Luke, it's time to take a break." Zuri looked at his greasy dehydrated face, "Let's smoke a bowl and eat something."

"I can't do any of that right now. I got a mess in here. I need to get it together." He turned away to sort things out in a large plastic tote.

Zuri knelt behind him and gave him a hug. He stopped what he was doing. She gave him a kiss on the neck, "Please babe, you're stressin yourself out in here. You need a break."

"What I need is another shot, maybe some water too. I can take a break once I get this house cleaned up. So if you want me to take a break then help me," he said.

"Every time I try to clean up your messes you accuse me of throwing your stuff away. Maybe you shouldn't start twenty different projects all over the house. Maybe you should do one thing at a time. And I think right now the most important thing for you to do is eat food and drink water."

"I've been drinking Ensure, that's got water and it's even better than food." Luke replaced a few more things in the tote then slammed the lid closed. "Fine, fuck it. I'm taking a break."

"Good, I'll grab the pipe." They sat together on the floor and smoked weed. Luke turned on some Dubstep during the session.

"After this I'm gonna go into the attic. There's got to be a fucked up reason why the landlord told us not to go up there."

"I don't think it's a good idea," she said.

"Why? I've got the chemical suits. Even if there's asbestos I'll be fine."

"It's not that. I just think it's a stupid idea. I don't think you'll accomplish anything good by digging around up there."

"Well, you told me he said to not go up there. Now because of that, it's all I want to do," he took a hit from the pipe. "Fuck. I also have to study for that motorcycle license test. Why is life so demanding?"

"You make it way too hard on yourself. You don't relax... Ever." She left the closet and came back with pizza bites. Luke was already starting to re-organize again. She stopped him, and forced him to eat. After eating, Luke forced himself to smoke a cigarette. Since starting MDPV, he lost all cravings for anything but MDPV. If there was a perfect time to quit smoking, it was then. If he had the desire to quit, it would have taken almost no effort.

He took a shot and geared up to investigate the attic. Zuri forced him to drink some water. Luke felt something terrible was happening. He tried to hide his paranoid feelings from Zuri. "Why are you taking that thing up there?" she asked.

Luke was all sealed up in his NBC suit, holding an AK-47 in one hand and a shop-vac in the other. "Oh, this?" he tried to sound casual, "I'm just gonna see if I can find a good hiding place for it up here."

Zuri didn't believe him. She knew he was paranoid. She could only hope he wouldn't be stuck up there for hours pointing that thing at the neighbors.

Luke climbed on top of the dresser, breaking a lamp and knocking over a bunch of Zuri's stuff. "Oh my god, Luke!" Zuri examined the lamp, "My grandma gave this to me before she died."

Luke kicked everything off the dresser before pushing up the opening into the attic. A thick cloud of dust and dirt came down. "You're a psycho." She left the room angry and hurt by his disrespect.

Luke threw the gun and shop-vac up into the attic, then he ran an extension cord up so he could have light. Luke was sweating by the time he was in the attic.

~~~

It didn't take long for Luke to fill up the shop-vac; the place was filthy. Luke could see the particles in the air. He believed it to be asbestos. An eerie quietness ensued when the vacuum turned off. There were voices coming from outside. They didn't sound like normal civilian voices; more formal and deliberate.

The voices came from the front of the house.

Luke found a vent and peeked out. He had a clear view of the street and front yard. No one was out there, but a few suspicious vehicles were parked down the street. More voices. *Oh fuck, they're already inside!* He scrambled to the safest corner of the attic.

There was only one entrance into the attic and he was almost completely out of sight from it. He could hear people in the house. They were going up and down the stairs, probably looking for him. With the mess in the bedroom it would be obvious he was in the attic. They would probably come up through the hole, and they would expect him to be armed. Whether they came through the hole, or crashing through the side vents, he would kill them all. *I hope they use a smoke grenade. Maybe they don't know I've got this suit. Maybe they don't know about the AK-47. Just try it you stupid fucks. Try coming in here without properly announcing your presence. I have every right to kill you pieces of shit.*

Time went on. They were stalling. Luke started to hope they would come smashing in. At least then he would know he was sane. *Please just do it already you pussies.* Time kept going by. The voices didn't stop. He wished Zuri would come check on him; he wanted it to be a delusion.

He needed to peek out of the vent again, but he was to scared to move. He couldn't be caught off guard; not after being in battle position for so long. *Nope, you're not getting me that easy. I can wait forever. I can wait so long and silently that they'll doubt I'm even up here. I'll be the one with the element of surprise.*

Hours passed. Luke hadn't moved a muscle, but was sweating profusely in his
~~~

suit. He was starting to think of an escape plan. Would they expect him to escape out of the ventilation duct? probably not, but they were surely watching all angles of the house. In Luke's mind, this could only end a few different ways: They give up; he gives up; they all die; or he dies.

Finally the voices grew louder. They were coming from the bedroom. He had his sights on the hole, waiting for someone to poke their head through it. Light flickered at the entrance. His body pumped with adrenaline. *Finally, time to confirm my suspicions.*

"Hey Luke," came a familiar voice, "you up here?"

Luke hid the gun under a piece of cardboard as his father's head popped into the attic. "Hey yeah, there's asbestos up here and shit," said Luke, trying to sound reasonable.

"Are you sure? What the heck are you wearing? Where did you get that suit?" said Allan.

"Just hold on. You'd better get outta here, I'm coming down right now." Luke crouched as he stepped on the rafters, trying to avoid the nails poking down from the roof. He made it down and took off the mask. His face was sweaty and looked like an AIDS victim. The place was filthy, there was dirt all over and Zuri's things were still scattered on the floor. "What do you have going on here?" said Alice.

"Just checkin things out. I really do think there's asbestos up there. My lungs have been all messed up the past few weeks." Luke was having trouble adjusting from combat mode to normal sober person mode. But he did feel safer with his parents. They were an anchor of logic in a sea of delusions.

"Is everything okay? Zuri's in the living room, says you're being an asshole," said Alice.

"I don't know. I've just been starting too many projects, it gets frustrating," said Luke.

"What is up with the suit?" said Allan, " It is sweet, how did you get it?"

"The internet. I've got four sets, so we're safe if shit starts to go down."

"Well that's good. Those suits can't be cheap, how much did it cost you?" said Allan.

"Oh, they didn't cost too much. I found a good web site. They were on sale. But anyways, I've been stocking up on weapons, too.

You can never be too prepared."

"No!" said Alice, "Guns, Luke?" You don't need to be buying guns."

"Oh shhh," said Allan, "We live in Montana now. He is an adult, he can buy as many guns as he wants. Lets see em, Luke."

Luke went to the closet and grabbed the 357 and the Walther. He brought them both out, "Careful, they're loaded," he handed them to Allan.

"Oh, cool!" said Allan.

"Not cool. Those are scary," said Alice.

"I've got an AK-47 too. It's up in th attic, I was gonna keep it stashed up there."

"I wanna see," said Allan.

Luke put his mask back on and crawled up into the attic. He came back down a few minutes later carrying the vicious weapon.

"No way," Allan took it and admired it carefully.

"Luke, that's so scary!" Alice was almost in tears, "You're not supposed to have those. It looks like an army gun!"

"It's an assault rifle, and it's perfectly legal for me to carry."

"I don't like it. Not one bit," she said.

"Are you sure your not selling other drugs?" said Allan,

"Because it looks like you've been taking other drugs. You don't look healthy, Luke."

"I've just been stressed out, and I haven't been eating good either. Adderall might have something to do with it," he said.

"You know you can come home and eat anytime you want," said Alice, "I wish you would come visit more often."

"You guys should go in the living room. I need to set up air purifiers and change out of this stuff." said Luke.

~~~

Luke came outside to join his parents. They were talking with Zuri while she smoked a cigarette. Luke lit one for himself as well.

"So, is Luke the one making messes all over the house?" Alice asked Zuri.

"Yeah. He's got some really bad ADD."

"Luke, you weren't messy when you lived at home," said Alice.

"I've just had a busy couple days. It's all gonna be cleaned up by the end of the day."

A delivery truck backed into the driveway. Paranoia returned for a few moments, then he realized it was his scooter.

"What's happening?" said Alice.

"It's my moped. I ordered a moped. Technically it's a scooter because it doesn't have any pedals."

"What do you mean 'scooter?' Why would you want one of those?" she said.

"Because they're sweet. It goes sixty-five and was only $850," he said.
~~~

"Sixty five miles per hour?" Alice was shocked.

"Yeah, I'll have to get my motorcycle license for it," he said,

"That's a lot of money. Your spending is getting out of control," she said.

"That seems cheap for something like that," said Allan, "It's not a Honda, is it?"

"Nope. Some brand new company out of China. I think it's called TNG or something, but it doesn't matter, it's gonna be badass," said Luke.

"I think it's gonna fall apart on you," said Allan.

"Well, I will prove you otherwise. I'll take good care of it and it's gonna be super sweet."

After the box was unloaded the man came up with a clipboard, "Which one of you is Luke Baker?"

"Me," Luke took the clipboard and signed for the delivery.

~~~

The man drove away. Luke's hands were already turning blue and splotchy. The box was too heavy to move, so he started opening it in the driveway. "Jesus, these are some heavy duty staples in this box. I'm gonna need a knife." Luke went inside, his fingers numb. By the time he came back out, Dave was parking on the street.

Dave came up and greeted everyone. "This is the scooter? Oh, I came just in time. You want some help with this?"

"Yeah. I could sure use your help putting it together, too," said Luke.

The box was opened enough for Dave to see how incomplete it was. "I think we should mount the front tire so we can wheel it down to your basement. We're gonna want to go over it very thoroughly. This being a new company, it might have inexperienced workers on the production line," said Dave.

"There would be no mistakes if it was a Honda," said Allan, "I think it will break down within a year."

~~~

Zuri had gone inside. Allan and Alice went to scope out the neighborhood and check out the house. Luke and Dave were still in the driveway with the scooter. The progress was minimal, Luke was cold and frustrated.

Luke's parents came back when the front tire was assembled. Allan had a worried expression, "Hey Luke, you should come check this out." They went around to the alley. Allan pointed up at the abandoned antique shop next door, "Do you see that device up in that window? That's one of those video/audio monitoring devices. The feds use those to monitor people they suspect are doing illegal activity. They can even hear what's going on inside your house."

"Are you serious?" Luke was horrified.

"Dead serious. Check this out, there's another one across the street." They walked across the street where Allan pointed to another device. It was in the top window of an ordinary two story house.

"So, is that house staged to look like a normal house? Because I've seen normal people coming and going from there. Are they fake people? Paid by the government to pretend to look like a normal family? Just to keep me from suspecting that I'm being watched?"

"What? No! Are you serious?" Allan was worried.

Luke realized how insane it sounded. "No, it was a joke," he lied, "but what do you think it means?"

"I think the DEA or whoever will ask people if they can set up a monitoring device in their home." There was a pause..."You're not dealing with any bad drugs, are you?"

"No, I'm not," Luke said through clenched teeth, "lets not talk about drugs."

Dave yelled from the driveway, "This is ready to go inside." Luke and Allan helped Dave wheel the incomplete scooter through the back door and down the stairs. Luke was thankful to be inside. His feet and hands were frozen and he was craving another shot.

~~~

Luke supplied weed while Allan and Dave worked on the scooter. Zuri and Alice talked while watching them work. Luke was upstairs peeking out the windows. It was beginning to get dark.

Luke had Dubstep blaring upstairs to distort the conversations. From now on, he decided, there would never be silence in the house; not as long as those audio devices were set up. Luke was already devising a plan to disable the video part of the device. He'd seen a movie where they just shined a laser into the lens to disable it. The only solution for the audio was to play loud music.

Luke was desperate to take a shot. He grabbed what he needed and stuffed it into his pocket. With the music playing he couldn't hear if someone was approaching. He couldn't risk having his parents see the terrible procedure. It was bad enough that his dad thought he was going insane.

It was almost a relief now that he was sure he was being watched; now that he had proof. He didn't have any doubts before, but it was entirely different to have a sober person confirm it. Especially when the news came from his father, who he trusted absolutely. For so long Zuri had assured him that no one was watching; that the DEA or Monkey Police had better things to do than watch small time tweaker kids. But these people weren't just normal small time
~~~

tweakers; they were part of an experiment; they were self-administering lab monkeys.

Both of Luke's phones were in the closet with the batteries out, even the untraceable one under the name of Frank Crankspooner. There were many desperate clients, but he didn't have time for them. He was trying to have some quality time with his parents.

There was a knock at the door. Luke scrambled to hide his paraphernalia. He looked out the peephole and saw Blue with his usual tweaker determination. Luke opened the door, "Dude, this isn't a good time." Blue came in anyway. "Hey, there's some weird shit going on right now. There's fucking surveillance devices pointing at my house!"

"Get your shit together, bro. I need thirty grams," said Blue.

"Did you not just hear me? We're being monitored." Luke was thankful for the distorting Dubstep music.

"Nobody's monitoring nothing. It's all in your head," Blue insisted.

"Dude, my dad's the one who found the fuckin devices. He's here right now, and he's totally sober."

"Where's he at?"

"In the basement. Him and Dave are doin some shit with the scooter I just got."

Well, lets go do this shit real quick. We can lock ourselves in the closet if it makes you feel safe."

"Fuck, dude... fine." They went to the closet. Luke made the transaction as quick as he could. He was terrified the entire time, and had to mentally restrain himself from grabbing a weapon. The monkey police would come crashing in at any moment.

The deal was finally done. There was no small talk. "Thanks bro, I'm gonna bounce."

Both Blue and Luke left the closet. Alice was in the kitchen, Oh, hi Blue. How are you? Haven't seen you for a while," she said.

"Hey Alice. I'm doin good. What's new with you?" said Blue.

"Just checkin out Luke's fancy new moped thing. You should come see it, it's really pretty," she said.

"Sure, yeah, lets check it out." They went to the basement.

Dave was experiencing the disorderliness that is suffered among MDPV addicts. The frustration was showing in his face. Loud music was still blaring from upstairs, hip-hop lyrics with electronic beats. There were three air purifiers strategically place around the house. Still, Luke could see and taste the asbestos molecules floating in the air. "We should all be wearing gas masks; dust masks at least. I can feel the asbestos going into my lungs."

His parents gave him odd looks, "You probably just stirred up some insulation from the attic," said Allan.

Luke decided to say no more about the asbestos. Blue was inspecting the scooter while Luke's parents tried to make conversation with him. They knew he was a meth user. At this point, it was obvious. Blue's appearance was sickly. He could convince people he was fine on meth, but MDPV made him look like a psychotic AIDS victim.

The situation was strange, but Luke felt comfortable around his parents. The monkey police wouldn't dare come smashing in with them around. They were innocent civilians, not a part of the experiment. Luke's parents also felt good being around their son, even though he was mentally ill. Luke had been neglecting them lately.

Dave was muttering things to Allan as he continued to take things apart, "You see this kinked hose? They clearly put this on upside down. The diagram shows it on the other way."

Allan had no faith in the piece of junk. "Luke, you want to throw some knives?"

"Sure, lets do it." He grabbed the knives and distanced himself and crouched in his ninja stance. The first one stuck. The second stuck. The third stuck right in the forehead of the target.

"That is crazy good!" said Allan, "Nice form."

"Yeah, I been practicing. I can make it stick like that almost every time that way."

Allan had to pry the knives out of the board. All of his throws bounced off the board. "Suck. Do yours again. I wanna try it like you do it."

~~~

Blue found an excuse to leave. Zuri and Alice were enjoying each others company while Dave was getting more flustered.

Luke was no longer just jonesing for MDPV, he *needed* a shot, or else he would soon collapse with fatigue.

"I gotta take a dump," said Luke. He locked the bathroom door to the basement. There was nothing pre-made, so he had to mix some up in the bathroom.

The shot was finally ready. It already felt like he'd been locked in the bathroom too long. He hurried up and injected it.

Everything got louder, voices from outside, radio static, all audible over the
~~~

music. *Jesus, what the hell is going on around here? My parents are downstairs, I need to hide this shit.* There was a knock on the bathroom door. Luke panicked. His spoon dropped and clattered on the floor. *Fuck!* He hid the drugs in a towel on the shelf.

"Luke?" came Zuri's voice.

Luke opened the door, "What the fuck is your problem?" he whispered through clenched teeth.

"Nothing." She was disgusted with his aggressiveness. "I was just gonna grab a beer for your dad. You've been up here forever. Please don't get weird around your parents."

Zuri walked past him and into the kitchen. Luke felt a need to grab one of his guns, but resisted. *Fuck it. Even if they do come busting in, I'm not gonna have a shootout with my parents here.* Zuri came back and headed down the stairs. Luke was scared. He didn't think he could hide his paranoia. His instincts told him to look out the window; that danger was lurking out there. Finally Luke went downstairs and tried to act normal.

~~~

It was dark out when Luke's parents left. The paranoia got worse. He expected the monkey police to make their move now that there were no innocent civilians around.

Dave was desperate for MDPV while Luke double checked every window in the house. "C'mon Luke, everything's fine. Just give me the stuff and I'll make it up myself."

"I'll give you the stuff, but everything is *not* okay. Don't ever tell me that. There's all sorts of surveillance gadgets pointed at my house, and it's not all in my head; my dad's the one who found the shit," said Luke.

These words had no effect on Dave. His eyes showed impatience. Luke gave him a small bag of MDPV to last a few days. Dave took it to the bathroom and satisfied the craving. After the shot he was ready to get back to work on the scooter. Luke stuck the Walther in his waistband and attempted to clean the house. Zuri convinced Luke to turn the music down so she could do some reading.

Out of frustration, Luke went on a frenzy throwing things in the garbage. Anything that was out of place either went in the garbage, or in a box to be stored in the basement. *How did I end up with so much stupid shit? Fuckin Walmart, that's how. All these stupid storage bins and containers. Why am I so mesmerized by all the clear plastic organizers? They were meant to get things organized, but all it did was make a mess.*
~~~

Luke decided to try and study for his motorcycle licence test. There was no snow on the ground for the moment. He hoped to take his exam before winter hit.

After a few moments of reading, he realized it was hopeless. He couldn't retain a single sentence. Zuri saw his frustration and tried to comfort him, "You should come out of that closet and lay down with me," she was lying on the bed and held her arms open invitingly. Luke obeyed. He was feeling agitated. As he laid down she squirmed with discomfort, "What is this? Put this stupid thing away, please," she said.

"Shhh!" Luke pulled the pistol out of his waistband and set it on the nightstand.

"Can I please have you for the night? No Dave; no projects; no being-paranoid? And also no being an asshole. I just want it to be you and me... like it used to be." He nodded. She kissed him on the cheek and held him tighter.

Death is not the greatest loss in life, the greatest loss is what dies in us while we are still alive.

-Norman Cousins

Chapter 23: The Monkey Police

Sunday 1-19-2011 4:00am

Winter had struck, and it was there to stay. Driving in the snow was fun, but the cold was vicious on the circulation. Constricted blood vessels were bad enough, and the cold made it ten times worse.

Luke was at his old friend Zack's house. They had ran into each other at Walmart one night. Zack had the paranoia. Luke knew he was on MDPV. Luke felt sorry for his old friend; for whatever vicious price he was paying for the dirt cheap chemical.

"Dude, Zack? What are you doing out this late?" the conversation started.

"Whoa, hey Luke. I don't know what I'm doing here. I came with a couple people. I don't think I should be here," said Zack.

"Do you still live at the same place? We should kick it. I can get that stuff for really cheap."

"I don't know what stuff you're talking about," he tried to sound innocent.

"That *stuff*, bro. The fake coke shit. I know you know what I'm talking about," said Luke.

"Right, yeah, this brand of motor oil is by far the best. Thanks for the advice," Zack said loudly.

"Yep, Valvoline. Sure thing." Luke played along. He was familiar with this paranoid tactic. Say something normal, any thing to make it look like they were normal citizens.

Zack was still holding a Valvoline bottle, pretending to be interested. "Yeah, we should kick it sometime," he said in a fake jolly voice. "How have you been?" Everything he said was an act. It was obvious. Normal people don't joyfully shop for motor oil at 5:00am.

They'd been hanging out often since then. Zuri had become good friends with Zack's girlfriend Tylar. Luke hadn't been spending much time at home since he's been aware of the cameras.

Currently, Luke hadn't been to his house in six days. He also hadn't taken his shoes off in those six days either. Zuri was going through a meltdown. She thought he was going to leave her. That wasn't what he wanted at all, but her emotional outbursts made him paranoid.

There was one incident he was particularly ashamed of. Zuri woke up late one night with an AK-47 resting on top of her. Luke was crouched behind the bed, using Zuri as his barricade. He had been sitting there motionless with his sights on the door waiting for the monkey police to come crashing in.

When Zuri woke up she started whining something about wanting him to get in bed. He gave her the signal to shut up. The whining continued, it came out as a loud squealing sound to Luke. "Quit your goddamn squealing!" he whispered. The squealing continued. Whoever was listening could surely hear. She didn't understand the danger they were in. The whining would soon compromise both of them. He acted quickly, grabbing a pillow and smothering it over her face. Her squeals turned to muffled screams.

Once she was quiet and no longer struggling, he lifted the pillow. She had tears in her eyes, and was finally ready to cooperate. In retrospect, it was the most disgusting and cowardly thing Luke had ever done.

~~~

"Hey Luke, what is going on with Zuri?" said Tylar, "She hasn't been over for a while."

"She never wants to leave the house. And I don't like spending much time there. The place is bugged. I'm not shitting you. She's a psycho for staying there. I'd rather be on the move, that way I'm untraceable."

"Oh. Well you should bring her over tomorrow. I miss her," she said.

"Okay, I'll try. You can always text her. She needs some friends in her life," he said.
~~~

"Do you think she's awake right now?" Tylar pulled her phone out.

"Probably not, but go ahead and try," he said.

Zack was sitting at his computer singing along with Daft Punk's "Harder, better, faster, stronger." Luke had let out the secret that none of the MDPV was pure. Zack was a diabetic and used that in his argument, "C'mon man, I need to know exactly what I'm getting. I'll pay whatever you want, it's important for my diabetes.

So Luke started selling the pure stuff to Zack, and eventually to everyone who wanted it. Luke charged $80 a gram for pure MDPV. He charged $35 for a gram of 50% MDPV, which most people preferred. The pure stuff made people go insane quicker, so Luke gave a discount for the 50% stuff.

Luke's Mexican friend Alex was there too. He was an MDPV smoker, along with Zack and Tylar. Smoking was easier to hide, but was much less efficient and very time consuming. The smokers couldn't stop; they had to keep smoking every twenty minutes or so, sometimes less. Luke was the only one who was allowed to shoot in Zack's bedroom. He was quick at it. Plus, he was the guy with the supply. There were syringes all over the room anyways, so Zack's dad would never notice.

Luke was playing around on his new pre-paid smart phone. It was untraceable, under the name of Han Solo. He felt another surge of guilt about skipping Christmas. Him and his family would go to Oregon every year for the holiday. Most of Luke's extended family still lived in Oregon. It broke his parent's hearts to have Christmas without Luke. He talked to them once over the phone during that time. He tried to explain himself. He told them he was going to spend the Christmas with Zuri's family, but that wasn't true either. Zuri had almost no contact with her family. She wasn't close to her parents or sisters, and had a bad history with one of her brothers; a sensitive subject for Zuri.

"Hey Luke, bro?" said Alex, "Do you think we could smoke a bowl? Of weed?"

"Yes, I think we could, and we should. Let's get baked." Luke loaded a pipe and passed it around. Zack wasn't interested in weed, but he went through the motions.

"Thanks Luke," said Tylar. She was grateful. The weed would reduce the paranoia. When Zack was paranoid he would get an ugly attitude toward her.

"Luke, do you think you could front me another gram until Friday?" said Zack.

Fuck, I shouldn't. "Dude, you're my friend and I feel shitty putting you in debt all the time. I'll front you a gram of the pure, but only if you take two grams of the fifty percent to sell. There's no reason for you to be broke," said Luke.

"Okay man, I won't let you down." Luke knew he meant it, but Zack blew the last couple opportunities he had given him. Zack had a two year old girl with his ex-girlfriend. Luke had seen the kid and was also good friends with the ex-girlfriend, so he felt a responsibility to help Zack succeed.

Luke weighed out some MDPV. He bagged it individually to make it easy for Zack to sell. Zack immediately placed some of the powder onto a piece of foil. Luke was ready to get high as well.

"Do you mind if I inject?" Luke asked.

"Sure buddy, just do it over here behind the bed," said Zack.

It was a strange request, but Luke was just as terrified of Zack's dad seeing the evil process. They had to be prepared for him to walk in at any moment, even though his dad had never intruded before.

The same Daft Punk song was playing. Luke finally realized that it was on repeat. They had been listening to the song for hours. It was insane, but Luke was guilty of the same behavior. He would listen to 'Moar Ghosts And Stuff' by Deadmau5. It was the perfect tempo for the attention deficit brain, and it never got old. "Harder, better, faster, stronger," Zack mumbled nervously as he glanced out the window. A hit from the foil instantly made him more on edge.

Luke took the shot and put everything away with shaky hands. He threw the used syringe into Zack's sharps container. *Jesus!* thought Luke, *Are we being ambushed? I need to take a peek, but I don't want to make people paranoid.*

"Do you mind if I smoke a cigarette on your roof?" said Luke.

"Umm... I don't know. I guess it's okay. Just don't do anything suspicious out there. My neighbors have been watching like hawks the past week."

"That's strange. Maybe they're doing the same stuff we are. Maybe they think we've been watching them," said Luke.

"I don't think so, man. Just be cool, and don't stay out there too long," said Zack.

"Sure thing." Luke grabbed a cigarette and crawled out the window. He lit the cigarette. It was cold. The house across the street seemed suspicious. The lights were dim with frequent passing shadows. A black Crown Victoria with tinted windows was running out front.

That house wasn't the only thing that made Luke uneasy; he heard movement and whispering voices that seemed to come from just below the roof. There was strange activity at the apartments down the street. Luke had a good view from where he sat. He could see any movement or flickering of light for a good distance. The apartments down the street had the most activity. There were three identical black SUVs parked right next to each other. All of them were running.

There's nothing wrong with that scene. It's just the drug; just the paranoia; all a figment of my frightened imagination. I just took a shot. This always happens after I take a shot. My brain is trying to go into fight or flight, I just need to ignore it. The frontal cortex needs to override the primitive mid-brain. Luke continued to hold his cigarette with no urge to smoke it. His head was facing down as his eyes focused on the parking lot in the distance. If they were real, he didn't want them to know he saw them.

There was more movement; a Silverado was pulling into the apartment complex. Luke couldn't deny it any longer, *They're assembling, and you're trapped on the roof with a concealed weapon. It's time to act before it's too late.*

Luke was still avoiding looking at them directly. He wanted them to think they had the element of surprise. That way Luke might have time to escape. Figures filed out of the SUVs with flashlights shining. Luke put out his cigarette and crawled back into the window. "Hey guys, I feel like taking a walk," he said.

"A walk?" said Zack.

"Yep. I'm feeling energized. You understand."

"Just be really quiet on your way down. My dad's sleeping."

"Right," Luke was already on his way out, leaving his weed, scale, and MDPV behind. He would have left the pistol behind, but Zack would have freaked. Luke wasn't supposed to bring any firearms into the house.

He made it out the sliding glass door on the back deck and went for the alley. It felt horrible to have the pistol hidden in it's holster. His instincts told him to carry it at his side. Luke made a break for someone's back yard. He ditched the gun and crept into a bush where he had a view of the apartments. At first it seemed as things were normal. He didn't have as good of view as he did on the roof. Then he saw the flashlights flickering in the distance. They were suited up in black NBC suits and carried AR-15 assault rifles. *They've finally come to capture their lab monkeys. This is real. This is life or death. The Monkey Police are out to get me.*

The masks made them look like monsters. They *were* monsters, preparing to take Luke away to some secret testing facility. They would do countless tests on him to see the change in his neurochemistry. They would inject him with more toxic chemicals, saying, "This is what you signed up for! You wanted to be the monkey!" He would be blindfolded and sedated. They would keep him forever; too risky to release. Or they would drop him off in a strange place, naked and covered in goo with a modified memory. He would think he'd been abducted by aliens, no one would take him seriously. The rest of his life would be a joke. He would live out his days as a walking vegetable with bubble brains; part of a drug experiment gone bad, and no one would believe him.

"That poor kid thinks he was part of a drug experiment," people would say.

"Ha, as if there's some secret research team that uses humans as lab monkeys. I also heard he thinks he was abducted by aliens."

"I think he did it all to himself, taking all that LSD and what not probably just had a bad batch of LSD and never came out right."

Jesus, I need to get the hell out of here; he thought, *The gun. Do I risk bringing the gun with me? It might mean the difference of me being captured or escaping. No, I just need to be stealthy. They can't be able to run fast or see well in those suits.* Luke took off stealthy as a ninja through backyards and alleyways. He crossed streets like a frightened deer, and disappeared into the shadows.

Once he was six blocks away he did something to confuse his pursuers. Luke played some music from his phone. It was electro, and was turned up as loud as it could go. He danced his way down the street. *No one would dare mess with someone who behaved this way. Maybe the cops, but that wouldn't be so bad. At least I would be safe from the Monkey Police.*

Luke decided he needed to text Zack to make sure the invasion was real. The Chrysler was still parked on the street by Zack's. Luke didn't know if he even wanted the Chrysler any more. If it was still there, it was surely bugged with every type of monitoring device their technology would permit. There was a reply from Zack.

(From Zack): Everythins cool man. U shud come back.

(From Luke): K

Luke stopped the dancing act, it made him feel stupid now. *So it's all fake. Nothing to worry about, then. Are the Monkey Police even real? Every time they seem ready to attack, they never make a move. Zack would tell me if those people were still out there. I can't be that much more paranoid than him. He would be checking out those windows just as much as I would.* Luke turned around and headed back toward Zack's. He told himself everything was in his head, that it was just a psychotic episode.

It took a while to get back to the street where Zack lived. Luke hadn't convinced himself that it was completely safe. The hallucinations were too vivid to ignore. He sneaked through the alley and hid in the same bushes where he had before.

Exhaust was coming from the parking lot where the gas mask men had been, but he couldn't see much from where he was. *Those fuckers are still there. How can Zack not see them? Maybe they already have Zack. Maybe that text was from the Monkey Police. They probably have his phone and are trying to trick me into coming back.*

Luke grabbed the gun he had left behind and snuck off to a safer hiding spot.

He traveled through alleyways and backyards to find a vantage point. There was an empty GMC Yukon with tinted windows. It was unlocked, so he got in and crawled to the back so he could see Zack's house. *Now let's see what happens when I do this.* He pulled out his cellphone and texted Zack.

(From Luke): Hey, Im here.

The text wouldn't make any sense to Zack, because Luke could just walk up if he pleased. But to the Monkey Police, it would signal their time to infiltrate. If the Monkey Police were lurking, they would be monitoring Zack's text messages.

Finally there was some commotion. Zack's bedroom light turned off when a black Silverado turned onto his street. Another Silverado and Suburban came out of the parking lot across the street. They parked in front of Zack's house. One Silverado drove around the block into the alley behind the house. The gas mask men got out of the Suburban. They set up tripod devices in the front yard. Luke's heart was pounding and he was horrified. His reality was ripping apart at the seams. Lights were flashing. The Monkey Police were in the house. *What happens when they realize I'm not in there? They'll come searching every inch within a mile radius!* He snuck out of the Yukon and closed the door quietly behind him. He ran down the street with the pistol in his hand.

The fear of death is more to be dreaded than death.
-Publilius Syrus: Maximus

Chapter 24: Fuck You Lady!

Wednesday 4-16-2011

The painful winter was finally over. It had gone by in a blur of psychosis for Luke and Zuri. Everyday was filled with the same exhausting nonsense until they took a short trip to Oregon. The trip was an impulse decision, motivated by paranoia. Luke believed his parents were plotting to rehabilitate him.

Now Luke was in the Walmart parking lot preparing Jared for a secret mission. The sun was shining and Luke had both vehicles parked side by side. "Now, you're sure you know what you're supposed to do? You know what you're going to say?" asked Luke.

"Yeah, I do," Jared said nervously, "but I still don’t understand why I have to do this. If you think these people were going to do something bad to you, what makes you think they won't do something bad to me?"

"Because they only want me. I'm sorry, but you're worth nothing... to anyone. If they try something crazy before they find out it's not me in the car, then I know I can't trust them."

"But why *me*?" the filthy fat kid looked like he was about to cry. "I don't even have a drivers license."

"Will you stop being such a fuckin baby? You're being compensated. I'm paying you. And there's nothing that could possibly go wrong. The car's completely clean. Nothing illegal in there, at all. If you get caught for driving without a license, I'll pay double whatever your fine is. The GPS is set with the exact destination, so you won't get lost. Now tell me what you're going to tell them."

"I tell them that if they want the stuff they have to give me the money. And if they give me the money, I tell them to be at Walmart at two o'clock tomorrow, where they will find a Mexican wearing a rasta sweater. I'll tell them to ask the Mexican if he needs a ride, and tell him that they're not with the Monkey Police."

"Right, good. And you know why I'm making them do all this?" Jared shook his head. "Because I need to know if they trust me. How can I trust them if they don't trust me?" Jared said nothing. "It's time for you to go now. I can't have you being late. This is very important."

Jared got in the Chrysler and adjusted the seat to his preference. The car started to roll forward as he put it in gear. He turned too sharp and scraped the car next to him. Luke cringed, but Jared seemed oblivious. Luke hoped he would get his car back in one piece.

It was time for Luke to relocate. He didn't want to be around when the owner of the damaged car came back from shopping. He re-parked at the movie theater. It was there that he decided to take an injection of MDPV. Moments after the shot, he received a phone call. "Hello?" he answered as he made sure all the doors were locked. He was driving the Suburban, since Jared had taken the Chrysler.

"Hey Luke," it was Stacy.

"Oh, hey," he looked around nervously.

"What are you doing?" she said.

"Nothing. Just over by Walmart," he said.

"I wanna see you. You should come to Woodland Park."

"Well, I don't really—"

"Will you just come please," she cut him off.

"Umm... sure, I suppose I could." He headed to the park after wasting fifteen minutes being paranoid.

~~~

Luke drove past the skate park to the back of Woodland Park. Stacy was standing by her Pontiac while smoking a cigarette. Luke parked next to her and got out, making sure all the doors were locked. Stacy gave him a long hug. He
~~~

never realized how much he missed her until he was finally with her. It was the same for Stacy. They had an unbreakable bond, bound by passionate sex and psychedelic drugs. The bond was spiritual, they both acknowledged it even though they were dating other people. "You wanna go for a walk?" she asked.

"Sure," he said.

Stacy led the way. They went up the hill through the trees and onto the railroad tracks. She pulled out her pipe and handed it to Luke. He took a hit and handed it back. She tried to hold his hand.

"I don't think we should do that," he said. "I mean... I'm just as tempted as you are, but it's probably not good for us."

"I understand," she said, not regretting her attempt.

They walked in silence. There was no awkwardness between them, they could just enjoy each other's presence. "So, how's Zuri?" she asked.

"She's good, I guess. I've been being a dick to her lately. I don't know, she's probably not doin to good, actually," he said.

"Why do you be mean to her?" she said.

"I don't know. She's a very emotional girl, and she treats me really good, actually. But for some reason, when I'm high, she irritates the shit out of me. Her voice is too loud, and sounds like squealing," he said.

"Maybe you should leave her," she said.

"No, I shouldn't. It's not her fault. It's the drugs. I know it is. If anything, she should be the one leaving me. I'm kind of a dirtbag. She doesn't do the drugs that I do. She's like super innocent and stuff and for some reason she's totally in love with me. I'm pretty sure she would kill herself if I tried to leave her."

"Are you in love with her?" she said.

"Totally, but my capacity to show it seems pretty limited lately. It's hard for me to show much love to anyone these days. And that's not normal; not for me. I need to get some psychedelics back into my life. The true psychedelics, not all these experimental tryptamines and phenylthylamines."

"What do you mean?" she was confused.

"I been doin all these weird chemicals that make you hallucinate and stuff, but I haven't had a good spiritually cleansing LSD or mushroom trip lately."

"I think you just need to stop that stuff you've been doing for so long now. That's what's causing all of your problems. It wouldn't hurt to have a nice acid experience. I'll do it with you. We could eat some molly too." She gave him a suggestive smile.

"We both know where that would lead us. I know I don't have the kind of self-control to restrain myself in that situation." LSD and ecstasy used to be their favorite combination. The perfect recipe for an endless night of spiritual sex; too much twisted pleasure for the average mind to comprehend.

"Well, it might just be what you need to learn to love people again."

~~~

"Hey, it's hobo Joe. Hobo Joe! What's up, dude?" said Luke. The homeless Native American sat in a patch of grass next to the railroad tracks. He didn't recognize Luke, but seemed thrilled by the warm greeting. "What are you drinking there?"

The man looked at his bottle of sherry cooking wine. His name wasn't even Joe, and his face looked acid fried. "Do you have any smokes?" the man mumbled.

"I do have smokes and I even got some weed. If you wait right here I'll run down to my truck and get you something to drink.

"Drink?"

"Yeah. Something that will get you fucked up, man."

"Ahhaha!" the man let out a savage laugh while shaking his hands together in gratitude.

"Kay, we'll be right back. Don't go anywhere." Luke and Stacy headed back through the trees down to the park.

"Were you being serious?" Stacy asked.

"Heck yeah, I run into that guy all the time. For some reason I feel compelled to give him drugs and cigarettes."

"You think that man needs drugs?" she said.

"Did you see what he was drinking? Have you tasted sherry cooking wine before? It's like freakin salt water! I drank some with him before. All the salt in his brain has made him confused. We need to give him water and drugs. And today, I have the perfect chemical for him."

They made it back up to the homeless man, this time with the proper supplies. "So, you're gonna have to have an open mind here," Luke told the hobo as he sat down next to him. "This stuff isn't alcohol, but it will make you drunk." Luke pulled out a tinted glass vial and a syringe. Hobo Joe didn't flinch, but Stacy seemed anxious about what was going to happen. "First you need to chug this." Luke handed Joe a water bottle.

The hobo opened it, smelled it, then asked, "What's this?"

"It's water, man. I don't want you to get dehydrated." The man drank the water, finishing off the bottle.

Luke refilled the bottle a fourth of the way full with another water bottle. "How much do you weigh?" Luke asked Joe. The hobo just shrugged, watching
~~~

Luke mess with the syringe. "Okay, we'll go with 1.25 milliliters." He uncapped the vial and stuck the tip of the needle into it. Once he'd measured the proper amount, he squirted it into the water bottle. "Now, drink this," he held the bottle out for Joe. The hobo just shook his head.

"Can I just have a cigarette?" the hobo mumbled.

"I'll give you a bunch of cigarettes, but you have to drink this first." The hobo shook his head, watching Luke cautiously. Luke turned the bottle upside down and chugged it himself. After finishing he recoiled from the painful taste.

Luke repeated the process. He refilled the bottle a fourth of the way with water, then diluted the same amount of chemical into it. "Here you go, man. Give it a try. You won't regret it."

The man was still apprehensive. He didn't want anything to do with the strange liquid. "Here, I'll do this one." Stacy grabbed the bottle and chugged it down, "Yuk!" she handed the empty bottle to Luke, "What is that stuff?"

"It's a structural analog of GHB," Luke said as he began to refill the bottle. Once it was ready he handed it to the hobo. The hobo took it, feeling better after seeing Luke's beautiful companion drink it fearlessly.

The man drank it and handed the empty bottle to Luke. The effects were already taking hold before his equipment was put away. Stacy was beginning to feel it too. "Is there any way that this stuff could be kicking in already?" she asked.

"Yeah, it takes less than five minutes. I don't understand how it absorbs so quickly. It's a pretty bizarre substance," said Luke.

The homeless man wanted a cigarette. Luke fumbled for his cigarettes and handed a few to Joe. "It's about to get to the good part; we should go for a walk." Luke got up, grabbed Stacy's hand and led the way.

"Whoa," she said, "I do feel drunk... and fuzzy like ecstasy," she started laughing as they stumbled down the trail, fighting to keep balance.

They stumble around the park for the next hour, trying to walk and talk properly. It was good quality friendship time. They checked up on the hobo once during their walk; he was laughing, crawling around the same spot where they had left him. Apparently he was too messed up to smoke. There were signs of struggled attempts with the cigarettes still lying in the grass.

Stacy and Luke were walking on the railroad tracks when Luke began to get tired. "I think I need to leave," he said. Time for fun was over; nothing was more important than getting that dose of MDPV.

"Where do you need to go? Can I come? I'm having fun spending time with you."

"Well, to be honest, I wanna go get high, and I won't feel safe doing it here. There's other things I probably need to do also, but I need to do that first. Otherwise I'll be crashing hard really soon."

"Can I come with? I've still got time, and it would be nice to go for a ride in your truck," she said.

"Sure, I guess we could go for a quick cruise," he said.

They drove to a secret spot by a nearby creek. It was a place where Luke felt he would be safe if a bad case of paranoia took over. He started mixing up a solution when Stacy asked, "Can I try one of those?"

"I don't know if that's the best idea," he said.

"Why not? You do it all the time. I just want to try it once; I wanna do it your way," she said.

"Well, you see, there was a time I would have injected you in a heartbeat, but I can't be doing that any more."

"Why not? What do you mean?" she said.

"I think it's evil. Zuri was totally right about this stuff, it's done horrible things to me and everyone I've introduced it to. I've shot up at least thirty people for their first time with this stuff, and every one of them is a junkie now. It turns people into the worst kind of drug fiend."

"I'm not scared to try it once. I don't really even like speedy stuff, you know that. I just want a glimpse of the reality you've been living in all this time," she said.

"Kay, fine." Luke began preparing another shot for Stacy.

He gave her the shot, then took his own. As the rush hit, he was trying to put everything away. Stacy seemed totally fine. She was enjoying the experience. Not Luke; his heart was beating viciously as he saw someone approaching the rear of the vehicle. He reached under the seat and grabbed the monster-size revolver. It was another psychotic episode, just like so many before. Each one just as convincing as the last. His instincts told him the threat of death was imminent. Just like the experience at Zack's a few months before. He was sure it had been over for Zack, Alex and Tylar, but none of them had any memory of the event. It had been so real to him. So real, it was easier to believe they'd been brainwashed by the Monkey Police; that Luke was the only one who kept the memory because he was the only one who'd escaped.

Stacy was watching Luke as he held the revolver between his legs. Her confusion turned to fear, "Luke? What are you doing?"

Luke didn't say anything. He was certain the intruder was crouched right behind his truck. "Let me just try something real quick," he said in a phony calm voice. He locked the door and slammed the truck into reverse. If anyone was back there they would have been crushed. "Just needed to re-adjust my parking." He put the gun under the seat once he was convinced no one was lurking.

"Are you good?" she asked.

"Yep, good to go. Pardon my paranoia. It gets pretty bad sometimes."

"I don't feel any paranoia. But the way you were just acting made me kind of nervous though."

"I'm sorry. It's been a residual build up of psychosis for me. It gets worse over time. I don't remember getting that way when I first started."

"Yeah, this is weird stuff. I see why you like it though. That rush is crazy; kind of scary in a pleasant way I guess."

Luke wasn't listening. His eyes ware glued to the rear-view mirror. "Luke?" She grabbed his leg. "Everything's okay, I promise." Her hand slid higher up his leg and he relaxed. It was difficult to be paranoid when a pretty girl was grabbing his crotch. She scooted closer and started kissing him. He started to kiss back. She reached into his pants.

"We should not be doing this," he pulled her hand out of his pants.

"Oh c'mon, Luke. I'm really horny and I know you are too. Don't fight it," she tried to grab him again.

"Nope," he held her hand away, "You have a boyfriend and I have a girlfriend."

"So?"

"So, I'm not doing it. I've never cheated on anyone and I don't intend to start now. I would have to break up with Zuri first."

"Then break up with her right now."

"No, I don't wanna do that. She would kill herself immediately. Plus, I love her. I don't want to leave her." Luke put the truck in gear and drove up to the road.

"Where are we going?" she said.

"I really do have some things I need to do," he said as they headed back to the park.

"Luke, I'm sorry. I shouldn't have done that. I respect you wanting to stay faithful to Zuri. Will you forgive me?" she said.

"Sure," he said.

They drove for a few minutes in silence. Stacy was thinking hard, trying to look remorseful. "What kind of errands do you have to run?" she asked.

"Gotta meet some people," he said.

Stacy started looking through Luke's I-pod that was plugged into the stereo.

"You need to sell PV?" Luke didn't answer. "Who do you need to see?"

"I'll see Tim first. He's been waiting," he said.

"Can I please come? I haven't seen him for a long time."

"Umm..."

"I won't do anything weird, I promise. I just wanna spend some time with you and see your friends," she pleaded.

"Yeah, I guess we can do that." Luke drove on past the park and headed to Walmart. He made a few texts as he drove. Stacy picked out a song she liked; 'Never Grow Up' by Chiddy Bang.

They made it to Walmart. It didn't take long for Tim to show up. He got in the back of the SUV and was surprised to see Stacy. "Hi Tim!" she greeted.

"Hey Stacy, long time no see," he didn't feel comfortable. Was she cool? Was it okay to do business in front of her? Why was Luke hanging out with his ex?

"How much did you need?" Luke asked.

"Umm... well," he said something too quiet for Luke to hear.

"Dude, you're mumbling," said Luke.

"I want twenty-five grams of the fifty-fifty. I also want a gram of the pure stuff."

"Alright." Luke went to work. Stacy made conversation with Tim while controlling the music. Once it was all bagged up, Luke handed it to Tim. Tim handed over 800 dollars.

"I only have this much right now, but I should be able to get you paid off after I sell this stuff."

"Jesus man, you're supposed to be working your way out of debt. What happened this time? Did another one of your friends steal from you again?"

"No. Something weird happened. Monkey Police. I panicked and flushed some of it down the toilet."

"Damn, dude. That's fuckin stupid, it's not even illegal. How much do you owe me now? Let's make sure we both have the same thing written down."

"I owe you nineteen-fifty now," Tim said. They each updated their lists of debts. Luke's was getting long with some big numbers. Tim's was even longer but had smaller numbers next to each name.

"Alright man, I gotta go. Thanks bro. Bye Stacy, it was nice seeing you."

"Yep, see ya Tim," she said.

"Later, dude," said Luke.

A few minutes later another car pulled up. The girl saw that the passenger seat was occupied, so she hopped in the back. "Hey Kimmy, how you doin?" said Luke.

"Pretty good, dude. I need ten for three-fifty," she said.

"Sure thing." Luke had it weighed up in a few minutes. There was an awkward tension between the girls. Suspicion and paranoia filled the air. Kimmy got out and left as soon as the transaction was complete.

The next person to pull up was much younger. It was Zuri's friend Ernie. Luke liked dealing with Ernie. He didn't do MDPV, so there was no tension; no paranoid feelings. It was easier for Luke to stay sane with people like Ernie around. Paranoia feeds off paranoia; Ernie's lack of worries canceled out any paranoid thoughts. Stacy introduced herself when Ernie got in the SUV. She spoke with her usual confidence, as if this was where she belonged. Luke had the feeling that bigger things were at work here; that Stacy was trying to plant a seed of mistrust, something that would get around to Zuri and make her wonder.

"So, what do you need, little buddy?" Luke asked.

"I wanted to get some of that molly stuff."

"I don't sell molly," Luke cut him off, "but I do have methylone. Not for human consumption, of course."

"Yeah, sorry. I want two grams of that and I was also thinking about getting some of that liquid stuff you let me try."

"Kay." Luke started to weigh out some methylone while debating weather to sell the GBL. He hadn't sold any yet and didn't know how to price it. To sell it in liquid form would be difficult, but that was the only form it came in. It would also need specific instructions on how to use it; 1.25ml for the average person. Any more than that and a person could black out or even die. It was a new drug, not enough was known about it. Luke was the lab monkey, not this kid. "I can't sell the liquid stuff. But we can hang out and do some experimenting sometime. I just don't feel completely comfortable selling the stuff quite yet."

"Okay, that's cool man. I would enjoy doing that again some time. What's Zuri up to, anyway? You two are still together right?"

"She's at home I think. And yeah, we're still together. This is not my girlfriend," Luke pointed at Stacy.

"Oh, ha. That's cool," said Ernie.

Luke handed the drugs to Ernie. Ernie handed over two crispy $100 bills. "Me and Stacy have known each other for a long time though. We used to date, and we partied hard. She had the best ecstasy pills in the world. No joke, the best. If you ever did any of the pistols, they came from her."

"Except for the yellow pistols!" she clarified.

"That's right. The yellow pistols were just meth pills; nothing like the others," said Luke.

"I think I did one of those yellow pistols. It just kept me awake all night and the next day," said Ernie.

"You never tried the blue, red, purple, or green ones?" said Stacy.

"No. You're saying the yellow ones were meth?"

"Yeah. The blue were coke; the red were PCP; the purple were LSD; and the green were mescaline. And they all, of course, had MDMA," she said.

"Yep, they were the truth," said Luke, "The yellow ones came later on. I remember being at this big high school party where all these preppy kids were eating those yellow pistols. No one had any idea they were doing meth. I knew, but I wouldn't tell anyone. They would have been horrified, and my friends were the ones selling em," said Luke.

"That's crazy, you guys. I should get out of here, though. I got girls waiting for me."

"Good. Awesome. Go take care of that," said Luke.

"Thanks dude, see you later."

Luke tried giving Jared a call. There was no answer. He was beginning to worry. "What's going on, Luke?" Stacy could feel his concern.

"It's Fat Jared. He has my car and he's not answering."

"Why would he have your car? Do you trust him with your car?" she asked.

"I don't care about the car. I sent him on a mission—nothing illegal—but there was definitely a good possibility that something could go wrong. He might be in trouble."

"What are you talking about?" she said.

Luke's phone started vibrating, "Ohh, that's probably him," he answered it, "Hello?"

"Hi Luke, It's Natalie. What are you doing?"

"Oh, hey. I don't know what I'm doing. I'm at Walmart, kinda stressin out," he said.

"Really? Why? What's wrong?" she said.

"Well, you know... you remember Fat Jared? I think he's lost or something. I can't really explain it over the phone."

"Jared's lost? Why? What's wrong with him?" she said.

"Nothing. Never mind. What's going on with you?"

"I'm just hanging out with my friend Molly. We're kinda bored, and I feel bad that we haven't talked for so long. Molly has a car now, would you want to hang out?"

"I don't know, it's probably not a good idea right now. How about tomorrow? I've got my own place now. Give me a call tomorrow, okay?"

"Sure. That would be sweet. Talk to you then," she said.

"Who was that?" Stacy asked.

"Friend from school. Pretty unexpected. I need to get high real quick. Then I need to go find Jared." Luke pulled out his supplies and prepared some MDPV.

"Where exactly would he be?" she said.

"Really far away. Stupidly far away. You want me to drop you off?" he said.

"No. I wanna help you find Jared; Whatever that even means, it's a mystery to me. And you should make an extra one of those for me," she said.

"I should?"

"Yeah, I might as well do another one. It's not like I'm gonna get addicted in one day."

"Kay." Luke restarted the process and eyeballed a larger amount of powder onto the spoon. He drew it all up into one syringe, then squirted each half into two separate syringes.

"Alright, gimme your arm." She gave it to him and he injected the solution. It was a thick one, carelessly measured out. Stacy was visibly overwhelmed by the rush. Luke took his own. It was too much. He couldn't get the supplies put away. Panic set in. The terrible weight pressed down on his chest. He could barely breathe, further limiting the oxygen supply to his heart.

"Are you okay?" Stacy asked.

"I don't think so," his voice was panicky, he hopped out of the truck and walked through the parking lot. Normal people were going about their business while Luke walked to his death. It seemed more appropriate to die in the parking lot than in front of Stacy. Better to die this horrific death in front of strangers; no need to traumatize Stacy during an excessive dose of MDPV. *In through the nose, out through the mouth,* he reminded himself, *I'm not ready to die yet! I'll go straight to hell.*

A woman was loading a minivan with her children. Luke made her nervous, so she hurried the kids into the van. Luke felt there was no blood left in his face. He looked sickly and psychotic with dilated pupils. The woman didn't know whether to help him or leave as quick as possible. Stacy caught up with him. She grabbed him and shoved a handful of aspirin in his mouth, "Chew em up!" She had tears in her eyes. She thought he was dying.

The woman was still watching in horror. It was a terrible scene, and from her view it made no sense. "Do I need to call 911?" she asked.

"Yes!" said Stacy, " He's having heart problems!" The lady started dialing.

"Don't fuckin call the cops!" Chewed up aspirin spewed from his mouth.

"Are you on drugs?" the lady demanded with the phone pressed to her ear.

"Fuck you lady! I'm dying!" The scene was getting ugly. Stacy grabbed his hand and pulled him back towards the truck. The lady was no longer concerned for his health, she wanted him jailed. The sickly teenager was a threat to himself and others.

Stacy drove while Luke sat in the passenger seat. "Where are we going?" Luke asked. Oxygen began to replenish his cells. The aspirin thinned his blood enough to compensate for the constricted blood vessels.

" I don't know... go find Jared, I guess. We needed to leave that parking lot. That lady was calling the cops."

"What the fuck was her problem?" he said.

"I think you scared her. I was scared. You need to stop doing that stuff, it's going to kill you," she said.

"I didn't think we did that much. I've done that much before. Did it mess you up, too?" he said.

"It gave me a scary rush and lots of anxiety, but it didn't hurt me like it did to you."

"But you did the same amount as me."

"Yeah, that's the scary part. Your body can't handle it any more. It's killing you. You need to stop immediately," she said.

"I know. I will."

~~~

It was getting late as Luke and Stacy headed west from Kalispell. Luke was driving, and Stacy was controlling the music while forcing Luke to smoke weed. "So Luke, you should explain to me exactly why Jared is way out by Thompson Lake in your car."

"I sent him to meet up with some people. It was their idea to meet all the way out there. They were expecting to meet me, but I sent Jared instead."

"Why would you send Jared? And why would he be in trouble?" she said.

"I don't trust the people. I've heard bad things about them."

"Then why don't you just not deal with them?"

"Because they could make me a lot of money. They've been persistent. This is my way of giving them a chance."

"And these people want your MDPV?"

"Yep, and they could sell big quantities of it."

"So what could they have done to Jared? Are these people dangerous?" she said.

"They could have kidnapped him, ditched him in the woods, tied him up and left him in the trunk of my car. I have no idea. That's why I'm a little nervous
~~~

about the situation; it could be a trap or something."

After 45 minutes, Luke started climbing to the back seat. "Take the wheel, please," he said. She was used to the procedure and slid into the drivers seat. "Turn down Thompson creek road."

"I remember this road," she said, "Do you remember getting lost down this road? Remember how pissed you were at me for making you drive down it?"

"Yeah, I remember," he said.

She turned off the empty highway onto a gravel road. "You were so angry. Remember how we got a flat tire after driving down this road for like two hours?"

"Yeah! And I kept trying to turn around, but you insisted it looped back around to the lake. It's like 150 miles of vicious gravel road for no fuckin reason! What's the point?"

"Then we ended up staying the night in Thompson Falls. What are you—what is *that?*"

Luke was perched in the back seat with the AK-47. He switched his vision from each side of the vehicle, looking for Jared.

"It's just in case something bad happens. I have no idea what these people are capable of."

"Are you expecting to have a shootout with them?" she said.

"No, but I'd rather have it and not need it than to need it and not have it."

Just holding the gun encouraged Luke's paranoia. It sent signals to his brain that disaster was immanent. He would hallucinate that headlights were approaching from behind them. *At least it's not the Monkey Police were up against. For once we have a tangible enemy; An enemy we can be certain is out there; An enemy that is just as human as us, and probably just as paranoid, too.*

They kept the speed over 45mph. Any slower and the road would rattle the truck to pieces. If they went fast enough, the truck would glide over the washboard gravel surface. After a half hour of nothing but darkness and trees, Luke began to wonder, *If that fat piece of shit isn't out here I'm fuckin him up. He'd better not be avoiding my phone calls while driving around in my car.* All of the waiting and suspense made Luke crave a crisis. He was ready for an ambush; ready to find his Chrysler plugged with bullet holes on the side of the road; ready for *something.* He was tired of being frightened and prepared for nothing. If something terrible would happen, it would mean he was sane; it would justify all his precautions.

"I think I see something," said Stacy, "I think it's Jared."

Luke tensed up, not knowing what to expect. As they got closer he knew it was his helpless fat friend. They stopped in front of Jared and let him in. Luke kept the assault rifle ready.

"I need to get high," said Jared. He wanted sympathy, but Luke wanted answers.

"What happened? Where are they?" Luke kept scanning out the window, prepared to open fire. Stacy turned the truck around.

"They fucking ambushed me! And they have your car," said Jared.

"Why'd you give it to them? Where are they now?" he demanded.

"I didn't give it to them! They took it from me. That crazy bitch stuck a gun in my face and made me get out! They just took it and left me to die. That was like six hours ago, where have you been? Do you even care? I need to get high. Right now, please," said Jared.

Luke prepared the solution in the back seat with Jared. The bumpy road made it difficult. Jared continued to complain about what Luke had put him through. "There wasn't a single car the entire time I've been on this road. What kind of road is this? What's the fuckin point of a road nobody uses? Why did you send me out to meet those evil people? Why out *here?*"

Luke wasn't paying attention to Jared's self pity. He was listening to the music while focusing on the MDPV he was working with. Handling it was making him jones. He was ready for a shot. *Just a small one. I can do it quick enough that Stacy won't notice.* "Gimme your arm you fat piece of crap." The insult had no effect on Jared. The needle was too appealing. It was over quickly, and Jared's receptor sites were finally replenished. *And one for the doctor,* Luke thought before replenishing his own.

The mind is its own place,
and in itself can make a heaven of Hell, a hell of Heaven.
-John Milton

Chapter 25: Chemical Warfare

Wednesday 4-17-2011

Zuri heard the Suburban pull into the driveway. Luke came through the door a few moments later. " Oh Luke!" she hugged him tight.

"Hi sweetie." They held each other for a few minutes.

"You smell like *her*," she said with disgust.

"That's because I was hanging out with *her*. I almost died in the Walmart parking lot. I'm pretty sure she saved my life," he said.

"Did you do anything with her?" she said.

"Did I do anything sexual with her? No, absolutely not."

"Did she try anything?"

"No. She has a boyfriend, remember?" he said.

There was another pause. Zuri was getting emotional. "We need to talk. I need to know what's happening between us. What am I supposed to think when you disappear for a week?"

"Everything's fine. I've just been busy and distracted." Luke took off his shoes to reveal his crusty socks as they walked to the bedroom. "I'm also trying to keep you out of danger. There's some desperate people out there who are willing to do anything for the stuff I have." They laid down. Zuri rested her head on his chest.

"I don't care about any of that. The only thing I care about is you. And when you don't come home for a week, it makes me think you don't care."

"I do care. I love you and I'm sorry. I don't know why I treat you like crap. I thought that maybe if I spent some time away it would make it better," he said.

"I know why you do it. It's because of the drugs. And I'm not going to give up on you, because I know it's not going to be this way forever."

"You think I can stop doing this stuff?" he said.

"You're gonna have to eventually. Otherwise you're gonna die. And if you die, I'll just kill myself."

"That's fucked up! Don't say that shit," he said.

There were a few more peaceful moments. Then she said, "You smell bad."

"I know. I haven't showered for a while. I think this is the first time I've taken my shoes off for a week."

"You haven't showered since you went to Missoula?" she said.

"Nope. I'm pretty much coated in dried up hippie drug rave, research chemical sweat." Luke took off his socks to reveal cracked yellow feet with wrinkly toe nails.

"Oh my god, that's disgusting!" she said. Zuri had been shooting meth on her own, but still would not touch MDPV.

"I think I'm turning into a zombie. These are definitely zombie feet," he said.

"You used to have pretty feet! What's happening to you?" she said.

"I'm pretty sure MDPV is doing it. I saw Jared's feet and they looked the same."

"We should get in the shower." Zuri got up, picked up her cellphone and made a text. Then she grabbed Luke's hand and led him to the shower.

The shower was vitalizing. It brought blood to Luke's limbs and rinsed the dried up chemical sweat from his body. They kissed each other while sharing a long naked hug. "I love you... So much," she said.

"I love you too, sweet heart. Why are you so good to me?" he said.

"Because you're the love of my life. I'm keeping you. Don't ever leave me like that again. It would kill me," she said.

"I won't," he said.

"Promise me."

Luke heard radio static: "We got a ten eighteen on Harrison Avenue." *Cops!* Luke's heart raced as he got out of the shower.

"What are you doing?" she said.

"I'm leaving," he said.

"What are you talking about?"

"I know what you're doing, you stupid bitch!"

Zuri jumped out of the shower and tried to grab him. She was crying. They were both naked and slippery, so it was easy for him to get away. "Luke, please just talk to me!"

Luke ran out of the bathroom and found a pistol. He checked a few windows before getting dressed. He went for the front door. She grabbed his shirt, trying to stop him. "Get the fuck off me!"

"No!" she screamed. Luke threw her on the floor and ran out the door.

~~~

Luke couldn't believe he made it as far as he had. He was finally out of C-Falls after a frantic drive through side streets and alleys. There were flashing lights behind him that never caught up. Getting caught was not an option; he would fight until the death if he had to. His impending doom was certain. Every minute he kept driving felt like a miracle.

Finally he made it into Kalispell. He relaxed as he drove aimlessly through a residential part of town. Zuri had been calling, but Luke had already taken the batteries out of his phone so no one could triangulate him. *I sure hope that wasn't all in my head. That would make me a real dick. The poor girl is probably traumatized. I shouldn't have been so mean; even if she did set me up. I hope she doesn't kill herself. Maybe I should call her.* Just as he was about to put his phone together, a black Silverado pulled behind him. He wasn't following close, but it seemed suspicious. Luke made a few unnecessary turns and the Silverado stayed behind.

Luke sped up, but couldn't shake him. The Silverado stayed close behind. One man was in the Silverado. He was bald with dark sunglasses. His expression was fierce as he made eye contact in Luke's rear-view mirror.

Luke made it to main street and waited for an opportunity to cross. The Silverado was right behind him. An opening came, but Luke waited. He waited until the very last second so the Silverado couldn't follow. As the gap was closing he sped across the street. Tires were squealing and horns were honking as he sped off into the residential streets.

He made a few wild turns, ignoring all stop signs until he felt he'd safely distanced himself. He parked the truck and jumped out, locking the doors and leaving his cellphones behind. After running a few blocks he decided to get rid of the weapon. He ditched behind a dumpster and kept running.

A block later he decided to go back for the gun. He felt vulnerable without it. The gun was drawn; completely exposed in broad daylight. There was a yell. He
~~~

slipped in some gravel as he scrambled to hide behind a car. There was another yell, he decided it was coming from someone's backyard.

Time to get moving. I've drawn too much attention. I need to get rid of this gun, or at least conceal it. What the hell am I doing? He stuffed the pistol in his waistband and continued down the alley. After a couple blocks he slowed down to a walk. *I'm just a normal everyday citizen, doing normal everyday things.* He tried hard to be inconspicuous, but his frantic movement was sure to give him away. The feeling that someone was following him was impossible to ignore. *Am I fuckin insane? This can't all be in my head, I'm sober!*

~~~

Luke managed to sneak across town to the apartments where he knew Tim would be. The Silverados were becoming more abundant. They were surely looking for him. *Maybe they just want to see what MDPV addicts do under pressure. They're putting the test subjects in stressful situations to see how they will respond. Maybe they want to find out how dangerous we really are.*

Tim was on the porch smoking a cigarette as Luke approached. No words were exchanged. Tim handed the cigarette to Luke. Luke understood that Tim was going through the same thing. "It's coming to an end, isn't it?" said Luke.

Tim nodded, "Have you been watching all the Silverados?"

This confirmed everything for Luke. He was not insane; the Silverados *were* real. "Yeah. I'm pretty sure they've set up an outpost a few blocks down," said Luke.

"Oh yeah, I've seen it. That three story building to our left? Don't look at it," Tim whispered.

"Did you see how many Silverados are parked behind it?" said Luke.

"Yeah. They've been setting up some sort of equipment on the roof. They can see my place from the roof. I'm pretty sure theres an undercover in my house right now. This dude is acting completely weird."

"Let's do a little experiment. Like a fake drug deal. I'll pretend I have some shit and you pretend you're giving me money. Then if they decide to attack we'll be totally clean."

"I'm down. I don't have anything bad on me," Tim whispered.

"Good. Me either. Keep whispering, it makes us look like we're up to no good. Our goal is to force them to make a move," said Luke.

They moved over to the sidewa lk and began the act. "I've got that stuff you wanted," Luke said in a normal voice.

"Awesome. I've got your eight hundred dollars right here." Tim held out a clenched fist. Luke pretended to grab the money and stuff it into his pocket.
~~~

"And here's your *drugs*." Luke stuck his fist out, full of make believe drugs.

"Thanks man. I'm gonna get really high and sell this to kids in elementary schools." Luke gave Tim a disapproving look. "Just kidding," Tim mumbled.

An innocent looking lady was walking toward them with her dog. Tim pretended to be caught up in normal conversation, "Yeah, uhh... it's a pretty nice day, isn't it?" he said to Luke.

"Sure," Luke played along with Tim's poor attempt at normal conversation, "It's a totally nice day. We should be out doing things... like skating... and stuff." It was a desperate attempt, but the lady was gone. As she was walking away, Luke noticed her speak into a microphone on her wrist.

That was their cue, thought Luke, *Our antagonizing has worked; they're moving in.* There was strange activity in a house across the street. Uniformed men were in the living room. They were setting up equipment on tripods, pointing it toward Luke and his friend. "I have to go. I'm very sorry." Luke walked away. He didn't have time to explain what was happening.

"Wait, don't leave yet." Tim followed.

"I'm sorry." Luke started running.

"Where are you going?" said Tim.

Luke didn't answer, but kept running. He felt guilty for leaving his friend to suffer the mysterious fate.

~~~

Luke had managed to escape the situation. He used backyards and alleys to avoid detection. Silverados were everywhere and he would take any measure to avoid them.

It was dark finally. He tried to be stealthy, but was hindered by vicious dogs. No dog was friendly toward Luke. They could sense the fear and desperation, which left them no choice but to attack.

Luke finally gathered the courage to walk the streets. The residential neighborhoods seemed abandoned. There was no normal human activity. *Did they declare martial law?* The Silverados became less frequent. Luke still hid every time one drove by.

A normal vehicle began to follow, keeping a safe distance behind. Luke would turn down dark streets and continue walking. It wasn't until he'd made it a block or two that the car would re-appear behind him. Once the vehicle got close enough he could see it was a black Crown Victoria. He made one last turn to see if they would follow him. A block later the Crown Victoria turned the corner and parked.

The people in the car got out and opened the trunk. They pulled out the
~~~

tripod equipment and started setting it up right there in the street. *Fuck it! I'm done. I'm tired of running.*

Luke turned around and walked toward the Crown Victoria. They disassembled the equipment and stuffed it back into the trunk.

The three men watched Luke as he approached. They each were bald and wore sunglasses with Hawaiian T-shirts. Luke kept walking toward them, ignoring the fear of the unknown. All he could do was hope that they were gentle. His mind was made up; it was time to surrender to the Monkey Police.

He stopped when he was face to face with the strange men. Each of them were identical; bald with matching sunglasses. Luke wished he could cry. These were the same men who had been following him since the beginning of MDPV. These were the men who spied on Luke when he first moved into his house. These were the men that set up all the cameras. These were the men who drove the SUVs and Silverados. These were the Monkey Police.

Luke turned around and put his hands behind his back, "I'm done. I surrender. Do your fuckin monkey business." He closed his eyes, anticipating the cold cuffs around his wrists.

"I'm afraid you have us mistaken," said the man closest to Luke.

Luke peeked around, hands still behind his back. "What do you mean? I know what you're up to; it's no secret anymore. I'm tired of hiding, just take me away."

"What do you think we're up to?" said the man.

"The experiment, man! I'm tired of the games. I don't want to be a part of the experiment anymore. I quit. You can stop faking."

"We're only looking for Colter's Coffee. Would you give us directions?" The man's expression had humored arrogance to it, showing that he knew things that he wasn't going to tell Luke.

"Colter's Coffee is on Main Street, and there's no way it's even open right now. Stop the bullshit!" said Luke.

"Thank you. We will be going now."

"Wait, do you have a cigarette?" said Luke. One man came forth and handed Luke a Basic. "I need a lighter." The same man gave him a lighter. Luke smelled the cigarette before lighting it. "I'm keeping this," he stuck the lighter in his pocket.

The three men smiled and got in the car without saying a word. They drove off, leaving Luke on the sidewalk to smoke his cigarette. *What the fuck is happening to me? Is this the fuckin Matrix?*

Luke started walking again. He pondered the mystery that seemed to get deeper as the night went on. The energy from those men was cold and inhuman. *Who wears sunglasses in this kind of darkness. Maybe the Monkey Police aren't human. Maybe they're aliens conducting chemical experiments on humans. Maybe they're shape shifters. Maybe I'm just fuckin crazy.*

~~~

Things got worse as the night went on. Silverados were still swooping all around him. He avoided them out of instinct, but knew it was hopeless. At one point a person started to follow him. They kept safe distance, using the same tactics as the men in the Crown Victoria. Luke made a few strange turns to make sure the person was following. Once he was sure, he turned around. He would confront this person just as he had with the three men.

Luke was ready to be aggressive; ready to interrogate this person until he got some answers. If the Monkey Police wouldn't take him before, they wouldn't take him now. As Luke got closer the person slowed down. The person wore a long trench coat and combat boots. Luke noticed something shiny attached to the man's belt. The man turned around and walked away. "Hey! Get back here!" The person stopped and turned to face Luke. Luke caught up to him , "What are you doing right now?"

"Umm... I... uhh," the man stuttered.

Luke could sense the fear in his stalker, and that gave him even more confidence.

"Why are you following me, fuckface?" said Luke.

"I... uhh," he took off in a sprint. Luke chased after.

"Get back here! I just want some answers!" The person ran through someone's yard and jumped a fence. Luke was over the fence an instant later, but the trench coat man was gone. A dog came snarling out of nowhere and bit him in the leg. Luke kicked the dog in the face before disappearing into the darkness.

Disgusting! What the fuck is happening to our country? Luke thought. He noticed many houses being invaded by the gas mask people. *Why gas masks? Why do they need to convert innocent people's houses into military outposts?*

He walked past another house that had their lights on. The gas mask men were unloading boxes and setting up equipment in the living room. One of the men with a Hawaiian shirt and sunglasses walked into the room. The gas mask men went about their business while the Hawaiian shirt man watched.

Well, this is beginning to make sense. The chemical suited men work for those arrogant, Hawaiian T-shirt wearing creatures. The man with sunglasses gave Luke an evil smile.

"Fuck you!" Luke yelled with his middle finger in the air. The man shook his head and went back to supervising his gas mask men.
~~~

I need to get out of this town. How long would it take to get to my parents? Could I possibly make it on foot? I need some fuckin water. Damn it, is that radiation I taste? Luke noticed strange particles floating from the sky. It burned his lungs. *That's it, our world is fucking dead. No hope. Let's see how these people are holding up.* Luke walked up to a dark house. A house that wasn't occupied by the Monkey Police. He knocked on the door. A light turned on and a man cracked the door open, "May I help you?" he said.

"Hello, sir. Is everything okay over here? Have you been watching the news?" said Luke.

"No," he said.

"Can I please have some water? I think I'm dying."

"Would you like me to call 911?"

"No, water is fine." Luke tried to sound reasonable.

The door closed with the sound of the dead bolt locking it shut. A couple minutes later the door opened. The man peeked out and handed Luke a glass of water. Before Luke could thank him, the door was shut and dead bolted. "Fuckin weirdo," Luke said as he walked off with the glass of water. *I wasn't being unreasonable, was I? He'll wish he'd listened to me when he wakes up covered in radiation.*

~~~

Luke made it out of town. He was on the country road that lead to his parent's house. It was only a few miles away, but he doubted if he would ever make it. His mind had flipped back to being afraid of the Monkey Police now that he had a purpose. He *needed* to make it to his family. That was all he had to live for.

He would dive into the tall grass whenever a Silverado would drive by. It was always a Silverado. There hadn't been anything but Silverados since he'd been on the country road. The radiation was getting worse. He could feel it burning into his skin. *I spent all that money on NBC suits and don t even have them when I need them.* His mission was to warn his parents. They needed to get the NBC suits.

Luke was making good distance, completely terrified, but at least moving fast. As he was walking, he noticed glowing lights out in a field. He got closer and saw that it was the gas mask men. There was a whole squad of them, all armed with AR-15 assault rifles.

It was too late for Luke; he was already spotted. The whole bunch of them were staring right at him. The glowing lights were a part of their survey equipment. "I hate you!" Luke was so close to saving his parents, and these assholes were going to stop him. "I'll fuckin kill you!" Luke charged into the field after the gas mask men. The men started climbing down into an underground
~~~

bunker. The lid was closed before Luke could get there. The entrance blended so perfectly with the landscape that Luke couldn't find it. Luke stomped around in the field for fifteen minutes trying to find it.

He made it back to the road and continued walking. Time was running out; the radiation was dissolving his flesh. The Monkey Police knew it; that's why they disappeared into the bunker.

A vehicle was approaching. It didn't look like a Silverado; it was too small. It was a Geo Metro. Luke ran into the road and waved his arms in distress. The vehicle slowed down and came to a stop. A guy was driving with a girl in the passenger seat. Luke approached the window, " Are you guys okay?"

"Yeah, we're good. Are you okay?" said the driver.

"No, I'm not. Can you taste that shit? Have you been listening to the radio? Is there any sort of emergency broadcasts?"

"No, I don think so. Why? What is happening?" said the driver.

"We're all dying, there's radiation in the air. Do you see my arms? It's fucking eating me!"

"Do you need a ride? Do you want me to take you to the hospital?"

"Well, I don't have much further..." Luke was staring down the road. A vehicle was approaching; a Silverado. "Shit, here they come, go, go, go!" The Geo drove off and Luke made a run for it.

~~~

It was the final stretch. Luke could see his parent's house. Monkey Police were in the fields, and he was sure they weren't going to let him make it to his parents. Glowing lights were monitoring him from all angles. He started running.

He made it to the house and crawled through the doggy door into the garage. He scrambled into the house and jumped onto his parent's bed. They both woke up and saw him perched up at the foot of their bed. "Luke, is that you? What are you doing?" said Alice. He didn't speak, but stared toward the window, expecting the Monkey Police to come crashing in.

"Is someone outside?" said Allan.

"I don't know. I don't even know how I made it here."

"Your friends have been looking for you," said Alice, "They said something was wrong with you. Are you okay? It's almost five in the morning. Where have you been?"

"I don't know. It's hard to explain."

"Your eyes look weird," said Allan, "Why do you keep looking out the window?"

"I'm sorry. I'm so sorry. I think the radiation is messing with my brain. We
~~~

need to get my chemical suits."

"I'll go make sure there's nothing nuclear happening," said Allan. He went outside to check.

"Do you need any food?" said Alice.

"I'm starving and thirsty," he said.

"Let's go get you something," she said.

Luke and his mother went to the kitchen. She made him some cereal. Allan came back in to assure Luke that there was no radiation then went back to bed. Alice stayed up to talk with Luke.

Stacy and some friends had been searching for Luke. Zuri had been calling everyone, trying to find out what happened. Alice kept explaining these things as Luke tried not to look out the windows.

It was time for Luke to sleep. Alice helped him up to his old bedroom and got him into bed. Luke still couldn't help but look out the windows. The horror had been too real. He could still feel the radiation burns on his arms and in his lungs. "Goodnight sweetie, get some sleep. I love you."

"I love you too, mom." She went downstairs and left Luke in silence. He had to fight the urge to peek out the windows. The shadows and noises outside were frightening, but he had to believe it was fake. He would pretend it was fake.

You change for two reasons:
Either you learn enough that you want to, or you've been hurt enough that you have to.
-Unknown

Chapter 26: Bad Reaction

Sunday 4-20-2011

It was evening when Zuri pulled into Luke's parents driveway. For two long days she had been searching for Luke. No one would answer her calls. No one wanted to help her find Luke, especially Alice. Finally Zuri was desperate enough to investigate for her self.

She walked up to the front door and knocked. Allan answered with a smile,"Hi Zuri, how have you been?"

"I've been looking for Luke," she said.

"Oh, right. He is upstairs. I'm pretty sure he is still sleeping. He's been sleeping for a couple days now, but go ahead and check on him if you'd like."

"Thanks." She walked past and went up the stairs. Her fears were confirmed; Alice hated her and didn't want her to have anything to do with Luke. *As if I'm the one who's causing the problems. Like I'm the one who's causing him to do the drugs.* Zuri was hurt, but was relieved to have finally found Luke.

There were two people in the bed. It was Stacy. She was awake and had herself wrapped around Luke. "Hi Zuri," said Stacy.

"What the fuck, Luke!" The betrayal was too much, she wanted to die.

Luke woke up as Zuri was running down the stairs. He noticed Stacy, "What the fuck are you doing?" he pushed her off and ran after Zuri. Halfway down the stairs he noticed he was wearing a clean pair of boxers he hadn't seen for a long time.

He ran into the driveway as Zuri was starting the car. She backed out as he was pulling on the passenger door . It wasn't opening and she was going faster, so he jumped through the window, Zuri was crying as Luke's face smashed against the floorboard. "Will you just fucking calm down? I don't know why she was in my bed. You have no idea what I've been through!" he said.

"You have no idea what *I've* been through! Three fuckin days I've been looking for you! Then I find you sleeping with that disgusting whore!" She stopped the car in the middle of the road and burst into sobs.

Luke sat in the seat and continued to defend himself, "I was not sleeping with her! I just woke up and she was there. I don't know how she got there."

Zuri wanted to believe him. Her agony began to recede. "Do you mean it?"

"Of course I mean it. If I wanted to be with her, I wouldn't have chased after you. Can we go somewhere please? Cars are coming," he said.

Zuri started driving again. She pulled over into a parking lot as soon as they made it into town. They held each other for a few moments. "Did you really think I was setting you up?" she asked.

"Yeah, at the time. I know you weren't though," he said.

"What happened to you? Where did you go after you left me?" she said.

"Well, it's a long story. And it was a pretty fucked up experience. I don't really know what was real and what wasn't. We need to go see if my truck is where I left it, then I'll try to explain what happened," he said.

"We have to go find your truck right now?" She was still squeezing him and didn't want to let go.

"Yeah, sweetie. I'm kinda worried about it. There's important stuff in there and I don't know for sure if I locked it," he said.

"You're not going to do more PV are you?" She said, still holding him.

"No... well, maybe a little. I definitely need to do a *little*."

"No! Please, no more."

"I'm gonna quit, but I can't do it all at once. I don't think you understand how fuckin miserable I feel right now. Getting a shot of that stuff is pretty much all I can think about. Its fuckin torture."

"You need to stop! Its killing you and makes you crazy. I can't take it anymore."

"Zuri, I love you, and I promise you I'm going to quit. I don't want to keep doing this to you; I'm not going to keep doing this to you. I want us to be happy."

"Then don't do anymore PV. Do some crystal instead or something. Will you please try that instead?" she said.

"I have tried that, remember? Meth does nothing for me anymore. PV is the only thing that works."

"Just try it again, please. You haven't done anything for like three days. It will be different this time," she said.

"Sure, I'll try it. Now lets go find my truck."

~~~

It was only a five minute drive. The Suburban was just where he'd left it. A few days ago he would have been terrified to approach the vehicle. But now that he was rested, there was no paranoia.

"You're not going to drive away, are you?" said Zuri.

"No. I'll be right back. I just need to grab something."

"No PV," she said.

"Right." Luke got out and ran to his truck in his boxers. He came back a few moments later with a case of Ensure and a grocery bag.

"Who's boxers are those, anyway?" she asked. "I've never seen them before."

"They're mine. I just haven't had em for a long time. I don't remember ever putting these on actually."

"Oooh I hate that bitch. Was she wearing those?"

"Yeah, I'm pretty sure she has a bunch of my clothes," he said.

"She keeps your underwear?"

"Well, she used to wear my clothes all the time," he said.

"Why don't you ask for your clothes back. I think it's fucked up," she said.

"Because I don't really care. I have plenty of clothes, and she likes them."

"What the fuck? Do you keep her underwear?"

"No! Jesus, get a hold of yourself. You're digging way too far into the situation," he said.

"I don't think she should be wearing your underwear."

"Fine." Luke pulled a sunglass case out of the grocery bag and began to make a shot.

"None of that!" she said.

"Just a tiny one."

"No!" she tried to grab it, but he shielded it from her.

"You're supposed to do the other stuff instead."

"I'll do meth also. But I need just a tiny bit of this right now. See, look," he
~~~

showed her the spoon with a speck of powder in it. "That's all I'm doing."

Zuri knew it was a harmless amount, but she still wasn't happy about it. "I wish you would not do it for just one day."

"I've gone almost three days without it. This won't get me high; it will just give me a chance to wake up." It wasn't just to wake him up. It was a terrible craving that made him feel that his survival depended upon it. Nothing was going to stop him from getting his dose. "I am going to quit. I know I have to, but you can't expect me to do it all at once."

Zuri accepted defeat. She knew he was sincere, and that's all she could hope for. He took the shot and felt better, but he wanted more. His reptilian brain sent signals to the frontal cortex, telling him he would benefit from a large dose. He was determined to give meth a chance. He knew he would be much healthier addicted to meth, but it seemed so useless compared to MDPV.

"Kay, that's it," he said, "no more PV. What do you want to do?"

"I just want to spend time with you. I think we should drive to our special place," she said.

"Sure. Let's do that." Luke gave her a kiss and grabbed her hand. He was amazed by the amount of love he felt towards her now that he was rational. There was terrible guilt, and he wanted to make it up to her. *How could I have treated this wonderful girl so terribly? I love her, and she loves me no matter how horrible I've been.*

~~~

They made it to their spot; a secluded place on top of a mountain, only a short ways outside of town. There was a beautiful view in all directions. "I'm so sorry for being such a prick lately. Will you please forgive me?" he said with Zuri in his arms.

"Of course I forgive you. I know it's not really you when you get that way. Sometimes when you're like that, I look into your eyes and see a completely different person."

"Yeah?" Luke gave her a kiss on the neck.

"Seriously, it scares me. It's like, not even human energy; like you're being possessed or something," she said.

"That is scary. Do you really think I could be possessed?" he looked into her eyes, "Do I look like I'm possessed right now?"

She stared into his eyes, "No. I see you in there. This is the Luke I love."

"Good. I don't wanna be possessed. No more demons allowed here." He started to kiss her again. They were both happy. It had been too long since they had shared feelings. "I think we should both get completely naked," he said.
~~~

"Ha, I think that's a good idea." They took off their clothes and got in the back seat. Being on MDPV had turned Luke into a selfish lover, but this time was finally payback. Today it would be all about Zuri.

~~~

They made love for hours, taking cigarette breaks every thirty minutes or so. Finally they just cuddled naked in the back seat while celebrating with some weed. "Mhmm, I love you," said Zuri as she gave him a kiss.

"I love you too, sweetheart." Luke was feeling drained. His mind kept directing his attention to MDPV. "I'm feeling pretty tired," he said.

"Maybe you should take a nap. I'd be fine laying right here like this forever," she said.

"Well, I'm not that kind of tired. I've slept for three days." he said.

"Do you want me to make some up?"

"Yes please." Luke put his boxers back on; it was still all he had to wear. Zuri crawled to the front and got dressed. The craving for MDPV was gnawing at Luke's soul. He could only hope the meth would make it bearable.

She handed him a loaded syringe. "How much did you put in here?" he said.

"I don't know. I just eyeballed it. There's a lot thought. Yours is bigger than mine." Zuri was already tying off. Luke went for it. The process of injecting was half the high. His brain expected MDPV, but he was let down with a meth rush.

He coughed, and lost his vision for a moment. He looked in the mirror when the rush was over. His pupils were dilated, but there was no energy. *Hmh, better drink some Ensure.*

He drank his Ensures while Zuri injected. She coughed and was energized. "I think I should do more," he said.

She looked at him with disbelief. "Maybe you need to get up and walk around or something."

"Sure," Luke lit a cigarette and got out of the car. He walked barefoot. It was a beautiful day, but he couldn't appreciate it. He walked down a trail until his feet started to hurt. The energy wasn't coming, and his craving was getting worse. He went back to the car.

"I'm gonna see how much meth it takes to cure MDPV craving."

"Okay, here you go." She handed him the supplies. "Is this stuff pure?" he asked.

"Yeah. I did that thing with the acetone as soon as you gave it to me."

"Okay. I'm gonna measure this out proper." Luke decided he was going to try 250mg. 10mg is psychoactive in normal people. He knew it was way too much, but he didn't believe people could die from meth. Even with that belief, he knew
~~~

it wasn't going to be pleasant.

The needle went in and the plunger depressed. He coughed, and his vision went black as the chemical made it through his jugular. He was incapacitated for five minutes before his vision came back.

His skin was cold and clammy. He could feel the disgusting chemical coarsing through his bloodstream. Everything was terribly bright. He looked in the mirror and saw his pupils almost fully dilated even though the sun was shining.

"Are you energized yet?" said Zuri.

"I'm not sure. I feel gross. We should go for a walk," he said.

They both got out of the car and walked down a steep trail. Most of the hillside was logged. It was rough terrain, but Luke decided to tough it out with his feet.

Luke's cravings were still strong. He was dirty inside and out, and the meth had only made him feel dirtier. "So, do you think when we get back to the car that I could do a little bit of my stuff?"

"Please don't do PV. Anything but that," she said.

"What if I do just a tiny bit? I could even write up a ween down schedule. That's how they get people off of methadone, right?" he said.

"You're seriously not high right now?" she said.

"Not at all, and the craving is unbearable."

"I thought today was *my* day. I just want you, *without* PV. If you do it you'll turn into an asshole," she said.

"I'm fuckin miserable. The meth isn't working; I need *real* drugs. I promise I won't do much; not enough to become an asshole," he said.

"Whatever. I don't want you to, but I know you're going to do it anyway. I think it's terrible. Don't you ever think about your freakouts? How you always think you're going to die? Do you have any idea what that does to *me*?"

"I know it's terrible, but I'm done with the freakouts. I'm starting a ween down schedule. I'll write it down as soon as we get home. I'll be completely done with MDPV in a month by gradually decreasing my dose each day. I'll follow it to the T. Nothing can go wrong," he said.

"I don't know. I don't see that working… Hopefully it does."

~~~

They made it back to the car. Luke was excited to finally take a decent dose of MDPV. "See how much I'm doing?" he held the spoon in front of Zuri. It wasn't much, but it was larger than his previous dose. "It's only twenty-five milligrams. Do you approve of this dosage?"

"I don't approve of any dosage." She sat in the driver seat while smoking a
~~~

cigarette.

"Alright then." He finished mixing it up. This was the wonderful moment he'd been waiting for. The first reasonable dose in three days. His earlier dose was less than 10mg; barely over the psychoactive threshold.

He injected it slowly, savoring the moment. It was everything he'd hoped for. The anxiety, the constricting blood vessels, the fear; that norepinephrin, the emergency/pleasure center chemical.

It was exactly what his brain had been looking for.

"Are you happy now?" said Zuri.

"I am," Luke said over short, shallow breaths. Ten minutes went by and everything was normal. Zuri was holding his hand; it was cold from lack of circulation.

"Aww, shit," Luke was worried.

"What's wrong?" she said.

"My face."

"What are you talking about?" she said.

"It feels droopy. Only this side, though," he pointed to his left cheek. Zuri was confused. "I can't feel your hand either. Or my leg. I think the whole left side of my body is numb."

"What does that mean?" she said.

"I don't know but it's fuckin freaky. I think I need to go to the hospital."

"Seriously?"

"Yes, seriously! This is not normal. I'm definitely fucked up."

"Okay, I'm going." Zuri maneuvered the Oldsmobile back onto the treacherous logging road.

"This is fucking weird... you have no idea. You should probably go fast, because I'm pretty sure I'm going to die," his words were beginning to slur.

"Kay, I'm hurrying." She was frantic, shaking from fear.

The vehicle scraped to a stop as it high-centered on a rock. She tried to gun it forward, but it wouldn't budge. "Yep, I'm fucking dead for sure," said Luke.

"I'm trying!" She started crying as she tried to reverse. The car scraped as she went forward and backward again.

Finally the vehicle broke free as she gunned it in reverse. The road got better and she drove more reckless than ever before. Luke was trying to prepare himself for death. His reality was turning magical. Light reflected differently. His thoughts were calm; none of the random, meaningless thoughts that usually filled his head. Zuri's terrible driving didn't phase him.

Maybe dying is like a DMT trip. Any moment now I might just blast off into the cosmos.

Everything will burst into fractals as I travel at light speed. Then I may manifest as some creature in another place; possibly another planet in another solar system. It would make no difference if I ended up in another galaxy as well.

Maybe it will be a primitive existence. Maybe they will have unimaginable technology, and a beautiful religion inspired by DMT. DMT certainly must exist everywhere life exists. It is, after all, the original building block of all brain chemicals.

~~~

They made it to the hospital. Zuri pulled into the ambulance drop-off and helped him out. Nurses came to assist, but Luke could walk on his own. The numbness in his face had gone away about ten minutes before their arrival. The nurses led him inside, while Zuri went to park the car. Zuri was in the emergency room with Luke five minutes later.

"What happened to him?" she asked the doctor.

"From the symptoms he described, it sounds like he had a stroke. It's clear he's been injecting some kind of speed, which would make it very likely that he did have a stroke."

"We've taken a blood sample and are going to do an MRI to see if there's any permanent brain damage," the doctor said before leaving the room.

"Oh Luke, are you okay?" she said.

"Yeah, I feel fine." He looked helpless with the IV tube in his arm. "I don't know why they hooked me up to this thing. Maybe to make it more dramatic or something," he said.

"Please tell me you're done doing PV," she said.

"Yeah. I'm done for sure. The doctor said I'm lucky to be talking and stuff right now."

"Luke, that's scary."

The doctor came back fifteen minutes later with the blood test results. "So, we found out the cause of your stroke. It looks like you mixed a certain kind of Mexican methamphetamine with a chemical that resembles bathtub crank."

"Bathtub crank?" said Luke.

"Yes, some kinds of crank, when mixed in the bloodstream with methamphetamine, will clot into a plastic-like substance. The plastic substance got stuck in your brain, cutting off blood flow and causing the stroke."

"That's freakin nuts," said Luke.

"Yep, I wasn't kidding when I said how lucky you are to be functional right now. If that substance hadn't made it through as quickly as it had, you could either be dead, or severely brain damaged. We're going to take you to the MRI now to make sure there are no dead spots," he looked at Zuri, "you'll have to
~~~

wait here."

Luke was gone for, twenty minutes before they brought him back. There was no significant damage. The doctor left for another half hour before coming back with his clipboard. "There's one thing I want you to know. If you keep using these chemicals interveiniously, you *will* end up here again. If you smoke or snort, you'll most likely be fine; not that I condone it at all. We've been seeing a lot of this crank lately. It must be going around, because lots more people are coming in here with related problems," said the doctor.

"More people are coming in than usual?" said Luke.

"Yep. Now, if you'll sign here, we can get you out of here. Happy four-twenty, by the way. Maybe you'll spend the rest of the holiday more appropriately." He gave a smile as he held the clipboard for Luke.

"I certainly will. Thank you." He signed the papers and handed them back to the doctor. Before long, they were walking out into the parking lot.

They got into the Oldsmobile. "You're really done with PV, right?" said Zuri.

"Of course I'm done. If that wasn't a sign, then I don't know what is."

"Good. I love you," she said.

"I love you too, sweetie."

Chapter 27: Tweaker Peeker

Sunday 4-27-2011

Luke drove the Oldsmobile into a dark neighborhood. Snoop Dog rattled from the 30 year old speakers. He reached the end of the cul-de-sac and parked in a driveway.

Dave greeted him, "Hey friend, I'm glad you could make it."

"Yeah. Who's house is this?" said Luke.

"It's Linda's friends. You know, Debora's friend Linda. But that's not where I've been stayin. *That's* where I've been stayin," he pointed at a trailer camper.

It was full of people. Wires and cords were strung over the walls. Drug paraphernalia littered the counter tops. "Isn't this nice?" said Dave, "I only paid 500 for it. It *will* be nice as soon as I can get it away from this flop house."

"For sure." Luke was thankful for the loud music. He didn't want to be overheard. "What did you need? I've got it pre-weighed I don't want all these people to know I got the shit."

"Well I don't have any money. It was Linda who wanted to see you. She should be back any minute. Would you like to do one quick? I've got a box of fresh ones."

"Sure man." Dave grabbed his kit. Luke filled the spoon with enough MDPV for everyone. Dave filled the drawback rig and squirted some solution into each persons syringe. People injected and the vibrations became tense. A few people left the trailer.

Linda came in, "Hi Luke. Long time no see."

"Hey Linda, how have you been?"

"I've been great. I hear you can find some of that good stuff," she said.

"Well sure. I've been hustlin small shit, but I'm pretty sure you'll want to talk to Debora if you want any good deals. She's got the connect."

"I don't think she is. I think you could help me out just fine."

Luke was getting paranoid. "You need a gram? Sure, I can help you, but it's going to be full price."

"How about an ounce. I know you can do it for me," she said.

"I might as well ask you to get *me* an ounce. We get our shit from the same people. I don't even know why we're having this conversation." Luke's anxiety grew stronger.

Another guy came in, "Does anyone have a half g?"

Luke set the bag on the counter, "Give the money to him," he pointed at Dave. "I'm gonna go smoke a cigarette."

"You should stay in here," said Linda.

"I'll be right back. My cigs are in the car." Something felt wrong.

Luke closed himself in the car and locked the doors. He grabbed a pistol from under the seat and cocked a bullet into the chamber. He shoved it into his waistband, lit a cigarette and stepped out of the car. There was the familiar feeling that something was watching him. He pretended to not suspect anything.

A twig snapped. The pistol was out with the safety off. The sound came from the trees between the neighbors property. Dave came out of the trailer, "Luke, Linda wants you to come back inside. You can smoke in here, you know?"

"Hold on a second," said Luke.

Dave came closer. "What are you doing? C'mon Luke, put that thing away."

"You're right. I'm just bein paranoid. Sorry." Luke leaned back into the car and pretended to put the pistol under the seat. Instead he just slid it back into his waist band.

They went back into the trailer. Luke tried to take a drag from his cigarette, but it was gone. He only took one drag off the entire cigarette.

Luke snuck a peek out the window every chance he could. He tried to be sneaky so his friends wouldn't think he was paranoid. Linda was talking while Luke pretended to listen. He wanted these people to think he wasn't paranoid. He wished he had more control over himself.

A nervous girl came into the trailer. She looked at Luke. She was unsure of herself. "What is it?" he asked.

"I think someones out there," she said.

"In the trees?" She nodded.

Luke went for the window. Linda told him not to be paranoid. Two other people agreed with her. "Yeah. Cut that shit out."

Luke went for the door. "Now hold on," said Linda, "let's do another hit real fast."

"No! Get the fuck out of my way." Luke pushed his way to the door and left the trailer.

Dave followed Luke to the car. "Wait a minute now. Will you tell me what's going on?" Luke stood by the car and stared into the trees. "Will you stop being so paranoid? Just take it easy and hang out for a while."

"You're right." Luke pulled the gun out of his pants and threw it under the seat. "There's nothing to worry about. It's all in my head. I'll just leave this thing in here." Luke closed the door and walked around to open the trunk. "Should I bring all of it in? Linda said she wanted lots. Should I show her the brick?"

The bait worked. Luke heard commotion in the trees. Dave was oblivious. Luke strapped an infrared lamp onto his head and pulled out the AK-47. He flipped the safety off and began to scope out the trees through his sights.

"Luke! Put that thing away. This is not the place for that," said Dave.

"Shut the fuck up and listen." Luke moved towards the trees. Dave followed.

"Luke, if the neighbors see—"

"I said shut the fuck up." Luke stepped further into the trees. He could feel his enemies nearby. It was life or death. He was ready to kill.

A person bolted. They saw the person's back as he sprinted off into the darkness. "Run you piece of shit! I should'a shot him," Luke looked at Dave, "See? Fuck this place. Why would you invite me here? It's a fuckin setup."

Luke got back in the car and took off. He kept the AK-47 in the passenger seat. He turned out of the cul-de-sac and drove toward the highway. A cop car drove past him. All the lights were off. *Fuck that sketchy place. Never again.*

Experience is a hard teacher because she gives the test first, the lesson afterwards.
-Vernon Law

Chapter 28: Observations

Friday 5-2-2011

It was a warm day. Luke was cruising 60mph down the highway on his scooter. He had all the accessories: a full-face helmet; a touchscreen cellphone attached to the dash with headphones and microphone plugged into it. He wore a black leather jacket. His 357 was holstered to his belt, and the AK-47 was slung over his back. Electronic music was playing into his headphones.

I can't stop-stop-stop-stop... The modulated baseline was mind rattling.

The music stopped and a voice asked him if he would like to receive a call from... James. "Yes," he replied. The call was connected, "Hello?"

"Hey bro, are you busy?" said James.

"I'm heading to Kalispell, but I think I'm gonna stop and do some shooting before I get there," said Luke.

"Oh, right on. You wanna give me a call when you make it into town? I got some money for you."

"Sure, I'll give you a call," Luke ended the call and the music resumed.

Luke noticed a black SUV was gaining on him. He couldn't go faster; the engine was air-cooled and operated best at night. The SUV decelerated to keep distance between Luke. He knew he looked like a terrorist and hoped they weren't after him. Everything was legal except for the used syringes. He wasn't breaking any laws. The guns weren't concealed, and the scooter was licensed and registered. None of this was assuring to Luke. These could be Monkey Police, and everyone knew that they didn't abide by normal law-enforcement protocol. Luke was still a part of the experiment and therefore, not exempt from being fucked with.

Luke wasn't afraid of the Monkey Police, or any police; he was afraid of their ability to take away MDPV. His primal instinct was to protect his supply. The thought of losing MDPV was as terrifying as losing his life. MDPV had replaced his basic needs. His brainstem sent signals to his frontal cortex, telling him that MDPV was necessary for his survival.

Luke slowed down and drove into a gravel parking lot. The SUV kept going, but made a suspicious turn up ahead. Luke didn't believe in coincidences, so he waited in the parking lot. Cars drove by. Every face seemed to stare right at him.

Luke decided everything was fine after fifteen minutes. He turned back onto the highway. His headphones blasted vicious trap music by Bassnectar.

He made it a few hundred feet before another SUV was behind him. He made a sharp turn onto a residential country road. The SUV turned after him. There was going to be a confrontation, and Luke was prepared for the worst.

There were many turns, but he kept his speed. He made a turn down another street. It was a dead end. He stopped in the street and took aim with the assault rifle. He was prepared to open fire as soon as the SUV turned down the street.

~~~

Zuri was on her way home from Kalispell. She was driving into C-Falls when she started to suspect she was being followed. A purple minivan kept a good distance behind her the entire time. They never got close enough for her to see their faces.

Zuri pulled into a gas station. The minivan drove past. She saw the van turn a few blocks ahead. *Hmm, that was strange. I hope I'm not getting paranoid. Maybe Luke's home.* She opened her phone and called Luke. There was no answer. The call went straight to voicemail. She tried his other cellphone. Zuri thought it was stupid that she had to address him as 'Frank' on this number. He would hang up on her if she used his real name. It went straight to voicemail. That meant the batteries were out and he was going through a paranoid episode.

She turned back onto the road, deciding the minivan was just a coincidence. She was unwilling to succumb to paranoia. After a few blocks, the minivan was behind her again.

~~~

The SUV didn't come down Luke's street. Luke didn't have to open fire. It made no sense to Luke, *Maybe they didn't see me turn down this road.* He stood there in the road for a few more minutes, waiting for them to come chasing after him.

His readiness to kill began to frighten him. *What if an innocent civilian came down this road? What if they were driving a black SUV? I need to get the hell out of here, I'm probably being watched.* He hopped on his scooter and sped down the country road.

He wasn't familiar with these roads. All the frantic attempts to escape made him disoriented. He was worried about more than just Monkey Police now. Any good samaritan was a potential enemy. He'd drawn too much attention, especially after the desperate stunt with the AK-47.

Driving around with the assault rifle was bad enough; looking ready for violence and bloodshed made him even more conspicuous. This kind of activity wasn't normal even for a hick town. He pictured nervous civilians reporting to the police.

Luke stopped at a stop sign. A vehicle was coming from his right. It was a black Suburban. The SUV drove past. The people inside were hidden by tinted windows. He waited in terror for the vehicle to disappear into the distance.

It didn't. The SUV made a U-turn. Luke panicked and made his own U-turn, heading down the road he had come from. He found an opportunity to drive off the road into a field of tall grass. It wasn't tall enough to hide the scooter, so he laid it on its side and crouched his way through the field.

He was in combat mode; two fully loaded 30 round clips and a revolver. A door slammed. In his mind they were approaching, surrounding the field. He proved himself to be too dangerous, so it was time to shut him down. The Monkey Police had finally seen enough. He was toast. Was it possible to kill the Monkey Police? Another door slammed. There were voices. They were talking about him. He army crawled to the edge of the field so he could see the road.

A vehicle was approaching. It was the black SUV, driving slowly along the field. They were surely looking for him. Did they know how desperate he was? Did they not understand that he was ready to kill?

Luke was confident in his hiding spot. He could barely see them through the grass. There was no way they would see him; not unless they sicked the dogs on him. Luke watched the SUV through crosshairs with his finger on the trigger.

~~~

Zuri still wasn't going to panic. It was only a purple minivan; probably harmless, but she still had a bad feeling. *Probably just need some sleep, that's all.*

She drove through a yellow light. The minivan was stopped at the light, allowing her to get away. It was only a few more minutes until she got to the house. She hoped Luke would be there, but he wasn't. It was sure to be another
~~~

lonely day at the house. She went inside, planning to smoke some weed and maybe read a book.

~~~

"You sure she's here alone?" said Wade.

"Of course I'm sure," said Mandy, "just stay right here. I'll only be a few minutes. If she doesn't give me the drugs, I'm taking that bitch hostage." She grabbed a baseball bat and got out of the minivan.

The back door was locked, so she went for the front. She walked into the bedroom. No one was there. It seemed odd that the closet was locked. She rifled though the bedroom before deciding to check the basement.

Someone came through the front door, "Hey! Who the fuck are you?"

Mandy made it through the bathroom and locked the door. Dave grabbed a kitchen knife and pounded on the door, "You'd better get the fuck out of here! The cops are on their way!" he lied.

Dave managed to kick the door in. When he made it through the bathroom, he saw the woman running for the alley. She jumped into the minivan as it peeled out through the dirt alleyway. He tried to get a good look at the criminals before they got away.

"Hey Zuri, are you here?" he yelled.

Zuri appeared at the bottom of the stairs, "Yeah, what the hell is going on?"

"Some maniac woman was up here with a baseball bat."

"What are you talking about? Where is she now?"

"She just took off in a minivan. A purple one," he said.

~~~

Luke was on the highway again. Somehow he managed to survive the terrifying experience. He couldn't tell whether he escaped, or if they just decided to let him go. *Maybe they don't want the experiment to end. Maybe they are gonna let it go until I end it myself. Maybe that's the point, to see what kind of demise MDPV can bring to a perfectly normal American kid.*

He continued to think as he sped down the highway. No more Dubstep; his brain was having enough problems as it was. The AK-47 was making him uncomfortable. It drew negative attention like a beacon. He wondered how he could have ever thought it to be reasonable.

It was time for a small dose of energy. A *small* one. He didn't need to dive any further into psychosis with an assault rifle strapped to his back. There were some storage units up ahead. He turned into the parking lot and cruised around behind it. There were some houses that could possibly see him, but it didn't matter; he wouldn't be long.

~~~

Luke had made it to Blue's tent in West Valley. Four hours went by without trouble. His clients were getting impatient, so he headed back towards Kalispell. He was on Highway 2, committed to meeting his friend James on a historical bike trail. James was supposed to be waiting on the trail under a train truss. It was close to the point where the trail merged into Kalispell. There were apartments all around it, but it couldn't be seen from the street.

Luke turned onto a country road where he could get onto the trail. He blazed the trail for a few miles until he got to the checkpoint. James would be arriving by bicycle, so Luke listened closely over the sound of the creek. He was in complete darkness and had his weapons ready. The bag of MDPV was weighed and ready for a quick transaction.

Ten minutes went by. Luke began to get nervous. A bike was approaching. It was only hobo Joe. Luke wasn't in the mood to be friendly, and the hobo didn't recognize him anyway. Hobo Joe rode off into the darkness.

Luke felt the fear; something terrible was going to happen. He pushed the scooter a little ways off the trail, and covered it with some brush. Once it was hidden he snuck off to find a safer vantage point.

He climbed up onto the railroad tracks and creeped over to some railroad cars. There was a ladder, so he slung the rifle over his shoulder and climbed up. He laid down on top and waited.

James had always been punctual, which made Luke even more worried about his delay. If James was to still come, Luke would see him. If not, he would see any other possible danger that decided to approach. He didn't want to be there any longer, but he had to wait to make sure it was safe. Waiting was his specialty, especially when his life depended on it.

He started to hear noises. There was whispering and rustling of leaves. The more he focused, the worse it became. There was strange activity in an apartment window; they were setting up the surveillance equipment. He aimed his weapon at the window. The person made eye contact. It took all his effort to keep from pulling the trigger.

It was a woman, going about her business. He realized his mistake. Did she really make eye contact? Did she know an AK-47 was pointing at her head? Hopefully not.

There was more noise coming from the field in the opposite direction. The grass was rustling; people were army crawling towards him. He opened the hatch on top of the train and shined an infrared LED light into it. It was empty. Was it too late to hide? Yes. If they were army crawling, they surely knew he was
~~~

on top of the train.

He was tired of it. They had finally brought him to the breaking point. This is where he would end it. He strapped the infrared light onto his head and aimed into the field. He fired a three round burst at one of the figures, then another.

There was no return fire. He realized they were fake and decided to run. Lights turned on in the apartments as he ran to his scooter. He drove down the trail and disappeared into the night. Luke was in for a terrible night of psychosis. It was a recipe for disaster.

Just because you're paranoid doesn't mean they're not out to get you.
-Hunter S. Thompson

Chapter 29: Broken Paranoid

Sunday 5-4-2011

Luke survived the night, but not undamaged. His brain was broken. He could no longer become paranoid. The nerve endings responsible for that function were fried.

Luke was at home. He had lots of friends over and was managing to have a good time. The fear no longer made sense to him. *Fuck the Monkey Police. If they make a move, it's going to be a bloodbath.* Being surrounded by people used to make him nervous, but now it was comforting. Even if *they* chose bloodshed, did they want *that* much of it. There were innocent bystanders.

Luke had a good visit with his friends Dan and Erica. Not much had changed with them except for some new chemicals. Dan had also been working on his new line of incense. It was called BrainSplat. He had a machine that would package and label his product. Luke would buy some, but Dan would mostly sell it on the internet. They perfected the combination of synthetic cannabinoids to create a psychedelic imitation of marijuana.

Making the incense was a complicated procedure. Dan would dissolve the chemicals in alcohol and spray it on mullen, mugwart, wild lettuce, and other herbs. He also had an assortment of delicious candy flavorings that he would spray onto the product. Of course there was the disclaimer: Not For Human Consumption.

There was plenty more than just incense. Dan had the latest research chemicals automatically sent to his house every week. Luke was proud to be the lab monkey. He tried most of these chemicals intravenously for the first time. Most of these chemicals were so new that there was little information about them.

Luke would start with the smallest of doses first; an obvious safety precaution. Then he would try increasingly larger doses until he reached the desired effect. Dan kept all of his reports documented. They were conducting *research*, after all.

Luke's house was a filthy mess. All of his friends were comfortable, enjoying the abundance of chemicals. The newest ones were MXE, 5-MeO-DALT, 4-FMA, 4-FA, 2C-I, 2C-E, PMEA, and dimethocain. Dan had also began to investigate a new website called Silk Road . A new digital currency allowed him to buy *anything* without it being traced back to him.

"What the fuck is this shit?" Luke found a rig hidden underneath the kitchen sink. He went to the basement to confront the issue. "Someone stashed a fuckin rig under the kitchen sink."

His friends watched as he accused them. "I didn't do it," said Fat Jared.

"Well, whoever it was, there's a sharps container right here."

Luke reached behind the stairs and showed them a two liter bottle full of used syringes.

"Umm, Luke?" said Byron. He was a new acquaintance to Luke. "I don't mean to be a bum or anything... I don't want to overstep my welcome, but could I convince you to supply us some more MDPV... and some of that MXE if possible?"

Byron was a shady character. He was missing his two front teeth and had a meth lab tattooed on his arm. "Would you like some jewelry? Here, take your pick," he opened his backpack and showed Luke.

"What the hell? Why do you have a fake arm in there? And what's with the fanny pack?" said Luke.

"That's the old gypsy arm. And never mind the fanny pack," said Byron.

"Gypsy arm?"

"Yeah, it goes in your sleeve so that your actual arm is hidden under your coat. You can reach out and snag things when it looks like both hands are in your pockets," said Byron.

"That's the stupidest thing I've ever heard. You're a genius! I'll go get some more chemicals," said Luke. He left the basement and re-stocked the community supply of chemicals for his friends. He encouraged his friends to do more than just MDPV. Straight MDPV could create nasty vibes. The scene was much more friendly with some entactogens, empathogens, hallucinogens, and dissociatives. It was harder for people to become irritable and selfish when they couldn't walk or see straight. Though the occasional death trip would put everyone on edge.

Luke walked into the bedroom. Zuri was using her laptop all by herself. "Luke, would you please come here?" She set the computer aside and held out her arms.

"Hold on a minute please," Luke proceeded to the closet, "I have to give these people some more drugs. Then I need to make a run to Kalispell."

"I just want you here for one minute, please." She held her arms open stubbornly.

"Aw Jesus, fine." He went to the bed and held her.

"Please don't go anywhere. It will take you forever and I don't want to be stuck here with your friends all night. It's my turn to have some Luke time," she said.

"And you will. I promise I won't be long, and I'll tell everyone to stay in the basement so they won't bother you."

"How can they not bother me? They're so loud and someone's been peeing all over the toilet."

"I'll make them clean it when I get back. I gotta go take care of this." Luke went to the closet and finished grabbing chemicals.

He went back to the basement with the assortment that included GBL, MDPV, 4-MEC, MXE, and BrainSplat incense. "Alright you guys, I have to go meet someone. I'll be back soon. Nobody do anything retarded."

"Right on," said Kimmy, "Thanks Luke."

Luke went back to the bedroom. He put on his black leather jacket and grabbed the AK-47. "You're not taking that thing," said Zuri.

"Of course I am. It's my right as an American citizen."

"No! It's gonna make you go crazy. Then you won't come home. You almost killed the mailman last time you took off with that thing!"

"I'm not breaking any laws. I'm just an ordinary citizen who chooses to stretch his civil rights to their limits. It's good for our country. Most people would think it's patriotic," he said.

"Most people are scared to death when they see that thing! I'm telling you, it's a bad idea," she said.

"Well, I disagree. Got to go now. I love you," he gave her a kiss on the way out.

"I love you too," she said in defeat.

~~~

Luke prepared for the drive. It was dark out. He had his headphones and microphone plugged into his cellphone that was attached to the dash with velcro. He climbed onto the scooter with the AK-47 slung over his back. South African rap music was playing. He felt like he belonged in Africa. The engine worked well in the cool night air. Driving was good. There was no paranoia, instead he had a dangerous feeling of invincibility.

He arrived at Walmart after a 30 minute drive. James was waiting in the parking lot next to his bicycle. Luke parked next to James who was shocked at his appearance, "Holy shit, dude." It was almost 3:00am; there was no hiding that this was a drug transaction. The assault rifle made it look even worse.

"What's up, man? How much did you need?" Luke stepped off the scooter and opened the trunk.

"Are you sure this is okay?" said James.

"This is absolutely okay. We're not breaking a single law, I guarantee you that. Unless you've brought something illegal with you, which I would hope you haven't because I've instructed you specifically not to."

"No man, I don't got nothin bad," said James. "Good. How much do you want?" said Luke.

"Ten grams of the fifty percent stuff," said James.

Luke grabbed the supplies out of the trunk. He weighed the MDPV on the seat of his scooter. James looked around nervously. He was only 17, but he was a hustler, and knew how to steal and sell drugs. Before MDPV, James was a meth user. Now that he'd discovered MDPV, he was a hopeless junkie, willing to go any length to ensure his supply. He would take shot after shot, pushing his body to the brink of death.

"Have you been watching the UFO's lately?" Luke said as he measured out the chemicals.

"No... I haven't. There's been UFO's?" said James.

"Yeah man. They were all over last night, and I expect them to start showing again here shortly. The sun only reflects off them at a certain time of night. You can't see them when they're in the shadow of the earth."

"What do they look like?"

"At a glance they just look like stars. But if you watch for a while, you'll see the crazy things they do. They're way up there. You'll see them coming together and flying in formation. You might even see the mothership. Other objects fly in
~~~

and out of the mothership."

"That's fuckin crazy," James was looking at the sky.

Luke put the scale away and handed the bag to James, "This is not for human consumption. Research purposes only."

"Of course it is," James handed the money over.

Luke took the money and looked up into the sky. "Yep, I think I can see it happening already. See those three moving slowly? They're moving slower than satellites."

"I think I see," said James.

"I'm pretty sure this kind of activity happens all the time, only most people don't pay any attention. Especially at the proper time of night. It only happens around three and four in the morning," said Luke.

"Crazy. I think I'm gonna go. I have a long bike ride."

"Alright dude, later." Luke pulled his visor down and hopped onto the scooter. He turned on the music and drove off. People were watching. They were terrified just as Zuri said, but Luke didn't care.

~~~

Luke made it home safely. He walked through the front door, still wearing the helmet and rifle. He found Jared and Nick in the kitchen. "I thought I told you assholes to stay in the basement. And why the fuck are your shoes on in my house?" said Luke.

Nick was notorious for wearing his shoes in the house. "They're absolutely clean. I bought them two days ago. They're cleaner than your floor."

"I don't give a shit. You take them off now, or I take them off for you," Luke threatened.

"Jesus, Luke. You look completely psychotic. Go look at yourself in the mirror," said Nick.

"I don't give a shit! Take off your shoes and get in the basement!"

Nick obeyed. Luke was getting irritated. He went to the bedroom to remove his gear and take a shot. Zuri didn't try to stop him. If he wasn't going to stop after the stroke, he wasn't going to stop now.

Luke was dehydrated, so he forced down a glass of water and two Ensures. He was frightened after taking the shot. His kidneys hurt. His chest was tight. He could see his heart beating through his shirt. His brain was tingling. He worried about his circulation. He thought of the stroke.

Zuri was playing tetris on the bed. Luke went to sit next to her. He hugged her and buried his face against her neck, "I love you," he said, just in case he was going to die.
~~~

"I love you too. What's wrong?" she said.

"Can you do that thing you do for me?" He took his shirt off and laid down with his arms straight out. "I'm not circulating."

She knew the routine. He believed the blood was restricted underneath his armpits. She started at a vein on his left wrist, and forced the blood all the way up to his armpit with her hand. She would do a similar motion with his right arm at the same time. Luke believed this was the way the blood flowed; into the heart from the left arm, and out of the heart through the right arm. He believed this could keep him from dying.

Ten minutes later he was fine. "I'm gonna go downstairs and see what everyone's doing," he said.

"Hurry back please. I want some time with you. And I think that crazy lady has been driving around the neighborhood. I saw a purple van drive by when you were gone," she said.

"You're absolutely safe. If she comes after you, you have every right to shoot her in the face." Luke had given her the Walther PPK and showed her how to use it. He even made her shoot it a few times for practice.

Luke went back to the closet. He grabbed a supply of chemicals and herbal remedies to share with his friends. When he got to the basement he laid everything out on the fold-out picnic table. "Alright everyone, it's time for DMSO and goldenseal." He dipped the wet Q-tip onto some powdered goldenseal root.

"I'm not doing it," said Nick.

"Yes, you are. It's mandatory. If you don't, you'll have track marks for the rest of your life," said Luke.

"Why don't you just worry about your own track marks."

"Give me your arm," said Luke.

"No, it burns. And it makes my skin yellow for days," said Nick.

"You stick needles in your arm. How can you complain that it burns? Give me your arm, or else you're getting pinned down," said Luke.

Nick held his arm out, "For a drug dealer, you're opressively health conscious."

"It's my way of restoring the Karmic balance. I give drugs, but I also teach you people how to use herbs as medicine." He applied the solution to Nick's arm. "Now everyone needs to take a capsule of Hawthorn and grapeseed. It will strengthen your arteries and help with circulation." Everyone was forced to take an assortment of capsules along with the DMSO/goldenseal application.

It was time to smoke BrainSplat. Luke was trying to promote Dan's product, but MDPV addicts didn't seem to care much for anything but MDPV. Even pot became unimportant.

The BrainSplat made everyone forget how to speak. Still, Luke managed to prepare a large solution of 4-MEC and inject everyone with it. Twenty minutes went by in a blurry, silky rush. Next was 5-MeO-DALT. Luke threw some in a pipe and passed it around. Everything got colorful and began to vibrate. Electronic music blasted and the cycle continued. There was no end in sight.

~~~

Luke made it out of the basement after a few hours. Zuri was on her computer when Luke came into the bedroom. Since she started using MDPV, she couldn't read like she'd been able to on meth. She gave up and started using PV when Luke relapsed after getting out of the hospital.

"That weird guy walked in here earlier with his hands in his pants," she said.

"Which weird guy?"

"The one with the missing teeth and tattoos. He asked me if I knew a place where he could jack off. I told him to get out. I thought I was gonna have to shoot him."

"Oh yeah... that dude's really confused right now. He took the 2C-E and smoked way too much BrainSplat. I think MDPV has that effect on him as well." Luke went on to the closet and came out with a syringe and a bottle of GBL. He filled up the syringe, "Open your mouth."

"No, that stuff is disgusting," she said.

"Open it, I'm date raping you," he said.

"I don't need to be high to have sex with you. When is the last time we've made love without being high?" she said.

"It doesn't matter. We're doing it like this." He climbed on top of her and pointed the syringe at her face. She opened her mouth. He squirted it.

"Aww, disgusting!" She grabbed some water and chased it down. He took the same dose even though he hadn't come down from the last one.

Luke grabbed two more syringes full of 4-MEC. "Quick, we need to inject these before that shit kicks in." He gave her the shot, then did his own. He tore her clothes off in a blind rush of blurry silkiness. They both got naked and tried to have sex.
~~~

Every negative event contains within it the seed
of an equal or greater benefit.
-Napoleon Hill

Chapter 30: Hypertension

Saturday 5-10-2011

Luke came home Saturday evening with an old friend. Zuri was in the bedroom. "Hey girly, this is my friend Sam. Sam, this is Zuri." They both said hi. "We're going down to the basement. You should load a bowl and bring it down."

"Okay," she said. Luke grabbed his plastic organizer full of chemicals. He grabbed the one full of herbs as well, then went downstairs with Sam.

Zuri came down a few minutes later. Australian rap music was playing. She handed the pipe to Luke, who was explaining his assortment of designer drugs. "Thank you sweetie," he took a hit from the pipe and handed it back. He held her from behind and kissed her on the neck. She smoked, then handed it to Sam. Sam wasn't interested, but smoked out of good manners. He was excited about the research chemicals. Until now, he'd been getting MDPV through a chain of middlemen.

"Damnit Sam, why did we ever stop kickin it? We had the craziest of times. Remember that little hippie commune up in the North Fork? You had that bag of pills; hundreds of ecstasy pills, and those hippies wanted no part of it. They had some good acid. That shit was epic," said Luke.

"Yeah bro, that was good times."

"Those hippies were the *real* freakin deal. I wish we could find them. I can't believe we *did* find them."

"Smoke that," said Zuri. She had to remind him to smoke.

They each took one more hit before Luke got distracted with his chemicals. He loved talking about his chemicals. "Why don't I make up a solution of methylone? You want to try it? It's fun, let's do it."

"I'm totally down for that," said Sam.

Luke was concentrating on his work. There was a loud smack on the basement window. Zuri screamed. "Jesus!" said Luke, "It's only Blue. Will you go let him in?"

Zuri let him in and came back down. "I'm sorry for being so jumpy. There's been some weird things happening around here. That same minivan keeps driving by," she said.

"The purple one?" Luke asked.

"Yeah."

"See, I'm scared of black Silverados, and she's scared of purple minivans."

"Yeah, but those Silverados never actually tried to abduct you," she said.

"That's because they only want to observe. How can you think she wanted to get you? She was probably just trying to steal stuff," he said.

"She followed me home. She knew I was the only one here," she said.

"Kay, fine. What's up, Blue?" said Luke.

"Not shit. Just need twenty. What are you makin there?"

"This is methylone."

"Well, let's make some of the good shit," said Blue.

Luke gave him some MDPV, "Make some for me too." He weighed out the MDPV while Blue mixed up another solution.

$700 for Luke; 20 grams of MDPV for Blue. A syringe of PV for each of them. They each took their shot. "I'm outta here," said Blue, "Thanks cousin."

"Later dude." Luke showed Sam a vial with green liquid in it, "This is for freakouts. Like, if someone gets too paranoid or has a panic attack. It's Xanex."

"Way to be prepared. I've seen some people freak the fuck out on the shit. Sometimes it makes you feel like you're having an actual heart attack," said Sam.

"Yeah, that's why I started goin hard on the herbal meds. We've got the cure for all our problems right here," Luke went on to explain the herbal remedies, and insisted they take some capsules.

~~~
~~~

Luke and Sam pulled up to a trashy house in Kalispell. "Remember the plan," said Luke, "You're the dude who found some shit from an unreliable source. I'm tryin to find some shit, but we can't get a hold of your guy. So I'll see if I can buy some. Someone in here will be able to sell me some, right?"

"Yeah, for sure, but it will be shitty. I'm tellin you, these people are straight junkies for the shit," said Sam.

"Cool, let's do it." They hopped out and went to the house. Luke had been there a few times in his high school days when he was in desperate need of overpriced, stomped on crystal. He had never been there since the MDPV hit.

They made it inside. It was even filthier and smelt worse than it had before. The carpets were encrusted with dirt. There were holes in the walls and everything was broken. Some people called this place home. They were the slippies; the cesspool of society.

"Hey Sam. Hi Luke, long time no see," said a young girl named Hannah. She was cute and innocent in a sad way.

Luke and Sam worked there way through the house. There were people in every room; some huffing dust-off, some eating cold medicine. "Who wants to get high?" said Sam. "I've got some shit if anyone wants to go in."

"And I'm tryin to throw in also if anyone's got some to get rid of," said Luke.

"Hell yeah," said a girl that Luke didn't recognize. They went to a crowded room. These people were smokers; the worst kind of drug addicts. Luke bought a quarter gram for thirty dollars. He threw it on a piece of foil, took a hit, and passed it to Sam. It was disgusting. Luke hated the taste of MDPV. It tasted like burning butt fungus to him.

Another foily was passed to Luke. It left an ashy residue behind as it burnt; not normal for PV. PV usually left an amber colored resin behind. Luke knew it was a poor attempt to cut the PV with baking soda.

Everyone got high, but they craved more. "We should smoke some of that shit you found," Luke told Sam.

"We totally should." It was all part of the plan. Sam threw the MDPV onto a piece of foil. The small amount of powder made it all the way around. He threw some more on, and sent it around again.

Luke was disgusted by the taste in his mouth, but the smokers were pleased. The vibe started to change. People were getting paranoid. One person got up to close the blinds. A couple people left. Hannah had gotten the butt end, and was still trying to smoke whatever was on the foil. Sam gave her some more.

The bigger girl seemed like she was the one who could find shit. Luke asked her how much he could get a gram for.

"I could probably find you one for a hundred," she whispered. She was paranoid, and didn't feel comfortable talking about it. It was a hideous price. Luke wondered if she was the one who put the baking soda in it. He wondered how many hands the stuff had gone through to get to her. Luke found it comical that this girl was too paranoid to sell anything. Things were conspiring against her. Luke knew the feeling, there was no hope.

"We should probably smoke some weed," Luke suggested. He wanted to ease the tension. These people could probably use some weed in their lives. It would also cover up that terrible taste.

~~~

It was 2am; six hours since the mission with Sam. Luke was driving with Zuri after doing some errands in Kalispell. Luke had to go to Walmart, and Zuri had a friend who needed crystal.

Luke didn't know anyone who did meth anymore. Meth was obsolete to anyone who had been exposed to MDPV. Zuri knew some sheltered people who still ran around obsessing over crystal, so that was her department.

Luke and Zuri had fun at Walmart with the blood pressure machine. Zuri's was the highest by far. It was in the pre hypertension stage. Luke used this as leverage to try and get her to take his herbs. He prescribed her a few capsules, but she refused. She would not cooperate with his natural medicine.

Luke found a safe place to get high. They were in a quiet neighborhood right off Highway 2. Zuri made her own solution. Luke made his doses much smaller than hers. His heart couldn't handle the big ones anymore. It was always tempting to do a big one, but after the repeated near-death and paranoid experiences, he learned to restrain himself. Not Zuri though, she could still do shots that would kill Luke two times over.

Luke injected. He scoped around the vehicle to make sure no one was sneaking up on them. "Hurry up with that shit already," he told her. The neighborhood looked dangerous.

"Kay, hold on," she fumbled around, trying to get her vein to pop out.

"Here, let me do it," he took the syringe. The liquid was yellow; way too strong for Luke's taste. But this is how she'd been doing it, so he gave it to her. Her breathing changed. She was in pain. Luke cringed at the thought of taking a syrupy shot like that. *Jesus, why did I just give that to her? I should have squirted some out or something. Is she trying to kill herself?*

Zuri started breathing quick shallow breaths. She went pale. Her hands were cold. "Do we have that paper bag?" she asked.

"Maybe," Luke climbed around the truck to look for it. "Hurry please," she
~~~

was beginning to panic.

"I can't find it!" He was panicking too. The shot was too big. Her death would be his fault.

Zuri was hyperventilating. She needed the brown paper bag, but it was nowhere to be found. Luke climbed up to the front seat to try and comfort her. "You need to calm down," he said.

"I can't!" she gasped, "Something's wrong."

"Yes you can! Please sweetie, just breathe," he pleaded.

"Luke, help. Something's wrong," she could barely speak through her shaking and hyperventilating.

"No, no, no. Zuri please, it's gonna be okay," the symptoms were getting worse.

"Luke, I'm dying."

"No you're not! You're going to live a long happy life. We're gonna stop doing drugs and get married. You'll have lots of kids and live a long beautiful life." Luke was crying the first tears since he began using MDPV.

Zuri couldn't respond. Luke drove off as fast as he could. He said a prayer, promising to never do drugs again if she survives. He drove through town as fast as the truck would take him. His hazards were on as he swerved through traffic, disregarding all traffic laws. If she died, he could never live with himself.

~~~

Luke pulled up to the ambulance drop-off. Zuri was getting worse. Luke jumped out to help her get inside. Nurses and doctors were there quickly. They put her in a wheel chair and took her in. Luke had to move the truck to a proper parking spot.

It took Luke twenty minutes to find Zuri. She was fine. "What happened to you?" he said.

"They said I went into hypertensive shock."

The doctor walked in; the same doctor that dealt with Luke when he had his stroke. "Hello again," he said.

"Hi," said Luke, feeling ashamed.

"You're lucky you got her here in time. She wouldn't have made it five more minutes."

"How did you save her?" said Luke.

"Beta-blockers. It eases the hearts pumping action and widens the blood vessels by blocking the effects of adrenaline."

"You didn't use benzodiazapines?" said Luke.

"Not in this case. If this happens again I recommend having her breathe into
~~~

a paper bag. Hyperventilating depletes the blood of carbon dioxide."

The doctor left the room. Luke held Zuri's hand as she laid on the hospital bed. An IV was hooked into her arm. Luke was done with MDPV. He was so thankful to have her alive. "I love you," he said.

"I love you too."

"I'm sorry… I'm sorry for getting us into all this. I'm done. Forever. I couldn't stand losing you," he said.

"Now you know how I've been feeling all along. That's why I've been trying to get you to stop since the beginning. The thought of losing you is unbearable. It kills me every time I see the drugs hurting you," she said.

"I know. I'm done. We're absolutely done with it." Luke's eyes started to water again. He couldn't hold it back. The past years worth of pain was finally coming out. He couldn't cover it up any longer.

"I can't believe you're finally crying," she said with sympathy. "I've been trying to get you to cry for so long now."

"You're an ass," he said.

"It's healthy to cry. You've been needing it," she pulled him in for a kiss.

... the way to perfection
is through a series of disgusts.
-Walter Pater

Chapter 31: Mountain Tigers

Sunday 5-25-2011

It was fifteen days since the hospital visit. Paranoia was creeping back into Luke's psyche. He had relapsed immediately after leaving the hospital. The urge was too strong.

Luke was riding his scooter down the highway. It was dark out. He was drafting behind his friends Jack and Alison who were driving an old Jetta. The 150cc scooter could get close to seventy when he kept the right distance from the car.

They were on a mission; a mission to escape the paranoia. Jack had it and so did his girlfriend. Luke suggested that escaping to the wilderness was the best way to escape the paranoia. No cops out there; no prying eyes; nothing to worry about.

The Kila cliffs would be their safe haven. Without external factors to cause paranoia, they would have a good time. That was the theory. Any paranoia they did experience would be easier to overcome. They could even laugh at it.

The turnoff was coming up. Luke flashed his lights so Jack would let him pass. There were a few more bends in the road before Luke had to start slowing down. He turned onto the gravel road, then drove through the tall grass onto the logging road.

He had to drive slow and careful. The road was treacherous. He stopped at the spot he knew Jack would have to stop. There was no hope past this point without four wheel drive. The darkness was intimidating. All he had was a pistol; Jack had the big stash of weapons. Luke left the scooter running.

Jack arrived a few minutes later. Luke hopped in the Jetta. He was ready to get high before their expedition, and so were Jack and Alison. They each had their own. Luke pulled out his junkie kit while his friends snorted the powder. The problem with snorting was that it was easy to do too much. Jack and Alison had become just as psychotic as Luke in a short time.

Luke took his shot and was instantly terrified. He put his supplies away with shaky hands. "Here you go guys. You'll need these," he handed his friends each a pistol.

"I want two. Can I have two?" said Jack.

"Why do we need these?" said Alison.

"In case we come across some aggressive animals. It's better to be prepared," said Luke as he grabbed another pistol out of the backpack. Alison didn't argue. The prospect of an animal attack brought new fear.

"It's kind of scary out there," said Jack as he stared into the blackness.

"Yeah, you should turn your lights on for a minute," said Luke, feeling frightened as well. The headlights illuminated the forest. Luke saw something scurry off into the darkness. "There could be mountain tigers out there. Possibly bears as well. They can sense our fear. We'll have to be careful."

"I don't think I want to go out there at all," said Alison.

"I could shoot off a few rounds. That would scare them off for miles," said Luke.

"No way," said Jack, "That would draw too much attention. There's gotta be people that live around here."

"Okay then, if you see any animals, just start shooting. But we probably won't see anything. The animals are actually supposed to be more scared of us. Just don't be scared. They can smell it," said Luke.

No one felt any better. "Let's just go, it's getting late. As soon as we start a fire we'll be safe."

"Who's carrying the backpack?" said Jack.

"Me. Now let's go." No one moved. "On the count of three we get out of the car. One. Two. Three!" Luke cracked his door. No one else budged. "C'mon guys. It's not that scary out there. We used to spend lots of time out here. No one just gets attacked." He tried to convince himself. "Fine," said Luke, "I'll go first." He put the backpack on and wrapped a sweater around his neck. *Mountain tigers always go for the jugular.* He strapped his infrared light to his head and grabbed the AK-47. He opened the door, *locked and loaded, safety off.*

Luke went to the scooter and started it up. There was no way he was leaving it behind. Jack and Alison got out of the car. "You know where to go. I'll meet you at the top."

"You're taking that thing up there?" said Jack.

"Yeah. I have to. All my drugs are in here. My lifes work is in here. I'll see you at the top." Luke ran beside the scooter while giving it gas. The AK was slung over his back. He pushed the scooter while the back tire peeled out up the hill. The backpack was heavy. Luke ran along side the scooter the whole way up. Too top heavy for the scooter; especially at low speed. Luke made it to the top in five minutes. He left the scooter running.

Jack and Alison made it up soon after. They built the fire up against a fallen tree. Luke managed to start some conversation. He felt bad for his friend Jack. Jack was hopelessly addicted to MDPV and was having problems with his family because of it.

Luke had known Jack since he first moved to Montana in junior high. Jack had never been into meth, but went straight to PV. His cheekbones and eyeballs protruded, which was common among PV users. His parents knew he had problems and were trying to keep his two year old son away from him because of it. MDPV turned Jack and Alison into unfit parents. They had alcohol problems before, but this was much worse. They spent every penny on the stuff. Luke tried his best to help them make money with it. There was plenty of room for profit.

Luke was caught staring fearfully into the darkness. "Who is it?" said Jack, "Is it the Monkey Police?" He made a parody to the song *Dream Police.*

The Monkey Police,

Are out to get you…

Luke laughed, "It's pretty stupid, huh? Totally paranoid for no fuckin reason."

"That's why we came out here, right?" said Alison, "So we should probably just not be paranoid. We told ourselves there would be nothing to worry about."

"Yes," said Luke, "that's exactly the kind of reasoning we need right now."

"I agree," said Jack, "We must use logic and reason if we are to overcome our fearful instincts."

An hour went by. Luke talked about the Oregon Country Fair. It was less than two months away. He always wanted everyone to come, but only one or two people would make it. "I would really like you both to come with me to the hippie fest. I'll cover everything. There's gonna be spiritual healing. We have problems. We need the healing. I feel like I owe it to you. Please let me take you there. There's no good excuse not to go."

"Well," said Jack, "it sounds great. I appreciate your offer, but it would really be tough."

"Yeah," Alison agreed, "We have the baby, you know."

"And I don't think I could get the time off work. Even if I could, I need the money," said Jack.

"Man, I told you that money's not a problem. If you can't go to the fair, then I guess I'll just have to bring the fair back with me. We need some good old fashioned LSD. That, and some DMT. I believe we can heal ourselves that way. It's our only hope. Either that, or we need a shaman. A spiritual healer. Have you taken a look at your soul lately? I don't know about you, but mine's fucked!"

"Speaking of all that, I could go for a small bump right now," said Jack.

"Me too," said Alison, "Did you bring the stuff?"

"No, fuck. I thought you did," he said. There were a few moments of angry silence.

"Hey, did you guys bring any water?" said Luke.

"There's some in the car," said Jack.

"Then I guess we'd better bust a mission," said Luke.

"All of us?" Alison did not look ready for a mission.

"I'm too scared to go out there by myself." said Luke.

Alison didn't want to, but Jack thought otherwise. "We should all go. We'll need to go down there eventually anyways."

"Better wrap something around your necks. Mountain tigers always go for the jugular," said Luke. "We need to stay close. We're more intimidating that way. Plus, everyone knows that they always go after the straggler in the back."

Jack had two pistols. Alison had one. Luke had his rifle and Katana sheathed to his side. They were just about to leave when they heard a grunt. "What the hell was that?" said Alison.

"Shh!" said Luke. "Do you smell that? I think it's a'bear."

"Oh shit!" said Jack, pointing his weapons into the darkness.

Luke turned on his infrared headlamp. He gazed into the forest through his crosshairs as he crouched behind some rocks. There was deadly silence; the silence that happens right before the attack.

Bushes moved. Another grunt. *There's bears out there. They're surrounding us. Mountain tigers are probably in the trees, waiting for us to venture underneath.* "I'm gonna start shooting," Luke announced, "They think they've got us surrounded. We need to scare them off. Our fear is too delicious to them." No one objected. Luke let off six deafening rounds into the darkness. "Alright guys, let's go."

They stayed close together and made their way to the car. Luke kept his gun pointed up and his eyes on the trees. The mountain tigers could still be up there.

They made it to the car. Their cravings were terrible. Jack and Alison re-dosed immediately. Luke had to prepare his own. He rolled up a piece of cotton with his filthy fingers before throwing it into the spoon. He believed that filthiness made for a strong immune system. So far, he had never been sick since he began shooting up.

Everything was fine until he injected. He visualized a bear crashing through their window. "You should turn the lights on for a minute." Luke scooted to the middle with his weapon ready. Jack turned the headlights on. Luke looked around, sweating and horrified. Something terrible was happening, he was sure of it. There was movement in the distance. The movement stopped. It looked like a bush. It was a man in a guile suit. The man lowered his binoculars and tried to blend by crouching deeper into the bush.

Luke needed to make a decision. He decided he wouldn't tell his friends. "Turn off the lights. All of them! We need complete darkness." Luke felt helpless. He knew what was happening, but he couldn't control it. *They* were out there. Every part of his being was certain of it.

A similar situation had happened a few months before. He was with a different friend; a friend he had abandoned in the forest. Luke ended up covered in dirt and branches he used as camouflage. He had his sound amplifier, infrared, and assault rifle. His face had been smeared with mud. It was a waiting game. Luke could hear the voices plain as day. It was life or death. There had been a gunfight. He killed people, but there were no bodies to be found.

"Is everything okay?" Alison asked.

"Is it the Monkey Police? Jack started humming the tune."

"No!"

Alison started smoking weed. She passed it to Jack, who then passed it to Luke. It was a calming ritual. Luke felt hopeless. He was in danger, but he tried to ignore the terrible things he felt were lurking. It was embarrassing. He brought these people to this place to make them feel safe.

Jack and Alison were busy doing nothing in the front. They bickered while trying to organize things. Time was slipping away. There were too many distractions. "We should probably get back up to the fire," Luke suggested.

"Hold on, I'm looking for my tooter," said Jack. The distractions continued.

There were way too many things happening in the car.

"Let's fuckin go. I'm going," said Luke.

"Hold on... let me just get this stuff put away."

Luke waited a couple more minutes while Jack did what he needed to do. He wanted to leave quickly, but was too scared to go alone. *All this fear... the savage animals.* There were enemies all around. No matter where he went, there would be enemies.

"Fuck! Hurry up, dude. We didn't come here to sit in the car all night." Luke was irritated.

"Alright. I'm ready, let's go." They went in the same fashion they came. They stayed close to each other. No one wanted to be in the back. They walked along the cliffs. It was the shorter but steeper way to get there.

As they got close, Luke noticed a terrible glow. It was the fire. It had gotten out of control. "Oh shit!" Luke took off ahead of his friends. *Not a fuckin forest fire! Anything but a forest fire!*

He made it to camp. The grass was on fire. It had spread to a fifty foot radius and was extremely close to the trees. Luke took his sweater off and started swatting at the perimeter. The shirt started smoldering and soon became worthless against the fire.

"Whaaah!" Jack ran up the hill screaming. He looked as if his life was over. Jack panicked and started dumping their jug of water into the center of the fire.

"Nooo!" Luke took the jug from Jack. He took off his pants and soaked them with the remaining water. He used the wet pants to swat at the fire and tossed what was left of his sweater to Jack.

Jack didn't understand Luke's strategy. He wasn't thinking with logic. Instead of swatting at the fire, he threw all their food into it.

"What the fuck are you doing!" Luke yelled, "That shit is flammable!"

Jack screamed something unintelligible. His girlfriend was stomping at the edge of the fire. She went for the half burnt sweater and started copying Luke.

"We need to get out of here!" said Jack, "We can get in huge trouble for this."

"Just fuckin do what we're doing! We can stop it."

"They're still gonna charge us a huge fine! Are we even supposed to be up here?" said Jack.

"I'll pay whatever fine. Just calm yourself," said Luke. The fire was soon under control, but another conflict was approaching.

"I think someone's coming up here," said Alison.

"Fuck!" said Jack. He saw a headlight beam in the distance, "We are so fucked."

"Will you get a hold of yourself?" said Luke, "We're gonna need to act sober. We need to suppress any kind of paranoia so we can handle this situation rationally."

"What about those guns? Why would you bring all those fuckin guns?" said Jack.

"The guns are fine. They're mine. Let's just get all of them in the backpack." Luke was paranoid, but had to ignore it. The pistols could have been reported stolen.

The vehicle was getting closer. Jack decided they would sneak down to their car. He didn't want to be around when the cops arrived. The car he was driving wasn't his, and he was too paranoid to deal with authority figures. Luke decided to man up and face whatever was coming. He threw his dirty syringes into the fire; they melted quickly. The only risk he was taking was with the pistols.

The approaching vehicle became visible. It was a firetruck built for off-roading. It crawled up the treacherous trail. Luke's friends had gone down along the cliffs, he expected they would make it to the car undetected. There were two ways Jack could get back to the highway. Luke was sure he would go the long sneaky way that winded through the mountains. Jack and Alison would be long gone before Luke made it out of this mess.

The fire truck made it to the fire. Luke gave them a friendly wave, trying to look like an innocent civilian with nothing to hide. The firemen got out. Luke told them he had it under control, but they continued with the procedure. The hose came out and the fire was extinguished.

"Where's your clothes?" said one of the fire fighters.

"I used them to put out the fire. They're ruined." He pointed to the pile of burnt clothes.

"Would you mind unloading that?" the fire fighter pointed at the AK-47.

"Oh sure, absolutely." The rifle was up against a rock. Luke took the clip out and cocked a bullet out of the chamber. "All these horror stories about bears and mountain lions... you can never be too prepared, right?" The man gave him a weird look. Luke felt stupid in his dirty underwear. He was suspiciously skinny. No wonder these people were nervous. There was no way Luke could present himself as a normal person; not like this.

"So, I don't know what I'm supposed to do about this," said Luke, "Do I have to pay a fine? Am I in trouble? Do I just tell you I'm sorry?"

"No, it's fine. There's a sheriff down talking with your friends. He might ask you some questions."

Oh shit, here we go. "Can I have some water out of your truck? I'm like...

dehydrating to death."

"You don't want this water. It came out of a pond."

"I do want that water. I don't care how bad it is. Can I have some, please?" The man let Luke fill up his jug. The water had a brown tint. Luke drank it anyway.

The fire fighter scanned the area picking up trash. Luke helped. The fire fighters noticed the scooter and asked if he wanted them to bring his backpack and rifle down. Luke accepted; it would have been a rough ride down the trail with it on his back.

Luke headed down on the scooter. The fire truck came down after him. Jack was standing next to his car, looking sick with fear. Luke parked in front of the sheriff and took off his helmet. The sheriff was confused by Luke's appearance. Luke pretended to be calm and harmless. No matter his appearance, he had to convince this cop that he was a reasonable person who'd just had an accident.

The cop asked if Luke had any ID. Luke grabbed his wallet out of the scooter glovebox. He showed that everything was legitimate. "So, you had some guns up there with you?" said the cop.

"Yep. They're all in the fire truck," said Luke.

"You had other weapons besides the assault rifle?"

"Some pistols. You know... for my friends. You hear about all these bear attacks and I felt it would be good to have protection," said Luke.

"How many pistols?" said the cop.

"Five." Luke decided to be honest and hope for the best.

"All of them are in this backpack?" He examined the backpack that was leaning against the fire truck.

"Yeah."

"Do you mind if I take a look?" said the cop.

"Well, I guess not. Go for it." Luke thought that was the least suspicious thing he could say.

The cop put his fingers on the zippers, "Which pockets are they in? Are they loaded?"

"They're loaded, and we kinda threw em in there in a hurry. So I don't really know which pockets they're in." It was a metal framed hiking pack and was extremely heavy. "You want me to get them out?" Luke went for the backpack.

"No, no. I think we'll just leave em." The cop went back to talk with Jack and Alison. Jack looked pale as he expected the very worst. The cop told him everything was fine and that he could leave if he wanted. Jack couldn't believe it. He couldn't believe they were getting away with this. Jack left without a word to

Luke.

"Your friend isn't leaving any clothes for you?" said the cop.

"No, I guess not," said Luke.

"You're gonna be driving in your underwear with that giant backpack?"

"I don't live that far away," he lied, "It shouldn't be too bad."

"Alright then, you're good to go if you'd like."

"I'm good to go? No fine? No ticket?"

"You're good to go." The cop was starting to sound impatient. Luke went for the backpack. He managed to strap the AK-47 to the backpack and threw the clip into the side pouch. The pack was heavy with guns, wet clothes, and garbage. He tightened it up and put his helmet on before getting on the scooter.

~~~

The drive was miserable. Luke was freezing. His muscles ached from being so tense. It had taken almost an hour to make it into C-Falls. He pulled into his driveway. Zuri's car was gone. It was 3am.

Luke made it in through the front door and went straight to the bedroom. An SUV drove slowly through the alley. It didn't look good, but he was too tired for paranoia. He needed PV. He went to the closet and did some. There was an evil feeling in the house. He dug all the pistols out of the backpack and loaded the AK-47. There was strange activity happening in the neighborhood. He could feel it.

Luke went to the kitchen for some water. He was trying to ignore his paranoia. There was a noise in the basement. It wasn't the friendly ghost that lived in the house. The ghost would only whistle on quiet nights or maybe walk up the stairs. This sounded like a broom handle falling against concrete.

Luke went back to the bedroom. He blasted Dubstep, closed the blinds, and grabbed the assault rifle. Luke assumed the worst. He would kill them if they resisted in any way.

He creeped through the kitchen and into the bathroom, completely consumed by fear. Luke peeked down the stairs into the basement, "Hello?"

"Hello?" replied the familiar voice. It was Fat Jared.

"Jesus Christ, dude. What the fuck are you doing here?" Luke went down into the basement.

"Zuri let me in. She left and said she would be right back. She left like three hours ago. I think something's wrong. Weird things are happening. They're watching this place. The same SUV has been driving around this place since Zuri left."

A shadow passed by one of the basement windows. Luke could hear radio
~~~

static. "Jared, I need you to go up to my room and grab some guns. Get my extra clip, too," he pointed to the banana clip.

Jared obeyed, and made no comment on the way Luke was dressed. He came back down whimpering with fear. "They're out there!" he whispered, "A whole fuckin squad of them got out of an SUV that's parked down the street. They're wearing all that gear and everything! They mean business, Luke. What are we going to do?"

Luke grabbed the clip from Jared. "Get under the stairs and keep an eye out that window." Luke found a different spot to keep a lookout.

This is it. The experiment is over. We've taken it too far. Pushed it to the breaking point. Now it's decided; they're finally going to put an end to this.

"Jared, what's happening out there?" Luke said from the far corner of the basement.

"The SUV is still parked down the street and another one just drove by real slow." Jared was terrified. They were in total darkness except for the streetlight coming through the dirty windows.

Luke shivered, mostly from fear, but partly because he was only wearing the dirty underwear. *Fuck this shit. I shouldn't have to go through this. I'm not ready to die. I'm just a kid. Should we surrender? Can we surrender?*

"What do we do, Luke? I think they're at the front door. I can hear them."

"If they come in without announcing, we have to kill them." There was no other option for Luke. *Where's Zuri? I should have listened to her. She tried so hard to convince me that this would end horribly.*

Luke had a friend who's grow operation was raided and robbed by fake FBI agents. This would be Luke's defense in court. He didn't trust sneaky black clad militia looking groups. He would kill them all—legitimate law enforcement or not— and get away with it.

Luke noticed one of his spare gas masks on a table. He strapped it on and hid under the table, keeping the sights on his rifle pointed at the top of the stairs. Fat Jared adjusted his position under the stairs. He looked ready to start shooting through the steps at the potential invaders.

"They're outside the back door!" said Jared. "I can hear them talking. They're coming in."

"Are the doors locked?"

"All of them. I even locked the bathroom doors on the way down," said Jared

Good, thought Luke. There was only one way they could come in; unless they came through the windows, and Luke hoped they would. It would make them easy targets. Luke was ready for anything, even tear gas, but he would have to be careful of flash bangs. He would probably lose Jared, and that was acceptable. Jared would make a good decoy.

Tension rose as things got quiet. Minutes went by as condensation built up in Luke's mask. *Any second now, they can't wait all night. Thirty minutes went by. Neither Jared or Luke moved a muscle. They both had the same mind set. They would not be caught off guard.*

Maybe they think we'll forget about the situation. Maybe they think we'll attribute it to the drugs. If they've been studying us properly they would use these tactics. They should know how our brains operate by now. If it's a waiting game they want, they've met their match.

Jared's breathing changed. It was labored. Luke suspected he was trying to inject himself, but he couldn't risk asking. *Go ahead you fat retard, make a distraction of yourself.* There was rustling under the stairs. Luke expected this would prompt the invasion. He tightened the grip on his rifle.

There was a flash of light at Jared's end. Jared looked out the window. "Hey, that SUV is leaving. We're safe now, right? Luke? Does that mean it's over? Luke? Luke, where are—"

Glass broke upstairs. It was all coming together. Jared had given up his position. Luke was still under the radar; still under the table, right where he wanted to be. There were footsteps upstairs. Three people; maybe five. They checked the living room, then the bedroom. Back to the kitchen. Luke could visualize them trying to open the bathroom door. They couldn't get to the basement without going through the bathroom. Not unless they came from outside through the back door.

The front door opened. They went outside. Jared looked at Luke waiting for instructions. Luke gave him none. Jared had served his purpose as a diversion. Luke's face was sweating terribly, but the mask refused to fog. They would be coming through the back door and straight down the staircase. *Here it comes; the moment we've been waiting for. There was a tap on the back door as they tried the handle. SMASH!* The door flew open, followed by gunfire.

"You stupid mother fucker!" said Luke. Jared ran out of bullets and was whimpering under the stairs.

"What the fuck is going on down there?" Blue yelled from the back door.

"You almost killed my cousin," said Luke.

"I panicked!" Jared had unloaded his clip into the stairs. "What the fuck?" said Blue.

"It's safe. You can come down here," said Luke.

Blue came down the stairs, "You guys need to get your shit under control! This is fucked up. You're gonna end up killing people if you keep this up."

"I know, I'm sorry. Why'd you kick down my door?" said Luke.

"I came to check on you because you weren't answering your phone. The bathroom door was locked and you wouldn't answer. I thought you were fuckin overdosed or some shit. I came around and kicked in the back door."

Extreme remedies are very appropriate for extreme diseases.
-Hippocrates: Aphorisms

Chapter 32: There's Hope at the Hippie Fest

Thursday 7-3-2011 7:00pm

Things continued in a steady decline since the basement shoot-out a month before. It reached a breaking point, and Luke finally made a plan to turn it around. He was going to Walmart for a few last minute things before heading off to Oregon. His new car was in the parking lot, and he was bringing an odd assortment of people.

Alice was concerned for Luke's health. She was certain that Stacy was the one who could keep him safe. Luke agreed to bring Stacy under the condition that they were *just friends.*

Nick was coming as well. He had feelings for Stacy and hoped to start a relationship. Luke hoped this trip would bring Nick and Stacy together. Zuri wanted no part of Stacy, let alone a road trip, but Luke assured her there would be no problems.

Stacy and Nick were just as addicted as anyone. Luke wanted to help them recover as well. They hoped to have a spiritual awakening at the hippie fair. It was decided that they would not come back to Montana until they stopped doing PV.

Luke was carrying a case of Ensure as he saw a familiar face approaching.

"Natalie?"

"Luke? Oh my god!" She gave him a hug. She was with her friend Molly. "What's going on? Are you okay?"

"Yeah I'm good. Kinda. Why?" he said.

"You look different. Your face..."

"Oh. Well, I been kinda stressed out. I'm leaving town right now."

"Where are you going?"

"Oregon. You should come smoke a bowl or something. I got a new car," he said.

"Yeah. Lets do it." They went to the checkout and proceeded to the parking lot. "This is your car?"

"Yep. This is mine." It was a 1999 Cadillac Deville; burgundy with buckskin interior. Luke got in the passenger side. The girls piled in back with Nick and Stacy. The tinted windows gave a feeling of security.

Luke introduced everyone. Stacy was in her happy social mood. She was happy to be going to Oregon even though she was coming down from heroin and had just gone through a breakup with Logan. Luke suspected that she only wanted to go to Oregon for the heroin. Without Logan she had no heroin. She facilitated the weed smoking. Luke also suspected she had stolen all the weed from Logan.

Zuri was pissed and wouldn't talk to anybody. She was sure Luke would have sex with Stacy by the end of the trip. Luke gave her no choice in the matter. If she didn't like it, she could leave. That was Luke's favorite line, no matter how vicious it was.

Stacy and Nick were excited. Nick thought he was finally going to get the girl of his dreams. The pipe went around. "Are we okay to be smoking here in the parking lot like this?" said Natalie.

"Oh yes," said Stacy, "I have my medical marijuana card."

"We're also hidden by my awesomely tinted windows," said Luke. He turned up the music to show off his sound system. Luke clung to the feeling. He created this. He was the master of the vessel.

"So Luke, what have you been doing lately. Are you working now? Are you still doing the spirit quests?" said Natalie.

"I'm not really working. I haven't been doing much spirit questing either. I guess I've been neglecting the spiritual part of my life; which is terrible; which is pretty much the reason for this trip. I've got some big problems, so I'm going to a hippie festival to try and heal myself."

"Have you been doing meth?" Her friend was frightened by the ugly word.

"Umm, no. Why would you think that?"

"You kinda look like you could be on one of those meth commercials. Your cheeks, and your eyes are sunken in. You seem way skinnier."

"Well, I honestly wish I could say my problem was meth. My problems are much worse actually."

"But there's nothing worse than meth," said Molly.

"There is now."

"What is it? Why haven't they put up advertisements against it or anything?" said Natalie.

"Honestly, I don't want to get into any of that right now. The stuff isn't even illegal. I think there's a big conspiracy behind it all. But I promise you that I'm not coming back from Oregon until I'm better."

The weed smoking went on for a few more minutes. Natalie was getting bad vibes. Something was wrong with these people. She only got a few glimpses of Zuri. Zuri looked terrible just like Luke. She didn't seem natural for him; not the way he used to be. Natalie felt bad for Luke even though he had a beautiful car. It made sense now why he hadn't made any time to hang out with her. Luke was ashamed. She could see it. He was ashamed of what he'd become. "I'd better get going," she said.

"Yeah... right. Me too."

"Bye Luke... Good luck on your quest. It was nice meeting you guys." The girls got out of the car and headed off.

"Let's get going then," Luke signaled for Zuri to start driving. She hated driving, but Luke insisted. He was the boss and she was the chauffeur. She tried telling him she didn't want to put the expensive car in danger. But of course he told her, if she didn't like it, she could leave. They were brutal words. It brought her close to suicide a few times.

Luke started preparing an MDPV solution for everyone. He decided he was going to control everyone's intake. No one would be allowed to go crazy on this trip. They *needed* to at least make it to the fair, and that was still six days away. It would be rough time in Portland if everyone started getting psychotic.

Luke injected Zuri first. She was impatient, and very needy when it came to that. Luke handed two syringes to the back. Nick and Stacy could handle themselves. "Make sure you're drinkin water. And give me those dirties when you're done." Luke took his own injection and felt the paranoia. He had an arsenal of terrible things. Some were illegal. Most all of it would be illegal as soon as they left Montana. There was a duffle bag full of guns in the trunk. Some of them were reported stolen. Luke had a buyer for all of them. Also,

Oregon was one of the few states where most of Luke's chemicals were illegal.

Before the trip, Nick had asked Luke's permission to be with his ex-girlfriend. Luke encouraged it. It would make the trip much easier, and would hopefully make Zuri more comfortable being around Stacy.

Luke turned around to tell them to hurry. Stacy was jabbing at Nick's arm like a sewing needle. A shoelace was tied around his arm. "What the fuck are you doing?" Luke said.

"I'm sorry," said Stacy. "I'm starting to go into opiate withdrawal. I'm not very steady."

Luke took the syringe. There was some blood in it. The point was dull from so many attempts. He squirted the solution into a new syringe and injected them both.

~~~

They pulled into a truck stop somewhere in Idaho. Nick was driving. Zuri was laying on Luke in the back behind Stacy. Stacy was acting strange, but Luke ignored it. He wanted to prove to Zuri that it wasn't a mistake to bring Stacy.

They found a secluded parking spot. Nick tried to comfort Stacy. Stacy didn't have to pretend to like Nick now that the trip had begun. Luke could see this. Zuri had seen this before anyone. She was always the one who got to say, 'I told you so.'

"Are we stopping?" Luke slurred, Him and Zuri had been lacing their drinks with GBL. "We just stopped. We need to get out of Idaho. This place is evil. They'll crucify us if they catch us you know."

"Stacy has to use the bathroom," said Nick.

"Damnit. Hurry up, and turn the music back up." The GBL was stronger than anything. It didn't matter how much speed he injected, he would still stumble around like a drunken fool. He was having fun. The music was sensational, and it felt good being so close to Zuri.

Stacy stormed off to the bathroom. Nick went after her. "She's such a drama queen," said Zuri. Luke was oblivious to whatever she was sensing. They started making out. They told how much they loved each other. Things were looking up for Luke and Zuri. It was a good start on their road to recovery.

Stacy and Nick came back. They were acting weird. Luke didn't have the capacity for it. They wanted more PV, and wanted Luke to make it for them. Luke said no. He told them to drive. They complained. "I'll give you the drugs if you start driving. We don't have time. I need to be at the dope house in like… a few hours." Nick drove. Luke handed the kit up front for Stacy to deal with.

Stacy complained about something. Nick gave her some soothing words. He
~~~

tried to put his hand on her leg but she pushed him away. Zuri could sense what was happening, but didn't care at the moment. Luke had no idea; he was preparing to inject Zuri with 4-MEC.

Stacy injected Nick. He started getting weird. It was too much. Red and blue lights were flashing in the rear-view mirror. "Are we getting pulled over?"

"No, dude. There's no one even behind us," said Luke.

Stacy took her shot and got weird as well. She wasn't making sense. She was having a breakdown. Luke laced a cigarette with AM-2201 and gave it to her, "Don't share that with the driver," he instructed. Nick was having enough trouble as it was. Stacy took a couple drags, then handed it back to Luke. He took a couple, then put it in the ashtray.

The 4-MEC was ready. He couldn't do it; the cigarette had warped his perception too bad. Zuri did it for him, then did it to herself. Nick had turned the music down out of fear. Luke screamed at him to turn it back up as he rubbed his face all over Zuri. Stacy attempted to speak. Nick was panic stricken. It was pandemonium. They created a blender of mental confusion that traveled at 65mph.

The sun was beginning to rise as they approached Portland on highway 84. Luke was driving. He didn't trust his small town companion in the aggressive traffic. They listened to the radio. Luke made it a tradition to listen to the radio as they came into Portland. The stations were good and played new music Luke had never heard. 'Addicted' by Black Eyed Peas came on. It melted Luke's heart. *I'm addicted and I just can't get enough...* This song would forever remind Luke of Zuri and this adventure.

The vibes were crazy. Cars and lights flashed by at tremendous speeds. " Hit me girly-friend." Luke held his arm out to the passenger side.

"Seriously? I just gave you one. That was like a half hour ago," said Zuri.

"I know, but it was a small one. My eyelids are trying to close."

"Okay, you're gonna have to stop driving so crazy."

"I have to drive crazy. Everyone's driving crazy. I don't care if you fuck me up, just get it done."

She got it done for him. His blood flow felt restricted, so he held his arm in the air and squeezed his fist. He was having anxiety. He forced himself to operate like a robot.

"Cristina's ready for us," said Zuri, "I just texted her."

"Nice. Tell her we'll be there in about an hour." It was nice to have drug dealers that would be awake at 6am.

"Where are we going?" said Stacy.

"Oregon City," said Luke.

"That's where the stuff is at?" Stacy was becoming more miserable as the heroin withdrawals progressed.

~~~

They pulled into a park next to the Willamette River. "What are we doing here?" said Nick.

"I have to drop you guys off for a little while. I'm not supposed to bring other people to this place," said Luke. They found a parking spot. Zuri wasn't getting out.

"Why does *she* get to go?" said Stacy.

"Because these people are *my* friends," said Zuri, "and he's *my* boyfriend."

"Bitch, I'll fuck you up!" She went for Zuri; Nick held her back. Stacy babbled accusingly at Zuri for having sex with Luke in the back seat during the drive.

"I can have sex with my boyfriend whenever I want!" said Zuri.

"Shut the hell up and knock it off!" said Luke. "I'll send all of you straight back to Montana." Stacy was crying and mumbling. Nick was trying his best to comfort her. Zuri was angry and looked ready to fight. "Don't antagonize her," he said to Zuri.

"Don't defend her! She's being a fuckin drama queen."

Nick went to Stacy's defense, "She needs that H. She's coming down hard. You should hurry up and get that stuff, please."

"Alright, I'll go get the stuff, but I can't promise I'll be quick."

"Why not?"

"Because we have a lot to talk about. I enjoy these people. Plus, I need to try and advertise my research chemicals to them. The faster I get going, the faster I'll be back."

~~~

Luke and Zuri pulled up to the house. The house was hidden in the trees. The driveway leading to it was rough. It was a different place than before. Last winter they had been living in a camper trailer parked behind a double wide. Zuri texted. Cristina came out and waved. It was 7am.

"Hey guys. How was your trip?" Cristina said as they got out of the car.

"It was good," said Luke.

"It was horrible," Zuri countered. Cristina already knew most of the story through Zuri's texts.

"Well, at least you've got a nicer ride than you had last time." They followed her inside. There was an old man on the couch in the living room. He was smoking meth while watching television. They continued down a hallway and went into a small bedroom.

Clint was in there, looking content with a piece of foil. He was Cristina's boyfriend; a skinny guy, helplessly addicted to meth and heroin. "What's goin on guys?" He looked more withered than before.

Zuri told them about the trip. They smoked some crystal out of a monster-size glass pipe. It didn't make much difference. They might as well have been smoking cigarettes because they were all IV users. The process of smoking was just for fun. Luke took one hit off the piece of foil; only one. Two would have made him sick. Zuri despised heroin with all her heart.

None of them had slept recently. Their conversations were strange. Luke talked about his new chemicals and his DJ researcher friend in Montana. He boasted about all the new drugs he would try each week. MDPV was a big topic. Cristina and Clint were only interested in meth and heroin. They asked what Zuri thought of MDPV.

"MDPV isn't better than meth in a good way, but it's definitely better in a bad way. It's way more addictive and the high doesn't last as long," she explained.

Cristina was preparing a solution of meth in a spoon. "Are you guys gonna want any of this?"

They both said no. Luke explained how he had gotten a stroke from mixing MDPV with meth, and that he was only safe doing meth by smoking or snorting. Zuri pulled out the supplies she needed to inject some PV. She made enough for Luke and herself.

Luke bought an ounce of crystal. It was only 800 dollars and it was the best. Luke wanted to give out samples of his chemicals. If he could get these people to promote MDPV it would mean good money for him. Luke wanted to quit doing PV, but he wanted to keep making the money it provided. He was sure he could retire in a couple years if he could buckle down and get organized. To do that he would need to be sober.

Luke went to the car and came back with the suitcase-safe. Zuri had a syringe ready for him. He injected it, trying to ignore any unpleasant side effects so he wouldn't scare off his potential customers. Luke opened the safe and started showing off chemicals. He busted out the scale and measured out single dose samples of each and put them into capsules. Luke explained the different drugs and labeled them properly. He even ate a few capsules of 4-MEC to goad his friends into trying some. They promised they would try the stuff later on. He also gave them a 10 gram bag of PV to share with their friends.

Luke received a text. Nick was having trouble with Stacy. She needed heroin, and Nick wanted Luke to hurry. Luke was going to take his time. It was a coincidence that Clint was out of heroin. Clint needed a ride from Luke. If Stacy wanted the heroin she would have to wait until they did this errand.

Luke explained the situation to Clint. Clint said he would just give Luke a glob of chiba for the ride. They headed out. Luke was happy to show off his Cadillac and crazy music.

If there is no struggle, there is no progress.
-Frederick Douglass

Chaper 33: Crazy White People

Friday 7-4-2011

Luke drove around Portland looking for somewhere to stay. If it were just him and Zuri he would stay in his car or at friends.

There were also family members he was supposed to visit. He could stay at those places but would rather not.

Stacy and Nick were in the back seat smoking weed. They were much more pleasant now that Stacy had her heroin. Luke gave her the glob, but he kept a chunk for himself as well. He made her promise to only smoke it; no shooting. This chiba was stronger than anything in Montana. Luke needed everyone to survive until the hippie fair.

So far they tried two hotels, both of them said they had to be 21. It was decided that they would rent it in Nick's name. Luke was convinced he was still being watched. The Monkey Police were persistent. It was an experiment; Luke was certain of that. The guns made him nervous. He wanted to get rid of them as soon as possible, and he couldn't do that until he dropped off Nick and Stacy.

It was 4pm when they found a motel. It was run down and owned by Asians. Luke paid for it and didn't plan to stay long. He was eager to meet with his friend Smokey to get rid of the guns. They all went inside and settled in. Zuri hated the idea of staying in the same room with Stacy.

They went to the bathroom and covered the counter with paraphernalia. Luke enjoyed the freedom to make a big drug mess without having to clean it up. They all injected PV. Luke got distracted and stayed busy doing nothing. He started to unpack, then changed his mind. He didn't know what he needed to do. They all *needed* sleep. The beds looked useless, and the thought of sleep was repulsive. They were in a new place, and there was much that needed to be done.

Luke texted his friends. They wanted to come see him. He didn't know where he was, and was too paranoid to turn on his smart phone. Luke decided to only use his throw-aways until he got rid of the guns.

It was time too meet with Smokey. He took one more dose of PV before the road. More distractions. Luke forgot what he was doing. He was dysfunctional. They got high again. Then again. And again, until the room became a mess.

"I'm leaving! Right now!" Luke announced. It was 8pm. The day had been wasted away in confusion. Luke walked around grabbing everything he needed.

There were drugs scattered all over the room; small baggies of different chemicals lying around. Luke gathered them all and threw them into his suitcase-safe. Nick and Stacy insisted he leave some PV for them. He left a small pile on the bathroom counter; enough to last them until he came back. Luke and Zuri left. They were off to meet with the Mexican gangsters.

~~~

Luke turned down a residential street in Northeast Portland. He found a place to park and Smokey walked up to the Cadillac.

He rolled down the window. Luke was wearing a black fedora and his leather jacket. Smokey was what they call a 'cholo.' He wore dickie shorts with the long socks. His head was shaved and he was Mexican. "Ey fool, nice ride you crazy white boy." He got in the back and they were off.

"What the fuck is this?" said Smokey, pointing at the AK-47 that was wedged behind the front seats. "Is this shit for real?"

"Oh, yeah. I like to keep it in plain sight. It's perfectly legal that way," said Luke.

"Ey man, you can't be cruisin around like this. You're not in Kansas anymore, fool."

"Oh... well, you can throw it in that duffle bag if you want." Smokey did, and as he opened the duffle bag he saw all the other guns. "Oh shit! What is this?" He was surprised by the turnout. Luke had never brought more than one or two. "Those are the ones I'm selling," said Luke.
~~~

"What, you're not gettin rid of the chopper?"

"I wasn't plannin on it. I like that thing."

"Sell it!" said Zuri.

"Yeah fool, sell it! Listen to your girl. You don't need that shit." Smokey pulled out the 357 revolver, "I think this is more suitable for you. Get yourself a big belt buckle and some cowboy boots. You're into some real redneck shit up where you live, ain't chu?"

"I don't know, man. I probably don't need any guns. I'll end up killing people with em if I don't stop doin drugs."

"Man, you're crazy fool. You're the craziest white boy I know. Look at chu. Your leather jacket, what's that shit? You look fucked up fool. You're like a straight up dope fiend, ain't chu?"

"I'm a junkie, man. I got some serious problems, to be perfectly honest. But I'm tryin to fix it. I'm not going back to Montana till I quit PV."

"You still slingin that weird shit? Cuz you're ballin, fool. I don't know any junkies who got the shit you got."

"Yep. I'm sellin all sorts of chemicals. But PV is the money maker. Do you think your people would be interested?"

"I don't know, man. They're down with the coke and chiba, that's what makes money around here. But I tell you what, the homies gonna be psyched when they see this shit," he slapped the duffle bag.

"Well, do you think you could give them a sample? Give them the chance to share it with some people. I'm tellin you, pretty much any speed freak is gonna go nuts for this shit. It's a big opportunity. I could bring shitloads of it from Montana. As much as they need."

"That's tight. I'll talk to em about it."

Smokey gave directions. Zuri talked about how much she hated Stacy. Luke defended the situation and explained why they had to bring Stacy and Nick. Smokey met Stacy a few years before, and couldn't believe that they were all addicted to the needle now.

"Man, remember seventh grade?" said Smokey, "All we did was smoke weed and shit. I blazed you up for your first time, now look at chu. I feel like this shit was my fault."

"Nah. I woulda done it anyway. It's my destiny. I was meant to experience this. I'm not ruined for life because of it."

The rest of the ride was filled with stories; Luke's crazy stories of Montana and Smokey's stories about the gang life.

~~~
~~~

They arrived at the apartments. Luke found a parking spot and told Zuri to stay in the car. They convinced Luke to sell the AK-47. Luke gave Smokey a sample bag of MDPV to give to the Mexicans.

They got out of the car. Luke grabbed the heavy bag from the back and slung it over his shoulder. He was nervous. There was a chance he could just get robbed. He trusted Smokey, but these people were MS 13, and they weren't friendly with white people. The only reason Smokey associated with Luke was because they had been friends since fourth grade.

Mexican rap music grew louder as they approached. Luke tried to suppress his paranoia. Three of the pistols were reported stolen. He wanted them out of his possession.

The door opened and they walked in. They Mexicans eyed Luke with suspicion. He was an unusual visitor in a place like this. The living room was full of Mexican men and women. They all spoke only Spanish. Smokey greeted people in their unique way. He explained Luke's presence to a vicious Mexican. The Mexican's expression showed he was pleased. He motioned for Luke to bring the bag over. Luke set it down and signaled that they were welcome to explore.

Another Mexican came over and opened the bag. The AK-47 was the first thing he pulled out. It was fully loaded and ready to go. The Mexican held it with pleasure. Luke told Smokey to let them know that it was unregistered and completely legal. Smokey explained. Luke also pointed out which three were reported stolen.

The Mexicans laughed when they pulled out the .22 cal hunting rifle. It was in pristine condition and had a nice scope. The guy looked at Luke with humor. Luke shrugged. There was plenty of ammo for everything. It was a complete arsenal of seven pistols, a rifle, and an assault rifle.

They offered Luke two ounces of cocaine for the guns. Luke accepted. Someone gave Luke a beer. He drank it out of courtesy.

Smokey was having an exciting conversation in Spanish. These people were his friends and they were in no hurry to leave. Luke drank a second beer and pretended to enjoy the scene. He felt out of place. He was just a skinny tweaked out white boy who somehow ended up in this cholo gangster pad.

Luke found a spot on a couch. A blunt was passed to him. He drank a third beer. Smokey was trying to explain MDPV to a few people. They listened with interest. Smokey pointed at Luke and imitated an injection. It was a shock that the white kid was injecting strange chemicals.

Smokey explained how Luke came up with all the guns; that people in

Montana would steal them and trade them to Luke for his chemicals. He explained that the chemical was addicting and easy to make money with. Smokey gave them the bag of PV and instructed them to try it or sample it in small amounts at their leisure.

Smokey gave Luke his payment and they headed out. Luke felt better without the guns in his possession. It was eleven o'clock when they got in the car. Zuri had been listening to the radio. She was happy to see him come back without the duffle bag.

Luke got in the driver seat and drove off. He was jonesing hard and told Zuri to prepare a shot for him. Smokey was shocked. "You're not seriously doing that while driving, are you? I don't approve of that shit. You white people are fuckin crazy."

"It's fine. We do it all the time," said Luke.

"Naw man. What if you black out and drive us into traffic or something?"

"I'm not doin that much. And the only way I would black out was if I was dying. It's not like shootin opiates or nothing. This stuff wakes me up; makes me more alert."

"Fuck, you're crazy, fool." Zuri injected Luke. Smokey watched in disbelief. He was disgusted by the process.

"It took all of Luke's concentration to make it through the rush." After a few minutes he mentioned the fair. "Man, you should come to the hippie fair."

"I don't know about all that shit. There's a few people I wanna bring, but I don't think they'd be down. It's hard to explain that hippie shit to people. I don't even understand what happened to me at that place. All those white people..."

"Well, I could certainly benefit from some hippie white people. I've been away from that scene for too long, and it's eating at my soul. Hallucinogenic drugs are kind of my religion."

"Your bitch ex-girlfriend is freakin out on Nick," said Zuri. "It sounds like they're fighting over drugs or some stupid shit."

"Well, that's shitty. You should check my phone for me. It's been vibrating pretty much non stop for the past few hours."

He handed the phone to Zuri. She opened it, "Oh geez." A few minutes went by as she read through the texts. "I don't want to go back there."

"Why? What's going on?"

"Stacy want's us to hurry up. She wants to get away from Nick. Nick is pissed, because Stacy did all the PV. They're just freaknig out. There's like ten texts from each of them, and a bunch of missed calls."

"You said they got a hotel?" said Smokey.

"Yeah."

"You should leave them there for the night. They probably need sleep. And you look fucked up too, fool. When was the last time you slept?"

"A couple days ago. I usually sleep every day, just only for a few hours. I can't go for weeks like I used to," said Luke.

"I think you need a full nights sleep. You should get another hotel and force your friends to sober up for a minute. Then we can kick it tomorrow when everyone's straight."

Luke's phone started vibrating. "It's Stacy," said Zuri.

She handed it to Luke. "Hello," he answered.

"Where are you? I need to get out of here or else I'm gonna kill Nick." Nick could be heard arguing his defense in the background. "Get away from me!" she told him.

"I don't think I'm coming back tonight. You guys need sleep, and so do we. I'm gonna stay somewhere else for the night. We can meet back up tomorrow."

"Are you serious?" she said.

"Yeah. We have a big adventure ahead of us. We need to get some sleep if there's any hope for us. You're just gonna have to get along with Nick for the night."

"No! Please just take me with you at least," she said.

"Not doin it. Our primary objective is to make it to the hippie fair. I feel like shit's gonna get fucked up if I come back to the hotel."

"No, Luke. Just come talk to me. I need you here," she said.

"Not doin it. You're on your own for the night. I gotta go," he said.

"Wait, don't go!"

"I'll talk to you tomorrow." Luke hung up the phone. Everyone in the car knew he did the right thing. Zuri grabbed his hand and held it.

~~~

Luke and Zuri found a nice hotel after dropping off Smokey. This place was familiar to Luke. He had driven past this hotel many times as a kid. Those days were innocent. He never expected he would stay at this place; especially in the circumstances he was in.

"I think you should send them both back to Montana," Zuri said as they waited in the lobby.

"Maybe. We'll see how they're acting tomorrow." Luke had a hopeless feeling. He wanted to do more drugs even though he knew he needed to sleep. His instincts told him to take a shot of PV as soon as they got to the room, but past experience told him that it would lead to another, then another, and another. He
~~~

would pass out around 6am, then wake up at 9 craving another dose. That's what his drug habit had evolved into. It seemed impossible to overcome.

They lugged their bags up to the room. It was five floors up and had a great view of Luke's homeland. Luke spent a few sad moments looking out the window, then he went for the suitcase safe. "What are you doing?" said Zuri.

"Just need to re-organize a few things," he said.

"No you don't. Come to bed." She was already lying down.

"One second," he acted quickly to prepare a shot of PV.

"Stop it, Luke. Get over here." Luke didn't reply. Zuri got up and went over to the desk he was at. "Luke no!" she grabbed his arm.

"Get off me! I'm just doing one before bed."

"Liar!" She went for the spoon. Luke grabbed the paraphernalia and went to the bathroom. She tried to follow, but he pushed her away and locked the door. Zuri pounded on the door a few times and started crying.

A few minutes later the shot was ready. Zuri was still sobbing outside the door. He injected it. Something went wrong. It was too much. He thought his life was ending.

Luke stumbled over Zuri as he rushed out of the bathroom. He landed on the bed, lying on his back with his arms straight out to the side. His heart was visibly beating through his shirt. Zuri ran to him, "Are you okay?"

Luke shook his head. He could barely breathe. Deep breaths felt like they were suffocating his heart. There was a terrible pain in his head as well as his chest. He thought he was having an aneurism.

Zuri was terrified. Luke's face was deathly pale and his hands were cold and blue. She tried circulating his blood by massaging the blood through his veins in his arms; up the left arm and down the right. *Please don't die, we're so close to getting better. Don't leave me now.* The thought of Luke dying right here like this was sickening. She was prepared to kill herself if that happened. PV would be too horrifying; a lethal dose of heroin would do the trick.

This horror lasted for twenty minutes. Luke started to come back around. A gas mask Monkey Police man was hanging upside down, staring in from outside the window. Luke didn't care if he was real or not; he was just glad to survive. His head still hurt. Something was different. Luke feared he'd caused himself some serious brain damage this time.

Zuri comforted Luke. She was emotional. Luke apologized. He didn't know why he had wanted to get high so bad. There was activity happening out the window. He knew he was hallucinating, but couldn't help but glance out the windows.

Sleep was coming fast for Zuri. She undressed Luke and crawled into bed with him. It wasn't often that she had him sitting still like this while he was awake, so she clung to him. The traumatizing experience was exhausting. Luke fell asleep even though the drugs were potent in his blood. Zuri fell asleep as soon as she was certain Luke went to sleep first.

There are things known
and there are things unknown,
and in between
are the doors of perception.
-Aldous Huxley

Chapter 33: Oregon Country Fair

Wednesday 7-9-2011

Luke and Zuri pulled into a Chinese restaurant parking lot. They were in Salem, only an hour away from the hippie fair. Stacy and Nick didn't make it. Luke had to put them on the Greyhound and send them back to Montana. There was too much drama, it was destined to fail.

"Well, here we are," said Luke, "this is the last restaurant we'll be going to for a few days. So we'd better munch down hard." They both had refrained from using PV for four hours just for this eating binge. They went inside. The place was rundown, but at least they were playing the Chinese music. Luke had located the place on his phone.

"This place is kinda gross," said Zuri.

"Shh! This place is the real deal. They're back there speaking Chinese and shit." The waitress brought them some tea. She was perfect. Luke loved the place already.

"When do you think we're gonna go back to Montana?" said Zuri.

"Hopefully a few days after the fair. I've got some family I should probably visit. And there's still a bunch of friends I haven't seen yet." Luke had been putting off visiting family. He didn't want them to see him in this condition. It was shameful. Things would be different after the fair.

The food came, "Heesh yo kung pao sheeken." Luke loved her. He had such compassion for Asian people. So much that he believed he had lived in the orient in another lifetime.

"Thank you very much," he said. She left and Luke ate until he hurt.

~~~

They walked out of the restaurant after leaving a generous tip. Both of them were craving a hefty dose of PV. "Hey, excuse me. Could I bother you for a cigarette?" said a stranger.

"Sure man," said Luke, "I got some in the car." They walked over to the Cadillac. Luke opened the door and pulled out a pack of American Spirits.

"Thank you so much. I just got out of jail today. I was in there for an entire year."

"That's crazy, dude. You're welcome."

"You got a nice car, bro. I noticed the Montana plates. What are you doin here?"

"Well, we're headed to a hippie fest right now. That's the main thing."

"You're shittin me! The Country Fair in Eugene?"

"That one," said Luke.

"I was arrested on the way out of the OC Fair last year! The fourteenth actually."

"Wow, crazy." Luke lit up a cigarette of his own. "What are you doing right now?"

"I have no idea. I have absolutely nothing except for these clothes, which aren't even mine either. I have no money and no place to go. I literally just got kicked out of jail less than two hours ago. I'm from California and don't know anyone here. I wish I could go to the Fair. My crew is probably gonna be there. They go to all the big festies around the country. We just sell shrooms and shit. That's what I got busted for. I sold to an undercover outside the campground and got busted with almost ten pounds."

"Hop in buddy. You're goin to the fair," said Luke.

"Are you sure, bro? I don't got no money. And I'm not even sure if my people will be there."

"Naw man. This is destiny. You're goin to the fair, I got you covered," said Luke.
~~~

"Seriously?"

"Hell yeah dude, get in."

"Damnit bro, you're awesome." They all got in the car. Zuri gave Luke a look. She didn't trust this person. She didn't want to bring this transient on their adventures. "My name's Vince by the way."

"I'm Luke. This is Zuri. That shirt has got to go. It's a bad trip waiting to happen." It was black with DEA spelled in white letters.

"Yeah, I know. I wasn't wearing a shirt when I got arrested. This was left in property so they gave it to me."

"Do you like drugs? You want anything?" said Luke.

"Well, I like weed, but I haven't done anything in forever so I'll probably get straight retarded."

"That's cool, man. You're safe to get retarded. This is a perfectly safe place to get retarded. Is there anything that makes you uncomfortable? I'm into some weird shit and I don't want to make you uncomfortable," said Luke.

"I don't care what you guys do. Nothin is gonna bother me," said Vince.

"Very good, then." Luke grabbed his sunglass case from the glove box and proceeded to prepare a shot. Slightly Stoopid was playing. Zuri loaded a bowl of weed and handed it back to Vince. Vince was amazed by how far he'd come in just a few hours. From a jail cell to this. It was luxury.

Vince ascended into a magical world. The weed took effect. He didn't even notice Luke and Zuri injecting themselves. The previous weeks he had been stressing about what would happen to him. Homeless shelter? Hitchhiking? Stealing to survive? But no, instead he was blessed by two ambitious teenagers who seemed generous and trusting.

~~~

They approached the Fair. The country roads were packed with vehicles. Herds of hippies walked on the sides. Cops were everywhere. They knew this was a drug fest. They drove past topless hippie girls without interfering. Public nudity was acceptable here. Cops were not allowed into the campgrounds either.

Luke was forced to drive slowly past an ugly scene. A Mitsubishi Lancer was pulled over. People were in handcuffs and there were large bags of marijuana and colorful bags of ecstasy pills on the hood. The officers examined them with satisfaction. Vince had terrible flashbacks of his own arrest.

"This is fuckin weird you guys," Vince said. "My whole perspective on reality is so messed up right now." There was a brief pause. Luke was trying to understand. "Fair… Jail… More Fair… that shit isn't normal. What's happening to my life?"
~~~

"That is definitely not normal. Your perspective must be very unique. I wish I could say I understand what you're going through," said Luke.

Luke pulled into the Shady Rest campground and parked the car. They got out and went up to the booth. A friendly hippie woman was there to take their money. It was fifty dollars per person. Luke handed over the money and they each received a green bracelet. They went back to the car and crept through to find a spot.

Shady Rest was crowded, but it was the mellower of the two big campgrounds. The Darling Reunion campground was the crazy one, but they were both connected. A fifteen dollar bracelet would allow people to travel between the two. Luke's two cousins had a spot in Darling. They had to reserve their spot a year in advance.

Luke found a nice camp spot. It was under some trees in the furthest part of the campground; good privacy considering their surroundings. It would be a place of refuge from all the inescapable noise, lights, and people.

Luke grabbed two tents out of the trunk, "Call it fate, but we actually have an extra tent for you."

"That's nuts! Why two tents?" Luke explained that they started the journey with two other people, but had to send them back to Montana.

"Where's your cousins at?" Zuri asked as she set up the tent.

Luke was in the car preparing a small dose of PV. "They're in the Darling campground. We'll go look for em after we get set up and shit." Zuri knew what he was doing, and she wasn't happy about it. They were here to fix themselves. She didn't want him losing his mind.

Vince finished setting up the tent. He went over to the car. "Hey Luke, can I bum a smoke?"

"Sure," Luke gasped. He was trying to catch his breath from the shot he had taken. He gave the rest of his pack to Vince. "You can keep em. I got something else for you too." Luke went into the suitcase safe and handed Vince a bag of methylone. "There's a gram. Go ahead and sell it or whatever. I know you need some cash."

"Thanks bro, I appreciate it. I hate to ask you, but could I bum fifteen so I can get into Darling? I wanna see if I can find my crew over there."

"Not a problem." They smoked some more weed, then Vince was off to enjoy his freedom.

~~~

Zuri wanted to stay in the tent. But Luke got her to leave with him after an hour. It was 4pm and 90 degrees. The two camp grounds were separated by a
~~~

creek. They held hands as they approached the bridge. Luke paid and they each received and extra bracelet. "Happy Fair," said the lady with the bracelets.

"Thank you," said Luke. He was so happy to finally be able to show this place to Zuri. This was the promised land he'd been waiting for. This was the place he would find his spiritual freedom.

Luke had eaten a heavy dose of methylone, which was magnifying the experience. Some hippie bluegrass music was playing in the distance. "Oh, this is so special!" He pulled Zuri close and kissed her on the cheek, "I've never brought a girl to this place. This is exciting!"

They walked past all the beautiful camp spots. There were stands where people sold their handmade merchandise. Topless women, naked people, beautiful people walked around casually.

"Should we take our clothes off? Do you want to be naked with me?" said Luke.

"Nooo way. Not a chance," she said.

"Me either." Luke tried to picture it. It didn't look right. Him and Zuri were shamefully skinny and pale. The people around here looked natural being naked.

"Sid," a passerby whispered.

"How much?" said Luke. The person stopped.

"Ten a hit."

"No thanks." Luke turned around and kept walking. "Anything more than five is gonna be shit. I'm determined to find a vial of the best LSD in this place. Maybe I can heal our friends in Montana with it."

"Sure, it's worth a try," she said.

~~~

It took two hours of aimless walking to find Luke's cousin. "Stan!" Luke hollered at his cousin. He had long straight red hair; hard to miss.

"Hey Luke, you made it." Luke introduced him to Zuri. "I just got back from the Fair. Spent entirely too much money." The actual fair was a mile away from the campground. It wasn't an ordinary fair, instead it was full of hippie stuff. No drugs, just good family fun. That is, if the families were okay with some nudity. It was a whole village that only manifests once a year.

"That's cool," said Luke, "we only got here about four hours ago. We been looking for your camp for a while now."

"Oh, yeah. We got a different spot this year. There's a trampoline," said Stan.

"Serious? Let's go see!" said Luke.

They had an enjoyable walk to the campsite. It was beautifully located in a
~~~

section of trees. There were two spray painted VW busses forming a perimeter on one side. Tents formed another perimeter. A full size trampoline was in the middle, a group of hippies were on it while passing around a joint. Luke's other cousin Scotty was on the ground playing a bongo drum while a dreadlocked man strummed a guitar. "Luke!" Scotty got up to give Luke a hug, "Damn, cousin. You're getting skinny."

"Yeah man, I noticed that," said Stan, "It looks like life's been rough on you."

"Yeah, it has. A lot has happened since I saw you guys last year."

A girl with dreadlocks came up to give Scotty a kiss on the cheek. "Hi love. Who are your friends?"

"This is my little cousin Luke. Luke, this is Jill." Scotty was taller than Stan. They were brothers, but Scotty had long curly blond hair. He was barefoot, with brown corduroy pants and no shirt.

"It's nice to meet you. This is Zuri," Luke put his arm around her and gave her a squeeze. "This is her first time at the Fair."

"Oooh yay! You're gettin your peach popped," said Jill, "Thats groovy."

"My peach?" said Zuri.

"It's like the symbol for the Oregon Country Fair," said Luke, "The peach... I don't know why, or how that came to be."

"Weird," she said.

"It's like losing your virginity," said Jill, "It's gonna be beautiful."

"That's cool. I'm excited. You guys have a really cool camp spot. This place is nothing like I expected."

"You're gonna love it. Just wait until the sun goes down."

"I've heard it's crazy, but what about all the little kids?"

"Nothing bad happens here. You'll see that. Only good vibes here. That's what it's all about."

It was hard for Zuri to imagine. There had been so much hideous negativity in her life lately, she didn't see how this place could be immune to that. So far it seemed okay. Luke was in good spirits for a change. It was rare, and she savored every moment that he was being sweet. She put up with his abuse for these moments, and in hopes that the old Luke would someday return for good.

The hippies were smoking something different now. They passed it from the trampoline to Scotty. It made it to Zuri. She asked what it was. "It's weed, with a big glob of opium on top." Zuri took a hit, but didn't look happy about it. She hated heroin, and this was just as bad in her mind.

A few people left, making more room on the trampoline. They all piled on and continued to get faded while telling stories. Luke told of his adventures with new chemicals and all the drama that went with it. His cousins told of their own adventures, and how life was treating them in Oregon.

~~~

Saturday 7-12-2011

The first three nights yielded no spiritual progress. Neither had Luke been able to cut down on his MDPV use. Luke had moments of enlightenment during the previous nights, but it would all fade away before the sun came up.

Luke wasn't spreading the good vibes he hoped to create. Instead his presence was harmful to the collective. He was getting irritated with Zuri. He even had some violent outbursts. She had lost all sense of adventure, and would rarely leave the tent.

They ran out of needles the second day. Luke blamed Zuri for wasting them. Her needles got dull more quickly. Now Luke had to sharpen dull, dirty needles on paper. Zuri's arms were looking mutilated and seemed close to becoming infected. Luke had his healing herbs, which Zuri refused. This added to his frustration.

Injecting drugs while under the influence of hallucinogens was hideous. It was ugly. It was the most evil thing Luke could imagine doing to himself. He found that PV gave him no chest pain as long as he was under the influence of LSD. The mushrooms he ate on the first night prevented him from shooting anything at all. Not only was it disgusting, but also an impossibly difficult operation.

The mushrooms were good for Luke and Zuri. It stripped away every physical and egotistic attachment and showed them the truth. The experience shed light on the ugliness of the way they had been living. It gave them hope.

Zuri and Luke went to the actual fair after the first night. It was fun at first, but became miserable as they started to crave PV. They left the PV at the camp as a test for themselves. The mushroom experience inspired them to do so. They bought some expensive food at the fair. It was delicious as they were coming down from PV. They also bought some other hippie shwag: a hackysack, a pipe, mood rings, and some glass gauges for Zuri.

The mood rings seemed to be broken, because they would just turn black when they put them on. But Luke and Zuri bought them anyway. It was a beautiful scene full of culture and interesting people.

Luke walked around in the hot sun in search for the best LSD. He'd found a couple people who had plenty of LSD. But his cousin had found some that was pure Jesus. Luke's mission was to trace it back to its source.

He was irritated that Zuri wouldn't come explore with him. *Stupid girl. Might as*
~~~

well have left you in Montana. What a waste. Probably reading or writing in your diary right now. No doubt doin some lame shit. Luke had been an emotional roller coaster since they'd arrived. One minute they loved each-other to the point of tears; the next minute was filled with abuse.

Zuri was always the victim. She spoke gently, and never fought back. Luke said horrible things to her, and he hated himself for it.

Damn, there are some hungry hungry hippies in this place. Luke noticed people looking exhausted. Their ribs were showing. They were burned out. The life of this place was running out. It had reached its peak two nights before.

Luke was walking barefoot in only boxers. He was dehydrating so he headed back to the camp. As he approached the Cadillac, he saw the water jugs were empty. He grabbed the jugs and went to fill them up. When he came back, he found Zuri in the tent trying to get a needle into her vein. "Will you help me?" she asked.

"No. You might as well just kill yourself if you're just gonna sit in this tent for the entire festival."

Zuri didn't respond. All she could think about was getting the shot. "Please Luke. I've been trying to do this for a half hour now."

Luke grabbed the syringe. It was full of blood, water, and drugs. He took one disgusted look at the damaged needle and jabbed it into the floor. "What the fuck!" she tried to grab it from him.

"Shut the fuck up! We'll use one of mine. That thing was too fucked up." Luke put the syringe in a pop can that was being used as an ashtray. He went through his own collection and found a syringe that was in decent shape. Luke made a new mixture; enough for himself as well. "I'm not doing this unless you agree to use my herbal remedies."

"Fine, whatever. Just do it." He did it. She sat quietly and was satisfied. Luke still saw it as evil. He felt terrible. He wanted to stop. Luke did his own shot and felt the same uncomfortable satisfaction. It was the most rewarding thing he could do for himself, but the side effects were terrible as ever.

It took an hour of silent eyeball twiddling for Luke to get on the move. "I'm not getting stuck in here like you. I'm going to hang out with my cousins."

"Can't you just stay with me for a while. I just want you to hold me or something." Zuri looked filthy and miserable.

"No. I'm leaving."

"Will you do one more hit with me? That last one was small." The craving was there. Luke prepared another one, but decided he wasn't going to get distracted. He would leave immediately after. The syringes were loaded. He tried to do his own first, but she tried to stop him, "Do me first! You won't do me if you do yours first."

Luke ignored her. "Shut up!" she tried grabbing, "Get the fuck away from me!" He took the shot before she could stop him. His ears became sensitive. Zuri's voice got too loud. She was holding the syringe, trying to get him to stick it in her. She was whining, it was drawing attention. "Shut the fuck up!" he whispered. She didn't shut up. He put his hand over her mouth and held her to the ground. She tried to scream, "Shut the fuck up you stupid bitch! Are you trying to get us in trouble?" His heart was racing painfully. He could hear people talking outside the tent. They were talking about *him*. Zuri's whining turned to silent sobs. He lifted his hand from her face and she stayed quiet. He peeked out of the tent. There was no one out there, so he left.

~~~

By nightfall, Luke had managed to consume almost every drug the Fair had to offer. The combination included mushrooms, LSD, 2C-B, GHB, MDA, MDMA, and an odd assortment of ecstasy pills. On top of that, he'd been consuming his own chemicals as well. He even managed to obtain a bottle of Captain Morgan, which he carried and sipped on casually. This was his last chance; the final hoorah. He needed to realize something life changing or die trying.

Luke walked into a disorientating scene. There was electronic music and lasers that projected shifting patterns on the trees. He found himself walking down a narrow winding trail made of glow sticks; *Hundreds* of glow sticks. Luke was wearing a foily emergency blanket as a cape. His broken LED shirt flashed odd patterns with the music.

He looked drunk as he stumbled down the trail, but it was the GHB that caused the coordination problems. The sounds and lights were overwhelming. Everything was pulsating; the trees were alive and communicated by movement and vibrations.

The trail converged into a crowd of people. They were dancing to a sinister beat. Luke tried to move in harmony with the liquidy mass of glowing people. The trees above were shrinking and growing and intertwining with the people. The branches slithered and stretched. Luke made it out of the crowd. A glowy person aimed and array of green lasers at him, which he deflected with his foily cape.

The trail got darker. The psytrance music faded into the distance. Luke noticed a small, hunchbacked creature lurking in the shadows. "Weird ecstasy pills," it offered, "Weeeird ecstasy pills. Five bucks."
~~~

Is that thing talking to me? It looked like a deformed ten year old with a weathered face. Luke stared as he walked past.

A glowing figure was approaching. It was a man carrying a small woman who was laughing while holding a balloon. "Him!" she said, "Let's give it to that kid." She handed the balloon to Luke, "Careful, nice shirt dude!" And they were off.

"Thanks," said Luke. He inhaled the contents of the balloon. The euphoria came and he went down. He lost the rest of his motor function.

A noisy group of people walked by. "Hey, look at that guy. I wonder what he's supposed to be. Hi kid!" said one of the girls. Luke managed to give a peace sign as he rested next to his deflated balloon and bottle of Captain.

The effects of the nitrous dissipated. The place got quiet. Luke noticed the unmistakeable smell of burnt MDPV. *No fuckin way,* he thought, *people here are smoking that disgusting shit?* He looked around in search of the source. It was easy to find, he could feel the terrible vibrations coming from a camp spot hidden in the trees. Luke could see the people from where he sat. Four people were crouched around a small LED lamp. He had a terrible feeling. He wanted to run. All four of them looked right at Luke. Their faces were hideous with a look of hatred.

Luke was about to run when he felt something behind him. He turned around and the thing crawled up a tree. It looked like a skinny black monkey with a head of a bat and leathery skin. The creature clung to a branch and stared at him. Luke wanted to shout bible verses at it.

Luke tried to get away, but stumbled and fell back to the ground. He looked back into the tree; the creature was gone. He looked at the PV smokers. There were four of the hideous creatures. The people stared at the ground as the monkey demons clung to their backs. They all stared at Luke while the PV smokers sat limp without fighting.

Luke forgot where he was. He felt trapped. A tall figure was approaching. It was glowing, which told Luke it was friendly. Luke realized it to be a man on stilts. He was wearing a top hat and was decked out in glowsticks. "Where am I?" said Luke.

"All roads lead to Fair!" The man didn't stop, but kept walking and stepped right over Luke. Luke looked back at the PV smokers. They were looking human again, and there was no sign of the monkey demons. The people were acting suspicious while smoking more PV off foil.

Luke sat watching them for a few moments. The vibes coming from them were much too familiar. Luke felt this place was trying to consume him. He wanted to get away; he wanted to find the drum circle.

Two figures walked up to Luke, "Heyyy, nice shirt!" The lights flickered as she spoke. They were two girls, both looking like glowing butterflies.

"What is this?" The other girl examined his foily cape. "Can we sit with you?"

"Yeah... No!" he said, "This place is horrible and I've been stuck here for too long."

"Why are you stuck?" she said.

"It's something evil here and I'm lost. I just want to go to the drum circle."

"Okay, we'll help you get there. We can find it together!" she pulled at Luke's arm and helped him up. They linked arms with Luke and headed off.

The two girls had rescued Luke. His life became much better. They were *all* lost as they wandered around looking for the drum circle. No place was off-limits; they laughed as they stumbled through people's camp sites. The place turned beautiful. Everywhere they went was full of colorful lights and beautiful sound. These girls were on MDMA and the love was contagious.

They made it to the drum circle. Luke lost his butterfly girls and melted into the crowd. There were hundreds of people drumming the same beat. They were all spiritually connected. *Everyone* was connected. Topless women were spinning fire. A man was spraying fire out of his mouth. He was wearing a loin cloth, and had a torch in one hand with a bottle of Everclear in the other. There was a primitive kind of chanting; everyone was involved. Luke let go and lost himself to the movement. He connected himself to these people. Together they were strong.

~~~

It was around 4am. Zuri was by herself in the tent trying to mix up some MDPV. An LED light was hanging from the ceiling. She was irritated with the faulty syringes. She was also irritated at being alone. Luke had not been to the tent since dusk.

Finally she heard someone approaching the tent. She covered the paraphernalia and grabbed Luke's switchblade. She had the fear. The zipper unzipped. Luke came tumbling in and curled into the fetal position. "Close that!" she whispered before closing it herself. "Where have you been?" Luke said nothing, but covered himself in his emergency blanket cape. "Talk to me please!"

"What do you want? I've been out there trying to find what we came here for," he said.

"You've been trying to find drugs? That's pretty stupid, you have plenty of—"

"I've been trying to find spiritual healing! We're being consumed by evil. Can you not feel it right now?"
~~~

"What are you talking about?"

"Eat some fuckin drugs and you'll see! It's in here right now. They're watching us. They *own* us. We're fucked."

"Have you been seeing monkey police again? It's all in your head, you know?"

"No, this is much worse. They're monkey *demons*. I saw them. I broke through to the other side. We can escape right now! They won't follow us to the drum circle."

"Okay, whatever. Will you give me a hit first?" she handed the loaded syringe to Luke and held her arm out for him.

Luke stared at the evil tool with disgust. He could feel the creatures around him. They were coaxing him; pressing him to do the deed. He squeezed the syringe. "Hurry up," said Zuri. He looked up at her. Luke squeezed the syringe tighter, pointed it, then squirted the drugs in her face. "Aah! You fucking ass hole!" She was in shock. She couldn't believe what he'd done.

Luke stared at the empty syringe for a few moments, before jabbing the needle into the ground. "What's your fucking problem!" Zuri grabbed the broken syringe from his hand. She threw it in the pop can and started preparing another.

Luke could feel the anger from her. He could also feel the anger from the creatures. But he also felt safe. There was a protective glow he had acquired at the drum circle. He felt bad for Zuri. He knew the monkey demon had her, and he could tell it was controlling her right then.

Luke wanted to go back to the drum circle, but he was experiencing too much pity for Zuri. Luke believed it was all his fault.

Zuri finished flicking all the bubbles out of her syringe, "Are you gonna help me or do I have too keep trying to do this myself?" Luke didn't want to. He wanted to wrap himself up in the emergency blanket with Zuri. He held out his hand. "Promise you won't waste it?" she said. Luke nodded. She handed the syringe to him. He looked at it for a few moments. The LSD was still going strong. Zuri held her arm out and her fist. "Please hurry."

Luke felt her arm to see if the vein was ready. The injection site looked infected. He looked at the syringe, which began to have a seductive appeal. There was a gripping sensation in his chest. Before he could think, the substance was injected into his own arm.

"What the fuck!" She grabbed the empty syringe from him and was close to tears with frustration. All she could do was start over again.

Zuri was at the stage of taking reckless doses; much larger than Luke could handle. His heart had gone weak months before. But this dose caused him no pain. No dose of MDPV had caused him pain while on LSD. This was a strange phenomenon that he had discovered at the festival.

The next five minutes were emotional for Luke. He watched his girlfriend prepare more MDPV. His heart was fluttering without rhythm. *Is this really my life? How did I end up in this tent on this planet? Did I choose this?*

"Okay, I'm ready. If you don't do this then I'm just gonna keep trying until my vein collapses."

Luke took the syringe and zeroed in on the wounded vein. The monkey demons were pleased. He could feel this. He went for the poke, but it wouldn't penetrate. "Fuck this." He didn't want to hurt her.

"Do it. Or else I'm doing it myself," she said.

Luke went for it. He cringed as he forced it in with a jab. It was in the vein. He flagged it, then depressed the plunger. Zuri was satisfied. Then she looked afraid. Luke could feel her pain as his trip went from bad to worse. She couldn't speak, but signaled that something had gone wrong.

Zuri lied on her back while holding her chest. She was sure she was dying. *I killed my girlfriend.* This was too much for Luke. He was frying on acid as he watched his girlfriend die.

Why isn't he helping me? She thought, *I'm dying. Do something!* But no words came out. She couldn't catch her breath. There wasn't enough oxygen; not enough blood flow. Her blood felt like it was turning to jelly.

"I'm sorry," he mumbled. "I didn't mean to…" he didn't know what to do. He was terrified; too scared to touch her. What was he supposed to do? What was he supposed to tell people after his girlfriend died at the hippie fair?

~~~

They drove away from the fair the next day. Their mood rings remained black. It was 3pm on Sunday. Lots of people were leaving that day, although they could have stayed for another. Luke felt terrible. He had drank more alcohol than he realized. Once the drugs wore off, the alcohol kicked in. Now he was hungover and his brain chemicals were all messed up.

"So, where are we headed guys?" said Vince.

"I think we're gonna get a hotel or some shit," Luke said from the passenger seat. "We'll just find a place in Eugene so we can shower and stuff." Luke loaded a large chunk of crystal into a glass pipe. He hoped that developing a meth habit would make it easier to stop PV, even though the meth had almost no appeal to him.

They found a motel in Eugene. It was owned by an Asian family that yelled around in their native language. It was clear that they didn't like the Oregon
~~~

Country Fair or the people that came with it. Who could blame them? The three customers that walked in looked filthy, like they would leave a huge drug mess in the motel room.

The drug mess happened immediately. Luke and Zuri went to the bathroom with the suitcase safe. Vince insisted he get the laundry done for them. He took all the clothes and left. Luke and Zuri both took a small dose of PV before getting in the shower together. The hot water felt good on their constricted blood vessels.

Zuri's feet were as yellow and unhealthy looking as Luke's now. The water that went down the drain was filthy brown. They scrubbed down for the first twenty minutes. Zuri initiated some romance, which Luke knew she deserved in return. They were back in civilization, and had somehow bonded through their traumatizing experiences at the Fair. PV was still an issue, but they both learned much about themselves and their problems.

It felt good for them to finally be alone together. They loved each other, and acknowledged that MDPV brought out the worst in them. Zuri wanted to quit, and so did Luke. "I don't care how horrible things have been," said Zuri, "I won't give up on us. I love you."

"I love you too. And I won't give up either. I know we can make this better. I know I can change. There was a few times at the fair… I know I was close. I broke through, and saw everything for what it really is. The way I've been living; the way I've treated people, especially you, it's disgusting. I could like, feel the damage that's been done to my soul. It's real damage. I could actually feel the defects. If we don't do something to fix it, then we'll carry those defects with us into our next life, or wherever we decide to go. It's so much worse than I ever imagined."

Zuri had seen it too. She had seen it the first night at the fair when she had taken a heavy dose of mushrooms and LSD. "I know, love. You'd be surprised, but I've actually been watching it happen since the beginning. That's why I tried so hard to help you. But now we both have the same problem, so we have to do this together. It's gonna be okay. We'll make it through this." She kissed him. They just held each other close and kissed for a few minutes. Then things got sexual. It was the first *real* intimacy they had shared for a long time.

~~~

Vince returned to the hotel when the laundry was done. He had been considerate enough to give his new friends some alone time. The tension Luke and Zuri had been going through was obvious. He didn't know what to think of Luke and Zuri. They were a strange couple who lived a strange life.
~~~

Vince smoked on a joint while Luke smoked a tremendous amount of meth in a desperate attempt to curb his craving for PV. "Just out of curiosity," said Vince, "do you really need to smoke that much of that stuff? Aren't you high yet?"

"Well, it's hard to explain," said Luke. "That speed stuff is fuckin me up. Amphetamines don't effect me much because of that other shit. Have you ever tried this stuff? It's really not as bad as it looks. It's legally prescribed to children as Adderall and shit."

"Well, no, I havn't. I've probably had some nasty ecstasy pills that had meth in it, but I've never smoked the pure stuff. Do you care if I try?"

"I don't care, but you'll be up all night and tomorrow."

"From one hit?" said Vince.

"From one or two," said Luke.

"I'll try one I guess." Vince put the joint in the ashtray. He was stoned and feeling tired. He doubted it would keep him up all night, especially after seeing how much Luke was doing.

Luke held the pipe and lighter for Vince. He instructed him to inhale slowly. Vince took one hit and blew out a massive cloud. He could feel his pupils dilating and his eyes grew wide. "Holy shit, dude. That was fast." His heart was fluttering and his tiredness was gone. He felt like he could do anything, but he really wanted a cigarette. "Can I have a cig? I really need a cig. I also need water. Luke gave him some cigarettes.

All of Vince's worries seemed small now. He could accomplish anything. Previously he had been worried about where he would go. He knew he would have to part ways with his friends soon. He had some family in California, and felt like he could be there in a day or two. *With this energy, I could do anything*!

"I think I'm gonna head out tonight," said Vince.

"Really? Where to?" said Luke.

"Cali. I've got an aunt who lives close to L.A."

"You sure? You could stay the night and catch a bus in the morning."

"Naw, man. I'm up for the adventure. I'm clean; got clean clothes; even got a good chunk of cash, thanks to you."

"Alright dude. Sounds like fun. May the force be with you."

"Thanks man. Do you think I can bum a small chunk of that stuff for the road?"

"Absolutely. We'll have you at your aunts in no time." He measured out a half gram, "I think you'll make it with this. Just promise me you won't get in no trouble." Luke had inferred that Vince had problem with stealing. His friends had been at the fair, but they wouldn't accept him for reasons he was vague about. He had gone to jail for mushrooms, but the mushrooms were stolen from his hippie crew. Instant Karma kicked in and landed him in jail. Luke and Zuri didn't know this, but they had speculations that were close to the truth.

They talked for a half hour and shared a joint before Vince left. "Find me on Facebook," said Luke, "I wanna know where your travels take you."

"I will contact you soon as I can. I appreciate everything you've done for me. Take care guys."

"Happy trails, dude," said Luke.

"Bye," said Zuri. And with that, Vince was out the door.

"Well," said Luke, "I guess we have the room to ourselves." He jumped onto the bed and felt his muscles and joints rejoice.

"Yep, we sure do!" Zuri landed next to him and rested her head on his chest.

"Should we go to Portland tomorrow?" he said.

"No. Maybe. I'd like to stay here for a couple days at least. We'll never get alone time like this with all your friends around."

"Kay. We can chill here for a bit. We should check out the town tomorrow. Like... we should go for a long walk and find a good restaurant or something," he said.

"That sounds good."

A dream you dream alone is only a dream. A dream you dream together is reality.
-John Lennon

Chapter 34: Psychadelic Exorcism

Wednesday 7-23-2011

Luke and Zuri found a hotel around 11pm. They had left Eugene on the 17th and spent a week in Portland before getting a hotel. A couple of nights were spent with friends. They went to house parties during the weekend where Luke saw many of his old friends and schoolmates. His old friends were doing drugs now. They liked cocaine and ecstasy. They found Luke's chemicals fascinating although most didn't want to try any. Luke's old friends were new to the drug culture and were cautious about what they consumed.

Luke chose to stay most nights in the car. Zuri hated it, and would have much rather enjoyed the comfort and privacy of a hotel. They slept on top of each other, but their relationship was becoming distant again. Zuri felt neglected. Every waking moment for Luke was filled with distractions. Their MDPV use was increasing, and their romance was decreasing. Zuri was miserable and so was Luke. The love was gone. Their whole mission was falling apart.

They loaded everything into the room. The first thing Luke did was make a big drug mess in the bathroom. Luke took a shot of PV and drank some Ensure. Zuri had her own supply and dosed herself in the bedroom. Luke measured each dose on the triple beam scale. He enjoyed measuring and fondling his chemicals. The whole process was part of the high before the high.

Luke came out of the bathroom and began texting people. Zuri was writing in a journal she had been keeping. She bought one for Luke, but he didn't have the attention span to write anything. She looked up to see him pacing. "What's going on, Luke?" He didn't answer. "Will you come here?"

Luke was irritated and stressed. His lips were cracked and bleeding from dehydration. His kidneys hurt. He sat down on the bed, but not close to Zuri. She moved closer to him and rested her head on his shoulder. "What is wrong, love?"

"I don't know. People are coming over. I don't want you acting weird," he said.

"What do you mean?"

"I don't want any attitude. I don't want you creeping out my friends or whatever."

"Do you just want me to be quiet the whole time? Should I leave? Cause I know you're just going to ignore me the whole time they're here."

"I want you to act normal. Don't get pissed if I don't give you enough attention. I don't get to see these people much so I'm gonna give them most of my attention."

"You could at least show me some affection. I feel like you're disgusted with me around your friends. You make me feel ugly. Sometimes I feel like you don't even love me."

"That's stupid, I do love you, and I'm pretty sure it's your own insecurity that makes you feel this way."

"Maybe I am. I'm not pretty like all your friends here; like all those girls at those parties. And how am I supposed to feel when you pretend I don't exist in front of all your friends? Just tell me if I'm disgusting to you," she began to cry, "because that's how you-"

"Shh," Luke hugged her, "You don't disgust me, I love you." Zuri was crying. Luke kissed her on the forehead and felt bad for the way he had been treating her. She was the most loving girl he'd ever met, and he treated her worse than he ever would have thought possible.

~~~

Smokey and Carlos showed up around noon. Luo and Zhao came a half hour later. Luke had known all these people since fifth or sixth grade. Luo was 17. She was a pretty Asian girl. Zhao was her cousin and was the same age as Luke.

Smokey had gone the gangster path. Carlos was a high-achieving athlete. He hung with all the jocks and popular people. Zhao had gone his own independent way and was in close contact with Luo. Everyone was brought together when
~~~

Luke came to town.

"Luo! Zhao! You made it!" Luke hugged both of them and introduced them to Zuri. Zuri felt the insecurity again. Seeing Luo made her feel ugly. *How can he stand to look at me when other people are so beautiful?* The Asian girl was healthy. Zuri was pale and sickly. Zuri had been comfortable until they showed up. She had known Carlos and Smokey since her first visit to Portland.

Carlos and Smokey teased the Asians. "What's happenin chink?" said Smokey. They exchanged stories. Luke insisted they smoke weed.

"So, Luke, what have you been doing lately? I see you upgraded to a nicer car?" said Zhao.

"Oh, wow. It's a strange story. I sell chemicals. Research chemicals."

"What are those?" said Luo. She and Zhao both noticed that Luke's health was worse than before.

"They're new drugs that haven't been made illegal yet. So I'm not breaking any laws; not many, anyway."

"That's crazy!" said Zhao, "And you been making good money? I have no idea what you're talking about."

"Well, I can show you my inventory if you're interested."

"Sure, I want to see," said Zhao.

Luke went to the bathroom and grabbed the suitcase safe. He hid the nastiest paraphernalia under the sink. His friends would be grossed out by the needles and spoons. Luke opened the safe on the desk in the bedroom. The first thing they noticed was a bag of syringes. *Oh shit*, thought Luke.

"Eww!" said Luo.

"What the hell is that?" Zhao accused.

Luke tried to think of an explanation. "Measuring tools... for the GBL." Smokey and Carlos already knew what he did, which made it awkward.

Zhao grabbed Luke's arm, "Liar! You junkie now!"

"Damnit, sorry, fine." Luke pulled his arm away, "I'm trying to quit. I swear I am."

"That's horrible, Luke," said Luo. "So gross!"

"I know it's horrible. I'm not proud of it." Luke went on to explain the MDPV and how he discovered it. He described the addiction and how he discovered all the other chemicals. He told them about Dan, the DJ and chemical researcher.

"Why don't you just quit?" said Zhao.

"Yeah. Just say no," said Luo. That was easy for her to say. She had never done drugs, let alone MDPV.

"You have no idea. I've tried so hard. I almost died a few times. I had a stroke

—"

"A stroke!"

"Yeah, a stroke. And Zuri almost died, too. She went into hypertensive shock or some terrible shit," said Luke. Zuri looked up from the bed. She had been texting, but now everyone was looking at her.

"Oh my god!" said Luo, "That's bad. I learned about that stuff in medical class."

"You do the stuff too?" said Zhao, "Why?"

Zuri shrugged. "I didn't know what else to do."

"Who did it first?" said Zhao.

"Luke did."

"Why did you let him keep doing it?"

"I didn't. He didn't do it when I met him. Then he started doing it and wouldn't stop. I tried to stop him. I knew the stuff was evil from the beginning."

An hour went by. Luke was beginning to jones for a dose of PV. He didn't want to shoot up with his friends there. Not even in the bathroom. He shared some MDPV with his friends. They all tried it except for Luo. Luke gave them samples to take with them. "Share it with people who like coke. They'll love it. They'll want more."

'What's it called?" said Carlos.

"It's called MDPV. But people in Montana call it all kinds of things. Like monkey dust, or crank, or Nazi dope. The stuff is illegal in Oregon, so you can call it whatever you want. It's not illegal in Montana, and it remains legal as long as I sell it for what it really is."

"So, I can just tell people it's angel monkey?"

"Sure, tell em whatever." Luke went on to educate his friends about the chemicals.

~~~

Luke's friends left around three. They had to work and do other normal things with their lives. The rest of the day was full of potential for Luke and Zuri, as long as it wasn't wasted on MDPV.

"I think we should do some acid," said Zuri.

"*You* want to do some acid. Why?"

"I like what it does for us. I like the way it makes you. It lets me see the real Luke. You're so much nicer to me when we're on that stuff. It makes me feel like were in love again."

"Okay then," Luke went for the vial. "How much should we do?"

"I don't care," she said.
~~~

"Kay." They each did two drops. One would have been plenty in a normal situation. Luke put the vial away then went to the window and opened the curtain. *What a strange place for an acid trip.* They had a second story view of a busy intersection. There was a shopping plaza across the street. Lots of cars and people.

Luke was determined not to make plans. He would let the trip guide itself. It was fun to be around people on LSD, unlike mushrooms.

Luke paid close attention to the clock. He took the LSD at 3:15, which meant it would be kicking in between 4:00 and 4:15.

3:55 came around. Luke went to the bathroom to prepare his final shot. It would have to be a big one, that way he wouldn't have to worry about doing another during the acid trip.

The bathroom was a mess again. Luke measured out 50mg of MDPV. Zuri was preparing a similar dose in the bedroom, only she didn't have a mess and didn't care about precision. The syringe was ready. Luke flicked it a few times and removed the bubbles. He had the butterfly feeling in his stomach; a sign that the LSD would soon be creeping in.

He inserted the needle and depressed the plunger. All forty units of yellow liquid into the bloodstream. It was too much for him, but he was determined to talk himself out of the panic attack. He set the syringe down with shaky hands. He couldn't breathe. He stared into the mirror, stepped back against the wall and slid to the floor.

The floor tiles illuminated into shifting patterns while pulsating different colors. Luke was shocked that LSD could kick in so fast. He sat on the floor and lifted his hands to watch the tracer effect. There was still a tightness in his chest and his heart was beating out of control. He felt a familiar evil presence as his awareness expanded to an inter-dimensional level. The pain in his chest grew stronger.

Luke stood up and saw the source of the squeezing sensation. The creature was on his back, just like the monkey demon victims at the hippie fair. The scene was terrifying, but Luke felt a powerful confidence. The creature gripped into Luke's chest tighter; it's long fingers buried into his chest. Luke stared at the leathery bat-faced creature. He was disgusted by this thing that had taken hold of his life.

Luke became angry. The creature squeezed tighter. *You nasty little fucker!* He grabbed it's wrist and pulled the hands away from his chest. Luke swung the creature around and grabbed it by the throat and ran to the bedroom. He threw the creature under the bed, "Stay!" he commanded. Luke looked like a maniac.

There was another nasty creature on Zuri's back. She sat in fear while Luke glared at the creature in attack position. He made a dive for the demon. Zuri screamed. Luke ripped the demon off of her and threw it under the bed as well. He grabbed Zuri's hand and ran from the hotel with her.

They ran down the stairs. The LSD had kicked in hard for both of them. They made it to the sidewalk in front of a corner store. There was the screeching sound of a Tri-Met bus stopping for them. "Let's get on! It's trying to rescue us."

Luke lead the way as the doors opened. They were the only ones getting on; a couple people were getting off from the other end of the bus. "Money," said Luke, "Christ, we have to give these people money." Emotionless faces watched Luke and Zuri. The driver started driving while Luke fumbled around with his wallet. He didn't know what was which. The money had already turned into a meaningless mess of paper. There was too much pressure; he picked out a random bill and shoved it into the machine. They received their tickets. The machine didn't give change, so he would never know how much he gave it.

They found a secluded spot towards the back. "Did that really happen? Up in the hotel room? Did you see what happened?" said Luke. Zuri nodded. They escaped the terrible creatures. Luke could breathe easy. The monkey demon wasn't there to squeeze his heart and soul. "We're free!" he yelled. Some people glanced his way, but Luke didn't care. He hugged Zuri and kissed her on the cheek.

Zuri was happy. This was what they were after. They had re-connected with the source; with the universe; with each other.

Twenty minutes went by. Luke and Zuri laughed at the passing images. It didn't matter where they were going. A skinny guy with a nasty vibration sat in front of them. Luke and Zuri knew he had been drinking and doing drugs.

The person turned around to face them, "What are you guys doing? You're not from around here are you?" Neither Luke or Zuri had a chance to answer. "Do you want some tequila? I have some Patron." He showed them the bottle. "How about drugs?"

"You're insane! We don't want that. Especially not here," said Luke.

"Oh, okay. You don't like drugs either? What kind of drugs do you like? Where are you from?" His attention was only on Luke.

"Montana," Luke replied.

"I knew it. I knew it! I could tell you were different. You *are* different! Where are you going right now? I'm going to Dicks. What do you know about Dick's? Do you want to go to Dick's with me? How about the drugs?"

"I don't want anything to do with any of what you just said," said Luke. Zuri was trying not to laugh. It was too much to handle on an acid trip.

"You're telling me you don't like drugs? C'mon, I know you like drugs. What drugs do you like?"

"I'm not telling," said Luke.

"Oh, fine then. You know what? You *know* what? Here in Portland we do meth. What do you think of that, huh?" He said the 'M' word way too loud. People were watching now. "Do you want to go to Dick's with me and do some *meth*? What do you think of that?"

"I think you're a fuckin slave! That's what I think." Zuri started laughing. People were concerned. The crazy guy gave Zuri a nasty look.

"Hey look," said Zuri, "It's Dick's," she pointed at the sporting goods store. The bus stopped. The crazy guy tucked his bottle away and walked off.

"Dick's…" Luke repeated, "What the shit?"

"I don't know, but that guy wanted your dick."

~~~

"Train! Let's get off here," said Luke. The bus came to a stop on an overpass above a freeway. They were at a busy bus stop with stairs leading down to the train platform.

The whole place was magical; all the personalities. There were lots of black people wearing dew rags and talking loud. "This is like some gangland shit," Luke whispered to Zuri as he lit a cigarette.

"Soda! I got some ice cold soda! One dolla," said an old black man with a cooler.

"Oh my god, yes. We want soda!" Luke looked at Zuri, "Should we accept a drink from this man?" Zuri shrugged. Luke pulled out his wallet and tried to decipher the bills. "This shit is evil. Ugly meaningless garbage." He finally picked out two bills and handed them to Zuri, "Are these okay? Or is that too much?"

"It looks good to me," she handed the bills to the man, who opened the cooler in return. Luke picked a Hawaiian Punch and Zuri picked Mountain Dew.

Luke admired the can while smoking his cigarette. He felt a nasty presence behind him. There were two cops. They walked past in a hurry. "What a terrible job," said Luke, "They're probably going to try and capture a human right now. Ignorant slaves of the American Fear Machine."

They made it down to the platform and found the ticket machine to be difficult. Luke and Zuri could sense every situation that was happening around them. They eavesdropped on everyone; even people they couldn't hear. The
~~~

visible language was impossible to ignore. Zuri would laugh, then Luke would laugh because he knew what she was laughing about. Everyone else was oblivious.

They got on the train without knowing where they were going. As the train ventured on, the buildings grew bigger. Luke's emotions fluttered as he remembered some of the scenes from his childhood. *If only I could have known that one day I would see these places from this perspective.* "Things are changing," he said as he stared out the window. "Everything is always changing. The impermanence of it all..." He looked at Zuri, "This can't last. Nothing lasts!"

"But nothing is lost," she said.

"Oh my god... you are beautiful. I'm sorry I don't tell you that enough."

"You're beautiful," she replied.

~~~

They made it to the Rose Garden and got off the train. This was a busy place; a place where many of the busses and trains intersected. They could go anywhere in Portland from here. They hopped on the next train they saw.

"Does that say *China Town?*" said Zuri.

"Oh snap, we're going to China Town! I've never been there before." The train coasted onto a bridge that headed over the river. The view was beautiful in it's complexity. "Look at what our species has created. The machinery..."

"Picture time," Zuri leaned on Luke and took a picture while he was gazing out the window.

A short time later they arrived at another platform surrounded by old brick buildings. "I think we're in China Town," he said.

They made it off the train and headed off in a random direction. Both of them lit cigarettes. They walked past a fountain where a group of people were speaking Chinese. Street signs were subtitled in Chinese. "This is the real shit," said Luke, "we're not in Kansas anymore."

"Are we even supposed to be here? White people... in China Town," she said.

"Well, I guess we're still in America. We are Americans, aren't we? Hey look! A Chinese restaurant."

"I don't want to go in there, at least not yet."

"Me either. Food would be frightening. They probably don't speak our language anyway. We would have to telecommunicate."

They found a place to sit. Luke read a Chinese newspaper, "I'm keeping this, this is beautiful! It's starting to look familiar. I'm pretty sure this is the language we write with after we die. The universal language... or something close to it. Much closer than uptight bullshit English. English makes *no* sense, and it makes
~~~

us stupid. Why do you think Chinese people are so smart? Why do you think they can understand such abstract things so well? Chinese is deep shit. English is shallow." He set the paper down and hugged Zuri tight with his cheek pressed against hers. "I love you."

"I love you, too. I wish it could stay this way," she said.

"I believe we can naturally attain this state of being. We can probably achieve even better than this. Jesus did it, and he said we could too. I believe that LSD gives us a temporary window to see what we need to strive for. Like a reference point.

"Imagine if everyone was like this. There would be no greed; no violence. There would be understanding and proper communication. That's one of the biggest problems with humans on this planet; we don't know how to communicate. What do you think?"

"I think you're crazy, but I like it," she kissed him.

The psychedelic romance went on. It was a time for healing. Even just kissing was more intimate than some of the sex they had. Luke decided to see if he could operate the GPS on his phone. The images came in full detail on Google Maps. He zoomed in on China Town. One magical place on the map caught his attention. "Look at this. It's a Chinese garden. We have to find it!"

"Nice. Lead the way," she said.

They walked for twenty minutes, enjoying all the scenes. The Chinese theme was perfect for the LSD trip. They stopped to appreciate a piece of artwork. A group of Asian people approached them. One elderly man was being pushed in a wheel chair. "Do you know how to get to the Chinese garden?" said one of the Asians.

"Dude, that is exactly what I'm looking for! Check it out," Luke handed him the phone and pointed, "this is us, and that's the garden."

"Oh, thank you."

"Thank you, and bless your souls!" The Asians left. Luke and Zuri lit a cigarette and headed in another direction; a scenic route that would also lead to the garden.

They made it to the garden, but could not see inside. The place was surrounded by high walls and was built of traditional Chinese architecture. There was a lady in a booth at the entrance who looked ready to take their money. They would have to endure another transaction.

"Hello, how do we get inside the garden?" said Luke.

"Oh…" the lady looked down at a clipboard, "You not on the list?"

"The list?"

"Name?"

"I don't think I'm on any list. Is that the only way we can get inside?"

"Yes. You need reservation."

"I have money. How much does it cost?"

"No, sorry. This is reserved for today." She handed him a brochure of business hours and reservation policy.

"Thanks." They walked around the garden to try and at least get a peek through the wall. There was a section of wall they could see through, but most of the garden was bordered with vegetation. What they saw was beautiful. There was water and birds and Chinese people.

Zuri took another picture with Luke. "We need to come back here someday," she said.

"I agree. How about Chinese food? Maybe they will be more welcoming. Are you prepared for that?"

"Sure."

~~~

They left China town a couple hours after eating. Someone had warned them that China Town was not safe at night, so they took the train to downtown Portland and continued their aimless adventure. There was an array of water fountains by the river. There were like mini geysers that shot into the air.

Luke began to drink from the fountains. Zuri stepped on a fountain to watch another one get bigger.

"You're gonna start glowing if you keep drinking that," said a passerby.

"Glowing? Am I glowing?" said Luke. It was getting dark. He looked at his hands to see if they were glowing.

The man pointed at a sign. "It's contaminated. It's like radiated shit water from the treatment plant. "You're not even supposed to give it to your dogs."

"Gross," said Zuri.

"That's shitty," said Luke, "maybe it will strengthen my immune system."

"Right. I doubt that. We should get out of here. Don't the busses stop running soon?"

"Oh, yeah. They probably do." Luke set his phone to lead them back to the hotel.

They road the train until he needed to switch to a bus. Luke didn't like the idea of going back to the hotel. In his mind, the place was tainted with evil. Zuri felt this too, but she also felt strong. The spiritual afterglow was still bright.

"You're not doing anything when we get back, right?" she said.

"Of course not. I'm throwing all of that nasty shit away; all of the needles
~~~

and spoons at least."

"I don't want you to touch it or even look at it. We're going to the bed as soon as we get there. Then you're going to make love to me," she said.

"That sounds wonderful."

~~~

"Ooh, it says we're two minutes away." They made it to their stop and got off. A few more minutes and they were at the hotel.

It was quiet as they approached. They went up the stairs and found the door was still unlocked. "This place is scary," said Luke. He went towards the bathroom.

"Don't do it," said Zuri.

"I'm just gonna take a leak."

"Hurry please."

Luke walked into the bathroom. He stopped for a moment and stared at the ugly mess. There was a rush of emotion, then a sound. The hideous creature leaped onto his back, and before Luke could do anything, the long fingers were sunken deep into his chest.

Luke lost control of his motor functions, the monkey demon took over. The fingers inside Luke's chest caused him pain and forced him to move. Luke didn't have the will to fight. His hands automatically sprinkled MDPV in the spoon. He squirted water, drew it back, and shot it up. The monkey demon was here to stay.
~~~

Failure is simply the opportunity to begin again, this time more intelligently.
-Henry Ford

Chapter 35: Junkmonkey

Saturday 7-26-2011

Luke woke up in Blue's apartments after 16 hours of sleep. He was on the couch with Zuri still sleeping on top of him. The drive back to MT had been terrifying. Because of Blue, they avoided another visit to the hospital. Blue convinced them to come to his place, then he forced them to sleep.

Luke and Zuri had tried desperately to replace PV with coke, meth, and molly. It didn't work. They wound up doing all that and combining PV on top of it, which resulted in severe psychotic delusions. They were convinced that parasites were living in their bloodstreams. The bugs crawled through their veins. Luke tried to guide the direction of the bugs to keep them away from his heart. One of the bugs made it to Luke's brain, giving him a placebo stroke. They both saw the bugs and were certain that it was real. Luke was so sure that he actually *felt* the stroke, and acted it out accordingly. If it weren't for Zuri, Luke would have cut his veins out. There was plenty of crying, screaming, and reckless driving. Even some violent fits of rage on Luke's part.

They were an hour away from Kalispell when Luke called Blue. He explained the bugs and the stroke. He told Blue that he was going to die. Blue explained that the bugs were fake and told Luke to stay away from the hospital. He knew that Luke's car was full of illegal drugs and possibly guns.

Zuri woke up, and was happy to find Luke was still beneath her. Their minds were clear, which came as a surprise. It was such a contrast compared to the psychotic state they were in before going to sleep.

"Hey crazy kids, have a good nap? I made you some breakfast." It was Blue, and he was carrying three syringes that were loaded with PV.

"Awesome." Luke got up, grabbed a syringe and gave one to Zuri. Blue's shots were always thick; too thick for Luke. He injected 20 units out of the 30. His depleted receptors rejoiced.

"Thanks for keepin us out of trouble," said Luke.

"You're my little cousin… I gotta keep you in check," said Blue.

"Man, those fuckin bugs… I still think they were real. It's a miracle we survived."

"Naw bro. Tweaker bugs. Completely fake. I had the same shit from some real dirty dope back in Oregon. You guys need food. Want me to make somethin?"

"Umm… sure. I could do mac and cheese. And one of those breakfast drinks," said Luke.

"Me too," said Zuri. Blue went to the kitchen. Zuri got up and pulled out her smokes. "Want to come smoke with me?"

"Sure," said Luke. They went out the back door and sat on the porch to share a cig.

A few minutes went by in silence. It was noon and the sun was shining bright. "I'm sorry about everything."

"It's okay," she knew he was talking about the drive to Montana.

"I'didn't mean for things to go so horrible. Everything was so fucked up, I just lost control."

"I forgive you. Okay?" She put her arm around him.

"Kay," he said.

They finished the cigarette, "I think we should smoke some weed, because I'm not hungry at all," she said.

"Yeah. Me either." They went in and loaded a bowl. Blue sat with them and listened to them talk about the trip. They told of the Fair, the parties, and the transient they adopted for a week.

"What happened to Nick and Stacy? They fuckin hate each other now," said Blue. Zuri went on to explain how that happened; how it was such a terrible idea in the first place.

After an hour it was time for Luke to leave. His phone was exploding with messages. He was almost broke. He needed to check on his own house, which

Dave and Jared had been looking over. They each took another dose of PV before leaving. Luke only finished the 10 units he had left in the syringe from earlier. He wasn't giving up on quitting, even if they had failed their mission to leave Oregon PV free.

~~~

Luke and Zuri met with Tim in a church parking lot at 5pm. They hadn't been home yet. Luke wanted to get these deals done with first. His parents didn't even know he was back yet.

Tim got into the back of the Cadillac, "Hey guys, how was your trip?"

"It was weird," said Luke. He noticed Tim was looking skinnier and had an angry vibe about him.

"Can I get three grams of the fifty-fifty for this? I only got a hundred."

"Only a hundred? What happened?"

"Piece of shit thieves is what happened. I keep getting jacked. I can't trust anybody," said Tim.

"Hmm, sure I'll do it. You sure you're not just losin shit like always?"

"Yeah, I'm sure." Tim went on to explain and justify all of his suspicions while Luke weighed out 3 grams. Tim gave the hundred to Luke. Luke handed it to Zuri.

"Hey, what is this?" said Zuri. She unfolded the bill and showed it to Tim.

Tim looked close and acted surprised. "What the fuck? Somebody just gave me that. Piece of shit, I got ripped off again!"

Zuri handed the fake bill back to Tim. Luke put the drug supplies away. Tim tried to defend himself, "Hey, I swear I didn't know! Can't you front me some? I'm all out. You have no idea how bad my luck has been lately."

"Naw dude. I don't even feel right about selling the shit anymore. It's fuckin evil. A real friend would not give you that shit, no matter how much you were willing to pay."

"Please bro, I just need to make some money. My mom needs help paying rent."

"Fuck that. I'll tell you what I will give you," Luke handed Tim an 8 strip of blotter LSD wrapped in foil. "Eat half of that at once. Please just don't sell it to anyone. If your mom needs money for rent, tell her to call me. Me and you need help, and this is the closest thing to a cure I've found so far. I gotta go, dude."

~~~

"Where are we going? I thought we were going home," said Zuri.

"I need to see Dan," said Luke.

"For what? Shouldn't we at least go home first? You don't need anything right now anyway."

"I don't want to have to drive back to Kalispell. It's not about getting shit. He's my homey and I need to see him. So, unless you wanna go home and hang out with Dave and Jared, you can come with me," said Luke.

They arrived at Dan and Erica's. Dan opened the door, "Hey bro. How ya been?"

"Eh."

"C'mon in." Luke and Zuri walked in. Erica greeted Zuri with a hug and asked how the trip went. They stayed in the living room while Luke and Dan sat in the kitchen.

"You bring any bud?" said Dan.

"Sure did." Luke gave Dan a quarter ounce; the usual order. Luke had met with Shawn a few hours prior.

"So… how was your mission? Did you quit yet?" Dan said as he loaded a glass bubbler.

"Naw man. I came close a couple times…" Luke went on to explain the whole trip from the beginning. He explained what happened with Nick and Stacy; he explained the house parties; the hippie fest; Vince, the transient. Last of all, he explained the demon. "This might sound crazy dude, but I seriously think I might be possessed by a demon."

Dan opened his laptop. "You probably are, bro. And I don't think LSD is gonna be able to cure you. I've been thinkin about you a lot lately. I did some research and found that LSD has only been proven to cure alcoholism. Even with that, only forty-five per cent of patients treated with LSD improved.

"Now, look here. They've been using DMT for physical, emotional, and spiritual healing. It's the orally active DMT that shows results, more so than smoking or IV doses. There's even clinics in some countries that use this kind of treatment. Rich people go to these places to get off drugs and cure cancer and shit. When you combine MAOI's with DMT it becomes orally active and lasts much longer. If there's any way you're gonna conquer your demon, this is it."

"How do we get it?" said Luke.

"Well, I can make the DMT. It sketches me out because I like to keep this operation perfectly legal. Strictly research chemicals here." Luke was discouraged. "But, if it does somehow get made, you're taking all of it with you. I won't have it in my house."

"Good, because all my friends are slaves. Everyone needs healing," said Luke.

"Everyone definitely needs healing. There's some new info on PV by the way." Dan pulled up a wikipedia page, "Look at this. It says that MDPV permanently mutates your DNA. That's your genetics, bro."

"That's crazy. Does that mean this stuff could start the zombie apocalypse? Because I've suspected that before," said Luke.

"Are you planning on having kids someday? Because what you're doing now is gonna effect how they turn out. Your genes are getting fucked up. *They* inherit your genetics."

"Jesus, dude. That's horrible," said Luke.

"Yeah bro, the shit is evil. Speaking of that, I have the recipe to make it now. Got the CD from our manufacturer in China. So when the stuff finally becomes illegal, you can keep it pushin. There's also another drug coming out. It's called a-PV, and it's supposed to be like MDPV except the neurotoxicity is much lower. I should be getting a sample soon.

"I know you're making a lot of money with the shit and you're selling most of it to tweakers anyway, but I don't feel good about promoting it anymore. Especially after seeing the ingredients. I checked out the recipe and it is some *nasty* shit. Worse than any of the dirty crank I used to make."

"I'm starting to feel the same way," said Luke.

"I mean, I'll keep helping you make your money. You help me make my living, so it's only fair. Besides, if you don't make that money, someone else will. What bothers me is watching you hurt yourself with the stuff. You're one of my best homies. I care about you, bro."

Zuri and Erica came in the room, "Are you even gonna offer to share?" Erica took the bubbler, "I put the kids to bed by the way."

"Right on," said Dan.

Erica took a hit and handed the bubbler to Zuri. After she smoked she asked Dan how he was. Dan went on to describe an outdoor rave by Missoula. It was the Alien Abduction rave and Dan had been one of the DJ's there.

"That's sweet, I wish I could have seen," she said.

"It was sick. You missed out. I got Facebook now. DJ Junkmonkey. I'm gonna be doin a lot more shows now."

Luke took the bubbler, "That's tight, man. I won't miss it next time."

Nobody can go back and start a new beginning, but, anyone can start today and make a new ending.
-Maria Robinson

Chapter 36: Bear Creek

Friday 8-15-2011

Luke was riding his motor scooter when he got a text from Dan. The cellphone was velcroed to his dash, right below the speedometer. He read the message and made an immediate U-turn. The message was urgent. Music continued to play under Luke's helmet as he sped off toward Dan's.

During the past couple weeks Luke had digressed back to his greedy state of being. Money controlled him. It made him run from this place to that. He even sacrificed his health for money, then spent money in attempt to restore his health. The LSD was gone. He sold most of it and gave some away. Him or Zuri hadn't done any since Oregon, and it showed in their relationship.

Zuri was miserable and would hardly leave the house. She wanted Luke, but he was always gone. She hardly existed to him. His money and chemicals were all he cared for. She wanted him to stop. She wanted to disappear into the wilderness with him; away from money and away from PV. Luke justified his actions, and argued them to be logical and reasonable.

The house was empty besides Zuri. She made Dave and Jared leave. Much of Luke's time was spent with Dave. And Dave was now living with Debora. A romance had blossomed between them. Luke didn't spend much time with anybody but them or Dan. Everyone else was just a dollar sign. The people who did hang out with Luke had their own selfish reasons for that. He was no longer the psychedelic inspiration that people used to gravitate towards.

~~~

Luke arrived at Dan's. It was 6pm. He walked through the front door wearing his helmet and backpack. Dubstep music was playing loud. Dan was creating the music with all his gadgets. Luke sat on the couch next to him.

The song ended and Dan turned off the equipment. "What'd you think of that? I got this new program..." Dan described it while Luke tried to understand.

"*This* is for you," said Dan, "and so is this." One package was a brown paper bag, the other was a USPS package.

"What's this?" Luke knew the USPS was his MDPV, but the paper bag...

"It's your medicine; your spiritual tools. Don't open it now, all the instructions are inside."

"Oh wow," Luke held the bag as a holy artifact.

"My shaman buddy blessed it and everything. You remember Rikki? He wrote the instructions and found the Harmala alkaloids; the MAOI stuff."

"Aw, dude... I love you!" said Luke.

"Right? Did you need any methylone? I'm kinda anxious to get that stuff out of my house."

"Oh, yeah sure. Ten grams is good." Luke put the paper bag in the suitcase safe in his backpack. Then he counted out $850 and gave it to Dan. "What do I owe you for the medicine?"

"Nothing, of course. It's a gift from me and Rikki to you." Dan gave Luke the ten gram bag of methylone. "There's also a map in that bag. Rikki had a special place in mind. Said the place is full of protective spirits and all that."

"Thanks man. I'm gonna go now. The next time you'll see me I'll be cured."

"I hope so, buddy. Happy trails."

~~~

The orally active DMT was prepared the next day. This was more like 'pharmauasca' rather than the traditional ayahuasca brew. Luke combined the synthetic DMT with the harmala alkaloids to create an imitation of the ancient medicine. The result was a generous amount of nasty brown pellets. Everything was measured to ensure the proper dosage. Each mixture was measured and prepared as instructed.

Luke had hoped to bring some friends with. So far, no one wanted to come.

"Kay, I'm gonna try calling Tim," said Luke.

"I don't see the point," said Zuri, "he sold the acid you gave him to buy PV. Tim doesn't want to change."

The phone rang, "Hello?"

"Tim, dude. I have the cure."

"What are you talking about?" said Tim.

"We're going on a quest. You want to get better, don't you?"

"I don't want to talk to you unless you're gonna hook me up with some shit. You owe me. I've made so much money for you and you just treat me like shit. I can just start buying my own shit. I'll get it online so I'll never have to talk to you again. Then I'll be the one who gets rich."

"Take it dude, I don't want it anymore. Do whatever makes you happy. Just know that you're a fuckin slave! I'm sorry for dragging you and everyone else into this, but I'm trying to get better. And I won't give up until I heal everyone I've ruined."

"Whatever man. Talk to me when you're not so greedy." Tim hung up.

"This sucks," said Luke, "no one wants to go. Nobody wants salvation. Maybe we should wait until we can gather a good tribe of people to go to Bear Creek. Sooner or later people will want to change, right?"

"Who gives a shit? Let's just go," said Zuri. "If people don't want to change then screw em. We *need* to change. If we don't go now, we'll never go." Luke tried to think of another excuse. "I'm loading the car now. We're doing this," she said.

"Okay then," said Luke. Zuri was already grabbing all their food and throwing it into bags. Luke went to the bedroom and picked up his sunglass case. He went to the bathroom to avoid detection.

"Luke, don’t," Zuri said as she tried to open the door.

"Don't what?"

"Don't do that! You just did some. I don't want you to go crazy."

"Shhh!"

"Luke!"

"Hey, this is the last day I'll ever get to do this stuff. Don't tell me how much I get to do," he said.

"What about fasting? I thought we weren't supposed to eat or do any drugs before DMT."

"We can fast when we get there."

Zuri went back to packing. They were going on this quest no matter how crazy he got. She would inject him with Xanex if she had to.

~~~

The last of the loading was done. Zuri had done it all while Luke walked circles and attempted to re-organize things around the house. The truck was having problems so everything was loaded into Zuri's Oldsmobile. Luke would never undertake such treacherous trails in the Cadillac.

They were going to a place called Bear Creek. It was halfway between Big Fork and Missoula in the middle of nowhere. The handwritten map showed that the car wouldn't make it all the way to their destination. Once they turn off the highway, there would be 20 miles of dirt road. They would walk another mile to their destination. It was supposed to be a magical place.

Zuri walked back into the house, "C'mon Luke. Everything is ready."

"Aw fuckin shit." Luke was pacing back and fourth while texting.

"Let's go," she said.

"Kay. Five minutes," he said.

"Now, Luke. We don't need anything else."

"I just gotta grab some things," he hurried off to the bedroom. Zuri lit a cigarette. Ten minutes later Luke came out with the suitcase safe.

"No, Luke! We don't need that crap," she said.

"I can't have it get stolen. This is our livelihood."

"Whatever. Let's just go. Are you bringing a gun or anything?" she said.

"Nope. No guns. We're goin primal. Rambo knife and loin cloth."

"There's a lot of bears and mountain lions out there. Real ones," she said.

"I don't care. I'm leaving it in the hands of God. If it wants us to live, we'll live."

"Good. I'd rather get eaten than keep doing what we're doing anyway." They got in the Oldsmobile after locking the house. "Hopefully my car makes it there."

"Yeah. We gotta meet with some people at Walmart before we head out."

"Kay. They better be quick. Cause I'd like to get our spot set up before dark." She reversed out of the driveway. Luke started messing with the sunglass case. "What are you doing?" she said.

"Takin a hit. You want one?" he said.

She hesitated, "Sure."

~~~

"I think we're getting close," said Luke. "It says the road gets really bad after this rocky stretch."

"This must be it." The road ended. A rock slide had covered the road. No vehicle could have journeyed beyond this obstacle. The road was narrow and there was no place to park, so she just stopped the car where the road ended.

"Cool. It looks like we'll be all alone for our spirit quest. I can't see many people trying to hike past this."

Zuri popped the trunk and got out of the car. She grabbed the large bag of food, "Ugh, you can carry that. Luke c'mon. I want to get there before dark. What are you doing?" Luke was still in the passenger seat preparing a solution of PV. "This is ridiculous. Don't you even want to stop?"

"Of course I do. This is the last one ever." Luke went on to take his final dose. Zuri took one as well. They were large doses.

They grabbed the supplies with some fear and anxiety. The beautiful wilderness became frightening in a matter of seconds. The PV caused severe chest pain. Luke feared he had done too much. *Please don't die, please don't die,* he thought, *Not when I'm so close to being healed.*

Zuri tried to comfort him. It took fifteen minutes to get over the attack. "C'mon babe, let's go," she said. They started to leave, but at the last second Luke grabbed the suitcase.

"Luke, please don't bring that. We'll never stop getting high with that around. We should leave all the drugs behind except for the DMT. How much DMT did you bring anyway?"

"I brought enough for us. Most of it is still stashed in the house. I'm bringing everything. There's like twenty grand worth of shit in here. I can't risk getting it stolen."

"But what about the fast? I can just see us sitting out here doing PV for days. How will we do the DMT? I know how you are. You'll just keep doing PV until you go crazy or end up killing yourself," she said.

"We won't eat or do anymore drugs tonight. Then we eat the DMT first thing when we wake up."

Zuri grabbed Luke's hand and stopped walking. "Promise me," she said.

"I promise." She hugged him tight and buried her face in his chest. He dropped his luggage and hugged her back. At that moment Luke felt some terrible guilt. Why was he so weak and she so strong? "I love you," he said.

"I love you too. So much." She kissed him.

"I'm so sorry. I promise. I don't want to put you through this anymore. You deserve so much better." Luke almost cried. It was difficult to cry on MDPV.

"It's okay, Luke. Everything is going to get better."

~~~

The walking persisted for over an hour. " Are you sure we haven't passed it? That spot back there could have been it," said Zuri.
~~~

"No way. He said we would know when we've found it. He said it was going to be magical."

"Magical huh?" She stopped and sat on the suitcase-safe to light a cigarette.

"Good idea." Luke dropped the bags and laid down. He was sweaty and dehydrated.

The logging road was on the side of a mountain. The valley on their left had been getting bigger as they progressed. They also had been gaining in elevation. The valley was thick with forest, with the occasional grassy meadow. It was beautiful, undisturbed nature.

"Here you go," Zuri handed the cigarette to Luke. She pulled her journal out and began to make some notes.

"What are you writing about now?" he said.

"You."

"Me?"

"Kidding…kinda."

"What could you possibly be writing about?"

"Lots of things. Have you been writing anything in yours?" she said.

"No. It's hard for me. My mind just goes blank. It's impossible."

"Well, then you'll thank me someday."

"Will I ever be able to read any of it?"

"Maybe someday."

"Can you read me something from it?"

"Right now?" she said.

"Yeah. Please?"

"Okay, let's see…" she flipped back and glanced through the journal. "Oh, here we go. I think you'll like this one. Kay, this is from the 21st of July.

"*A homeless person just peeked through the window. I can't move. Luke is sleeping on me. He's in the most uncomfortable position I've ever seen. I don't feel bad for him. He's the one who insists that we sleep in the car. It's almost 4. We're parked in some scary street in downtown Portland. I can't sleep. These homeless people can't seem to sleep either.*

"Kay, I'd better stop," she said.

"Why."

"It gets depressing," she said.

"Keep going. I can handle it."

"Uh-uh."

"Please?"

"Fine. *I don't want to move. I'm scared to wake up Luke. He needs sleep really bad. He had another freak-out earlier. It scares me so bad. I don't know how many more times he can survive it. Each time seems like it's going to be the last. I love him so much and I'm afraid he's going to die. I know he wants to get better, but everyday he forgets and then it happens again."*

She couldn't hold the tears back. "Sweet heart, come here." Luke sat up and held her.

They laid down for some time, holding hands and staring into the sky. The temperature began to drop as the evening progressed. "We'd better get going," said Zuri.

"Yeah? How long do you think we should stay out here in the wilderness?"

"Forever," she said.

"Forever?"

"I would rather stay forever than go back to Dave and all of your infinitely demanding junky friends."

"I see... we are all just a bunch of slaves, aren't we? We run a million miles an hour in every direction and never get anywhere."

"Yep. It's so stupid." Zuri got up and tugged on Luke's hand. They strapped on their luggage and headed off.

The view became blocked by the trees as the road turned away from the cliff. They trekked on uphill for a 15 minute stretch before finding a turnoff. "Maybe this is it," said Luke.

The took the trail and found the cliff a moment later. There was a perfect clearing that protruded like a balcony from the cliff. A long neglected fire pit was positioned at the center, with enough room for 3 or 4 tents to surround it. The sun had dipped below the mountains, giving off an otherworldly glow as they looked out into the canyon.

"Holy smokes," said Luke.

"I think we found it," said Zuri.

We don't receive wisdom;
we must discover it for ourselves after a journey that no one
can take for us or spare us.
-Marcel Proust

Chapter 37: The Hell Worlds

Sunday 8-17-2011

The night had been terrifying. Luke continued to re-dose throughout the night and suffered the usual fear and physical pain. He woke up and obeyed the habitual impulse to go for the safe.

"Stop it Luke!" Zuri was holding an uncapped syringe full of green liquid.

"What are you doing?" he said.

"I'm gonna stab you with this."

"What the fuck for? Just let me do a small one to wake up," he said.

"No. You need to eat that DMT stuff. It's what we came here for."

"Fine. Then I can do a shot?" he said.

"Yeah. I even made one up for you. It's twenty milligrams so you don't go crazy."

They each ate their dose of DMT/MAOI resin and washed it down with Ensure. Luke took his 20mg injection of MDPV but wanted more. As he put the paraphernalia away he managed to sneak a syringe and small baggie of MDPV, I'm going for a walk," he said.

"Why? Aren't we doing this together?" she said.

"Yeah, I'll just be a few minutes. I want to scope out our territory." Luke left the tent wearing only his Smurf boxers. He wanted to find a place to mix up a reasonable dose of MDPV. Since he didn't have water, he would have to find the stream. Luke followed the edge of the cliff as he left the clearing. Soon he reached a point where the cliff made itself into tiers. It made for a massive staircase which he could descend. His feet were sensitive and withered from the MDPV. With slow and careful progress he made it to the forest floor. He expected the DMT to reach its effect in an hour or two; similar to mescaline. Luke had seen a stream from the cliff. He headed in that direction as soon as he'd found a trail.

There was a feel of magic in this wilderness. The landscape reminded Luke of a *Lord of the Rings* movie. He couldn't appreciate much of this in his current state. His only focus was to find water so he could inject. He wanted to take the shot before the hallucinations began. It was so wrong, and he knew it. His behavior went against Dan and Rikkis instructions. No drugs were to be mixed with the medicine. He feared the reaction could be fatal. Luke was told that there would be spiritual entities that would give him gifts and healing if he were sincere. He was sincere. Luke wanted the healing more than anything, but the primitive mid-brain had taken complete control. It was mentally and physically impossible for him to resist the craving.

Luke began to hear the rapids. The trail was made by animals and he regretted his decision to go barefoot. Luke reached the stream and found it to be inaccessible. He stood at the ledge. The water was 30 feet out of reach. Luke's palms grew sweaty with fear and anxiety. The anticipated experience was something his primitive, chemically dependent mind would rather avoid. The thought of change was terrifying. As confusing as it may seem, Luke's mind, at the primitive level, was horrified at the prospect of being cured. Losing the craving would mean losing MDPV; and for so long, MDPV had done an excellent job of falsely satisfying all of Luke's basic human needs. Food, sex, shelter, purpose; all of it was meaningless unless there was MDPV. The drug had firmly planted itself at the top of his hierarchy of needs.

The treacherous hike went on for 20 minutes before reaching the level of the river. There was a rocky beach where the land leveled out. The rapids widened and slowed to the pace of a river. Luke made his way to the bank and squatted at the edge.

He felt something watching him. He held the supplies close to his chest as he looked around. There was nothing to be seen. He proceeded to fill the syringe with stagnant water. The plunger cap contained a piece of cotton and was caked with residue.

Luke jolted at the sound of laughter. It was nearly inaudible, but enough to frighten him to the core. He capped the syringe and proceeded along the stream, keeping watch in every direction. He stopped for a moment to listen. "Hello?" he said. No reply. *Fuckin paranoia.*

Luke walked for another 20 minutes. Each time he found a place, it felt unsafe. Finally he found a place where he had a clear view in all directions. He sat down to finish the preparation, not taking his eyes off the surroundings.

There were voices. Luke hucked the drugs into the river and stood up. "Hello?" There was no one. Luke watched his drug supplies float down the stream. *Son of a bitch!*

Luke turned back in the direction he had came, vexed by the let-down and wasted effort. A few minutes went by as a subtle vibration began to emanate from the foliage. There was an uneasy feeling in his stomach. He hurried on in hopes of reaching MDPV before the DMT rendered him incapable.

The vibrations became strong. There were intelligent beings, innocent beings. Luke was beginning to hear them with his mind. They were curious about Luke. They wondered what was wrong with him. Luke was entering a realm unlike anything he'd ever experienced. His sensory perceptions stretched to new limits. Parallel worlds were almost conceivable, just beyond his reach.

Luke made it to the beach where he had first attempted the injection. He sat down, nauseous and overwhelmed. There was fear, as he questioned whether he could handle the experience on his own.

The situation became even more otherworldly as a musical rhythm began to permeate Luke's reality. The tone became a distinctive melody of a flute. The sound was mystical and carried in an unusual way. It echoed and reverberated. Luke was reassured by the sound and decided to seek it out. An animal trail led away from the river. He followed it and the sound grew stronger. A deep overtone accompanied the flute melody. There was a sense of deja vu as he entered the long forgotten realm of the spirit world.

Luke found the source of the sound as he entered a small clearing in the forest. There was an ethereal being who stood at the center. The structure was unstable. The vibrational frequency shifted in and out of sync with Luke. He approached the being, who did not look up, but continued playing his bamboo flute. It was an old Asian man. He had a whispy fu-manchu and the appearance of a hermit.

The music stopped. Luke was mystified. "Are you real?" he finally asked.

"Of course I'm real. Everything is real. You may call me Tamanash." The being was becoming solid. Luke could see the detail in his leathery hands and face. The mans ribs were visible beneath the patched together robe he wore. The sandals on his dirty feet were evident of endless travel.

"What's happening?" Luke managed to say.

"Your friend Rikki provide the proper admixture to ensure I would be here. I will invoke helpful spirits, and drive away the ones with evil intent. I will facilitate the flow of energy during the ceremony. There will be suffering. This is unavoidable."

Unavoidable? "What are you? What's going to happen to me?" The man's expression was solemn, no longer concerned with Luke's fear and confusion. He turned away from Luke and sat in Lotus pose.

There was another presence. This one felt friendly, almost familiar. She approached. Luke recognized her features and dress to be Middle Eastern.

"My name is Yasmin. I am your spirit guide. There is much to explain. You are wondering if this is a hallucination. It is not. The medicine you have ingested has helped you to change the channel. Our dimension is of a higher frequency. From our perspective, we can see much more easily into your dimension than you can see into ours. But do not worry, you are just like us. The only difference is that you chose to incarnate into the human dimension."

She sensed Luke's questions. "It is okay for you not to understand. You knew that you would undergo a form of spiritual amnesia as you entered the human dimension. The confusion is only temporary. Your spiritual memory still exists, and remembers every detail of your existence.

"I am like you. You chose to come to this planet. You chose to incarnate into the human dimension. I chose to stay behind and be your spirit guide. It is not easy, because I experience your troubles as well. But you are the brave one; you chose to incarnate into the human dimension on this dark planet. I lived one life on this planet. This is number two for you."

"I've lived two lives?"

"You have lived many lives. You are what we call a mystic traveller entity. You have lived on many planets in many different galaxies. Your lives are not forgotten. Nothing is forgotten. You only suffer amnesia as you incarnate into this human dimension.

"Other planets are much easier. This one is the worst. It is the final testing ground for many entities who strive to perfect their soul. This is an exception for the dark entities. There are more on this planet than any other. They live for this world; to reincarnate over an over."

"What about God and Jesus? Where does that fit into any of this? Are you telling me that bad people just reincarnate over and over? What about hell?"

"God the Father is the uncreated; the Nirvana. We are all sparks of God with the purpose of experiencing these worlds. God the Father is the mind of the Universes.

"Jesus is a messenger entity. He came to represent God the Mother. She is the one who performs miracles. She has the power to interfere. Jesus came from the planet Nuvo. His kind can be many places at once. This is how you can pray to him for guidance.

"The Holy Spirit is an energy. Its radiance can descend from God and surround a person. We can see it as a white light around people who embrace it. Dark entities cannot have this, nor would they want it."

"Alright, why did I end up this way, then. If you're my spirit guide, then how could you let me go so far into the addiction. You say that I chose to come here, how can any of this help perfect my soul. I feel damaged. My soul is tainted."

"It is not the addiction that perfects the soul; overcoming the addiction is what gives you spiritual growth. Overcoming any affliction gives you spiritual growth. We did not recommend you to subject yourself to this. Many of us objected when we were writing your life chart, but you were convinced you could complete it. It was very risky, because if you had died it would have been like suicide. You would have been immediately reincarnated and forced to live through similar tribulations."

"What's a life chart? Does that mean that everything I do is pre-destined?"

"A life chart is not exact. You have most of the say in it, but a council will help you decide if what you have charted is feasible. In my world everything feels possible. It is easy to over commit yourself.

"You chose the theme of an experiencer and a catalyst. You came to precipitate a change in the world. You will teach natural medicine and follow the shamanic path. You will promote the Ayhauasca and teach of the African Iboga. You chose to uncover these ancient medicines and bring them into the popular culture. The world will soon come to accept these medicines as cures for mental and physical illness. This will lead the human race on this planet to once again live in harmony with the natural world, sharing it's resources in a way that is not harmful."

"Holy smokes... this is huge! I'm just one person. I'm only nineteen! How can I make any impact? I don't even know anything about that African whatever stuff you said."

"You will learn of the African Iboga. You will learn of other medicine.

Natural medicine is your passion. This is why you incarnate into family that supports these things. You will learn much more in time. These things will become more clear as events in your life fall into place."

Luke's reality was becoming unstable. "What's happening? Everything's getting all staticky."

"The channel is changing. There are some things you must see. It may be unpleasant, but it is all a part of the healing process."

The last of her words were fuzzy. Then his reality disintegrated. All of the forest faded away. The ground became barren and cracked. Everything darkened, even the sky turned into a bizarre electrical storm. There was nothing except for empty beer cans and syringes scattered across the wasteland. The land remained flat for as far as the eye could see.

The scene was vivid as could be. Luke was sober, no longer feeling the effects of the DMT. It was more real than the most believable of dreams. Luke felt a terrifying sense of desolation. He grabbed one of the syringes and poked himself in the hand. The pain caused him to flinch. A bead of blood formed on his hand. The syringe looked aged with the numbers scratched off. *What the hell is this place?* He threw the syringe to the side and looked around. *It's not real. It can't be real.* Next, he examined one of the beer cans. It was old, empty, faded in color, worthless. The feeling was hideous. He threw the can to the side and allowed his mind to wander.

The cravings began. Luke started exploring. He examined every syringe that appeared to show promise. The initial fear of this place was replaced by the obsession over the needles. Each empty syringe created pain and frustration which added to the craving.

Luke became insane; expecting each syringe to provide something that would satisfy him. He paid no attention to how far he traveled. There was no way to judge time. He could have been there for years. Time became an endless illusion.

Luke snapped out of his obsessive trance when he approached a being. "Hey!" Luke started running. The person was squatting with his back facing Luke. "Hey, can you hear me?"

The person did not respond. Luke stopped when he noticed the ragged clothes and leathery grey skin. The dead looking creature turned around. He had a hand full of syringes. "Have you seen my soul?" he whispered.

Luke tried to run away, but running was difficult. His joints were stiff and his muscles felt weak. He stopped once he could no longer see the zombie. His body felt old. He looked down at his deteriorated body. "Ahh!" He screamed when he realized he was dead. His body had decayed.

Luke fell to the ground as he looked at his withered grey hands. He tried to escape into his mind. Memories of his life were too faint to imagine. All he had was *this*.

The silence was broken by the crackling of beer cans. Luke looked up and saw more of the dead people wandering in the wasteland. In the distance was a house. It was Luke's house! He ran for it. This time he could run.

He approached the house. It sat all alone, looking even more rundown than usual in the darkness of the wasteland. He walked up the steps and through the door. The kitchen was intact. Everything was the way it had been when he lived there. "Hello? Is anybody here?" No reply.

The bedroom was in perfect shape the way he had left it. Out the window he saw the alley just as it was meant to be in Columbia Falls. For all he could tell, it was a normal day in the normal life of Luke. Though he couldn't shake the sense that this was all an illusion; a scene right out of the matrix.

There was the closet. The light was off and the door was cracked. Luke felt a stir of emotions. He went for the closet and turned the light on. A junkie kit was ready on the shelf. He locked the door and began the preparation.

The wasteland was forgotten. It was just a normal day in the closet; the same as so many others. His heart rate increased as the anticipation built up. This was the most satisfying dose he would ever take. There was nothing he wanted more.

The solution was ready. He licked the tip of the needle and tasted the MDPV. *Finally*. He lined the needle up to his vein.

KNOCK!KNOCK!KNOCK! His syringe flew and stuck into the floor. "Luke?" It was Zuri.

"Not now! Give me one second." He tried to straighten out the damaged needle.

"Open the door please," she said.

"Shut the hell up!" His hands were shaky as he attempted to inject. He stuck the dull needle into his arm. The door flew open and Zuri knocked the syringe to the floor. "Nooo!" He dove for it.

"Stop it Luke!" She tried to take it from him. He punched her and kicked her; tried to push her away. He struggled to hold her on the ground, but managed to jab the needle into his arm. It wasn't in the vein, but he depressed the plunger anyway to try and end the madness.

There was a bubble on his arm. Everything began to change. The house, Zuri, everything disappeared. He was rolling in the dirt with the empty syringes and beer cans. He was all alone with an old, useless, dirty syringe in his arm.

"Nooo!"

His flesh continued to rot. The tribulations continued in every hopeless, deceiving way possible.

The MDPV and needle obsession was the constant focal point of his death trips. During this time, Luke made no contact with his previous state of living. If there was a Hell, Luke had found it. And as far as he knew, there was no getting out.

~~~

Luke was pulled out of the hell-worlds by a fairy-like being. His perceptions sizzled into static as leaves and grass of the wilderness began to materialize. He could feel the fairy seal off the hell-world, keeping the twisted darkness from seeping into this magical world.

Luke stumbled, puked, and fell in front of Tamonash. The old Asian man began to pull a dark cloudy substance from Luke. Luke continued to convulse as he started foaming from his mouth. He puked a black tar-like substance.

Tamonash gathered the last of the black cloud between his hands and the vomiting stopped. The Asian man lowered his hands and released the energy into the earth.

Luke curled up and began to cry. Tamonash walked away and Yasmin approached. "I am sorry this had to happen to you. It is an unfortunate part of the healing process," she said. Luke didn't know what to think. Yasmin gave him time to gather himself.

"Where was I?" he managed to say.

"You went as far as the fourth level of the lower worlds. It is the repository of human creation. We are now in the first level of the lower worlds. This is the dimension of mystical creatures; an innocent fantasy world, but very real. We are close vibration to the human dimension, that is why it looks much the same. The first of the lower worlds is still a part of God's creation. Everything beyond is human's creation. The closer you get to the seventh lower level, the more demonic it becomes."

"What was that fairy thing that pulled me out of there?" he said.

"That was Lilith. She is the protector of the first level of the lower world. She also protects animals and children of the human dimension."

"Why did you send me there? Why did I have to go through that?"

"You would have gone there eventually on your own. It would have been in your dreams. It is a simple cause and effect; a Karmic balance. The medicine has allowed you to restore this balance quickly."

"But… oh my god…"
~~~

"No more. We must go," Yasmine held her hand out to Luke.

"Where?"

"The sixth level of the upper worlds," she said. Luke took her hand. The landscape sizzled to static and changed once again.

A glorious city emerged. The architecture was futuristic. It was full of beings but did not feel crowded. Luke felt light. He was sure this was not his human body. They started walking. "What is this place?" he said.

Yasmin spoke in a strange visible language, *This place is for teachers and researchers.*

"What's happening with Zuri?"

She has already been through here. She spent less time in the lower worlds. Do not worry about her. She has her own guides and will not be left out of their care.

Luke followed Yasmin into a building. He observed that they were among some very advanced technology. This was a place of science. Everything seemed to be clean and sterile. Much of the surfaces appeared to be made of light.

They walked into an operation room. It was full of doctors. They were friendly and greeted Luke in the same visible language. This was Luke's appointment. They wanted him to lay on the operating table. Luke did so.

The doctors used instruments on Luke. They communicated with each other and were curious about him. Luke could hear their thoughts and was pleased to know that they intended to do good.

His nerve endings must be toast... and look at this! Luke was amused by the doctor's human characteristics. He could feel things being erased and modified in his brain.

One of the doctors sensed his questions. *Don't worry. Your physical body will synchronize to the modifications. You will be feeling as good as new.*

Yasmin sensed his other question. *Tamonash is watching over your physical body. No one else will be able to inhabit it while you're gone.*

This was a relief. Luke had come to understand his physical body as a vehicle. It was like a car he left running while he ran in for the doctor visit. His fear had been that someone else would hop into that vehicle and drive off.

After the operation it was time to leave. Yasmin held her hand out for Luke. "Can't we stay here a while?" he said.

"No. There is still purpose for you in the human dimension. You cannot stay here."

"But I want to know more. What is this place, really? How come humans can't find it?"

"95% of the universe is what your physicists call 'dark matter.' They know it is there, but they do not know how to observe it. There are layers and layers;

dimensions within dimensions. This is one dimension. You cannot live here until you finish your life chart in the human dimension. For now we must go." Luke took her hand, and once again the channel began to change.

Everything materialized back into the wilderness by the river. Luke was in his body and could feel it synchronizing to his celestial body. There was tingling in his brain. He felt neurons grow and receptors multiply. A radiance descended upon Luke. It was an energy of pure love. He knew it was the Holy Spirit.

Luke stood up. He felt the interconnectedness of the universe. Everything was pulsing with energy. He felt perfect harmony.

Zuri, he thought. Luke headed for camp. He couldn't wait to share his experience.

Zuri was at the camp. "Luke!" she ran up to hug him. They both cried and knew what each other had gone through. Luke didn't need to explain, and neither did she.

"Everything is different now," he said.

"We're fixed," Zuri grabbed his hand. "Look at our mood rings. They're not black anymore."

~~~

They sat around the fire and enjoyed each other in their new condition. Their improvements remained even after the DMT/MAOI's had worn off.

The cravings did not return. Even the cigarettes lost their appeal, though Zuri decided to smoke them anyway. Luke decided it was just as satisfying to watch her smoke as it would have been to do it himself. He could feel what she was feeling if he wanted to, and if she allowed him to.

Luke felt more aware than he'd ever felt before. He felt the God presence in everything around him. There was also an overwhelming sense of empathy and connectedness with Zuri. They had developed a refined sense for non-verbal communication. Each of them felt understood.

Some time went by. The vibes began to change. "I feel a disturbance in the force," said Luke.

"Me too," said Zuri. The monkey demon was nearby. Luke went to the tent. "Don't go in there," she said.

"I have to. I'll be careful."

"Okay."

Luke came out with the suitcase and a buck knife. He was still barefoot and wearing only boxers. He opened the safe and started dumping the needles into the fire. Then he opened his organizers and started dumping the chemicals. The monkey demon was furious. Luke could feel him watching from the trees. Luke
~~~

continued to throw away all the baggies and vials until all there was left was the massive brick of MDPV.

He stabbed the brick with the knife. It worked on the demon like a voodoo doll. Luke stabbed it again and again as powder sprayed into the fire. He ripped the bag open and dumped it into the fire with the package. The monkey demon's form appeared in the smoke. The demon withered in agony. This was Luke's official way of shunning the evil spirit for good.

The morning came. Zuri had been up before Luke. She blew a cloud of marijuana smoke in his face. He stretched his legs and rubbed his eyes. "Good morning, love," she said.

Luke squinted as he looked out of the open tent flap. The view was vast and colorful. "Wow, good morning. Since when has it been so magical out there?"

"How do you feel?" she asked.

"Fine... holy smokes, I do feel fine!" he sat up.

"Isn't it great?"

"It's the greatest. This is amazing! I love you so much." He hugged her and kissed her on the cheek.

Zuri put the pipe down and lit a cigarette. "Do you want to go for a walk?"

"Definitely."

Hand in hand, they emerged from the tent. They chose the trail Luke had taken the previous day. Luke's perspective was entirely different than his first venture down the trail. The vastness and complexity of the landscape was profound. It was another planet. He recognized the beauty in each tree, the songs of birds and the warmth of the morning sun. MDPV had been a terrible nightmare, and he had finally woken up.

The only way to make sense of change is to plunge into it,
move with it, and join the dance.
-Alan Watts

Chapter 38: Healer of Souls

Sunday 8-24-2011

Luke and Zuri had been in their paradise for a week. It was full of innocent fun and adventure. They ate plenty of food and took natural supplements appropriate for recovering drug addicts.

Luke woke up and went straight for the medicine organizer. Zuri was awake. "Do you even think we need that stuff?" she said.

"Well… I don't know. This stuff is historically and scientifically proven. I understand this stuff. It's still hard for me to understand how the DMT alone could cure us."

"But it did. We're all better," she said.

"I know, but we should at least take the L-Tyrosine. We need all the catecholamines we can get. It can't hurt, anyway."

"Kay." She took the capsules from Luke. "I'm going to make us some breakfast. Then we should go for a walk. I think we should go back to civilization today."

"Seriously? Civilization? That seems out of the question. Do you think they'll even be civilized anymore? I can't shake the feeling that the whole world is different now because of what we did."

"You're crazy. It's just our world that's different now," she smiled and kissed him as they sat near the cliff.

"Mmh, I love kissing you. It's magical." He gave her another kiss, this time holding her longer.

"It is magical. I feel like we're alive and young again," she said.

"Me too. It's kinda like we're getting to know each other all over again."

She kissed him some more, "I love you."

"I love you too, so much." He kissed her more passionately, this time not stopping. Making out was a long neglected thrill. They enjoyed the feeling of each other's tongues.

Emotions stirred. Luke's hand was under her shirt, feeling her small breasts. She reached under his boxer shorts, breathing heavily, "I want you to make love to me, right here," she said.

"You got it sweetheart." He took off her shirt as they rolled onto the ground.

This place had become their Garden of Eden. Luke's sexual drive had been revived by the DMT. Lovemaking was passionate and primal. Their conversations were profound and meaningful. They were human beings again, full of purpose and inspiration.

Zuri had some profound revelations in her DMT experience as well. Her Toltec spirit guide instructed her to do the ceremony again in three months. Zuri was also shown some strange visions of herself in the Amazon and Europe. She was told that this was part of her life chart, but she was skeptical. Zuri seldom ventured beyond Montana, leaving the country seemed like fantasy.

~~~

Luke and Zuri made it to Kalispell and headed straight for Luke's parents house.

There was a call as soon as Luke turned on his phone. It was a Jared (not so fat anymore). "Hello?" Luke answered.

"Dude, where the hell have you been? I've got a shit load of money for you. I need twenty right now."

"Well bro, I'm all out. And I won't be getting more. Ever."

"Bullshit."

"Seriously dude, I'm done. I found the cure. I got the medicine that works. I want to tell you about it."

"Fuck that. Where can I get some shit?"

"I don't know."

"Whatever, Luke. I'll talk to you later."
~~~

"Kay." Luke felt bad for his friend. Now he had the medicine, but Jared wanted nothing to do with it.

They pulled into the driveway. Allan and Alice were on the porch. Luke got out of the car still wearing only the smurf boxers and ran to his parents.

"Luke!" Alice hugged him. "Why don't you ever call? I've been so worried about you."

"I've been sick in the head, but I'm all better now, I promise. I found the cure to drug addiction. I swear its the freakin truth!"

"What are you talking about? Tell me." Alice examined Luke as he explained the DMT and his spirit quest. She believed him. She could see it in his eyes. This time was the first time Luke allowed his parents to see the damage that had been done to his body.

She saw the deteriorated muscles and scars on his veins. "Oh Luke," she hugged him again and started to cry.

Allan gave Zuri a hug. "Is this real? You went through this too?"

She nodded.

Allan held Luke and examined him. "My son, look at you... you're crazy. I can see the light in your eyes again."

"I know. My soul has been cleansed. I'm done with drugs. Never again."

"You really mean to tell me that a natural medicine cured your meth addiction?" said Allan.

"Absolutely! But I wasn't addicted to meth. It was some weird shit I got from China. It's pure evil; way worse than meth. I burned it. I threw all the drugs in the fire."

The family rejoiced. Luke told his parents about everything him and Zuri had gone through with the research chemicals. Until then, they had been in the dark. They had assumed their son had been lost into meth addiction, in which Alice was quick to blame Zuri. Luke told them that it was all his idea; that Zuri did everything she could to try and help him. Alice was emotional and apologized to Zuri.

Luke received a call from Tim, "Hello?" he answered.

"Dude, where are you?"

"I'm at my parents. I just got back from the spirit quest."

"Can I meet you somewhere?" said Tim.

"Well sure, but I don't got nothing. I quit, man. I quit everything. The spirit quest worked, dude. I found the freakin cure! Lets meet up, I want to tell you about it."

"Don't lie to me, man."

"What? I'm not. The ayahuasca mixture works. The DMT and the MAOI's are the-"

"I don't give a shit about that! You're fuckin lying to me. You've been selling shit to my customers and lying to me about it! I want some shit and I want a better price."

"Dude, I'm telling you I'm done. I have nothing."

"I saw that brick you had. There's no way it's gone already."

"I burned it."

"You what?" said Tim.

"I threw it in the fire. The whole brick. I burned the M-CAT, the methylone, the 2-C's, and the cannabinoids. It's all gone. No one will ever find me with that shit again."

"You fucking liar! You owe me! I've done so much for you and this is how you repay me?"

"Hey man—"

"I'll tear your house apart. If you won't give it to me then I'll just have to take it from you."

"Whatever dude." Tim hung up.

Zuri, Alice, and Allan were watching. "Who was that?"

"It was Tim. He's pissed. It's all my fault. I got everyone into this mess."

"Why didn't you tell him about the DMT? We could just send him to Bear Creek and he could do what we did," said Zuri.

"He doesn't want nothing to do with that. The monkey demons got him good. I don't think he'll stop that shit until it's gone. It makes no sense. How can he want to keep living that way? It's miserable; such a nasty dark existence. I wish I could show everyone what I've seen."

"They'll come for help in their own time," said Zuri, "You don't need to worry about them."

Allan agreed. "It's up to them to make their own decision. Just give them love and support. If the medicine you discovered makes that decision easier, then awesome."

"Yeah, they'll come around," said Luke. "Zuri says that MDPV will be illegal in September anyways. Hopefully no one dies from the shit by then."

"We should go see Dan and Erica," said Zuri.

"We should!"

"Who's that?" said Alice.

"He's the one who helped me out with the medicine. He's a genius and he's got a good heart."

"Well good. I'm sure he'll be happy to know how much he's helped you guys. Are you going to wear clothes?"

"Yeah, I'd better grab some clothes."

~~~

Dan, Erica, the kids, and their friend Rikki were on the porch when Luke and Zuri arrived. "Hello friends!" Luke said as he stepped out of the Oldsmobile.

Rikki was an old friend of Dan's. He was a rare breed of hippie; a hybrid religious hippie. Luke had only spent a few occasions with Rikki because he was usually off the map; nowhere to be found.

"How was your quest?" said Dan.

"Man, it was magic."

"The stuff worked then?"

"It definitely worked. It did so much more than I could have imagined."

"You're done doin PV?"

"Completely!"

Erica gave Zuri a hug, "Aww Zuri, you look so much better already."

"Thanks. Things are different now."

They went to the back yard to share stories and marijuana. Luke told of his experience and Zuri told of hers. They felt a newfound connection to Rikki because of the blessings he had given the medicine. Rikki verified that without the blessings and admixtures they could have been exposed to any wandering spirits. Without the preparations the experience could have been useless or even harmful.

Zuri told of her hell experience similar to Luke's and of the glimpses she received of her life chart. She told how it was all planned out before she came to Earth.

Rikki was moved by what she said. "Now, come to think of it, I have a suggestion you may be open to."

"What's that?" said Zuri.

"I have close family ties to the Merry Pranksters. There's a commune in Brazil that I've been meaning to visit. The Family has been wanting me to come for a while now. They could set you guys in the right direction, as far as your quest to learn the way of the shaman."

"Well, I don't know if I could do that. Not for a while, anyway. I need to get my life together," she said.

"Well, if you ever get the impulse, I would like to join."

"You said you saw yourself traveling to Europe?" said Dan.

"Well yeah, but—"
~~~

"I know they're very liberal about religious freedom and stuff. There's an ayahuasca church there; especially in the UK. It's a pretty progressive country when it comes to that."

"There's a westernized church that uses ayahuasca?" said Luke.

"Yeah. I read an article about it," said Dan.

"Well shit, that's where we're supposed to be!" Luke looked at Zuri.

"Will you just settle down," said Zuri. "We can't just leave the country. We need jobs and stability first. I don't even have a passport. And we can't just *leave* the country. It's kind of a big deal."

"Stability? Jobs? How about we just follow our feakin destiny!"

"I think we should go home. Let's give ourselves a chance to come back to reality," she said.

"Kay." Luke's head was churning. He was visualizing; full of inspiration.

~~~

"What are you doing?" Zuri said as Luke pulled into the Post Office.

"We're getting you a passport."

"Luke!"

"What? I'm not asking you to leave the country. We're just getting you a passport. Every person should have one."

"Don't start getting crazy. We just got our lives back. Let's just settle down for a while. I've had enough excitement."

"No, no. Don't you see the obvious? We go to South America with Rikki and take whatever it has to offer. The shamans down there have been doing what we did for thousands of years. They're masters at navigating those dark matter dimensions. 95% of our universe is dark matter, remember? It's time to explore it."

"Traveling costs money. Money isn't going to be free for us anymore. We're gonna have to get jobs and live like normal people for a while," she said.

"Are you kidding me? Do you have any idea how much money I have stashed in the wilderness? And what better way to spend that dirty money than to fund our research expedition. We could make a difference. All we have to do is take the chance."

"Luke…"

"We can come back to America when MDPV is illegal. That way our friends won't be so resistant to the truth. Plus we can give the teachings second hand straight from the masters. We can also spread the word to my people in Oregon. We can gather them at the Oregon Country Fair. It will be a mass awakening on epic proportions. The whole world will turn their heads and see the dawn of the
~~~

age of enlightenment.

Then we go to Europe and get things organized. I envision a world united; a world of people who live in harmony with the Earth. Those scientists and researchers in the sixth level surely know how to solve our energy and natural resource problems. It's you and me, sweetheart. Let's save the freakin world."

Zuri smiled. His ambition was contagious. "Fine. I'm happy as long as I have you."

Learn from yesterday, live for today,
hope for tomorrow. The important thing
is not to stop questioning.

-Albert Einstein

Afterword

On a personal note I would like to mention something about my own experience with addiction and my struggle for recovery. DMT was the brightest ray of hope in my dark pit of addiction. I had acquired an orally active form of DMT for the sole purpose of aiding in my recovery. I had made attempts to escape into the wilderness and consume the DMT/MAOI combination. I knew of it's healing properties and that it may have been the only way to end my slavery to MDPV.

The sad truth is that the DMT was never consumed. I never found out what it could have done for me. Something inside me was terrified of the healing. I just wanted one more day; one more dose. It went on day after day until my life inevitably exploded into a terrible mess. Now I am in prison for attempted homicide and wonder what would have happened if I had taken that blend of DMT and MAOI.

Since my incarceration I have dedicated countless hours of study to DMT, Ayahuasca, and a wide variety of esoteric teachings. All of my research has reinforced my faith in Ayahuasca, and other related plant medicine. I hope this book will bring awareness to this remarkable medicine. Much of the world relies on natural medicine and understands it as common knowledge, but the pharmaceutical industry has done its best to separate us from this. So western society continues to stumble along with rehab programs that provide less than 10% chance of recovery. I hope this book will encourage people to do their own research and find a recovery method that is best for them.

~~~

Ayahuasca Resources

Yacu Puma - **Ayahuasca** Healing **Center** - Home
www.yacupuma.com/
Hummingbird **Ayahuasca** Retreats and Healing **Center**, Iquitos
www.**ayahuascaretreats**.org/
Phoenix **Ayahuasca** Retreat **Centre**, Iquitos, Peru
~~~

phoenix**ayahuasca**.com/
7 Day Authentic **Ayahuasca** Retreat in Iquitos, Peru | Kapitari
www.kapitari.org/**ayahuasca**
Nihue Rao Centro Espiritual **Ayahuasca** Retreat Healing **...**
www.nihuerao.com
Blue Morpho Shamanic **Ayahuasca Center** & Retreat in Peru
www.bluemorphotours.com/
The Dark Side of **Ayahuasca** - MensJournal.com
www.mensjournal.com/magazine/the-dark-side-of-**ayahuasca**-20130215

Index

PMA: hallucinogenic amphetamine. Also known as Dr. Death or 4-MA. Found in Red/Blue Mitsubishi, blue transformers, Rolex and other ecstasy pills.

2C-B: Part of phenethylamine family. Causes colorful and cartoonish hallucinations accompanied by excessive laughing and smiling. There are unpleasant side effects that include body tremors, tachycardia and hypothermia, lasts 4-6 hours.

MXE (Methoxetamine): Derivative of ketamine. Very potent dissociative with some anesthetic properties.

Triple C's: See DXM

DXM (Dextromethorphan): Antitussive drug used in OTC cough and cold medicines. Adverse effects include difficulty breathing, increased energy/confidence, shivering, hallucinations, dissociation, out-of-body experience, blackouts, blurred or double vision, inability to focus and insomnia.

MDMA: Empathogenic drug of the phenethylamine and amphetamine class, otherwise known as ecstasy. Last about 4 hours.

GBA: Colorless liquid that acts as a prodrug for GHB. Effects are similar to alcohol and ecstasy. Also used as superglue remover and paint stripper. Also was used as nutritional supplement sold by GNC.

DMT: Psychadelic compound of the tryptamine family. Its presence is widespread throughout the plant kingdom.

Methylone: Also known as M1, MDMC, or bk-MDMA. Similar effects as MDMA ecstasy.

4-FA: Stimulant drug of the phenethylamine and amphetamine class.

5-MeO-DALT: Psychadelic tryptamine with entactogenic effects.

Entactogen: Any drug with effects pertaining to the sense of touch.

Empathogen: Any drug with effects pertaining to empathy.

Entheogen: Any drug with effects pertaining to religious or spiritual experience.

Dissociative: Involving a sense of detachment.

AM-2201: A potent but nonselective agonist for the cannabinoid receptor. Can cause convulsions and panic attacks even at low doses. Similar effects as marijuana, but much more psychedelic and sometimes painful.

JWH-122: Synthetic cannabimimetic. Effects similar to marijuana.

MDPPP: A stimulant drug sometimes used in imitation ecstasy pills. Similar chemical structure to MDPV and a-PPP.

MDPV: Stimulant drug developed in the 60's, first sold as designer drug in 2004.

a-PVP: Similar to MDPV, also developed in the 60's.

Pyrovalerone: A pharmaceutical drug developed in the 60's. Similar to MDPV.

~ ~ ~

2C-E: Psychedelic phenethylamine with similar effects as mescaline. Lasts 6 to 10 hours.

MDA: A psychedelic stimulant with less entactogenic effects than MDMA Also know as the "love drug". Lasts 3-6 hours.

2C-I: A psychedelic stimulant with entactogenic and empathogenic properties. Lasts 4-12 hours.

2C-P: Produces intense hallucinogenic, psychedelic and entheogenic effects. Lasts 10-24 hours.

Ibogaine: Naturally occurring psychoactive substance found in plants such as Tabernanthe iboga. It is sometimes used to treat addiction. The most studied theraputive effect has been on the reduction or elimination of the addiction to opioids. Ibogaine has also been reported to reduce cravings for methamphetamine.

5-HTP: Nutritional supplement used to help restore normal serotonin levels.

Molly: Nickname for any chemical sold as "Ecstasy". MDMA, MDA, and methyl one are often sold as "Molly".

Mephedrone (also M-CAT or 4-MEC): Similar to Ecstasy with fast onset and shorter duration.

Dramamine: Motion sickness medication. Induces realistic audio and visual hallucinations and delusions. Makes people dream while they are side awake. It's very difficult to decipher what is real and what is not. Dosage 6-24 pills.

~ ~ ~

MSM: Nutritional supplement for joints. Also sued as cut for methamphetamine.

Pistol: A series of ecstasy pills with an impression of a pistol.

L-Tyrosine: An amino acid. The primary nutrient required by neurons to produce catecholamines. People addicted to stimulant drugs are typically catecholamine deficient.

Chiba: Another name for heroin

Oscar: An ounce of weed.

SSRI: Selective Seretonin Reuptake Inhibitor. Used as antidepresents.

MAOI: Monoamine oxidize inhibitor. Prevents the body from breaking down certain chemicals.

DMSO: A solvent capable of penetrating the skin and other membranes without damaging. Also able to help carry other compounds into the biological system.

Made in the USA
Monee, IL
29 January 2020

21011279R00233